the LAKE

and the

LOST

GIRL

a novel

Jacquelyn Vincenta

sourcebooks
landmark

Grateful acknowledgment to the following poets for use of their lines that are now in the public domain: Gertrude Stein, "Sacred Emily," "Sugar," and "Preciosilla"; Amy Lowell, "The Letter"; Christina Georgina Rossetti, "My Secret"; Lola Ridge, "Dedication" and "The Ghetto"; Elinor Wylie, "Escape," "Fire and Sleet and Candlelight," and "Incantation"; Fannie Stearns Davis, "The Dream Self"; Mary Elizabeth Coleridge, "The Witch"; Hilda Doolittle (H.D.), "Demeter"; Sara Teasdale, "The Net," "What Do I Care," and "In a Darkening Garden"; Georgia Douglas Johnson, "The Heart of a Woman"; Elizabeth Oakes Smith, "The Drowned Mariner"; Edna St. Vincent Millay, "Ashes of Life" and "The Poet and His Book"; and to Mildred Amelia Barker, "Not Again," about whom no biographical or copyright ownership information was located.

Edna St. Vincent Millay, excerpts from "The Plum Gatherer," "The Bobolink," "The Anguish," "There at Dusk I Found You," "Mist in the Valley," and "For Poe-Chin, a Boatman on the Yellow Sea" from Collected Poems. Copyright © 1928, 1955 by Edna St. Vincent Millay and Norma Millay Ellis. Reprinted with the permission of The Permissions Company, Inc., on behalf of Holly Peppe, Literary Executor, The Edna St. Vincent Millay Society, www.millay.org.

Reprinted by permission of Farrar, Straus and Giroux, LLC: Excerpts from "Casabianca," "Imber Nocturnus," and "The Wave" from *Poems* by Elizabeth Bishop. Copyright © 2011 by the Alice H. Methfessel Trust. Publisher's note and compilation copyright © 2011 by Farrar, Straus and Giroux, LLC. Excerpts from "Kept," "The Crossed Apple," and "The Crows" from *The Blue Estuaries*.

"The Flume," by Louise Bogan, is used by permission of The Louise Bogan Charitable Trust.

"The Study of Lakes," by Becky Cooper, is used with her permission.

Published by Sourcebooks Landmark, an imprint of Sourcebooks, Inc.
P.O. Box 4410, Naperville, Illinois 60567-4410
(630) 961-3900
Fax: (630) 961-2168
www.sourcebooks.com

Library of Congress Cataloging-in-Publication data is on file with the publisher.

Printed and bound in the United States of America.
VP 10 9 8 7 6 5 4 3 2 1

For Bob Sperling, whose love for the lakes,
the lights, and me changed my life

Prologue

Put something down.
Put something down some day.
Put something down some day in.
Put something down some day in my.
In my hand.
In my hand right.
In my hand writing.
Put something down some day in my handwriting.

~ Gertrude Stein (1874–1946), "Sacred Emily"

Mary Walker crouched against the attic wall, waiting. Two floors below, her husband hurled an ax into logs stacked near the woodstove, and she could hear chunks of wood clatter against the walls and floor as he cursed her. The fire was cold, there was no supper prepared, and she'd brought her coat up into the attic with her so that he would believe she was out. But hidden upstairs, her body was attuned to his every motion and his exact location in the house.

Eventually he would leave. He would leave either to go looking for her or to get drunk and forget about her. She just had to wait. Patience was so difficult for her. But she was just hours from freedom now—she and Robert would depart tonight. Tonight! She clutched the two small bags she had packed for the crossing to Chicago on the *Fata Morgana*. If all was going as planned, Robert was waiting for her this very minute, just half a mile away in the Lake Michigan channel.

In recent weeks, Bernard's fits of fury had intensified, almost as if he sensed Mary's intention to leave him. And his rage about her inability to conceive a child made it clear what she was to him, and that he would never truly support the woman and the poet she had been before they married. She had no doubt about the importance of getting away from him. But in this moment, when she was finally packed and ready to make this cold water crossing, the lake's violence and the unsettling purple sky made Mary afraid.

Pulling her gaze from the round window beneath the attic's peak, she turned to the sewing box in her lap, for it had always comforted her. A loose knob jiggled just as it had when her mother owned the box, and a quilted lining held needles and pins purchased before she was born. She had loosened a few tacks in the lining so that she could hide the special needle, and she reached in with one finger. Yes, it was still there—the needle that had nothing to do with sewing. She tucked it deeper, yearning for the relief of her medicine. Up against it, she slid a folded poem that no one would read until she was far from this White Hill life. In Chicago she would be a different woman. She would use another name to publish her poetry, and thousands of people would read every line. But until then she had to hide the most dangerous words.

"If you think you can make a fool of me, Mary Walker," Bernard roared to no one, "you haven't learned a goddamn thing."

Her heart stuttered at the heavy thud of something being thrown to the floor, and she shrank closer to the wall, her hands clutching the sewing box more tightly. Bernard knew how she cherished it, and if she left it here, he would smash it apart. She stared into the box at the threads and buttons, running her fingers lightly over their gentle shapes. No, she wouldn't leave it behind; she must take it. The truth was, she'd need something

like this in her new life—she'd need *precisely* this! With no furniture of her own, with nothing of home, she might really go
mad. Part of her could live in this box.

The small window's frame rattled in a blast of wind, and she
leaned over to look out, hollow with fear. The night sky was
starless and black. It was past time to go. God help her if the
storm raged too long. Once they pushed off into that cold lake,
she could never return to White Hill.

At last the front door slammed, and seconds later, she saw
Bernard taking long strides down the road, away from the lake
and toward town. Her eyes caught on an object gripped in his
right hand. It was the ax. Her gaze swooped blindly around the
dim room, then returned to the dark form of her husband. Was
he looking for *her* with an ax? Even from the attic she could see
that his gait was drunken with anger. When at last he had been
swallowed by shadows and trees, she sat frozen, forcing herself
to wait. Just three minutes. Two.

"Gather your courage. Now, Mary. Get on with it," she said
finally, and the feeling of her voice in her throat gave her strength.

She stuffed strands of blond hair up under her hat, stood
beneath the low ceiling, and moved quickly, gripping the
bags' handles with sweating hands. She picked her way along a
memorized path through the dark attic, raced down the stairs,
and crossed the cold, naked floors of the house to flee through
the windblown sand and grass. The sewing box knocked
against her hip, her bags grew heavy quickly, and the sky began
to hurl rain. She scanned the wet darkness. No one was near.
No one following.

Then at last it was there—the channel light—and thirty steps
later she could see Robert's boat rocking wildly near the pier.
She wanted to laugh and cry. She searched the open, storm-
blown sand again, and then again, in every direction, but she
detected no watching eyes, and out on his boat that loyal man
was waiting, just as he had said he would be.

Her feet sank and slipped in the damp sand, and her heart smashed against her ribs. Wind threshed the grasses that hissed around her knees, and as her boots reached the solid pier boards, the *Fata Morgana* heaved up and down on turbulent waves, its prow slapping the lake.

The voices of the water and the night urged Mary to hurry, crying out that she was only doing what she had to do, that the notion she could stay in White Hill and make her life work was only a fantasy. She had never really had a choice at all.

1

Little cramped words scrawling all over the paper
Like draggled fly's legs,
What can you tell of the flaring moon
Through the oak leaves?

~ Amy Lowell (1874–1925), "The Letter"

L ydia Carroll had no idea what she would find among the dense woods off Gravenstein Road. The poet's house was now little more than a grave, and the driveway was squeezed to a footpath by wild growth. Dirty snow banked the north sides of trees, and ice pooled in the surrounding lowland that was once a celery farm. Mary Stone Walker would have walked this way a thousand times. Ten thousand.

> I begged the Spring, "Return,
> we wait beside the long, small fires of winter."

Facts about the poet were few beyond her writings, and Lydia was at the point of feeling almost desperate for answers about the woman's actual life—most importantly, how it ended, for even sixty years after her disappearance, no one was sure. Lydia knew that no matter how prolific the author, even if she had left behind stacks of journals, still there would be missing, as well as misleading, information. And now there was more at stake than simply answering an intriguing literary question. Mary Stone Walker's mysteries had gone unresolved for so long that they threatened the well-being of Lydia's family.

She pushed through the heavy vines that blocked the path, and there stood the house—dilapidated, gaping, as if silenced midscream. She took in the wooden shape of the place and the wooded yard around it, considering how it might have felt to come home to it, and her imagination contended with ghosts. Lydia had been in the place with her husband twelve years before, both of them giddy with excitement to roam the silent rooms where Mary Stone Walker had once lived, but the police had shown up, and Carson Community College administrators had warned Frank the next day that the college's relationship with the Evans family was no longer friendly and any visits to the house would be viewed as trespassing.

"Good morning, Mrs. Carroll."

Startled, Lydia turned to find a slight man of about forty-five walking toward her, his hairline receding, his pale-blue eyes cold. He extended his arm. "Lincoln Babcock."

"Good morning." She smiled and shook his gloved hand with her bare one. "Lydia Carroll. I so appreciate you doing this."

"And your husband, the professor?" The man looked around behind her. "He'll be joining us?"

"No. It's just me." She watched Lincoln's friendly expression slip. "He was not part of the plan today."

"Didn't you say that you wished to see the interior of the house for an academic project?"

"That's right."

Lincoln paused. "But you're a romance novelist."

"Yes," she said patiently, "that's how I make my living, although I write other things as well." Knowing that her small size and unruly red hair made her look younger than she was, Lydia put forth as professional an attitude as possible, even though Lincoln's attitude was immediately irritating. The common assumption that the writing of genre novels and academic essays was incompatible still stung.

"These photographs are for Frank's book about Mary Stone Walker's life and work, which are also subjects of his PhD dissertation. The book is planned for the general public." She lifted her camera case, then unzipped it. At the confused look still lingering on Lincoln's face, she added, "Frank is my husband, the professor."

"Yes, I am acquainted with your husband's name. And his work." Lincoln's mouth twisted. "Why isn't he here himself? Call me suspicious, but I must ask: You're not thinking that *you* will turn the fiasco of Walker's life into a romantic novel?"

Lydia flushed. "As I said, I am gathering information about Mary Stone Walker for Professor Carroll's *nonfiction book*, but seeing as how *he* believes that Mary went on to live and write for years after she disappeared from White Hill, his perspective on her is actually more *romantic* than mine."

"Precisely, yes, she ran off," Lincoln said, grabbing on to a subject that apparently distressed him even more. "In that respect, your husband would find supporters among Mary Walker's husband's family." Sparks of anger lit his eyes. "In fact, Bernard Evans issued rewards for information about her because he was certain that when she 'disappeared,' she had merely fled."

"Yes, I know that." Lydia hoped she didn't sound impatient, but she wanted him to realize that she hadn't walked into this moment like some uninformed tourist. He was obviously skeptical, and she needed to get into the house.

"So we have continued to feel she was not a tragic victim," Lincoln went on emphatically. "She was in fact a liar and a thief. You probably aren't aware that she stole money and jewels before she left."

"Stole money and jewels?" Lydia frowned. She had never heard this accusation before during all their years of research, although they had often stumbled onto other odd, unsubstantiated rumors.

"Oh yes," Lincoln answered firmly, crossing his arms over his chest. "So far, the problem has been that those who like Mary Stone Walker the artist tend not to like the truth about Mary Walker the woman. After she abandoned Bernard Evans, he lost his mind and ruined their assets, so as far as most people are concerned, she does not deserve any further consideration, let alone the reverence academics like your husband espouse."

Lydia took a slow breath and tried to ignore her rapidly growing dislike of Lincoln Babcock, letting her gaze rove the thick branches crowded protectively around the sides and roof of the abandoned house. Last year's russet oak leaves rattled in the slightest currents of air.

"I gather you're close to the family, Mr. Babcock?"

"They have entrusted me with a great deal. A very great deal." He turned the collar of his wool coat up. "And I think everyone can agree that a stack of poems, no matter how exquisite, does not make up for an immoral life."

He gazed at her, folding his hands behind his back, and his expression was so absurdly superior that Lydia had an urge to laugh. In her mind, she heard what Frank's response would have been, and she pictured the crushing expression he typically wore during conversations with those he perceived as intellectually inferior.

The dark truth was, one theory of Mary's disappearance held that her husband, Bernard, killed her in a fit of jealousy and hid her body within the shuttered house for weeks before burying or destroying it. When Lydia first met Frank at the University of Michigan where he was a graduate student teaching English and she was in her junior year as an English literature major, she had gained his attention at a literary event when she spoke at length about Mary Stone Walker and her poetry, explaining who the White Hill poet was and how she had disappeared and never been found. Frank had approached her afterward, and the two of them had talked about poetry in

Lydia's apartment until sunlight burned around the edges of her paper window shade.

The weaving of their thoughts and emotions that night had been more intimate than anything Lydia had ever experienced, and over the following months, they'd read Mary Walker's poems and journals out loud together, wondering and theorizing. Murder was the scenario Frank had initially believed, asserting that it was the most realistic when Bernard Evans's documented violence and Mary's unrecovered body were taken into account.

The subject was one they went on to discuss into the wee hours of many nights, and the search for clues within Mary's words, which had begun in an Ann Arbor apartment, had continued for almost two decades. But Frank's belief in the murder had dissolved years ago when he became captivated with his own, much different version of Mary's fate.

"Between you and me"—Lydia decided against a discussion of the murder theory and tried to adopt a more collaborative tone—"since no one has been able to figure out for certain what happened, doesn't it seem likely that something completely unplanned and tragic occurred? Like suicide, for instance?"

"Well, that would be its own sort of betrayal, wouldn't it?" Lincoln blinked, staring at Lydia with no visible trace of emotion.

"That seems harsh." She took a step back and adjusted the camera bag strap on her shoulder. They studied each other with mutual mistrust. "So…exactly what is your connection to the family, Lincoln?"

"I'm a businessman with a soft spot for ruins—human as well as structural. I'm also distantly related to Bernard Evans." He looked at his watch, then swept his hand out toward the house. "Shall we go in? I don't have a lot of time."

Instead of heading toward the front door, Lincoln led Lydia around to the back of the house. After turning the doorknob to find it locked, he eyed a low, shattered window and began chipping a crust of crystallized snow from its sill.

"I couldn't find the keys to this place this morning," he said irritably. "New hardware and security are planned, but in the meantime…" He nodded toward the window. "We'll make use of the most recent vandalism."

"I don't understand. You want me to *climb in the window*?"

"Mrs. Carroll." His voice was pinched. "Entry through this window is our best option, and we should not waste any more time."

"Well, pardon me, Mr. Babcock, but you said that you would take me in and show me around. I could have trespassed through a broken window by myself."

"As you know, Mrs. Carroll, for decades, the Evans family has stated their unwillingness to memorialize Mary Stone Walker," Lincoln Babcock said. "The fact that I have procured permission to bring you here indicates a slight shift in their mistrust of the public, but the family is still not at the point of offering official tours or condoning trespassers." He gestured toward the window. "Shall we?"

"After you," she answered and watched him deftly swing one leg and then the other into the house.

Attempting to avoid the broken glass, Lydia followed slowly, standing up into a room that contained a heavily stained porcelain sink, chunks of fallen plaster, and piles of decomposing leaves, sticks, and trash. Mary's kitchen. Lydia's attempt to remember lines written about this room was eclipsed by the intimate, dead smell of rotting things.

The past is beyond your reach, the smell whispered. *It has lost its skin.*

"The house wasn't in this condition when I last saw it," Lydia said, glancing at Lincoln, but he was focused on a newly acquired smear of dirt on his suit pants. Cupboard doors had been torn off, fixtures and doorknobs were missing, and dead bugs littered the surfaces. She peered beyond the kitchen, her disappointment rising. "So much vandalism. Almost criminal neglect."

Ignoring her comments, Lincoln Babcock walked into the next room, his feet crunching unidentifiable things beneath them. Lydia followed, and there in the front room stood the iron woodstove. The black heart of Mary Stone Walker's home life, heating the days of both misery and hope with equal effect. It tilted on rotted floorboards, its surface rusted by decades of trespassing rain and snow. Lydia lifted her camera and took several pictures of the room. It was worse than abandoned—it looked abused. But Frank would be fascinated.

"It was the attic you were most interested in, if I remember correctly?" Lincoln said. "It would be best to go there straightaway. My time is limited."

Lydia eyed the stairs. Narrow, without a rail, they rose steeply to a shadowed second story. They didn't look safe, but she had to climb them, for it was the third-story attic she most wanted to capture on film: Mary's hiding place. It had been referenced in multiple poems, both overtly and, in Frank's opinion, through metaphor. What image could be more perfect for the cover of a book about a poet who had wrestled with her fears, as well as the circumstances of her life, and then disappeared forever?

Inside these time-battered walls, it was even easier for Lydia to believe that the right pictures could finally prompt Frank to assemble the stacks of notes and essays he had produced over the course of fifteen years into a book that would bring Mary alive for mainstream readers. To Lydia, this was not just a nice idea; it was an urgent need. She would develop these photos, have the best ones enlarged, and persuade Frank that he owed Mary Walker's memory the honor of sharing his writings about her with a waiting public. Lydia had become certain that it was essential to her husband's career—and mental health—to finish the project. *And then move on.* His life in the real world had been almost completely replaced by an obsession with the poet that had grown static and strangely decadent.

As she followed Lincoln Babcock up the stairs, she recalled the high expectations she and Frank had entertained twelve years before. Frank had planned to return often to search the house for documents that the paranoid, emotional poet might have hidden in the interstices of the structure itself. Lydia had imagined holding small poetry readings in the living room, when the woodstove had not yet started falling through the floor. But even back then there had been no furniture or belongings left inside. Legend had it that Mary's husband had buried or burned every item the poet had ever touched.

"Do you think it's true that Bernard Evans destroyed Mary's belongings, Mr. Babcock?"

"Undoubtedly." He paused and turned briefly back toward her. "Papers and books would have gone first."

"In the woodstove?" Lydia mused, but Lincoln Babcock said nothing.

As they passed the second-story rooms, she felt disturbed. One of these was the bedroom Mary had shared with Bernard. Yes, there it was, its arched windows familiar from a poem about night terrors. Lydia stepped inside to take a few shots. How provocative these images would be, printed in Frank's book next to Mary's words.

Lincoln Babcock stood uneasily at the door to the attic.

"Mrs. Carroll, I am a bit claustrophobic. I will wait here to escort you out when you are finished. Mary Walker did set up a makeshift desk in the attic, much to Bernard Evans's surprise when they cleared the place out fifty years ago. She obviously spent time up there without his knowledge. One of many places she hid from her obligations."

Lydia swallowed her response, for there was nothing to be gained by alienating Lincoln Babcock. Hiding from her obligations indeed. "The Evanses have gotten rid of everything that was part of her daily life?"

"Except for the spaces themselves," he said. "The views."

Lincoln's eyes drifted from hers as if some nervousness was whittling at his confidence. He looked again at his watch.

"I will have to ask you to hurry. Five minutes."

"What?" Lydia raised her eyebrows. "This is silly. I should just return here alone sometime."

"Do not consider it," he insisted. "That wouldn't do at all. It would be trespassing. Really, it isn't safe. For you or anyone else."

Lydia turned toward the attic door, peering up into the space beyond: the attic staircase that she and Frank had never had a chance to climb. With narrow steps blotted out by darkness, it was foreboding. She had not even thought to bring a flashlight.

Heart pounding, she inched up through the dank air until she stood beneath a slanted attic ceiling glazed by weak sunlight. Five long strings hung eave to eave across the space, perhaps for drying clothes in the attic heat, and on the west wall facing Lake Michigan there was a round window under the roof peak where wind slipped in around the crude frame.

> With the father's arms that could have held me,
>   buried
> in the earth, I reach beyond the treetops toward
>   the sea.

Lydia crept carefully to kneel before the window and was delighted to find that she could open it, lean out, and see a portion of the dirt trail that had once been the road into town. Patches of Lake Michigan flashed silver between the tips of cottonwoods, oaks, and pines, in glorious contrast to the haunted space behind her. She backed up a few steps to photograph this scene that Mary would have been so deeply familiar with. The partly overcast sky left the images flat, but Lydia intended to return sometime soon, in spite of Lincoln's warning.

Then a shout from below shattered the wooded silence. Lydia

pushed the window open wider and peered out. A man's voice called again, and it was not Lincoln Babcock's.

"Yes, *you*!" An ancient-looking man pointed up toward the attic window, limping forward with slow determination, his voice strangled by age and emotion. "*You crazy bitch, come out of there!*"

She pulled back into the shadows, out of his view, as the sound of Lincoln's footsteps descended the stairs from the second floor to the first. The old man hobbled forward a few more steps and pointed toward her again, his breathing visibly labored. He was tall and broad, with a pink scar that was spread and distorted by time angling across his left cheek.

"Don't you think I heard ya?" he called, punching out the words and shaking his head at her. "Don't you think I heard *everything you said*?"

Lydia couldn't tear her gaze from his face, made grotesque by rage. He waved arthritic fingers furiously toward the window as if to scratch out what he saw.

"Answer me!" he screamed, the energy in his voice growing.

Lydia heard the heavy front door open, slam closed, and then she saw Lincoln Babcock rush toward the old man. Lincoln grabbed the man firmly by the shoulders and struggled to turn him back toward the road.

"I asked you to wait in the car," Lincoln said, anger and anxiety battling in his voice. "You see how it is, don't you? If you don't stay safe, they won't let you go out."

The old man shook his head, made a sound like laughter, and shoved an elbow at Lincoln.

"Mr. Babcock!" Lydia called out the window.

Lincoln Babcock raised his hand in the air in response but did not turn around. Lydia heard their footsteps in the still morning air, then another shout from the old man and Lincoln's increasingly tense voice in response. One car door slammed, then another, and the car started. The crunch of tires on ice and gravel faded to silence.

> Leave me now, cruelty—crooked hand on my
> soul…

Mary Stone Walker's words skittered across Lydia's mind, as if exhaled from fibers of the attic. She peered through the window uneasily. The light on the lake had been snuffed out by cloud cover, and cold, moist air wrapped around her skin.

Fingers shaking from a rush of anxiety, she packed up her camera and avoided glancing into the thick shadows hunched around her. She ought to stay. Lincoln Babcock was gone, and she was free to look around. But no—it wasn't necessary to do that right this minute. She turned, eyes fixed on the ghost of light floating up from the second story below, feeling her way across the attic floor and down the stairs. She needn't stay; she could come back another time. She would bring a flashlight and return some bright, clear afternoon.

Lydia hurried past the wreckage of the other rooms, an irrational fear growing that her breath was constricted. It suddenly seemed quite possible that she could lose consciousness or fall through weak floorboards before she escaped the house. The air felt thin and infected. She yanked open the front door and rushed into the yard, and the door slammed shut behind her.

She had let her imagination open too wide, she told herself as she took deep breaths of the outside air, nearly running to her Jeep. She had let her mind entertain thoughts of Mary's struggle in the house at just the moment when the stranger had shouted up from the yard. She started the engine, turned the heat up as high as it would go, and locked the doors, shivering as she looked to her left, her right, and then behind her, certain someone hidden was watching her.

Lydia stared at the deteriorating house, filled with conviction that the search for the poet had gone on too long with too little gained. Mary Stone Walker was not Frank's goddess or Lincoln's criminal, and yes, her life had been worth examining, but maybe enough was enough. Picking around the verbal skeletons that the young woman had left behind and making up theories about what happened to her suddenly seemed a bit obscene. Had anyone given serious thought to the bones, breath, and heart that Mary Walker was in life? Good lord, she'd been a human being without family or any worldly goods of her own, trapped in a small town and a dangerous marriage. Trapped and in peril. And what was she left with, in her fear and hope? In her efforts to make a life, or to escape danger? Words, little strings of words?

The sense of this washed through Lydia's mind, and her heart expanded with pity as she seemed to see directly into Mary Stone Walker's life circumstances. Her young hands had cooked meals in that kitchen, her eyes had searched for deliverance of some sort through the glass of that attic window, and finally, she had fled across this very yard. In the end, the versions of Mary conjured by Frank, Lincoln Babcock, and the Evanses did not contain that human being.

Lydia peered up at the attic window where she had just been, at the dead blackness it framed, and it glinted with blame. She shifted the Jeep into Reverse and backed away. Yes, it was time to find a way to put this issue to rest. She and Frank needed to publish his work about the poet, get it into the world, and let her go. Who knew? Maybe even Mary Walker herself needed a release from their acquisitive searching. The hour was late for a woman who had been missing for sixty years—far too late for anyone to hope for good news.

2

White Hill, Michigan——March 1999

...the little dirty city
In the light so sheer and sunny
Shone as dazzling bright and pretty
As the money that you find
In a dream of finding money—
                    ~ Edna St. Vincent Millay (1892–1950), "The Bean-Stalk"

Sparrows scattered as Frank's truck turned into the dirt driveway and rolled toward the small, gray barn. Nicholas watched from the kitchen window as birds rushed to the bare apple tree like one person split into a dozen feathered bodies, but his eyes quickly went back to his father wrestling with the wide, crooked barn doors that had never slid easily. His father cursed, but succeeded in shoving the doors open, and Nicholas sighed. A large object stood covered with a tarp and strapped down in the pickup bed.

He backed away from the window, tipping the cereal box toward the blue ceramic bowl, and frosted corn flakes jingled into it. Hurrying to pour the milk, he sloshed it onto the counter, grabbed a spoon, and rushed back upstairs to his bedroom. As cartoon figures bounced around on the TV screen, he shoved his long legs under the sheets and pushed his glasses back up the bridge of his nose.

"Nicholas!" Down below, Frank entered the house and slammed the kitchen door.

"Crap." Nicholas set down the half-eaten cereal to find jeans in the pile of clothes on the floor. T-shirt, sweatshirt. He heard heavy steps on the stairs that led to steps getting closer and closer in the long hall, and then his door burst open.

"Ah! You *are* up! Don't try to tell me you didn't hear me."

Electrified by his own quick-fire emotions, Frank was capable of instantly filling a room with his mood. He was six foot four, his eyes sharp blue and magnified by thick glasses, his face surrounded by wavy black, graying hair that fell to his shoulders. Nicholas's frame and coloring resembled his father's more than his mother's, but he was skinny and awkwardly tall for a fifteen-year-old, while his father had expanded over the years into an imposing presence.

"How come you always tell me to knock first?" Nicholas mumbled, but his father paid no attention.

"I should have gotten you up and taken you with me this morning. You're getting lazy, Nick."

This was one of his father's standard comments, but it still provoked Nicholas. "It's Saturday, Dad. Jeez."

"Just get going. Hurry up, I want to unload this armoire into the barn before your mother gets home."

Outside, the March air was wintry and crisp, but within minutes Nicholas was hot from the effort of easing the immense piece of furniture to the edge of the truck bed. When they began to lower it, with Frank's back braced against it from the ground while Nicholas attempted to steady it from the truck with canvas straps, the boy lost his grip for a second, the strap slid a few inches, and the thing leaned too heavily against his father, who shouted at him to pull back. With more shouts, teetering, and a couple of loud thuds, they got the armoire safely to the ground, Frank huffing and Nicholas shaking.

"Okay, we've got to get it inside the barn. You're just going to have to put more muscle into it, Nick. Concentrate now."

"We could try to find something to put under it to pull it along. One of those drop cloths." He pointed.

"No, no, come on now. We'll just muscle it over there. It's only twenty feet."

Fifteen minutes later, unveiled in the fluorescence of the barn's shop lights, the armoire was impressive, although the finish was mottled with water damage. Rich cherry wood, a carved headpiece, and copper antique drawer pulls with a heavy patina made it look expensive to Nicholas's amateur eye.

The barn was cluttered with other pieces from about the same era—trunks, mirrors, chairs, dressers, and even an old stove and an icebox, along with less-significant items, like shoes, suitcases, and wooden boxes of various sizes. Anything from the early twentieth century that had been in Michigan's lower peninsula a long time, and which possessed a space within in it where a piece of paper could be hidden. Anything, in short, that Frank Carroll imagined could have belonged to the vanished poet Mary Stone Walker and become a vessel for secret, unpublished writings.

Frank's eyes gleamed, and he smiled as he stared at the antique. Nicholas watched him think, run his hands through his hair, and finally approach the armoire and gently open one of the drawers. Frank was captivating to watch when his mind was engaged, but the intensity of his desires was unnerving, so when at last he turned to his son with a large smile, Nicholas was filled with a familiar relief. He smiled in return, breathed deeply, and asked, "What do you think, Dad?"

"I think… I really think this one might have been used by Mary on a daily basis for a while, Nicky. When I read the letter she wrote to Dr. Sherwood at Hope College, this was almost exactly the design I pictured in my mind when she was describing the cherrywood armoire at her aunt's friend's house where she was staying. And there's every indication that she was writing a great deal of poetry that summer."

When Nicholas looked back at the antique, standing like a significant historical figure there in their own shabby barn, and envisioned it without flaws—ensconced in some cozy Michigan bedroom, full of a poet's clothes, her writing papers, pens, maybe purses and white gloves—he easily entered his father's dream, as he had many times before. He asked, "So when are you going to start examining it?"

"Today, for sure. Later today, after I break the news to your mother that I had to get it!" He laughed, Nicholas laughed, and Frank put his arm around his son's shoulders, gazing down at him. "Look at you! Almost as tall as I am all of a sudden! You going to have time to help me?"

"Yeah, of course! After we go to the folk arts festival with Mom." Frank said nothing in response, although Nicholas waited, continuing to look at him. "Remember, Dad?"

"What?"

"The folk arts festival near Traverse City. Every March."

"Traverse City… Christ, that's a two-and-a-half-hour drive! Is that today?"

"Today and tomorrow. We're staying at that cool old motel. The one with the round pool and the pinball machines, remember?"

"So it's a whole weekend deal?" Frank's face darkened. "That's too much time. I can't make that kind of commitment for a folk arts festival. Your mother shouldn't make plans like that for me. Or for you either, for that matter. I don't think I wanted my mother planning my weekends when I was your age."

Frank winked at Nicholas, who glanced uneasily toward the road where his mother would appear soon. "I don't mind festivals. They're usually okay. She's been talking about it all week."

"Oh, she doesn't need us to go," Frank said lightly, heading toward the house. Nicholas followed. "Give her some time to herself, Nick. You can help me here. This ought to be fun."

Nicholas said nothing. His eyes caught on a snow-streaked patch of mud in the perpetual shade on the north side of the house, not ten feet from sunlit jonquil shoots. After interminable Michigan winters, attending the show full of colorful artwork and live music had become a welcome family tradition.

"It will be great, Nicky. We can examine every possible hiding spot in that armoire. We'll boil up some hot dogs for dinner and pop popcorn. Just the two of us."

They headed toward the house. When his father glanced back for his son's nod, Nicholas forced a small smile as his mind clouded with frustration. His parents would certainly end up in a fight about this, and then maybe no one would go out of town at all. He'd be stuck in the house with two irritable jerks. "I don't know, Dad. It's the weekend—a good time for a festival, it seems like. But also, I haven't hung out with Joe or Kevin for, like, two weeks."

"Well, see, there you go. They can help us! Call 'em up!"

"Examining old furniture isn't exactly fun, you know." His father raised his eyebrows. "For them, I mean."

Moments after the back door bounced shut behind Nicholas and Frank, the front door opened and his mother called into the shadowed rooms, "Anybody home?"

"We're in the kitchen. Want coffee?" Frank answered cheerfully as he measured out coffee grounds and water.

"Whew!" Lydia walked into the kitchen, set her purse, briefcase, and camera bag on the counter, then leaned against the sink to look out the window just as Nicholas had done an hour before. "No, thanks. It's been a very long morning full of coffee already."

"That so? Where you been?" Frank flicked the coffeemaker switch and focused on Lydia.

"Where have I been? You're kidding! I went out on a little photo shoot, and then, remember, my agent's passing through, so I met with her…which I've been talking about—"

"Right, right."

"—for weeks."

"So, any good news?"

"No. She said that the new Asquith editor sees my talents differently than I do."

Frank gave a laugh. "They're idiots. I keep telling you."

"Yes, you certainly do. It doesn't help. I wish you would stop. Their position doesn't make sense. A year ago, we all agreed that this year would be a good time for me to branch out into mainstream fiction, and that's part of the reason I put so much time into doing three romances last year instead of two. *We agreed*."

"The publishing industry is in constant flux. Nothing's predictable. You know that." Frank gave her a few shakes of his head and a small smile.

"But I've been with Asquith House so long. If they won't give me a chance with something else, who would? I'm not asking to forgo the romances entirely. I've got one in the works. This is highly unprofessional of them, in my opinion."

Nicholas poured himself a glass of orange juice and sat down on one of the wooden chairs he had been using since he was a toddler. The set of six, with the table, had been a gift from his mother to herself and his dad when she sold the movie rights to her first romance novel, *A Dream Remembered*, when Nicholas was a baby. The chairs were finely crafted pale birch with inlaid mahogany designs, and many times his mother had proudly pointed out that they were nearly unique in the Carroll household: furniture purchased for the use of the family, with no possible link to the vanished poet.

Nicholas tipped his chair back to listen to his mother talk about her meeting at the Blue Sky Diner downtown with her agent, envisioning the scene that she recounted with her characteristic flair. He would sit right here and wait for the subject of the trip to come up—and then make sure she knew he wanted to go. Leaving town with her was the only way he was going to get out of another night examining furniture with his father, and he'd had enough of that this winter to last the rest of his life.

"Well." Frank crossed his arms and leaned down onto the counter to focus intently on Lydia's face with a professorial attitude. "You know you can't depend on them or wait for them to come around. How many times have we talked about this over the years? For better or worse, you chose the genre novel path. You have the obstacle of being known almost exclusively for romance writing, right? That's just how it is, but that isn't all you are. Or, at least, not all you once were."

"You're right. It isn't all I am. Though I don't want to jinx the romance writing. We've all benefited from it."

"But the price? You have the obstacle of an agent and editor who think of you as having certain limitations, so you have to either change their perspectives or get them out of your way and find others. You're still partly in charge."

"I know. That's true." Lydia's energy rose with Frank's attention. "Yes. I'm thinking all the time about how to change my course. And"—Lydia set her hands flat on the counter and paused—"I have a confession, Frank. Listen. Lately, I have been revisiting the idea of having our own press."

Nicholas hadn't heard this line of conversation before. His gaze shot to his father, who pulled back from the counter with an attitude Nicholas recognized but couldn't put words to.

"That'd be cool," Nicholas said with a smile that he hoped would make his mother feel good.

"I know, wouldn't it? Imagine the freedom!" his mother went on with an expansive gesture of her arms. "Not only to publish whatever we believe in, but also to push our standards through the roof!"

"Some truth to that." Frank nodded as if deep in thought, then walked to the broom closet where he began hunting through a stack of shoe boxes.

"It's just gotten so hard to listen to Barbara saying those dismissive things again and again about expanding my repertoire, which is the only vision for myself that I see a future in."

She watched Frank. Nicholas wondered if there were any more doughnuts in the pantry, and if he could get up to look without his father asking him to do something for him.

"You know what I mean?" Lydia prompted. As if she'd read

Nicholas's mind, she fetched the box of doughnuts, took one out for herself, then placed it on the edge of the counter near him.

Frank kept rummaging and said nothing.

"What are you looking for, Frank?"

"This…thing," he muttered. "Don't worry about it."

"No one involved wants to take even the slightest risk, but I don't know why that surprises me. It's a business that always proves itself to be more conservative than I wish it were."

"Any publishing venture is risky," Frank said, standing up and pointing the handle end of a small tack hammer toward her. He cocked one side of his mouth. "Don't think your own wouldn't be."

"Risky, oh yes," she said. "I'm ready. Because I'm risking literary death if I don't take myself seriously."

"Remember, romance novels *are* the only fiction you've written. For quite some time. Sounds like you may be taking yourself a bit *too* seriously."

"Well, thanks a lot." Lydia's pale face closed up, her mouth twisting as if to stop her own words, and Nicholas felt a pang of the hurt he knew his father's jabs like this caused. She aimed her gaze out the window. After a few seconds, she squinted and asked, "Did we leave the barn door open all night? Or have you already been doing something in there?"

Frank rose to his feet, red-faced from exertion, and took a tiny screwdriver to the loose handle of a jeweler's magnifying glass. "Nick and I had to put the armoire in there."

"What armoire?"

"I told you about it." He glanced at her, then back down at the magnifying glass, his tone mildly annoyed.

"No, you didn't. What armoire? Something new?"

Frank set the screwdriver and magnifying glass down on the counter with exaggerated patience. "Of course it's not *new*. It's probably over a hundred and twenty years old."

"You know what I mean. Where did it come from?" She

looked over to Nicholas, then back at Frank. Nicholas tipped his chair silently down to the floor and took his glasses off to wipe the lenses.

"Nancy's place. She went to an estate sale last week." Frank pocketed the glass and walked to the coffeemaker.

"Wait, wait, wait. Hold it. You *bought* another armoire. How much?" The fingers of Lydia's right hand started to work over one another, as if trying to remove dried glue.

Frank exhaled loudly without looking at her as he poured a cup of coffee. "The cost... Is money really the point here?"

"Come off it, Frank. You just bought that other thing last weekend, that steamer trunk. Overpriced, as you finally admitted. And yes, *someone* has to think about our budget."

"Here we go," Frank mused, shaking his head slowly. "The work of finding an answer to one of the most important mysteries in women's literature has ceased to mean enough to you to back me up while I take it on."

Nicholas stood up slowly, planning to slip out of the room, but his father rapped him on the shoulder.

"Stay here, Son. I want your help in a minute."

"I have homework I should do," Nick said too quietly to be heard. He knew how this conversation was going to go; he didn't need to listen to it again.

"Oh, Frank, come on," Lydia said warily. "You know quite well that I, more than everyone else combined—except you, Nicholas—have been fully involved in this enterprise from the start. From *before* the start. You never would have paid any attention to Mary Stone Walker if not for *my* interest in her years before you'd even heard her name. The truth is, I'm the reason you're here teaching about her!"

"Lydia, that's just silly. You don't think the quality of her poetry would have led me to her eventually? Not to mention her beauty, the intrigue of her disappearance?" He smirked, then continued as if talking to himself. "Definitely taking herself too seriously."

"You know how it was," Lydia said. "Our conversations literally gave birth to this quest of yours."

"Lydia, my dear, you are overestimating your effect on my life," Frank said casually, almost sweetly.

Nicholas looked down at his hands. There were dark scuffs on his palms, dirt from the armoire. He clenched them shut.

"I see," Lydia said in a subdued tone after a moment. "Well. Speaking of the intrigue of Mary Walker…lately, I find myself thinking about things like your trunks, your armoires…you know, our search that never bears fruit. And then I cross paths with someone like Lincoln Babcock. Do you know him?"

"Maybe. What's the relevance?"

"Well, I met him this morning." Lydia seemed to be expecting a strong reaction from Frank, but he thumbed obliviously through the contents of his wallet. "If you know who he is, then please tell me why we haven't interviewed him about Mary Walker and the Evans family. You've never even mentioned him to me."

Frank shook his head as he shoved his wallet into a back pocket of his jeans and shifted his jaw.

"Lydia. You have not examined my research notes in quite some time, nor sat in conversation with me about my latest thoughts. So this is no longer *our* search, and *we* don't interview people like Babcock because *I* have standards. You don't know the reasons why I choose which leads to follow, although you knew at one time. It seems to me that Mary Walker issues are not part of your life any longer."

"Are you kidding?" Lydia interjected, slapping her hand on the counter, but Frank ignored her.

"*I* am the one in possession of the big picture. I am the one continuing the work—*not you*. If I thought it would lead to any new and genuine knowledge, I would go to Babcock this afternoon." Frank gave an expression of interested innocence.

"So as far as you're concerned, I'm suddenly not part of this thing we've shared forever?" Lydia's voice was shaking slightly, and when she glanced at Nicholas, he knew that she wished he wasn't there to witness this scene. "You're so mean sometimes."

"Oh, Lydia, grow up." Frank pretended to lighten his tone, nodding his head once toward the barn as he pulled his coat off its hook. "If the search still matters to you, then come take a look at my latest acquisition."

"The search matters to me," she said flatly. "That's what I'm trying to say. It matters to me." She stared past him out the window.

"So come on!"

"The search matters to me *so much* that I want to pursue some form of gathering information *other than prying apart antiques*." She took a glass out of the cupboard, filled it with water, and held it without drinking. "The way this is going, it's likely to continue for the rest of your life without results. But…maybe that's how you like it."

Again, Lydia watched Frank's back, waiting for a response, but he silently bent down to tie the laces of his boots.

"Besides, we have made other plans, and we should get going." Her face was still tense as she gave a noisy sigh, took a sip of water, then poured the rest out. "I just have to gather a few things. I hope you're remembering the folk arts festival?"

Frank straightened and forced an exasperated laugh.

"Look, I've asked you before not to arrange things for me. I don't have time to spend two full days on nonsense. I'm going to run some errands in preparation for this evening, including getting the hot dogs *you*"—he pointed at Nicholas—"are going to cook for us."

He opened the back door and tugged it shut behind him, walking across the grass toward the barn. Nicholas could hear him whistling.

"Wow. He's a real downer sometimes," Nicholas said, then injected some enthusiasm into his voice, hoping it would help switch his mother's thoughts to the trip. "I'll get my backpack so we can go. It's ready and waiting."

"Oh. No. That's okay, Nicholas. You can stay here," Lydia said distractedly. "I'll go alone."

"But I want to go, Mom. I'd *rather* go. *Please.*"

She took a deep breath and glanced at him before she started fussing with items in the kitchen sink. "You're nice to say that… but let's just make a different plan. I've got a lot to think about."

"So my plans get trashed because of another stupid piece of furniture?" His voice shook with irritation. "It's not fair! I wanted to go."

"Well, I'm really sorry." She looked into his eyes, and he could see that she was. "But the weather's not great, and now Dad needs your help."

"No he doesn't! He really doesn't. You know he only drags me into his stuff to keep him company. I just run around getting things for him," Nicholas said, watching his mother dry her hands and pick up her briefcase. It was so obvious that she just wanted to avoid another confrontation with his father. Over and over, he was dumped off in the middle like some object without feelings.

"We'll find something else to do soon," she said unconvincingly.

"Yeah, sure," he muttered angrily, and he put on his coat and went outside. "Same old, same old thing," he said to himself as he walked away from the house. He ducked out of view of his father, who was holding a tape measure across the back of the armoire in the barn. It was too early to knock on a friend's door, and lately, he had begun to feel even lonelier around all of them anyway. How could he talk to people about stuff like movies and sports and girls when it felt like his world was crumbling and he was never calm? No matter where he was or what he was doing, thoughts raced in his mind constantly, spinning into tight wires of dread and fear.

He lifted his eyes to the clear sky, and as he waited for his breathing to slow, he spotted, almost too thin to see, a stream of cirrus clouds in the otherwise naked atmosphere, pulled by a wind too high to feel. He envisioned that invisible force caught in white sailcloth and walked quickly away from home, toward the wooded shoreline one mile west of town.

3

If there's not too much sun nor too much cloud,
And the warm wind is neither still nor loud,
Perhaps my secret I may say,
Or you may guess.

~ *Christina Georgina Rossetti (1830–1894), "Winter: My Secret"*

At five years old, Lydia Milliken watched her mother leave the house with a strange man, never to return to or contact her family again. John Milliken raised his two daughters alone while he worked in town as a family law attorney. With an unusual level of freedom, Lydia was free to explore the streets, alleys, and corners of White Hill unsupervised, secretly looking for her mother in little fenced backyards, the checkout lines at stores, and the windows of strangers' homes. Even now, decades later, White Hill was slightly haunted by elusive memories of the woman whose absence had had a far more powerful effect on Lydia than had her brief presence.

When Lydia discovered Mary Stone Walker's poetry in the town library and realized that this legendary writer wrote about the town and lakeshore that Lydia knew so well, she felt a joy she'd never experienced before, newly identifying not only with the poet's perceptions, but also with the power of language itself. And when she came to understand that Mary had been motherless, too, this fused a powerful psychological bond with the poet. Hours spent reading Mary Walker's poetry in the window seat of her tiny bedroom were some of Lydia's oldest, most beloved memories.

In Mary's era, there had been fewer female poets who wrote openly about the pain of feeling unseen and unloved. Themes of nationalism, Christianity, romantic love, and death were common, but Mary wrote about everything. It seemed that no remembered moment, no internal experience was insignificant. As a young poet herself, Lydia had held Mary Stone Walker up as an idol, so her adult years of searching with Frank for the vanished woman and any unpublished words she might have left behind felt like an honorable quest.

On this Saturday so many years later, Lydia Milliken was Lydia Carroll, who had gone away at eighteen to Ann Arbor to study literature, then to Boston for an MFA program, finally returning to White Hill to write novels far less complex than the poetry she admired and expected to compose. But the novels supported her, and they supported Nicholas and Frank. Security seemed worth the compromise. Even if her own husband voiced no appreciation of it.

Lydia kicked at a bottle cap on the sidewalk and furrowed her brow. Frank's opinions about her career hurt, she had to admit; but even more unsettling was the fact that she had reached a point sometime in this past year where she found her romance writing difficult and awkward. She had always been able to do what a professional does and write the novels that fed her family, regardless of her mood or conflicting aspirations. But in the last few months, she had struggled with even the simplest, most familiar writing tasks for her next novel, as if her mind were protesting the entire process.

Approaching Charlotte's Book Web downtown, Lydia had a flash of the bike shop it had once been, with an aqua tandem bike hanging over the front door. Her older sister, Louise, had saved up allowance money and bought her first "big girl" bike there at ten years old, a bike that was passed down to Lydia and pedaled along this very sidewalk countless times. But today, books about gardening, birds, and outdoor sporting destinations in Michigan were arranged among gardening tools and pots of artificial flowers in the shop's front window, and an electric camping lantern beamed its light out onto the chilly street.

Charlotte, the shop owner, stood at the counter with a pen held over a stack of papers, and as Lydia stepped into the shop, a wave of coffee and book-scented air flew through the door. Even a simply plotted, thoughtful novel about a bookstore, she thought, would bring such rewarding changes to her writing life.

Charlotte looked up. "Hey, my friend, how are you?" she asked with a wide smile made all the more charming by her slightly crossed eyes behind large, round glasses.

"Just fine, except for a case of writer's block. Right now, I'm on my way up north to a folk arts festival, but first, I have a question for you." Lydia sat down in one of the fat, upholstered armchairs at the center of the book-filled room that was one of her favorite places in the world. She and Charlotte had developed a close friendship over the last decade, conversing sometimes until midnight about books, writing, and the mysteries of Mary Stone Walker and White Hill. "So I got to meet Lincoln Babcock this morning. Know him?"

"Sure." Charlotte put aside her paperwork and stepped over to a kitchenette to refill her coffee cup. "Coffee?"

"No thanks. What a strange character."

"He's one of those guys who's into a lot of different things. Local politics, real estate, church leadership. But not dedicated to any one. You know? Kind of like my brother. I mean, Orin's fascinating, but he's all over the page."

"At least Orin's likable. Lincoln was not pleasant. I guess one of his hats is as caretaker for the Evans property, Mary Walker's house."

"Mmm." Charlotte gazed at Lydia. "I remember that connection. I think he came on strong a few years ago about erasing Mary from history. Ha! As I recall, he even wrote an editorial or two."

"Ah, yes. I'd forgotten about that."

"I believe he said she's not worthy of being admired because she destroyed an entire family. Something like that."

"And he expressed that sentiment this morning. I don't understand how that old drama can still matter to him so much. Or why it ever did."

"I have a vague recollection that his grandfather became a financial partner of Bernard Evans's just before Mary vanished and everything fell apart. Some connection like that. So crazy Bernard lost what would have been Lincoln's inheritance maybe?"

"Huh. Maybe Lincoln's father was the old guy I saw with him this morning," Lydia said as the shop door opened.

Three middle-aged women strolled in and sat at one of the café tables, chatting. Charlotte leaned across the counter and took notes as the women listed the coffee drinks and pastries they wanted.

Lydia stood and walked to the front window, gazing at the line of shops across the street, the largest of which was the former general store, now an antique mall. At the other end of the block, the old Stevens Hotel was four stories tall, with windows aimed down Water Street toward Lake Michigan, a feature that had enticed an investment company to purchase it for renovation the year before. So far, the only visible step that had been taken on the project was the sign placed near the road. The small cityscape was so much like it had been in Mary's time.

"Babcock's fixation really is curious," Charlotte said when Lydia walked back to join her at the food counter. "Did you set him straight about Mary?"

"I said that she might have been so troubled that she committed suicide. His response was that *that* would also be a betrayal of Bernard. Not really interested in her side of things." They chuckled, then Lydia sighed and sank down into an armchair. "Well, I sure hope she wasn't that miserable. It would be such a gift to find out that she didn't take her own life or drown at twenty-five because of some stupid accident. Wouldn't you love to discover that she escaped this small-town trap and wrote incognito somewhere?"

"Oh my, you know I would!"

In the sixty years since Mary Stone Walker's disappearance, nine documents containing previously unpublished poetry and several paragraphs of prose had been found tucked skillfully into the structures of various objects Mary had had access to during her documented life. Two desks, a lamp, a sewing box, and many other items, some of which Mary had mentioned specifically in journals. Then there were also works Mary referred to by title or content but which had never been found in her manuscripts, so they were assumed to be hidden somewhere.

Why she had tucked the poems away was uncertain, but the quirk had created a strange and captivating literary mystery that revived interest in the poet every time a new piece was found. For years, Frank and Lydia had worked to decipher clues about where Mary had been when she'd felt compelled to hide her writings. It had seemed possible, likely even, that the woman had fled White Hill in 1939 and continued writing. The fact that nothing found so far was dated after her disappearance only inspired Frank and Lydia to keep looking, but they had never found a document themselves. Not yet.

"Sometimes I picture *The Lost Poems of Mary Stone Walker* up there in the window," Charlotte said as she pulled a box of pastries from a shelf behind her and added three éclairs and two lemon cupcakes to the covered glass plate on the counter. "A whole display of nothing else. It could be as exciting to serious readers as finding more work by any of the classic writers! Wasn't it the *New York Times* that compared her to Sylvia Plath?"

Charlotte gave Lydia a promising smile and raised both hands. "And there Frank will be, poised to publish that massive book of his. Your family can finally benefit from it. All the research. The endless patience."

Lydia nodded. Should she update Charlotte on the sorry state of Frank's endless tome? His original plan had been for his definitive account of Mary's life, work, and mysterious fate to be written and released in three volumes, and just a few years out of graduate school, he had created an outline for forty-five chapters total. When Nicholas was in elementary school, Charlotte had hosted an event at which Frank read from the opening chapter to a respectably sized audience heavily populated by young female fans from his classes, and at that time, he had seven completed chapters. Ten years later, the manuscript had hardly increased in size: he hadn't quite finished chapter eight.

If things continued to go on like they had for years, and neither Frank nor Lydia did anything to force change, a surge in Mary Walker's popularity or a discovery of unknown facts or writings would bring no benefit for the Carroll family. Frank was light-years from having anything like a publishable manuscript, nor did he seem to think about that aspect of his obsession anymore. No, just like every other time it had occurred to Lydia to confide in someone about this issue, it was too embarrassing to bring up.

"By the way, a woman stopped in right before I left for Chicago last week," Charlotte said. "And since you're here…"

She grabbed something from under the cash register and came around to sit on the wide arm of Lydia's chair. It was a large, old scrapbook that Charlotte opened to the first page, where *E. Van Zant* was written in script. She flipped past three or four pages of newspaper clippings.

"This is an odd collection of things," Charlotte mused. "I'm not sure what to make of it. Except that I think the common thread may be some sort of personal White Hill networking effort. A lot of these articles are about the businesses located in this region in the early nineteen hundreds."

"Who does it belong to? I mean, who is this? E. Van Zant?"

"Ethel Van Zant. She was an herbalist here in town for decades. Her daughter was a midwife, and then *that* woman's daughter followed in the tradition with a little homeopathic medicine operation up north. In Misquers, I think. It was that homeopathic woman who brought this to me. Walked right in with this single item and no other interest, saying she wanted someone to have it that could understand its value and hang on to it. And I think that means you and Frank, even if she didn't know it."

Charlotte leaned close to the paper to peer at a square, yellowed clipping, running her forefinger slowly under the names and pointing to the smallest female figure in the middle of the group photograph.

"That's Ethel, third one from the left," she said. "This was a gathering of rural health practitioners showing support for the new hospital. And here's why I thought you and Frank might be interested. In the article, down here, Ethel is quoted as saying she was the 'primary apothecary for White Hill's literati during Carson College's golden era as one of the finest liberal arts colleges in the Midwest.'"

"Golden era? I haven't heard that one before. Before it became a community college obviously."

"Considering that this was 1951 and she is quite old in the picture, I can only assume that she meant Mary Walker's era, 1920s, 1930s, when the Chicago poets passed through from time to time and Mary's mentor, Griffin Clark, taught here. Not to mention Mary, of course."

"You said that the granddaughter has a shop in Misquers?" Lydia felt a tingle of inspiration. "Still in business?"

"It is. I just recently noticed a newspaper ad for aromatherapy sessions there. It's called Northern Herb Sense," Charlotte said as she stepped around the counter to her computer to search for the shop's address online. "Yes. The shop is at 540 Oak Street, Misquers. Oak Street intersects with the main drag."

"You know…I think I'll go," Lydia said. "Why not? It's on the way to the festival."

"Looks like the place is open late for tea-leaf readings on Saturdays. Until nine. You're in luck," Charlotte said. "Here, take this."

She handed Lydia the scrapbook.

"Are you sure?"

"Maybe it will spark a new line of research for Frank."

Lydia nodded, standing up with a flash of agitation. She knew he'd never look at it. He hadn't even been open to hearing about her conversation with Lincoln Babcock this morning.

"I won't hold my breath. He prefers *his* own interpretations of Mary's written words to the 'wild, scattered notions' of other people, as he's fond of saying. Even if they might be the woman's peers with some little, gritty piece of real life in their memories that could unlock the entire mystery of her disappearance," Lydia said. "Don't get me wrong. I am invested in this search, Charlotte, and I always have been. But I'm so tired of dead-ending in the same old fictions and irrelevant antiques. I just want to know the truth. You know what I mean? There are real things that happened, so there has to be a path of facts, and I'm pretty sure we're not on it."

"I understand," Charlotte said. "I've sensed your need to change course for a good long while. It's time."

"There's nothing I'd love more than to regain the old mind-sync that Frank and I used to have for this endeavor. We had so much fun, such stimulating talks about words, writing, love and death and fear… Everything seemed to come together in those conversations when we were analyzing her manuscripts for clues and visiting the places she lived, and for a while the examination of the antiques was a real thrill. I think even now we could get back our partnership by brainstorming how to conclude his book and sell it. Don't you think that might be possible?"

She searched Charlotte's eyes as if her friend might know the answer, then looked down at her hands, opening her purse for her keys. "Ah, well. If he isn't willing to listen to my thoughts about any of this, I'm going to try to trust my own instincts. Bring these years and years of effort together into some kind of conclusion."

"You are someone who should indeed trust their instincts," Charlotte said with a gentle smile.

"Well, thank you. We'll see."

Lydia blew a kiss in Charlotte's direction and left the shop to seek Granddaughter Van Zant.

"Northern Herb Sense" was painted in silver, cursive letters on the door of an old Victorian house at 540 Oak Street. Lydia knocked and then tried the knob. The door was unlocked, so she pushed it open slowly and found herself in a long, narrow room with shelves full of books, candles, crystals, bottles, and dozens of other odds and ends. The exotic scent of essential oils filled the air. One milk-glass table lamp burned at the cash register, and another light glowed somewhere beyond curtains at the back of the shop.

"May I help you?"

Startled by the voice that emerged from a side room, Lydia looked up from a display case full of jewelry near the cash register. A middle-aged woman wearing a straight wool skirt and a tight, little pink cardigan gave her a brief smile, then raised her eyebrows.

"Are we expecting you?" she asked, confused. A square of brown shoulder-length hair framed a pale face of about fifty years.

"I heard that you're open until nine for tea-leaf readings," Lydia said, smiling.

"Oh, I'm afraid not." The woman sounded genuinely apologetic. "In the off-season, it's only by appointment. I guess the front door was unlocked because we've been going in and out all day. Spring-cleaning, you know. How did you hear about us?"

"Actually it was someone's visit to White Hill that led to my visit today!" Lydia said brightly.

The woman stepped closer, looking puzzled. "A visit?"

"Someone from your shop visited Charlotte's Book Web. I thought it must have been you."

"Oh!" The woman's expression darkened. "Yes."

"Charlotte showed me the scrapbook you dropped off." Lydia started to unzip her briefcase. "I brought it with me—"

"Excuse me, what is your name?" the woman interrupted, cool fingers on the back of Lydia's hand to stop her from withdrawing the scrapbook. "All this chatter, and I don't even know who you are."

Lydia was startled by the woman's suddenly critical tone. Mentally, she took a step back and told herself to calm down. She had, after all, just barged into this woman's place unexpectedly.

"Please forgive me. I'm Lydia Carroll."

"Okay. I'm Theresa, the owner. And you have come here why?" A second later she shook her head. "Never mind. Don't answer, please. Listen…" She opened her mouth to say something, but instead raised her hand and pointed across the shop toward the room she had emerged from. "Come in the consultation room for a few minutes. Would you, please?"

"Maybe this is a bad time, Theresa. I can come back another day."

"Oh, please don't be coy now. The interruption has been made." Theresa gave an irritated laugh. "Come along."

In the consultation room stood a round wooden table, four

leather chairs, and a clear-glass oil lamp with a low, blue flame. A deck of tarot cards was stacked near the lamp with several individual cards laid on the table in a pattern. Theresa pulled the curtains closed and gestured for Lydia to take the chair opposite the one she sat in. She raised a light cloth and lowered it gently to cover the tarot configuration. Her manner softened slightly.

"You'll have to forgive my discomfort, but your visit is distinctly unwelcome, to be honest. Especially today when we have been cleaning."

Lydia stared at her.

"I did not ever want that scrapbook back in my sight, not in our shop, not in this county. And yet someone has come and brought it with her." Her smile was tight. "And you probably want me to answer questions about my grandmother and Mary Walker, am I right?"

"Why, yes." Lydia was cautious. "My husband and I have been searching for clues about her life and disappearance for years."

"I figured as much." Theresa leaned back and crossed her legs. "I've heard about Professor Carroll's obsession and felt certain the scrapbook would end up secure in his hands and that he'd never let it go. I hoped, anyway. Likely there are interesting tidbits in it, but I wouldn't have any idea. As soon as I opened it to see what it was, I closed it, and for good reason." She shook her head slightly as her concentration appeared to deepen. "There are things… There are things, relics and scraps, that I needed to get rid of. You know how it is. The spring-cleaning we must do at times in our lives. There are objects with too much weight that I just need to let go of."

"Yes, I know that feeling. If this scrapbook was that disturbing, I think I would have just burned it," Lydia said sympathetically.

"But I don't really need your ideas about it, do I?" Theresa gave a brief, barren laugh. "Just please accept that I would appreciate it if you would take it away from here. Don't bring it back."

"Of course." Embarrassed, Lydia began to collect herself to leave. "I had no way of knowing."

"I'm sorry to be so strident." Theresa's gaze followed Lydia's hands as she closed up her briefcase. "But I've had a sorry amount of stress over this scrapbook and some other items of my grand-mother's. She would understand completely why everything has to go."

Lydia looked warily into the woman's agitated face. "So you had a chance to get to know her? Your grandmother?"

"Oh yes. She lived quite a long time." Theresa ran both of her hands up through her hair. "Yes, I knew her. But only as my grandmother. I did not know her as a healer. I would have liked to talk to her about such things."

"I can imagine. But she clearly made an impression on you." Lydia smiled and gestured to the shop beyond the curtains. "Here you are in your own similar business."

Theresa's mouth turned down. "You could say she made an impression. Or you could say she dug my grave."

Lydia was stunned.

Theresa leaned forward and said, "There are realms you don't think about. Don't know about. Don't *want* to know about." Her intensity grew mesmerizing. "Something happened. We don't know what, but something happened in Grandmother's life and practice that led to…irreversible events." She lowered her voice to the point where it was almost a growl. "Things were set in motion that I might not have chosen for myself. They were chosen for me. And I'm certain it started with her. I have suffered for it. We all have."

There was the sound of a door slamming at the back of the shop, then the footsteps and voice of a man.

"I dropped it off," he said loudly. "The deed is done."

Theresa froze.

"Theresa?" the man called.

"I'm here." She stood up and went quickly into the main

room. "We have a customer. Come on out, dear," she said to Lydia with a practiced smile. "I can help you with your nerves and your sleep issue right over here. We think of this as our little pharmacy."

When Lydia approached her, Theresa said, "This is my husband, Bill." She turned to the man. "Bill, this is a visitor who did not realize we are closed on Saturdays in the off-season. She only had a few minutes, but I think we've been able to help her out."

A tall, coarse-looking man with black hair stood with his hands on his hips and merely nodded his head once when Lydia said hello.

"You are probably interested in some calming oils for your evening away from home," Theresa said musically, reaching for a tablet of paper and a pen. "Are you staying the night in a hotel?"

Lydia followed the woman's lead.

"That roadside motel up the highway a few miles," she said. "I've stayed there with my son and husband several times, so it has pleasant memories."

"Yes." Theresa jotted some notes, held a hand to her mouth, then walked to her medicine counter where brown bottles of all sizes stood waiting for customized mixtures.

"I think lavender, bergamot, jasmine. Especially good for these bone-chilling early spring weeks." She poured small amounts from each of three larger bottles into a beaker, shook it gently, and poured the mixture into a small brown bottle, twisting a black cap on tightly. In careful script she wrote instructions on a label, peeled it from the backing, and smoothed it onto the bottle.

With a grunt, Bill left the room, and Lydia heard what sounded like water running and splashing around in a sink in the back, just out of view. Theresa stood up very straight and pressed the bottle into Lydia's hand.

"You'll enjoy this, and I am certain it will aid your sleep," she said as she came around the counter, put her hand on Lydia's elbow, and walked her toward the front door. "As for your other concerns, I wish you the best." Bill reentered the room, wiping his hands on a towel and watching the two women. Theresa added, "Just a few drops in your tea!"

"Thank you," Lydia said when they stood at the door, then she whispered, "But...the cost?"

Theresa closed her eyes, gave a shake of her head, and said, "Good night! Put everything out of your mind and rest deeply now." She opened the shop door. "This must be your Jeep?"

"Yes." Lydia's gaze ran over the parking lot, where there were no other cars and nothing but wet asphalt. "May I possibly return to speak with you tomorrow?"

"I'm afraid Sundays are not good. Drive carefully. The rain is heavy now."

Lydia prepared to respond, but as soon as she stepped outside, the door was closing behind her. She heard the knob lock, and then the dead bolt, then the inside lights went out. Lydia hurried through the cold rain into her Jeep, pulled the bottle from her pocket, and squinted at it. The herbalist's handwriting was tiny, but legible.

Lavender, bergamot, jasmine. For deep sleep. March 1999. Theresa V. Z. Evans.

Evans? Could this granddaughter of old Ethel Van Zant have married a relation of Bernard Evans? Evans was a common name, so there was no reason to assume a connection. And yet...

Lydia started the Jeep, backed up, and gave a last look at the dark house as she straightened her wheels to go north on the road. Something was not right at Northern Herb Sense. And it was pretty clear she wasn't welcome back.

So, that was that. The black road gleamed and hissed under her tires. What a futile, unnerving encounter. There must have been some other way she could have handled it so she would have gained something more valuable than another cloud of questions. How could it possibly help to know that Ethel Van Zant's granddaughter lived with torment that she believed had been set in motion decades ago by her grandmother?

Lydia imagined Frank gleefully laughing at her failed interview. His strategy of seeking information from written words alone, without involving unpredictable human beings, had obvious advantages.

4

Let it be so…
Better—while life is quick
And every pain immense and joy supreme,
And all I have and am
Flames upward to the dream…

~ Lola Ridge (1873–1941), "Dedication"

Bernard Evans watched the Carson College actresses from the front row, hungrily waiting for moments when a patch of skin might slide free of the silks and cottons. *Romeo and Juliet*, an all-female cast—his friends had howled with laughter when he said he was going, and then they'd come along.

He gave a low whistle when Mercutio swaggered onto the stage, dashing and agile in black velvet boots, her gold hair curling almost down to her waist. She reminded Bernard of… of what? Angels, probably. Paintings he'd seen of angels. Even her voice was seductive, and although the words sounded like incantations, he caught hints about their meanings from her gestures and expressions.

"That one," he said to his friend Conrad beside him, drawing the attention of audience members around them. "Who is she?"

Conrad shrugged, but Richard bent around Conrad to answer, jabbing his thumb toward the stage. "Mary Walker. She's one of those"—he pointed to his head to indicate Mary's intellectual bent—"and poorer than dirt, but too good for you or me. So they say, 'Don't bother.'"

Bernard looked back at the girl onstage, whose beautiful body and bright face painted a womanly image that matched his ideal and became even more appealing with Richard's words. If she were needy, then perhaps she would prove a quick victory.

"'I dream'd a dream tonight,'" a tall woman with a long, dark braid recited.

"'And so did I,'" the blond answered.

"'Well, what was yours?'"

"'That dreamers often lie.'"

Bernard smiled at the actress's provocative tone and physical confidence.

Mary Walker's body filled with energy as she leaned out toward the audience with lines that went on and on, dizzyingly senseless to Bernard, and then she seemed to focus on Bernard's face. His heart raced and he began to sweat. She ran her tongue along her upper lip, and one slender finger brushed a lock of hair from her face.

When Mary left the stage, Bernard rose from his seat and slid sideways past the knees of his friends, for he could barely breathe and needed fresh air. He couldn't stand it, just sitting there. He would have to find her. He needed to keep looking at her. He wanted to touch and smell her, and to feel her attention on him. Ignoring the silence that he was noticeably interrupting, he pushed out the side door near the stage into the cool May air.

Christ have mercy. As Bernard stared up into the night, his breath came hard and fast. What had come over him? Within a few brief minutes, nothing, *nothing* mattered but that woman. He paced the walk, inhaling deeply, and his eyes groped the darkness for something he could take backstage to her as a gift. He had to make an impression on her mind. Then he could work his way into her body.

His family's general store was three blocks away, but the

Methodist church was just a dash across the green. He ran to the arched front doors and found them unlocked. Beyond twenty rows of pews, where the altar lay in stained-glass moonlight, Bernard could make out a tall cross, the urns on either side of it filled with lilacs for services the next day. He swept the entire perfumed contents of both urns into the crook of his left arm and fled the building.

At the back end of the theater building, he found a door propped open with a stick, and he pulled it slowly, peering in. The scent of musty curtains and costumes filled his nostrils, and Shakespearean lines met his ears as Bernard Evans walked slowly inside through the shadows toward the stage light. Actresses in the wings looked at him questioningly, and he heard someone say "Sir?" but he ignored them, searching around for Mary.

When he found her, she was eyeing him from a bench where she sat retying her boots. Oblivious to everything else, he stooped down before her and pressed the blooming boughs into her arms with a motion that ensured that the back of his hand brushed her breast. He smiled at both the sensation and her challenging stare.

"I want you to bear my children," Bernard said in an intimate tone that he had developed over years, but as the blond laughed and raised her eyebrows, she seemed more amused than charmed.

"How dramatic! I doubt that I will ever have anyone's child, sir," she said, pushing the flowers back toward him. "Who are you?"

"You know who I am." Bernard's certainty was based on his family's prominence in the town, as well as the ease with which his looks typically lured women of all ages to accept his invitations, no matter how compromising they might be. Of course she knew; she was playing games with him.

"You clearly think I ought to."

"Ask any of your friends." He offered the lilacs again, and she set them on her lap.

"Mary!" The call came from a woman moving toward them

from the curtain. Mary stood quickly, setting the flowers on the bench, but Bernard grabbed one of her wrists and pressed his lips softly to the delicate, pale skin on the inside of it. She paused, as if she were taking in the sensation, then yanked her hand away.

"Mary," he whispered with a gentler smile as he stood up. "I'll bring my car around after the show. It's a Cadillac. Yellow. I will wait."

"You will, won't you?" she said, her gaze darting around his face. "Whether I want you to or not."

"*Mary!*" a voice hissed.

She flashed her eyes toward Bernard one last time, said nothing more, and floated back onto the stage.

5

Under the discolored eaves,
    Out of trunks with hingeless covers
    Lifting tales of saints and lovers,
Travelers, goblins, thieves...

~ Edna St. Vincent Millay (1892–1950), "The Poet and His Book"

Around seven o'clock that evening, there was a knock at the front door of the Carroll house—three crisp, dramatic raps. Seconds later, the door opened and thirty-year-old Drew popped her dyed-blond head into the foyer and stepped inside without waiting for a response. Watching TV in the living room, Nicholas turned to look at her standing in the hallway.

"Dad's in the study," he murmured. "Expecting you."

"Thank ye, love!" she chirped in her fake English accent, then disappeared across the rugs as if there were an emergency.

For as long as he could remember, Nicholas had shared his father's search for the poetry Mary Stone Walker might have left behind. His memory was full of images of his father's intense blue gaze focused on the legs, backs, and drawers of furniture as his hands worked along seams, carefully searching with a magnifying glass, pulling wood from wood, cloth from wood, detaching hinges, mirrors, knobs, and even inlays that looked tampered with, hoping to find the smallest scrap of paper or hidden compartment.

Nicholas listened to his father's speculations, poetry recitations, and stories. He handed him tools, held things in place, and hurried to the kitchen for more wine to fuel the search. Mary Stone Walker verses and his father's daydreams about the poet were etched into his memory along with the scents of alcohol, must, and aged wood.

The study door was open, so Nicholas could hear every sound from the room. He turned off the TV to listen closely for a sign that his father had forgotten about him and it was okay to leave the house. Kevin had called, bugging Nicholas to go to the dance at school, and there was something inside him so urgent to be released from his parents' world that even that dreaded event sounded like a decent escape plan.

"Josh Bailey and Amanda Vanderveen. I hope you don't mind," Drew was saying. "They were both so curious about the essay we were reviewing in class—that one from the fifties about some of the first of Mary's hidden poems that were found. But like I was saying, Conor Thiele told me there's a new critique—"

"Wine?"

"Of course! That one looks good. Gorgeous label. Anyway, a new critique of Margaret Lynne's notations on Mary's *Sea Shadows*. This guy from Stanford—don't remember his name— complains that Lynne's notes about the poem are based on the fabrication that Mary lived past 1939 when in fact we have no good reason to think so."

"Oh! I see. We don't." Frank chuckled.

"Right. He says that to critique her work as if it is part of a larger whole we know nothing about is fantasy. Bad scholarship. That's what he says."

"If that's what Lynne was doing, he would have a point." Frank's voice was loose and lively.

Stealthily, Nicholas took small steps toward the staircase, hoping to run up, change his clothes for the dance, and then slip out the back door.

"Exactly. Well, I mention it because the timing would be so fantastic to write about a new discovery! There's that Chicago symposium in November, the Female Poetic Voice. Margaret Lynne's always there. I'd like to be there, too, with something noteworthy to add."

"So let's get started on the armoire!" Frank said. Nicholas heard clinking sounds as his father gathered up the wine and corkscrew to take them to the barn. "Nick! Nicholas!"

Nicholas considered ignoring him. A silent dash up the remaining stairs and into his room, and maybe he'd be safe. But his father was suddenly there in the hall, and Nicholas felt his gaze on him like a hook.

"Hey, you're going to help with this, right?" Frank said.

There was a time when Nicholas would have gone to great lengths and even told lies to get out of a school function—like this stupid dance—in order to stay home, whatever the cost of staying home might be. How could it be that all of that maneuvering to hide from the social demands of school had been so much easier to pull off than simply saying no to his father now?

"I told Kevin I'd hang out."

"What do you mean? We already talked about this. You stayed home tonight to help me."

"But, Dad, you don't need me." His tone sounded childishly pleading to his own ears. "*She's* here."

"Don't tell me what I need, Son." Frank's tone was stern. "And do not go back on your word so easily. Come on out to the barn, and bring some snacks when you do."

Nicholas recognized the intensity that always lit his father's communication as soon as he started to drink, and his nervous system registered it as a warning. He watched his father and Drew head cheerfully outside, chattering energetically, and a prickling rage that began in his throat spread quickly through his whole body.

He stomped heavily back downstairs to the kitchen, yanked

a platter from the cupboard, clunked it down onto the counter, and crossed to the refrigerator, where he grabbed cheeses, apples, and nuts, then dumped everything, along with the contents of a box of crackers, onto the platter. Then he picked up the saltshaker and shook salt violently over all of it. He leaned close to the food, examining it to ensure that the salt was not visible, but was gripped by remorse and tried frantically to brush it all off.

At last, he carted the food out to the barn and slumped down in an old chair. What had happened to the hot dog and popcorn idea? Now who wasn't keeping his word?

"Sit up here, boy. I need your nimble fingers. Take the doors off first. Let's have a look under those hinges." With his toe, Frank scraped the toolbox across the dirt floor toward Nicholas.

"Who was it that turned you on to this piece?" Drew sank deeper into an old, cushioned wing chair, swirling a thimbleful of wine at the bottom of her glass.

"Got a call from a Craig DeVries, a Grand Haven dealer, who said it was owned by a professor at Hope College. He wasn't one hundred percent sure of the provenance before that, but when I saw this, I felt pretty sure it was a decent bet. I just have a feeling about it."

"Ooh!" Drew pitched her voice high and tapped her feet in excitement, widening her eyes with a broad smile directed at Nicholas. "Isn't this great?"

Nicholas raised his eyebrows to imply agreement, then turned back to trying to keep the tiny screwdriver point in grooves worn shallow with age.

"You know, sometimes I think it's her beauty that gets to them, makes her critics think she was inconsequential," Frank said as he pried at the hinges of a cabinet door. "That she was just fluff."

"Mmm. Maybe so." Drew shook her head, face sad. "Of course, these days it's different, in my opinion. Women poets are taken seriously now, regardless of what they look like. Don't you think so?"

"Just look at any of the photographs of Mary. She's angelic, with soul-piercing eyes. Gorgeous, curling gold hair. A perfect female form." Frank shook his head, lost in the vision. "They think she was a fake, incapable of genius. Chauvinistic bastards. Jealous."

"You got it, Professor Carroll." Again, Drew flashed a giant smile at Nicholas as he removed the first door.

These comments were all things Nicholas had heard in various permutations a hundred times, but Drew had been around for only a year or so, a favorite of his father's, an apparent standout from the string of faces that had been dropping by the house all of Nicholas's life to discuss Mary Stone Walker. Nicholas had given up trying to figure out how his father maintained interest in his collection of unchanging observations.

"Ah-ah-ah, wait! Let me take that." Frank lifted the door high and away so as not to splinter the wood. He brushed it off and handed it back to Nicholas, then put his magnifying glass up to the strip of wood that had been concealed beneath the edge of the door.

"You think she might have taken the door off to…write on the wood?" Nicholas asked, confused.

"Well, probably not to write *on* it." Frank was distracted. "But we have to consider…" He stooped down to look at the lower hinge point.

"Oh, look who's here!" Drew cried, standing up. Two dim figures stood a few feet outside the barn doors.

"What's up, Drew?" a male voice said.

"Come on in," Drew replied, pointing toward a folding chair and a crate for the two to sit on. The young man wore a black fedora, a yellow scarf, and a baggy, striped cardigan that looked as if it could have been his grandfather's. His eyelids were lazy over brown eyes that did not seem to notice Nicholas. The woman did not look any older than Nicholas, though he could tell she was by her demeanor, her casually spiked blond hair, and the crazy hodgepodge of her clothing, along with the fact that she also ignored Nicholas entirely, her eyes going straight to Frank, apparently enthralled. She stood close to him, radiating admiration. Frank's gaze remained fixed to the furniture with such ferocity that Drew stood and leaned over next to him to ask what he was seeing.

"I can't be sure…" Frank's voice trailed off, and after a moment Drew nudged his arm, gesturing toward the visitors.

"Joshua and Amanda, Professor Carroll," Drew said.

Frank stood straight, facing them as if he had not noticed their arrival until this moment. He held out his hand and gave a suave half smile that Nicholas referred to privately as his "I'm the professor" smile, tipping his head toward each student.

Josh, who was over six feet tall but slender, straightened as if he wished to meet Frank's height and pulled out a pack of cigarettes.

Drew put her hand on his. "No smokes in here," she said.

"Oh, sure," Josh responded vaguely, still holding his pack and a lighter. He nodded toward the armoire. "Is this in any way similar to some other piece of furniture where a Walker poem was found?"

Frank did not respond. He had moved to the back of the armoire and was examining the panels. Amanda cleared her throat. Drew offered the students wineglasses and poured a couple of inches of wine into each. Amanda cleared her throat again, then spoke in a high, querulous voice.

"Professor Carroll, I think it's so important what you're doing," she said. She glanced at Drew, who nodded. "I mean, I have this one anthology where there are hardly any women poets. There are, like, two." She gave a short, indignant laugh. "What's the deal, you know? It's like women were trapped in cages and not even allowed to express themselves or something."

Frank gave an appreciative, low chuckle and sighed, backing up from the armoire and reaching for his wineglass. Then he looked intently at Amanda and sat down in his favorite velvet chair.

"That's a good word, Mandy," he said. "A choice word. *Trapped*. That's exactly what we see suggested in much of Mary Stone Walker's work, especially from the last months of her time here in White Hill."

Frank paused for what was intended to be only a moment in a flowing narrative that Nicholas recognized well, but Josh interjected.

"What I don't get," he said, turning his left palm open, his eyes still apparently only half-interested in this gathering, "is how you can look for so long and find nothing and…just keep looking. You know, in the same way, over and over."

Both women looked into their wineglasses, and Nicholas closed his eyes and pressed deeper into his chair. Josh turned his head and gazed slowly around the dimly lit barn full of antiques. "Is this all stuff you've examined looking for something Mary Walker wrote?" He scanned the crowded landscape of dark forms, then shook his head. "Wow."

Frank's smile was patronizing as he looked at Josh and said nothing. The others were silent.

Josh shifted uncomfortably, and his eyes opened wider. "But yeah," he said, "I have to admire your…dedication." He tried to wrap up his interruption with a shallow nod of approval, but Frank continued to stare as if he were trying to identify an insect on his dinner plate. "After all, you did help find that one poem, right?"

"No," Drew said quickly with a nervous glance at Frank. "There were poems found, but—"

"Wasn't that… That wasn't you?" Josh looked at Frank, then Drew, whose brow was furrowed as she gave Josh tiny warning shakes of her head.

"Well, Joshua. You've stumbled onto one of the problems in the world of knowledge and judgment," Frank said. Elbows on his knees, he held out his hands and gazed between them as if studying the space there. "And that is, when you essentially don't have any knowledge about a subject, then it's hard to make a judgment that's worth a damn." He turned his eyes toward Josh, and the young man opened his mouth to speak, but Frank held up one index finger.

"Sometimes...sometimes," he said softly as he narrowed his eyes, "when you've entered someone else's area of expertise, and, let's say, you know very little about their work, and absolutely nothing about them, it's best to just"—he flung his hands open and smiled—"keep your adolescent nonsense to yourself. You know what I mean, son?"

Drew forced a laugh and leaned forward. "He's just curious, Frank. It's understandable, considering—"

"Hmm," Frank interrupted, appearing puzzled. "Curiosity wearing a mask of ignorance and rudeness. Fascinating, Drew." He shook his head and went back to examining the armoire as if no one else were in the room.

Nicholas barely breathed and hoped Amanda and Josh really had forgotten he was there. After a full minute of silence, except for the sound of Frank's file on the hundred-year-old cherry-wood, Drew stood up.

"Well," she said with a hearty exhale, as if she'd just finished cleaning a room, "I believe we're interrupting your concentration. Maybe we'll check back in with you later in the week, Professor Carroll. When you have had a chance to focus on your work here."

The three of them stepped lightly out of the barn while Frank made no response. Nicholas heard the jingle of someone's car keys but no voices as they crossed the dark yard. He feared that if he stood to leave, his father would continue the lecture meant for the student, so he slowly sat up straighter in his chair and waited. But his father worked in silence for more than ten minutes, at last saying simply, "Get to bed, Nicholas. I don't need any help."

For hours, Nicholas read in his bedroom and listened for his father to enter the house but heard nothing. It was after two in the morning when he was awakened by the sound of Frank's voice downstairs, and he cracked his door open to listen.

"No, no, no. Nothing like that." His father seemed to be on the phone, speaking loudly. "I'm telling you, no. Nothing's going on. It's natural, isn't it? To miss your wife, who's never home?… You are not… Maybe so. Soon. That's all I'm saying. Not a goddamn festival. A more romantic destination. Yeah. What?" He laughed, then after a long pause when Nicholas assumed his mother was talking, his father said, "Well, you can tell me about it tomorrow. No, not now. I'm whipped. And hopefully you'll sleep it off. Good night… Yep. See you then."

Nicholas carefully pressed his door shut and went back to his bed. In the not-so-distant past, when he knew his parents had made amends after an argument, his mind would be washed with relief and he could return easily to the simplicity of his world. More often now, however, he felt only partial pleasure that was not strong enough to dispel a growing unease as his mind groped helplessly for answers, and even questions, that he could feel but not quite identify. He turned his eyes toward the side window where stars appeared now and then from behind slow-drifting clouds, and eventually, though he thought it would never happen, he fell back asleep.

6

When foxes eat the last gold grape,
And the last white antelope is killed,
I shall stop fighting and escape
Into a little house I'll build.

~ Elinor Wylie (1885–1928), "Escape"

L ydia hung up the phone and lay back down on the paper-crisp sheets of the motel bed. Wonderful—Frank had told her to "sleep off" her curiosity about the herbalist and the strange man at her shop. She'd mentioned the scrapbook Charlotte had passed along, and Frank had laughed. When he was like that, she usually concluded that it was just a mood or drunkenness and that she might find him open-minded at another time.

But she was starting to suspect that such moments revealed a lack of respect for her intelligence, and those later times when she hoped he might listen to her ideas never actually came to pass. She no longer seemed to have any credibility with him—not like in the days when she was dedicated to the same viewpoints he had. Everything she did in the real world to try to pin down the truth about Mary Walker's fate met with his unconditional resistance.

Lydia had always theorized that Frank could write a fascinating book about their long effort to find the poet, even if the outcome of the woman's life remained uncertain, and he could conclude with an exploration of the numerous, intriguing questions that still remained unanswered. But he had never given that idea much credence, and as time went on, his vision had narrowed from the scholarly exploration of every issue relevant to Mary Stone Walker's life and work to an appealing string of daydreams about her beauty and mystique, her life after she disappeared, and the nature of the work she might have gone on to create. Any fresh, worldly information about the years of her life during which she actually drew breath and struggled to write in White Hill had become irrelevant.

As Lydia lay in the motel trying to ignore the occasional roar of semis passing on the highway twenty yards from her window, she contemplated her own career path. Was it just as repetitious and disengaged from real life as Frank's seemed to be? She did not know if the romance novels were increasingly difficult to write because her power to create was failing her, or if she was just bored with genre writing, but she suspected that the fact that *romance* had become disconnected from anything she could call real life made the endeavor dead for her.

Now Lydia felt compelled to write about those subjects that mattered to her: motherhood, poetry, the human struggle to find love and meaning, and the history of life here on Lake Michigan. But she had a contract to fulfill. She would have to do both at the same time, beginning with gathering facts from the past that might give rise to a new novel.

The scrapbook! Her circling thoughts had pushed the day's events far away. Lydia got up and brought the book to bed with her. The cover was deep red with a gold chain of fleurs-de-lis imprinted around the edge, although partly rubbed off by hands through time. When she lifted the cover to open the book, the spine gave a small creak. Inside were about forty pages of crumbling black paper. Newspaper articles had been attached with daubs of glue, but many of the articles were loose, and all were yellow and brittle. Lydia felt a tremor of excitement. Stories of real lives spilled from every page.

Due to the difficulty of obtaining meat on a regular basis—this article was from May 1931—White Hill's Greyhound bus station cafeteria was introducing Meatless Mondays, featuring macaroni and cheese and four-bean chili, and Spaghetti Saturdays when the protein source would be cheese. Hero Outfitters was expanding its line of sporting gear in July 1928 to include men's and women's winter coats, with plans to add more clothing items by the next year. Both articles had photographs, the first of a dish of macaroni, the second of Hero's front window full of fishing gear. Lydia scanned the rest of the pages and found that every article was a simple little story about an area business. Most included the names of key people, and some of those seemed to have been underlined in pencil.

She would read everything in the scrapbook for ideas, if not clues about Mary Walker. She set the book on the bedside table and stared at it for a minute, imagining it lying somewhere in Ethel Van Zant's cottage when Mary Walker visited the herbalist. She reached over and opened the cover again. No, there was no date. She turned to the inside of the back cover, and there the dates 1918–1953 were written. She smiled, closed her eyes, and felt the imagined companionship of both women.

At last she dozed off, but was awakened by a sound outside. Close to her motel room, a car door slammed, and then Lydia thought she saw a beam of light darting around. She sat up and inched toward the window.

A bulky form was leaning forward over the hood of her Jeep, beaming a small flashlight onto the windshield. The person stood straight, and it became clear that it was a woman. In fact, it looked like Theresa Evans in a rain hat and trench coat. Lydia gasped and backed away, watching through the gap in the curtains as the woman jammed something flat under the Jeep's windshield wiper, then got back in her own car and returned to the highway. When the taillights vanished, Lydia put on her coat and rushed outside.

She snatched the object from the wet windshield and went back to her room. It was an envelope inside a clear plastic bag, and the distinctive handwriting was the same as that on the label of the bottle Theresa had given her. Lydia tore the envelope open and pulled out a short letter.

Mrs. Carroll —

I can't let my husband know I am sharing personal information with you. But my instincts tell me that unburdening myself of a few facts will improve my situation. Bill thinks that we mustn't ever speak about Mary Walker, and I have seen enough unaccountable misery in our lives to understand why. We have been the victims of a curse.

My grandmother gave mixtures to Mary because the girl had night tremors and panics, and God knows what else. She was a morphine addict, but she hid it, even from Grandmother, which was devious. The last time my grandmother saw her, Mary confessed, but by then it was too late. The mixture Grandmother had been giving her for years should never have ever been used with an opiate. It can cause deadly nerve damage and depression that might lead anyone to take their own life.

This may be where all the darkness started for my family and Bill's. I don't know. But now someone else knows of the mistake, so at least my conscience is relieved of the weight of secrecy.

Lydia's mind raced. Her gaze flew around the small motel room, then she got under the covers and pulled them tightly around herself. She read Theresa Evans's note again. Mary, a morphine addict? How many times had Frank insisted this was not the case? That it was impossible for that rumor to be true without references to the addiction showing up in her journals? It was a good question…but Mary Walker's weird behavior had begged for a better explanation than they'd ever come up with. And what about the frequent gaps in the journals?

Lydia had always struggled with these issues, while Frank assumed they were caused by Mary's fear of her husband. It was true that Mary had written countless anxiety-riddled journal entries about Bernard's violence and regular violation of her privacy, but to Lydia it had always seemed that an important part of the story was still missing.

Morphine. Addiction. These were like wild cards in the puzzle of Mary's life. They changed the picture. Yet Lydia was willing to bet that Frank would never consider them as the significant realities they apparently were. Not even in the face of this letter.

"Oh, Professor Carroll," Lydia whispered into the stuffy air, her eyes wide open toward the ceiling. "Your Mary and my Mary are so different."

Half an hour later, Lydia accepted that there would be no sleeping for her. Not now. Not here. The Sunday schedule of events at the folk arts festival would not begin for six or seven more hours, and Lydia's mood had darkened to the point that she wondered why it had ever occurred to her to drive all this way alone for a festival. Had the days of having the lighthearted companionship of a husband and child come to an end so soon?

Okay, she was shaken up, tired, and suddenly maudlin. Time to get out of here. She hurriedly dressed and packed, and drove as fast as she could away from Misquers, Michigan, and toward home.

But before returning to her house, Lydia drove to the light-house and pier where Mary had last been seen so long ago. She turned the Jeep off, wrapped a blanket around herself, and watched the water rise and fall against the jetty. For a long time, she stared at its flow from the channel, until it rolled at last from black to mercury silver in the morning light. Fishermen came and went, and seagulls cried.

She stared so long and so intently that she felt herself standing on that pier, wind whipping, rain lashing, desperation and morphine racing through her veins. It was all too easy to imagine a domineering husband bearing down on her. To feel the reckless desire to escape. One thing that suicide had going for it was that death left no open doors from this world.

Nicholas made a point of rising early to leave the house that morning before his father awoke. He walked the mile to the lake, then along the shoreline until he found an old orchard that he had never seen before. Sitting down with his sketchbook and pencils, he worked for almost three hours.

When a cloudburst swelled from the woolly gray on the southwest horizon, he stuffed his sketchbook under his T-shirt, grabbed his backpack, and ran for cover, dashing through the trees toward two buildings he could barely make out in the downpour, one of which turned out to be a barn. He stood under the overhang of the roof. Ten minutes later, the cold, pelting rain stopped as suddenly as it had begun, and Nicholas stepped onto the wet path covered with brown pine needles to walk home. He opened his sketchbook to the last piece he'd done. Not bad. Not finished, but not bad.

A screen door on the house thirty feet away whined open, then slammed, and Nicholas turned to see a man walking slowly from the doorway, watching him. He appeared to be about Nicholas's mother's age, his face freckled, his hair slightly curly and the color of wet sand. When he spoke, his voice was clear and dry.

"Hey there, buddy." The man lifted a tangle of rope from the concrete pad outside his back door and wound it in a loop over his palm and elbow. "Visiting the lakeshore?"

"No, I live near town," Nicholas said quickly. "I was born here."

"I see. Me, too." The man hooked the circle of rope onto one of several nails by the door and stepped toward Nicholas, right hand outstretched. "Jack Kenilworth."

Nicholas extended his own thin arm. "Nick Carroll."

Jack Kenilworth studied his face for a few seconds, then scanned to Nicholas's feet and back. He reached into the breast pocket of his faded-orange denim shirt, pulled out a pack of Camel cigarettes, and lit one, inhaling and blowing smoke off to the side as he gazed toward the lake, then back at Nicholas.

"I knew your mother a little bit when she was about your age. High school." His eyes seemed to smile, then he glanced at the sketchbook. "Doing homework out here?"

"Just… I draw."

"Let's see what you got." Jack slid his hands into worn jeans pockets and waited.

Nicholas was startled. "Okay." As he stood next to the man and flipped from the unfinished piece to his completed sketch of a damaged sailboat half buried in the sand not far from the Kenilworth house, he could feel Jack's interest rise immediately.

"Good eye," he said, looking into Nicholas's face. "Excellent detail and proportions." He pointed to fancy letters along the side of the boat, a faint smile visible. "Who's Chelsea?"

Nicholas felt his face grow instantly hot, but he forced himself to look Jack in the eye and just shrug. Jack cleared his throat and gestured toward the barn. "Say, do you have time to come into the workshop? I run my business out of this barn here, and I think it might interest you. Got a minute?"

Nicholas looked at the man's open expression and found it surprisingly easy to imagine him as a kid at White Hill High School. He wondered what sort of job Jack Kenilworth did by himself up here in the woods, and curiosity answered the invitation for him. "Sure, that'd be cool."

Nicholas slid the sketchbook into his backpack and followed Jack into the vast building. Unlike the Carrolls' barn, this one was well preserved and finished off with drywall and long bars of track lights mounted into the rafters. Instead of dirt, the floor was painted planks, and a long pine worktable was built into the far wall. Shelves full of books and rolled paper stood at each end of the table, and a pegboard above it held a variety of measurement tools.

"This is a studio, of sorts," Jack said, gazing around the space along with Nicholas. "But I'm not much of an artist when it comes to pencils and paper. I do what I have to for my projects, but it ain't always pretty."

Nicholas nodded, confused. Then he noticed three enlarged photos of a single sailboat from different angles, along with correlating sketches, pinned to a corkboard. "You draw boats?" he asked.

"I *build* boats," Jack said, walking toward the table. Nicholas followed him. "Mostly I purchase plans that have been built before. But once in a while I have to loft one of them. This is where I do it, and for me it's damn tedious." He shook his head at Nicholas and seemed to expect a comment. "I don't have much of an eye for two-dimensional forms, and my math comes slow. All in all, lofting takes me forever. As I said, the results are rough. But usually they suffice." He gave a short laugh. "Usually."

Nicholas raised his eyebrows and pushed his glasses up, still unable to make any kind of intelligent remark.

"You know. When boat plans are new, you loft them—draw them full scale here on the floor. To make sure there aren't any errors, so you build the boat right."

Nicholas looked down. "On the floor? Wow. How do you do that?"

"Measure and then measure again, and then again. That's most of it. Math. Then the drawing, of course. Takes patience. I do better with the 3-D part—the wood, nails, glue, the process of making the actual boat."

It seemed magnificent to Nicholas. Drawings as large as ships, drawings that filled a barn. His eyes searched the floorboards for ghost boats.

"I start with this." Jack pulled out a blueprint that was about two feet by three and spread it on the worktable. "The blueprints of the designs I choose usually arrive by mail—a bunch of sheets containing the plans. One drawing is three views of the boat's shape, and those are called the *lines*.

"First you draw the baseline—with great care—and everything else will be derived from that," Jack said. "Like this." He tapped a small nail into the floor, walked several measured paces and tapped in another, stringing a wire between them. "Under this wire you put strong marks about every two and a half feet with chalk, then use the yardstick there to connect them. Here, give it a try."

"I don't know…"

"Don't worry about it. Just focus on making that one line as straight as you can."

Nicholas felt Jack watching him as he concentrated and then stooped down to make the line.

"That's right," Jack said encouragingly as Nicholas marked off several dashes and drew a careful line through them all. "See, we've made the baseline twenty feet long. Leaves plenty of room above it for the seventeen-foot boat, right?"

"Right."

"Then, you *must* look from both ends of the base to make sure it's true, because like I said, everything's going to be built off it." Jack walked to the worktable and picked up the top sheet of plans. "There's so much here to do. And I can see you've handled pencils for many hours. Am I right?"

"Definitely," Nicholas said, nodding. The man's interest encouraged him to talk. "I've copied the road maps of every county in Michigan. When I was younger, I used to imitate the signatures and drawings of famous people."

"Mmm, how useful." Jack looked amused. "Famous people like your parents? Got yourself out of class once in a while?"

Nicholas laughed, avoiding Jack's eyes. "Well, maybe. It feels like drawing is sort of—I don't know—where I live."

"I bet." When Nicholas glanced up, the man's eyes were resting on him with a studious look. "So…you want a job?"

Nicholas chuckled, but the man's expression didn't change.

"A job? Really? Well, I actually do need one." He tried to think of the proper thing to say. He was absolutely sure that he wanted *some* kind of change in his life. "But I don't know if I can do…serious drawing."

"We can give it a go, see if it works out. If you want to. Nothing to lose for either of us, right?"

Nicholas considered this and all that it might mean for his freedom. He would have somewhere else to go besides school and home. And he could save every penny he earned to buy a car for a long, long trip. Or maybe a boat. He smiled.

7

Our heaven will not come to us again…

~ Mildred Amelia Barker, "Not Again"

T he father of the bride sat on the back steps of the church, gazing across the arid depressions of former tide pools and holding an unlit, hand-rolled cigarette between two fingers. A widower for half his life and a loner for most of it before that, Leonard Walker knew that he was expected to walk his daughter down the aisle, but he didn't care for socializing and was uncomfortable around his future son-in-law, so he'd fled the crowd to wait until she came for him.

Mary stood near an arbor covered with wild roses as her three bridesmaids adjusted her hair and veil with fastidious attention that filled her with gratitude. She watched their fingers, lips, and eyes around her face as they fussed over details.

"It will be all right, Mary, whatever you do," Ruth said in the intelligent, cool voice Mary had learned to rely on. "You're so beautiful that no one and nothing in this world can harm you."

"So beautiful," Helen echoed, shaking her head with a smile, her own delicate features lit with excitement. "Bernard is lucky, Mary, even if people might think you're the fortunate one. The fact is, he couldn't possibly do better."

Helen's smile crumpled into tears, and she put a hand on

Mary's cheek. "You have to take good care of yourself, Mary. He isn't the kind of man who will understand everything you need."

"Helen," Ruth said. "Mary knows what kind of man she's marrying. And frankly, no man understands everything a woman needs."

Josephine laughed and stepped back, hands clasped together at her chest. "I hope I look so perfect when I'm a bride! Let me get the photographer!"

"But I think it's almost time for the ceremony, isn't it?" Mary asked as she spotted a boy entering the bell tower to pull the ropes. Then it occurred to her: Where was her father? She had hugged him an hour or more ago when he'd arrived, but she had not seen him since. Where had he gone? With the wariness she'd developed as a young child, she squinted toward the windows of the church. Had he gone inside? She scanned the lawn. He should be here. He should not make her worry today. It would be mortifying if he'd walked down the beach and gotten too far away, or if he'd gone into one of his disturbing trances and ended up—

"Ruth!" Mary's worry made her breathless. "Would you please help me look for my father?"

The desperate note in Mary's voice brought Ruth quickly, and she laid a hand on Mary's shoulder.

"Of course, dear! Where do you think he might be?"

Mary could not explain how to look for her father. Someone searching would have to walk slowly, trying to think from his point of view, while watching for sights that might have drawn his attention and lured him away.

"Oh, I'll just have to go myself because I don't know how to explain his crazy mind," she muttered. "Ruth, please do get the photographer to come over here, and I will hurry back!"

Surely he would not go far on such an important occasion, Mary thought, fuming. She wrapped her fingers into the thick, white fabric of her wedding dress to lift it and run around behind the church toward the woods and dunes. It was a cool September day, and wind gusted in from the lake, but the sunlight was warm. About a hundred feet behind the church, the beach stretched for empty miles in both directions. Suspecting her father had gone wandering too far away to hear her voice, Mary stood in the wind and searched the shore. But then she heard him call her name. She turned. He was just there, on the back steps of the church, and he stood up and walked toward her.

"Daddy, what are you doing?" Relief and frustration poured out in her voice, but when his eyes widened with alarm, she tried to lighten her tone to banter. "I am getting married, don't you know?"

She forced a laugh, and her father attempted a smile. She could feel his gaze taking in the bridal image of her, but she couldn't tell if the tenderness in his eyes was for her or for some distant, tender moment that wasn't even part of her life.

"Mary," he said, tossing aside what was left of his cigarette and brushing his hands together, his face pensive. She wondered if he was going to announce that he just couldn't do it, couldn't endure the attention to his "old bones" long enough to walk her down the aisle. He was the only member of her family in attendance, and she did not think she could bear the shame of such a refusal. His silence continued, and her fists clenched more fiercely around the white satin of her skirt.

"What, Daddy? *What?*" She wanted to scream at him to be stronger, to pay attention to time, to other people, to the world around them both that would swallow them whole if they didn't assert at least a modicum of strength. The first set of invitational church bells rang, but still Leonard did not speak. "*Daddy.*"

His gaze rose quickly to hers, and at last he focused. She knew her expression was angry, but she no longer cared.

"I had a thought last night, my dear," he said carefully, and his mind appeared to follow that thought down winding corridors, again losing track of the moment at hand. "And I find myself fearing that I missed some important moments along the way."

Mary set her jaw in a warning that he did not seem to perceive.

"Along what way, Daddy?" she said evenly. "What—"

"Your life. I think there may have been points when I could have…better prepared you for"—he searched her eyes, his own glittering with tears—"for whatever comes. I will always try to save you from wrongdoing, but—"

"Daddy," Mary said with all the patience she could muster. She felt bitter resentment at hearing him speak of saving her, when for as long as she could remember in their actual lives, she had saved him—from sadness, from distraction, from malnutrition, from mistakes, from dropping out of life altogether. She did not want to hear about his fears for her. "I don't think it's the right time to talk about this."

He looked into her eyes for a moment, and then his intention receded. "Right," he said quietly. "I don't suppose it is."

Mary caught sight of Bernard's powerful form in a dark suit that added class to his raw masculine appeal, and her spirits rose. Bernard Evans—with his beautiful, strong body, free laugh, and cerulean-blue eyes full of vitality—was the ship that would take her away from the foggy, dangerous waters that her father inhabited.

"It's a journey, Daddy." She forced a smile and reached for his hand to urge him toward the church doors. "That's all it ever is. A journey. You can't save me from that, and I wouldn't want you to."

Side by side, they walked to a still point before the camera, where the photographer requested that Mary loop her arm through her father's. Church doors wide behind them, sun directly overhead in a cloudless sky, neither father nor daughter cast a shadow in the only photo ever taken of them together.

8

A Dream Self in a world of dreams:
A Shadow Self, among the gleams
The arc-lights cast.

~ Fannie Stearns Davis (1861–1934), "The Dream Self"

At the dinner table Sunday night after his mother had returned from Misquers, Nicholas was too excited about his good news to eat, but he cut his lasagna into many small pieces as he ran through his announcement again in his head.

"Guess what," he finally began, looking back and forth from his mother to his father for a response. His father was reading a magazine, so after a moment his mother gave the obligatory "What?"

"Well, this afternoon I went to the beach," Nicholas began, still hoping for interest to rise in their preoccupied faces. "I went north in the dunes until I came to an old orchard I've never seen before. Down below there was a damaged sailboat, and I spent hours trying to draw it *exactly* like it was. I mean *exactly*. Not skip over a single detail." Nicholas's mother got up and went to the refrigerator. He waited for her to return. "Then this downpour started, and I ended up running to a barn and a cabin near the orchard, and the man who lives there showed me the workshop he has in his barn. It's amazing."

"In Carson Woods?" his mother asked.

Nicholas nodded. "He builds boats, so when I showed him my

sailboat sketch, guess what?" When neither of them responded, he went on. "He offered me a job!"

"A job, Nicholas?" His mother's voice was surprised. "What kind of job?"

"A job drawing boats."

"My goodness!" Lydia glanced at her husband, then back at Nicholas. "Who is this?"

Frank was still absorbed in his reading and had not seemed to hear the announcement at all.

"Jack Kenilworth," Nicholas said, and at this, his father glanced over the top of his reading glasses.

"What about Jack Kenilworth?" he asked as if these were the first words Nicholas had spoken.

"He offered Nicholas a job drawing boats," Lydia said.

His father gave a short, hard laugh.

"He's an idiot," Frank said, looking back down at his magazine.

"You mean because he's not an academic?" Lydia asked lightly.

"He'd be an idiot if he *were* an academic. He's a…parasitic hermit. Living on public land for nothing. *Doing* nothing."

"It was his family's land before it was a state park," Lydia said. "In fact, they didn't have to donate it at all." She turned to Nicholas. "What would you draw boats for, honey? Advertisements or something?"

"Lydia, don't lead the boy on. He can't work for Kenilworth," Frank said. "He's only fourteen!"

"I turned fifteen in December, Dad. Remember?" Why wasn't the birth of your own child the easiest thing in the world to remember? Pretty sure his father would not look up and catch him, Nicholas scowled at him.

"Fourteen, fifteen—he's not accomplished enough to do anything like that, for God's sake. With a guy like Kenilworth, Nick would just get blamed for doing something wrong." Frank turned a few pages of the magazine, smoothing them with a heavy hand against the table, but his expression was dark. "Hell, even if Nick did put in hours, he'd never get paid. Not by that… con artist."

"Jeez, Dad."

"You don't even know him!" Lydia laughed.

"The hell I don't. He came to a reading once, and I could tell right away what he was. A fake. A con artist."

Nicholas's mind fogged with regret that he had brought the subject up at all. He hated these moments. He felt like a pathetic little kid, a five-year-old or something. His father only had to get angry to mess up the brains of everyone else in the room—and he knew it, too.

"He sat in the audience at one reading, and you could tell he's a con artist?" Lydia asked.

"That's right. Doesn't take more than that with some people. Saw him making the rounds in the room afterward."

"What do you mean?" she asked. "'Making the rounds'?"

Frank glared at Lydia over the tops of his glasses. "I was reading from my fourth chapter about Mary, in which I compile the evidence and use her own lines to expand upon speculation about her marriage, and he asked some question about my sources, then went afterward to talk to a couple of my colleagues. A troublemaker. An arrogant asshole."

"Why did he question your sources?"

"Exactly. Why indeed? He was pretending that he had knowledge that he did not."

"With all due respect, Frank, it's possible he knew something you haven't heard. He's lived here all of his life. I'm asking, what did he have to say?"

"I don't even know. He was too ridiculous to listen to."

Lydia made an indignant sound. "Frank! We spend all this time on Mary Stone Walker, and all this *money*, and then when someone offers information, you turn it down? And who's the arrogant one?"

"As I said, he has no credibility. As a scholar, you can't run around gathering up people's family gossip and fairy tales. You have to research from a core line of facts, a strong hypothesis. Kenilworth falls way outside my line of facts. And note that he just came to a reading to provoke me, and there's never been another peep on any other front about his *knowledge*. That should tell you something. He was just entertaining himself at my expense, and if I'd indulged him, I would have gotten an earful of bullshit. I know the type."

Lydia shook her head, ripped off a piece of French bread, and pressed her elbows on the table. "It probably isn't too late to find out what he wanted to say. I mean, come on, you know how it is: a seemingly insignificant detail can trigger new understanding of the written material. This is what I have been talking about. There are people out there to speak with. There's this scrapbook to examine. And who knows what else we might find."

"The old herbalist's scrapbook, huh?" Frank grunted.

"Why not? *Somehow* you have to move forward with the Walker manuscript, don't you? Maybe Nicholas's association with Jack Kenilworth can reopen the door with him. He seemed like a decent guy in high school."

"Defend the idiot. That's right, Lydia, and get our son into a situation where he will be misled and taken advantage of." Frank scraped back his chair to leave the table and nodded his head toward Nicholas. "I have plenty for you to do around here that you don't get done, young man. You have a thing or two to learn before you go off playing at a job for a fool who squats on public land. And don't you try to tell me that a boatbuilder can help me finish my dissertation, Lydia," he finished, shifting his accusing stare toward his wife.

Lydia's jaw tightened. "You're acting like a snob, Frank. Great example to set." She cast a glance at Nicholas. "While attempting to insult a virtual stranger, you're hurting your son's feelings."

"The truth shouldn't hurt anyone's feelings. Right, sweetie? Isn't that what you always tell me?" Frank's tone made Nicholas turn his focus to his plate. "I believe I know a bit more about Jack Kenilworth than you do."

"Doesn't sound like you know much of anything about him," she muttered. "Doesn't sound like you gave him the time of day."

"*I* was there. *You* were not." Frank shook his head. "You know, I think I'll let you two talk this over without me since you're happier ignoring the relevant facts." He grabbed his truck keys, jerked the door open, and slammed it behind him.

"Good grief, where did all that come from?" Lydia said, leaving the table to scrape the food from her plate into the sink. Nicholas left the kitchen as quietly as he could.

For a while, Nicholas didn't dare return to Jack Kenilworth's barn, but when he did, the boatbuilder seemed genuinely happy to see him. They worked together for over an hour in the chilly barn, Jack explaining the plans point by point and showing Nicholas exactly how to transpose them accurately onto the wooden floor. While Nicholas used the colored pencils and compasses to repeat the process Jack had taught him for the water lines, Jack strode to a window cracked open near the end of the barn, sat down on a high stool, and lit a cigarette. When he finished the first, Nicholas noticed that he lit another and wondered why Jack didn't just go outside. Fifteen minutes passed in silence, and Nicholas grew almost light-headed with joy at how clear and easy this process was for him. He was startled from a deep concentration when he heard Jack's voice but didn't process the words.

"What?" Nicholas asked.

"I said, 'So how's life?'" Jack's chuckle turned into a cough, and he waved the un-inhaled cigarette smoke out the window.

"Life's okay," Nicholas said. He didn't think his lines would be accurate if he tried to talk while setting them. He nodded, waiting to see if Jack wanted to say more.

"How're your folks?"

"Same as always."

"Good, I guess?"

"Yeah." The comments his father had made about Jack popped into Nicholas's mind, and before he thought it through, he said, "I guess you know both my parents. My dad said he met you once."

"Did he?" Jack gave Nicholas a small smile. "Once, huh?"

Jack's expression sent a wave of nervousness through Nicholas's stomach, and Jack seemed to notice a change on the boy's face because he dropped his smirk and stood up, brushing off his jeans. He was businesslike as he stooped beside Nicholas.

"Let's see what you've got," he said. Nicholas watched the man's brown eyes become sharply focused on the colored lines Nicholas had drawn. After a couple of minutes, Jack said, "Looks great so far."

Nicholas's face and shoulders relaxed, and Jack slapped him lightly on the back.

"Hey, relax! What are you worried about?"

"I wouldn't want to mess up your floor," Nicholas said as he eyed Jack.

"Oh, don't worry about that." Jack shook his head. "That's not anything to think about, messing up a line. It's just not *catching* the errors when you make them. That's the real concern in this process. Once I lost a whole load of birch because I made one miscalculation early on and everything else was off. The lofting should protect against that, but as I've said, it's not my strength."

Nicholas wanted to keep working, preferring the abstractions of numbers and lines to words. Now his thoughts were prodded by the question of why Jack made it sound like his dad was lying about how many times they'd met. It seemed inconsequential, yet strange. The wind rolling through the open window was cold and ruffled the boat plans on the table.

"What's bugging you, kid? You're doing just fine. Better than I expected, actually."

Nicholas shrugged and straightened his shoulders. But he couldn't regain his concentration. Maybe if Jack would leave he could; more and more these days, he could hardly think when he felt other people watching him. "You can go ahead and work on something else. I'm fine, I think."

"Okay, good." Jack stood up, smiling, and headed toward the door. "I have some calls to make, bills to pay. Let me know if you need anything."

Nicholas exhaled happily and looked back down at the project, but Jack spoke again.

"And say, tell your dad he crossed my mind the other day. I was wondering how his…his work is going."

When Nicholas looked up, he thought he saw a glint in Jack's eyes, but then it seemed like nothing. "What work?" he asked, uncertain whether Jack even knew his father was an English professor.

"Well, the college… He still teaches, doesn't he?"

"Yes."

"And he was writing a book about Mary Stone Walker, last I knew."

"Yes."

"Did he finish it?"

"Not yet." There was a long pause. Nicholas thought about making something up about the book being accepted by a publisher and they were just waiting for details to be worked out, but Jack cleared his throat and spoke.

"Hard to finish a book, I guess, when the subject doesn't have an ending. Or at least not the ending you're hoping for."

It surprised Nicholas that Jack knew anything about his father's manuscript, and his apprehension about Jack's attitude dug in.

"What do you mean?" he asked, pushing his glasses up.

"You know what I mean," Jack said kindly, not taking his eyes off Nicholas. "He believes she lived for many years after her disappearance."

Nicholas's face grew hot. He didn't know where to put his gaze, so it stayed locked on Jack's. He had the urge to say, "My father says you're a con man," but the desire to hear what Jack had to say was stronger.

"Is he still caught up in that…quest?" Jack asked.

The only response that came to Nicholas was a false expression of confusion, so he said nothing for a moment, but Jack waited. "Do you mean looking for documents?" Nicholas said at last.

Jack nodded slowly.

"Well, sure," Nicholas said, as if he himself thought it was great fun. "It's a hobby of his. Kind of like a treasure hunt, I guess."

"Yeah. I heard him talk about the process. More than once, actually. Probably half a dozen times. It's interesting."

"Yeah," Nicholas said as lightly as he could. He turned his eyes back to the boat plans. Clearly someone was being dishonest, either his dad or Jack, although he could not imagine a reason for either of them to do so. "Why do you think it's interesting? Doesn't have much to do with boats."

Jack raised his eyebrows. "Well, I do have interests other than boats. But you're right. Some versions of the story don't have much to do with boats. Then again, some do."

"Some versions?"

"Right. There are no boats in the story where the poet drowns in the lake, or in the one where she runs off and goes into hiding somewhere in Michigan to write more poems."

Nicholas was well aware that various scholars had studied Mary Stone Walker and that different theories existed about her fate, but he wondered why Jack took an interest. It seemed impossible that the boatbuilder loved poetry or that he had studied the poet herself.

"Do you read a lot of poetry?"

Jack seemed slightly annoyed. "That isn't all there is to the story of a poet's life. Their poetry."

Nicholas shrugged, watching him. So his dad was right. Jack Kenilworth really didn't know much about the subject. He hadn't studied Mary Stone Walker, because if he had, he would care about her poetry.

"Well, did you know her?" Nicholas asked.

"Of course I didn't know her. I'm thirty-eight. She died sixty years ago."

"*If* she died," Nicholas said. Jack's casual certainty sparked a flash of combative feeling in him.

"That's right." Jack nodded his head. "Your father's hobby. As for yourself, take my advice and stick to a hobby like drawing, Nicholas. I'll let you work. I need to make those calls before five."

Nicholas watched the boatbuilder walk out of the barn and thought of his father's harsh comments about him—but the way Jack stood and walked, and the way he talked, just did not bring to mind a con artist.

9

A piece of separate outstanding rushing is so blind with open
delicacy.
A canoe is orderly. A period is solemn. A cow is accepted.
A nice old chain is widening, it is absent, it is laid by.

~ Gertrude Stein (1874–1946), "Sugar"

Hours of writer's block stacked up into days, then weeks, and Lydia felt her confidence cracking. She'd never experienced such dullness in her mind. What if it never went away? One night at two a.m., frozen awake by fearful scenarios of her life without income, Lydia took her notebook and went in search of an all-night diner. Observing strangers, speculating about their lives, and writing down random details and bits of dialogue had worked to stimulate her imagination during her college years. She'd been a different person then, but maybe reviving that "different person" was exactly what she needed to do.

At the Cherryland Truck Stop, she sat at a white Formica booth watching semis and the occasional car roll from the dark veins of the highway to the gas-pump islands, releasing strangers who entered the store needing something and left with bottles and little bags of things. For years she'd been lucky, she guessed. She had rarely gone more than half a day feeling creatively stuck. Now she felt as if she might never be able to give life to any fictional world again, and she was at a loss to explain why it was happening.

She could get by with one or two, maybe three, inferior novels and still sell books and earn royalties. But what if her income suffered at some point? She could, and if she had to, she *would* write other things—feature articles, advertising, whatever she could find to do—but those would pay peanuts compared to her midlist successes with the romance novels.

However, *she was married*. She had a partner who had a job with open-ended advancement possibilities. If Frank would finish his dissertation and obtain his PhD, and then agree to teach full time at Carson Community College, he could become an associate professor in two years. He also had a book he could finish and potentially sell to both academic audiences and general readers, if he would just decide to.

The University of Michigan Press had virtually promised to publish his book. He had discussed the possibility multiple times with at least two of the editors. That, in turn, could lead to speaking engagements, more articles, and—she would have to insist—a moratorium on antique spending. That budgetary change alone would leave several hundred dollars more in their account every month for savings and paying down debt.

After an hour or so, she flagged the waitress and got her check. These agitating thoughts were making it hard to sit still. It had been a long time since Lydia had felt scared about the future. She needed time—time to find new subject matter, a new approach, and a new way to put it all together into novels that would extend beyond genre writing but still reach a sizable audience.

Walking back to her car in the long winter coat that covered her pajamas and an oversized pair of boots, Lydia felt tears rising. Frank would not understand her concerns; he wouldn't get why she felt both changed and needing change. The circumstances of their lives had been the same for so long: *her* earning most of their income from the novels, and him playing around with minimal teaching, research, and writing while he examined antiques, fondled Mary Stone Walker's poems and photographs, and fell in love with his visions of the girl. They had shared fifteen years of that, but it had only become clear to Lydia in the last few months that Frank's work had slowly morphed into an off-balance obsession.

Together, they had called it *dedication* and *determination*, but the situation could be viewed from an entirely different perspective, and that's where Lydia stood now. Additionally, the conversation with Frank about Jack Kenilworth had given life to a new concern: was he actively avoiding information, or even hiding facts he'd stumbled upon that didn't fit his theory? There'd been something deeply unsettling about his reaction to Nicholas's mention of the boatbuilder the other night.

She started her Jeep and headed for the pharmacy. It was time to buy a simple sleep aid and a box of chamomile tea. Theresa Evans's potion had certainly worked, but the side effect was epic nightmares. White Hill Pharmacy was open all night, and its bright ordinariness was comforting. Lydia looked around for a while but couldn't find the sleep aids, so she sat down in a blue plastic chair to wait to speak with the pharmacist, who was talking on the phone.

She flicked her eyes toward the man near the gum ball machine by the back door. Something about him was familiar. He had his left ankle propped up on his right knee and was thrumming his fingers in a rapid rhythm on a scuffed, brown leather work boot. His eyes were directed at some vague point directly ahead of him and midway between the floor and the pharmacy counter—as if to avoid her, Lydia felt, tearing her gaze off him.

"May I help you?" the silvery-blond pharmacist asked with head-tilting concern directed at Lydia. Lydia had seen other people at this same store who looked as she most likely did at this moment: downtrodden, homeless perhaps, squashed by life into a jumble of barely functioning body parts and random accessories.

"I'm wondering where your sleep aids are," Lydia said with overcompensating cheer.

"They should be right down there." The pharmacist pointed. "Aisle 8. Bottom shelf near the pain medications."

"Okay, great!" Lydia was about to stand when she noticed that the man by the gum ball machine had turned his head toward her and kept looking. In self-defense, she met his eyes. They were light brown, and the recognition they showed was pleasantly engaging.

"Lydia Milliken? Carroll, I should say?" he asked. When she raised her eyebrows questioningly and smiled, he nodded. "Thought so. It's been a while." His identity floated just below the surface of her mind, and when she continued to smile uncertainly, he added, "I'm Jack Kenilworth."

"Oh wow!" It was as if her thoughts had conjured up Jack Kenilworth's presence. "What a coincidence!"

"How's that?"

"I've been hearing about you. From my son." She could not confess that she had been arguing about him with her husband, wondering if Jack really was a liar and what secrets he may have tried to impart to Frank, and basically thinking about Jack more in the last week than she had in all of her life up to that point. "What are you doing here?"

"What am I doing here at the pharmacy? I could ask you the same," he said lightly, looking at his watch, "seeing as it's after three in the morning."

"I'm not sure I could explain why I'm here." Lydia attempted a friendly smile, a casual shrug. "Maybe to meet you!"

Jack shook his head, leaned back, and set his crossed foot back down on the floor.

"Whoops, what did I say wrong?" Lydia said to his profile, which was looking more and more familiar as memories came into focus. They had been in the same graduating class at White Hill High School, and even though the class size was modest at just under one hundred fifty students, they'd hardly crossed paths. She was the newspaper editor and a theater performer, while Jack was part of the stoner crowd and a state medalist on the cross-country ski team, which no one of any social standing gave a damn about.

"Nothing. It's just...*you*," he said guardedly, as if to keep their conversation from the pharmacist.

"Me? What about me?"

Jack reached inside his coat to his shirt pocket and pulled out a square package of gum. Lydia noticed the word *Nicorette* before he punched out a piece and slid the package back. So he was a smoker. Still.

"You're saying one thing," he answered, "but your eyes have little fireworks going off that suggest something else entirely is going on in your brain. Reminds me of somebody."

"Who?"

"Your son, of course."

"I see."

"Mmm-hmm."

"I didn't know that about myself," she said.

Jack gave her a brief look of doubt.

"Mr. Kenilworth," the pharmacist said, holding a white, stapled-shut bag in her left hand as her right keyed information into the cash register. Jack stood up, took a few steps, and reached into his back pocket for his wallet. Without Lydia thinking about it, her eyes grazed slowly along his shoulders and over his back and jeans. He hadn't changed much since high school, and this gave rise to a faint sensation of desire in Lydia's chest. She'd seen Jack on occasion over the years but never paid attention, for reasons she could not remember at this moment.

A vision of her own disheveled appearance returned to Lydia's thoughts. She looked down at her flannel-covered lap and drew her jacket more tightly around herself, just as Jack turned and gave her a two-fingered salute, his body aimed at the exit. She felt a wave of dismay that in a few seconds he would be gone.

"Good to see you," he said.

"One thing." She spoke hurriedly, sliding forward on the folding chair. "I want to tell you that Nicholas so enjoys the work you're having him do."

"He's good. Talented."

"It's just great for him at this time in his life," she improvised. "His self-esteem and all... He's quiet and alone so much these days that I get concerned..." Lydia had no conclusion to this sentence. She tried again. "I mean, I hope..."

Jack crossed his arms and settled back on his right leg, giving a couple of nods. After a moment of silence he said, "Sure. Sure. He's a good kid."

"Frank was afraid he might not be up to the task. You know, that Nicholas would disappoint you maybe. And then get disappointed himself."

Jack seemed to consider this possibility for the first time.

"Frank's my husband," she added, half hoping to see an expression on Jack's face that would indicate he didn't know him. "Nick's father."

"Yeah, I know."

"Do you? Know him?"

"Little bit."

"How?" The word came out too quickly, too eagerly. Jack gazed at Lydia, and she felt exposed.

"Most people in town know Frank Carroll, or they know of him," Jack said casually.

Lydia knew this was true but blurted out, "Really?"

"Sure, it's just...common knowledge. He's taught, lectured, all that. As you know." His expression softened. "Most people in town know you, too. You are prominent citizens of White Hill, Michigan."

Lydia's shoulders relaxed as she laughed, then she slumped back against the hard chair, suddenly tired. "So you don't really know him, I guess. 'Know *of him*' is what I should have said."

"Hmm. Maybe I'm starting to see what you mean about coincidence," Jack said in a more careful tone. "Nicholas and I were just talking about this recently. Did he say something to you?"

Lydia pretended to try to remember, then shrugged and lied. "Don't think so."

Jack shifted his jaw and looked at her closely. "Okay. I was, uh"—he laughed—"uncertain about the significance to Nicholas of a few conversations between me and his dad. I don't want any part in making him uneasy."

"Oh, don't worry," Lydia said. So there had been several meetings. "Nick's always trying to figure out things that…that maybe don't matter that much. Being an unusually sensitive kid."

"Guess so. Glad it's okay, anyway. Catch you later." His eyes flashed toward the door, then back at Lydia. "You know, you're welcome to come out to the workshop with your son one of these days. See where he works, what he's up to."

"I will." Lydia smiled at him, stood up, and on an impulse strode to him and stuck out her hand. "Good to see you."

Jack squeezed it, tipping his head forward. "Get some sleep," he said in a low voice, pushing open the pharmacy's back door and turning out into the night.

In his truck, Jack paused for a moment in the private silence and took a deep breath. "Jesus," he said. He turned on the ignition and swung around with his arm along the top of the bench seat to back out of the parking space. His eyes searched the narrow lit door of the pharmacy for Lydia, but she was out of view.

It had been some time since he'd been so vividly reminded

of the pathetic shyness that had dominated his high school personality, and it irritated the hell out of him. He was a grown man, but a little woman in pajamas with crazy red hair could discombobulate him. He'd fought it, talked when he didn't want to, while his body pleaded for him to just go outside and wait for his muscle relaxant in the parking lot. After three in the morning, he'd had to run to the drugstore because of the worst back spasms he'd had in years, and Lydia Milliken was there? What were the odds? Reflexively, his hand went to his chest pocket for a cigarette, and he found the Nicorette gum that was supposed to change his life.

"Shit." He reached the open street and jammed down on the accelerator. It wasn't as if he'd ever had a thing for her—not really. That is, not obsessively. Although she had certainly caught his eye now and then. Over the last couple of decades when he'd seen her on occasion, she was usually with her lummox husband, and it had been even easier to dismiss observations of her unusual good looks and that intensity she exuded. She was married and thus a nonissue, just like other married women; that was an easy one for him. And Jesus, could the guy she married be any more unlike himself? Jack chuckled and shook his head. So there was no issue, no real issue at all.

He noticed a deer at the side of the road and glanced at the truck clock, then back at the deer, murmuring, "A little early for breakfast, Lady." His eyes caught the whites of the doe's eyes as she curled her legs, pulled back her head, and wheeled away from the road into the dark woods. "Good choice."

Of course Jack knew in his heart that Lydia had not been completely left out of the equation when he'd been trying to decide whether to attend one of Frank's lectures to talk to him about that search he'd been on for years for Mary Stone Walker writings. Jack had been warned numerous times by other Kenilworths that Mary Stone Walker's life was no one's goddamn business, and he agreed.

He respected the local poet for what she had been: a young woman with plenty of talent, a heavy dose of early attention and ego, and her share of problems. An ordinary person, and a dead one at that, so just leave her alone; don't participate in postmortem gossip. That's how Jack justified keeping the knowledge he possessed about the poet to himself. The truth would shake things up, make people mad, and then be sensationalized and misused. It would definitely bring new problems to his life.

Local men at the barbershop and the Backroads Bar had described Frank's protracted quest as "stealing the work of a local girl." Jack didn't see it that way, but it still struck him as unseemly somehow. The manner in which the professor talked about Mary Stone Walker and her poetry made Jack suspect that the man was in love with the dead girl, more or less. His idea of her anyway. And therefore mostly interested in his own stories and the way those stories made him feel.

In fact, Frank Carroll's "passion" was part of his popularity as an interpreter of the poetry. That's what Jack had heard anyway—that Frank was well known around the state for his "emotional interpretations," or whatever they were called, and as Jack thought back to the first reading he'd attended, he agreed that the guy was entertaining to watch. He'd also published essays that Jack found faintly interesting, although they contained more speculation than actual knowledge. But bottom line, it was a little weird, being in love with a dead person you've never met—more than weird, Jack thought. Fucked up, really. And the guy was married; how'd that square with his wife?

Who cares? he asked himself. Who gives a damn about the fantasies that circulate at Carson Community College, whether they concern inventors, explorers, or poets? Who cares? People conjure shit up if it makes them happy or serves their ends to do so. That's a fact of life.

But then there was this odd juxtaposition of earnest, hometown Lydia being stuck onto the silly enterprise. She was a better poet than Mary Stone Walker anyway, in Jack's opinion. He'd read several of her poems at the emotionally raw age of seventeen when they were printed in the school newspaper, and he was so moved by their vividness, particularly the images of Lake Michigan, that he'd thought about telling her. But that was an impulse he'd killed easily enough. At that age, he'd had good instincts and knew he could not afford to get attached to someone like that.

So who was he, Jack Kenilworth, morosely inarticulate, reclusive boatbuilder, to try to correct any notion in the man's romantic noggin? Who appointed him special guardian of the Truth? Now Nicholas and Lydia were both raising the issue, as if Jack had violated something by trying to talk to the bastard years ago, when he'd only done it out of a sense of…well, pity. He rolled down his driveway, shut off the truck, slammed the door shut behind him, and entered the house.

Okay, fine, he thought, going to the kitchen sink and filling a glass with water to swallow two of the new pills. Mom, Dad, Granddad, they all said to keep your business to yourself, don't be talking around town about anything unless you wanted it twisted into something else, so fine. Let Frank Carroll and his fans have their version of reality without any input from the people who'd actually known Mary Stone Walker, like the Kenilworths. It works better for them, and the past is dead, so why not? He shook his head wearily, went to bed, and set his alarm clock for six thirty a.m.

"That's what I get for going into town in the middle of the night," he said conclusively, as if this admonishment would dismiss the other issues at hand. He lay on his back, staring into darkness as minute after minute turned into an hour and a half. At last, he threw back the covers and turned off his alarm. "Fuck it," he said, and shoved his legs back into his jeans, pulled on a shirt, went to the kitchen where he started coffee, and left the house.

In the barn, he vigorously swept up sawdust from the board cuts he'd made earlier. When he reached the worktable, next to which hung several photos of family boats from different eras, he stopped and stared for over a minute at the yellowing black-and-white photograph of the *Fata Morgana* fishing yacht. It was an eight-by-ten glossy print of a shot that his grandfather had taken, and Jack kept it up because the old man had been so proud of that early chapter of his life.

Jack and his father had spent hundreds of days helping Granddad with the boat's maintenance. His father and grandfather could work for sixteen hours straight, stopping only to light cigarettes or swig the thick, black coffee Granddad percolated at dawn. These were three habits—the work, the cigarettes, and the pitch-black caffeine brew—that Jack had picked up by the age of fifteen.

When at last the day's work was dropped for the night and the men switched from coffee to whiskey, Jack was allowed to break out the sticky, dog-eared deck of cards at the little galley table in the boat, but the longer the night and its whiskey drinking went on, the more they just talked, about everything from boats to White Hill politics.

And Granddad always said, "Folks know they can trust a Kenilworth, boys." Then he'd add, "But *we* don't trust anybody without good reason, Jack. We don't tell anybody what we say privately, or where to fish or how to think, because people will believe what they want to believe. They will get angry if you try to take their stories away from them because those stories are their personal maps of the world."

Still, though, why shouldn't the truth matter? If he was a "trusted Kenilworth," then how was it right, year after year after year, to allow silly tales to masquerade as reasonable theories, when he—and in this case, he alone—knew they were impossible?

He clipped the broom back into its spot on the cleaning rack, chuckling bitterly. He wanted a cigarette. And he wished he could sit on the deck of the *Fata Morgana*, heading out into a cold, black predawn world of water with plenty of sleep behind him and those old men to listen to. Hell, the stupid cigarettes were all he had left of them. He gave the fading photograph an accusing glance and sat down to list his tasks for the day.

10

And now the motion
of a hand,
a tiny quickening
of the heart,
and it will fall
and nothing more
can keep the sea and land apart.

~ Elizabeth Bishop (1911–1979), "The Wave"

The scream of the enormous saw was deafening. Mary could see Bernard's mouth moving but heard only the rip of steel blade into wood. Shivering in the late-winter air, she paused to watch her husband talk with the stranger, pointing and running his hand along the base of the tree being cut as he explained something. The Chicago visitor was dressed in a black overcoat and a high-quality black hat, and as if he felt her gaze, his eyes rose to hers, and the ghost of a smile came to his lips. Bernard noticed and looked toward Mary, and his smile was broad—that magnetic expression of masculine energy that was the physical feature most responsible for her marriage to Bernard Evans.

"Please bring some coffee to my office, Mary." Bernard had turned off the saw and ambled toward her, speaking loudly, casually, in an unsophisticated display of power that made her feel embarrassed for him.

"Steven Shugar," the stranger said, holding his hand out to Mary, and she clasped it briefly. It was smooth and warm. "Shugar and Behm Furniture. Your husband is showing me around this operation of his."

"Yes, he told me you were coming. I'm Mary." Mary could feel the man's admiration, and it warmed her. It had been months since she'd met anyone from beyond White Hill, and even longer since she'd encountered such a handsome man. She guessed he was about thirty-five, healthy and intelligent looking, and not wearing a wedding ring.

"The coffee, Mary?"

She turned back to Bernard, whose appearance in contrast was so suggestive of a lumberjack in a folktale that she laughed. The smile remained on his face, but its sincerity waned.

"My pleasure, Mr. Evans."

Bernard had requested that Mary visit the Evans Mill this morning to give him added credibility in his negotiations with Shugar and Behm. They were a huge and growing fine-furniture enterprise, and Bernard had spent the last several evenings examining maps to plot the additional cutting required to fulfill the Chicago partners' projected needs. Bernard Evans was the oldest son and the mill manager. During this visit, Steven Shugar would see that he was also a married man now, and his wife was a prize, both beautiful and articulate. She would enhance his image, a fact that Mary knew had figured into his interest in her from the beginning, because Bernard was practical and intended to be rich—facts that had likewise increased her interest in him.

"I understand you attended college, Mrs. Evans?" Steven asked as they sipped coffee around Bernard's desk.

"For literature and poetry writing," Mary answered.

"She got a good basic education," Bernard said proudly. "All that Carson College had to give."

"Of course there are many centers of higher learning where you could continue to interact with other scholars with similar interests," Steven said seriously, addressing Mary. "Through continued study, through readings. The social life."

Mary smiled, and Bernard gave an unenthusiastic nod.

"There are highly revered schools in Chicago," Steven Shugar continued, and Mary felt her heart open gratefully to his attention to that most essential part of her. "Often I am fortunate enough to enjoy their guest speakers and performers—some of the best in the country."

"My, how wonderful," she said.

He took a sip of coffee, his gaze steady on Mary's face, which was lit with joy at the thought of such opportunities.

"But those places are far away," Bernard said with a censoring glance at his wife.

"Yes, that's true." Steven gave a light shrug. "But your business is doing well. You never know where the profits may take you. You and your wife must have many dreams."

Mary parted her lips to agree that she, at least, did have many dreams, and to ask Steven Shugar if he personally knew women pursuing higher degrees, but Bernard leaned forward and spoke again.

"Mary wants to have a family," he said in a confidential tone that suggested Steven Shugar was among the first to be told. "In fact"—Bernard turned to her and gave that beautiful smile, squeezing her knee too tightly with one powerful hand—"my guess is that if you visit this time next year, there will be three in the Bernard Evans family."

"Ah! Well, congratulations on that." Steven Shugar lifted his coffee cup in a toast, his gaze on Mary. "To the three of you. Perhaps before that time you two can visit Chicago for a little cultural enrichment. The city grows more interesting by the week. I know you would enjoy it."

Sensing the possibility of a tighter connection to Steven Shugar, Bernard grew more interested.

"That's a fine idea," he said, then looked at Mary. "We could take the shoreline train and stay somewhere nice."

She gazed at him for several seconds without answering, staring at his strong features with sudden objectivity and imagining them mingled with hers in the form of a child.

"I've missed Chicago," she said, turning away from her husband. "So often I have wanted to return."

"When were you there?" There was alarm in Bernard's voice.

"Many times. During college. The girls and I." She smiled at Steven Shugar.

"Then you must return," Steven said. "As soon as the spring warmth arrives!"

Bernard laughed. "That's dangerous, Mary, traveling with just ladies. Your recklessness worries me. Even if I like it sometimes." He winked at Steven Shugar.

Mary flushed and glared at Bernard, and Steven's half smile at Bernard was a little grim.

"Lumbermen," he said, shaking his head.

"We're a forthright lot," Bernard said. "It comes with being hardworking, Dad says. The Evans Mill turns out the best wood at the very best rates. Guaranteed to meet all specifications and on time. I'll be right back with the special price list we have come up with for your company."

Alone, Steven and Mary avoided looking directly at each other, and then he spoke in a low and intimate tone.

"I see how it is. I am more than happy to show you around Chicago, Mrs. Evans."

"That's kind."

"With or without your husband."

When she looked up, his eyes seemed to be seeking her soul, and Mary smiled into her lap as Bernard reentered the room. She heard their voices, but her mind had flown to distant, imagined cityscapes. When at last she lifted her eyes to the office window, Mary saw that the snow had begun to fall again. But winter could not continue forever. That just would not happen. No one could stop spring from coming.

11

Love has gone and left me,—and the neighbors knock and borrow,
And life goes on forever like the gnawing of a mouse,—
And tomorrow and tomorrow and tomorrow and tomorrow
There's this little street and this little house.

~ Edna St. Vincent Millay (1892–1950), "Ashes of Life"

As she walked across the community college green, Lydia wondered if Frank would be happy to see her. She had stopped visiting him on campus a few years before, and similarly he had stopped attending any of her career-related events. Both would probably say they were giving each other space. But at some point, this partitioning of their lives had started to feel like disinterest. The quest for Mary Walker was the one remaining shared intellectual activity they had, and that was also slipping away.

But tonight Lydia would formally present to Frank, in detail, her ideas about starting their own publishing venture. She hoped that if he would let her explain her vision of how to assemble his Walker writings—accompanied by photographs like the ones she had just taken at Mary's house, along with some historical photos from her life—that he could see this as not only a viable business project, but also a desirable step forward in his career. The book would be beautiful. She could envision him becoming enlivened by her ideas, immediately able to see how this would translate into increased opportunities to do public readings and interviews, which he loved. But on the other hand, it also wasn't hard to imagine him shutting down in defensive anger. She entered the central cluster of Gothic limestone buildings on Carson's campus with trepidation.

In the main hall of the English-Philosophy Building, a bell six generations old rang hoarsely. Shuffling and murmuring ensued inside the classrooms. Lydia waited outside as the door burst open and students flowed out. She could see that two remained speaking to Frank by his lectern, and in an instant, the years fell away and she recalled his handsome presence at the front of a women's poetry class at the University of Michigan. He'd never been extremely thin, but he was trimmer back then and always striking, with charisma that made it as easy for him to inspire a class to learn as it was to seduce young women. She could testify to his skill in both areas, and she watched his hands now on the book he held, flipping through in search of something to answer a student's question. They were still graceful, suggestive of intelligence and refinement, but strong.

"Ah! My beauty! Is it really you?" Frank met Lydia's eyes with curiosity when the students had cleared out. "I cannot recall the last time you met me right here in my humble theater."

"I know you prefer to keep teaching and family separate."

"Yes, true," he said, gathering files back into his briefcase. He put his hand on his abdomen and bent forward a few inches. "I seem to be coming down with something. I feel horrible."

Lydia fixed her purse more securely on her shoulder so she could carry Frank's bag for him, but he waved her hands away.

"I was hoping we could go for coffee," she said, "but maybe my timing's not the best."

Frank gave her a questioning glance.

"You know, talk in the student union," she said. "Like the old days."

"Very old." His eyes searched her face. "What's this about?"

"It's about conversation," she said with a smile. "Something we used to be fabulous at."

"I don't know. Sleep was more what I had in mind right now."

They left the room, and as they walked down the hall, Lydia felt him give her a long look. "You seem pretty nervous to me," he said as they approached the metal elevator doors where his image floated dark and large, while Lydia's appeared even more elfin and ethereal than it was in three dimensions.

"I'm not nervous, Frank." She gave a short, sharp laugh. "Are you going to try to make me nervous? You sure aren't easy to talk to lately. I mean, here's another example."

"Oh, yes. It's my fault," he said.

Lydia's hopes fell, and she instantly felt weary. "I just want to talk to you."

"All right, all right. Next time give me some warning."

The Aurora Student Union was attached to the English–Philosophy Building by a glass tunnel much newer than the historic buildings at either end. Tree tips knocked softly against the glass above Lydia and Frank as they entered the nearly empty café.

"I'll get some tea for you," she said and walked to the counter while Frank sat down and waited in one of the booths. The familiarity of the place, the scene of countless conversations throughout Lydia's adult life, revived her confidence. She returned to the table carrying two steaming tan cups.

"I don't know what's happening to us, but for two supposed communication experts, we aren't doing very well lately," she said.

"Maybe what's happening is not to *us*, Lydia," Frank said. "Maybe it's you."

"No," she said after a moment, attempting a jovial, matter-of-fact attitude. "I don't think so. I want to talk about both my life and your life. I want to talk about my career, your career, and our shared finances. *I* am going to lead this conversation. Okay?"

"I'm here. I'm listening," he said, setting down his tea and linking his hands together on the table. "Shall I ask these individuals to leave so there's no chance of interruption?"

"Funny." Lydia grabbed her purse, drawing out a pen and notepad, then flipped to a page full of numbers and circled one of them. She was going to dive right into the heart of the matter in spite of his maddening childishness.

"To the point: this is what we have in savings," she said, glancing up, then back down, pen tip digging into the paper. "This will last through several months of ordinary living expenses—as long as a year, actually, if we're careful. In addition, I'm due to receive two royalty checks this year, and I think the total will be approximately *this* amount *here*. So."

She flipped through a couple more pages of itemized numbers and calculations. "I think that very soon we will have a decision to make, Frank."

"Oh?" His expression was blank.

She took a deep breath. Her mind cleared as her thoughts shifted from tension to problem solving, and she sat up straighter. "We have talked for years about starting our own press. And as I've said, this seems like the most viable option for me in many ways. When I look at these numbers, coupled with my…" She spread her hands and searched for words that would make him understand. "My frustration, my need to push myself in a new direction, and my belief that you need to publish your work about Mary Walker, I conclude that this is what we have to do."

"What, our own press?" Frank furrowed his brow, inhaled deeply, and leaned over the pad of paper. "And you think this is enough money? Enough to do what?"

"Okay. I've made quite a few calls. I'm basing my conclusion on estimates for printing, advertising, travel for promotion…that kind of thing. For a book of my work and one of yours. I have a pretty good idea about what's required." To Lydia's ears, her tone was knowledgeable and encouraging.

"Hang on, one book of mine?" He frowned. "What the hell book are you referring to?"

"Well, of course you have plans for a detailed, extensive exploration of Mary Stone Walker, her work, her life, her unknown work and life. Three volumes. I know." She was extremely careful with her wording. "At this point, as a prelude to that extended project, I'm thinking of the condensed version we have talked about from time to time. A popular introduction, if you will."

"I see. The condensed version *you* have talked about."

"Okay. But you know the concept. I can do the editing, prep work, business end of things because I won't be spending the time I usually do on writing. I can focus on both of our new manuscripts—"

"Hold it, hold it," Frank said, pressing his hand down onto her fingers and pen. "What do you mean about doing these things instead of writing? You have a contract."

Lydia's mouth started to turn toward a smile, but stopped as she took in Frank's worried expression. "I thought I'd cut my romance production down to one book a year. For a year or two. Maybe three or four years, depending on how this goes. We know how to live frugally. We've done it in the past."

A panic that Lydia had not expected filled Frank's features.

"You're serious," he said.

"Of course. I'm completely serious."

"We have savings enough for 'several months,' and you're forgoing a contract for…for a mere dream?"

"Why is it a *mere dream*? We're established in our fields. We have successes to lean on. Frank, look, it's a way to get our work out there, our real work. Wouldn't you like to publish at least *part* of your analysis in order to stir up interest in the literary world? Not wait until the entire Walker tome is finished and someone else says, 'This is good enough'? We would have jumped at this idea fifteen years ago. We could never have imagined saving enough for this. And yet here we are."

"But it's not enough, Lydia." Frank laughed hollowly. "I wouldn't say that enough money for a few months without full income is enough for anything except a vacation. We're not kids, you know. There's a great deal to consider. This timing is…" He fumbled for words to explain his resistance. "I mean, Nicholas will need college money in two or three years."

Lydia leaned back against her chair and tried to breathe slowly without looking away from Frank's face.

"Okay, Frank. It's like this. I have come up against the realization that I may not be able to write these popular stories forever. I've changed, or I'm changing… People change. Basically, I want a new job, you could say. One that requires different things of me. This plan is a way to start that. A *realistic* way to start that."

Frank stared out the window and said nothing.

"And what about you? I believe that there was a time when you wanted to complete your PhD. To become a full professor and achieve tenure. Am I wrong?"

He turned toward her, then regarded his tea. "You are correct. That was something that mattered a great deal to me."

"Doesn't it still?" This was an obstacle Lydia had not considered—that he might no longer care about the development of his career in the real world.

"Other things are on a par with it. Other concerns." He interlocked his fingers in front of his chin. "But let's be honest here. You aren't talking about what *I want.* You're saying you want me to bring in more income."

"Well, I do want you to. Is that wrong? I'm concerned about my own ability to maintain our current cash flow, especially if I have to write other things."

"You don't *have* to write other things; you're saying you *would like to.*"

"I'm saying that I am thirty-seven and uncertain that I can keep doing this until I die, or even until I'm forty. And I'm saying that you and I have dreamed since grad school about starting our own press, and now that we can actually do just that with our savings, I think we should give it a shot. Starting with the publication of your book, which I happen to believe will be profitable and add to our funds."

"My book is not adaptable to a single volume."

"Not in the form it's in, no." Lydia fought to maintain her composure. Frank had more intelligence than most people she'd met, but when his mind was closed, it felt like his IQ dropped by half. "You would have to reconceive the whole, but I've thought about it a lot, and I think you could use most of the prose you've written and some of the text from your magazine articles. We would then have to produce and market it. But all of this can be done. And, in fact, done quite quickly. I think it will reinvigorate our lives! If we don't do it now, Frank…" She took his hand. "Frank, if we don't do it now, we may never do it."

A flicker of something—was it memories?—seemed to alter his gaze. The two of them had dreamed from the start of their relationship about starting their own literary press, as so many literary pioneers had done in the past.

"What if you lose your contract entirely?" Frank asked, pulling his hand away and crossing his arms. "What if you completely lose your audience? End up with nothing from this venture?"

"Or what if the administration at Carson Community College sees self-publishing with your romance-writer wife as an unworthy enterprise for a professor? Or your old friends from the University of Michigan?" The words were out before she considered them. Such thoughts had been waiting a long time to be spoken, and she could see the guilty acknowledgment on her husband's face and how he tried to hide it.

After a minute, Frank tilted his head and gave a smile she knew he thought was charming. "Don't put words in my mouth."

Lydia sighed. "I'm not a fool, Frank. This is not an illusion of mine. I know how your colleagues think. I just hoped you might not fall prey to the same weakness."

"Nobody else dictates my thoughts," he said, weighting his voice with disapproval. "I just don't see how your idea fits our lives right now."

She inhaled sharply and closed her notebook, capped her pen and slid it and the notebook into her purse.

"All right," she said. "I understand. You have your life and I have mine, so I need to think about doing it by myself. I've started putting together ideas from many sources, and I don't need you to be involved. I just *wanted* you to be. For you. Your career. And for the good of our relationship. As you know, my publisher is not interested in anything from me but romance novels, so I want to complete and publish a nongenre novel on subjects that I care about, and I'll do it on my own. Since I know the ins and outs of doing just that, I guess I'll get started on it. Maybe someday you'll see things differently."

"It's the same financial risk, Lydia, whether we do it together or you do it alone. It just doesn't make any sense. Poverty is crippling to creativity. We both vowed we'd never go back to that…place. In fact, I'm not sure what's behind this."

She sank back. "What's behind this? Take a look at the obvious! I'm burned out. You're spinning your wheels. Maybe you should hear all of the working details of the plan before you veto it."

"Oh, now I don't listen to you, huh? Well, I don't want that claim driving your determination, for God's sake. Okay." Frank threw up his hands. "Okay, let's hear it. The whole thing."

Lydia lightly lowered her hand to Frank's. "I need for you to actually listen."

He closed his eyes for a few seconds, then opened them. "Listening will be easier with ambiance. Let's drive to Jacob's Tavern. I don't know if I can eat, but a glass of wine might help burn out this flu."

"Jacob's Tavern, okay," Lydia said, almost smiling. Frank stood slowly, and she put her arm through his as they left the café.

Back home hours later, Frank picked Lydia up and tossed her, laughing, onto their bed. She bounced back up, dropped her feet to the floor, struck a match, and held it to the wick of a candle. Lying across the bed on his stomach, Frank snatched at her dress and pulled her closer. He slid his hand up between her thighs as she lifted the dress off over her head.

"Mmm." He ran a finger slowly up her black-nylon-covered pelvis. "Black nylons. Very nice, Mrs. Carroll. Just what I'm desiring for dessert."

Frank still had his coat on, and he laughed as Lydia tried to remove it from his heavy body. He sat up, wrestled it off, and rolled Lydia to her back, gently pinning her shoulders against the bed. Lydia fixed her gaze on Frank's eyes, but they were half-closed.

"My nymph…" Frank said it caressingly, growing hard against her thigh as he let his fingers skim her camisole. He felt around on the fabric and found tiny buttons that he attempted to undo, but his fingers were thick and clumsy from the wine. Lydia slid both of her hands under his and undid the buttons, then reached around his back to slide her hand beneath his belt and pants, over his skin. Her camisole was open, fallen away, and Frank wrapped his mouth around one nipple, then the other, as his hand roved the slick panty hose.

He knew her well, knew which touches and how long, how strongly or softly. Lydia unfastened his belt, his pants, and her hands wrapped hotly around his tight skin. Pulling, releasing, gripping. He wrestled with her stockings, and in moments their bodies were free of clothing and he slid inside her. He moaned, and Lydia clung and fiercely squeezed, her mouth against his neck. There was almost nothing that could stop the swell of her desire now. Her eyelids closed, and she opened her mouth onto his. He thrust his tongue into her mouth and pushed hard against her pelvis, pushed again, and again.

Then, unexpectedly, he was limp. Lydia wrapped her legs tighter around his hips. She gripped him urgently and said his name again and again, biting his neck too hard.

"Ow!" Frank tried to regain his rhythm, but she could feel him lose consciousness for a second. Lydia's hands made fists, and she dug her knuckles into his ribs. Then she punched the mattress and let her legs drop beside him. He rolled away.

"Damn it, Frank," she muttered. "Whiskey dick."

"It's that flu," he murmured.

For a couple of seconds, he rubbed his neck where she'd bitten him. Then his hand slid to the pillow. They both lay still and silent, Frank slipping into sleep.

Lydia bolted up and walked down the hall to the bathroom. When she returned, Frank was snoring but roused as if startled by a dream.

"Jesus… I wonder," he said, looking around as if he wasn't sure where he was.

"What?"

"Your love. Even now, I don't know." He paused, and Lydia thought he was falling back to sleep.

"Me? What are you talking about?"

"You're always…" Again his voice faded.

"What?" Lydia was intoxicated, too. She was fuzzy, but not nearly as confused as Frank was, and this comment about her love had sent a shiver of adrenaline through her.

"What?" He roused and turned his head toward her, but she knew he'd only been half conscious.

"I always…what? You said, 'You always…'"

"You don't love me anymore. I can see that, Lydia. I see that now."

"Are you serious?" Her mind tried to outpace his, to figure out where his snaking notions might go.

He rolled his head toward her, his eyelids heavy.

"The way you loved me once. Excited. Devoted. That's gone." He lifted his arm and let it drop heavily onto the mattress between them.

Her heart rate increased.

"Of course it isn't, Frank." She slapped her hand onto his and squeezed it roughly. "Why would you say such a thing?"

"It's just…so obvious. I try to pretend it isn't true. But it is."

Lydia's mind raced, and the well-being she had felt blossoming through the evening sizzled away like water on hot stone. A minute passed in silence. Her breath came rapidly.

"I'm sorry you feel that way, Frank. I didn't know this was on your mind."

"I'm sorry, too," he said with a heavy sigh. "And then you bring up the idea of turning our lives inside out for a press of our own. I'm supposed to abandon my career, I guess, or…what? What, Lydia? Is this the condition I have to meet to keep your love? It frightens me."

"What frightens you? Our own publishing company would help *advance* your career, not force you to abandon it." She sat up. "What frightens you?"

"Fulfill my work as *you* see it…on your terms. What frightens me is that this is what you have come up with—a manipulation of me as a means of changing *your* future. Because you're unhappy with *your* work."

"That isn't it at all." Her insides began to shake. "That isn't true."

He pushed himself up. "And I can't do that, Lydia. Not even for you. I have my work. My career. It hurts me deeply that you don't know something like that is out of the question for me."

"Wait a minute. Listen to me."

"That's reality from my point of view, Lydia. I have been watching how you've been lately. But I don't think you can see it." Frank sat at the edge of the bed with his back to her, shaking his head slowly. "No. You can't see that your little dreams run right over my existence as if I'm..." He raised his hands as if to strangle someone. "I'm *nothing*."

The last word was virtually roared, and Frank stood, turning toward her, his face full of venom. Panic shot through Lydia's body. She knew this tone, this demeanor, all too well. Frank's inebriated rage was on an unstoppable course.

"Frank, I mean it." She stood and held out her hands. "Listen."

"No, my existence is outside of your concerns," he went on, as if she had said nothing. "You see things *you want for yourself*. Time off. Some other life, exotic places, different men maybe. How would I know? Some sort of new image... Is that what you're after? The 'real Lydia'?"

He shook his head, gripping his hands together at his chest as if to mock her heart's longing. Lydia watched helplessly as alcohol, anger, and paranoia fueled his imagination.

"I don't know, maybe you want to be a poet again. Reasonable." He stuck his lower lip out, gave a couple of nods, and his eyes brushed over her face occasionally. "You were once. But *now*..." He picked up a hand mirror and shoved it in front of Lydia's face. "Who do you see now? Who's in there now, Ms. Romance Novelist?"

Lydia tried to push his arm away, but he held it firm, the glass inches from her face. "Enough, Frank."

"Don't like the person you have made yourself into? Want change? *At my expense?*" He hurled the mirror across the room where it hit a framed picture on the wall. Both shattered and fell to the floor. "Well, you can forget it. Your little ambitions aren't worth giving up my work for. So fuck off."

Like a threatened animal, Lydia held perfectly still, barely breathing, while her heart hammered in panic. Without another glance toward her or the broken glass across the room, Frank went to the closet, yanked out a robe, wrapped it around himself, and walked heavily down the hall to the bathroom.

"Just fuck off," he said again before slamming the bathroom door.

Lydia slipped away to her study across the hall. Silently, she locked the door and sat on her couch, still frozen, waiting. *I have a right to lock the door of my own study.*

"Lydia," she heard him growl when he returned to their empty bedroom. "Lydia, goddamn it, what game are you playing now?"

She waited, jaw set, breath shallow. Within minutes, she heard him snoring, heavily asleep.

12

There's a word unspoken,
A knot untied.
Whatever is broken
The earth may hide.

> ~ *Elinor Wylie (1885–1928), "Fire and Sleet and Candlelight"*

When Nicholas had heard his parents enter the house late the night before, laughing and shushing each other as they clambered up the staircase, he had felt a small lift in his heart. When the convivial sounds were replaced some time later by his father's loud curses and the crash of something breaking, he woke again with a jolt of adrenaline, and he was upset, but not surprised. His muscles tightened with anger as he pulled a pillow over his head to cover his ears, and he wanted to cry, but that almost never happened anymore. In such moments, he felt he hated them both, and while he knew it was love that made it all hurt as much as it did, he fantasized more and more often about earning and saving up money to run away.

Nicholas had lived with a small, niggling sense of confusion about his father's Mary Walker quest for several years, the earliest moment of it probably arising on the Christmas Eve when he was in fifth grade, when the house air was spicy with scents of woodsmoke, cider, and a visiting neighbor's pipe tobacco. Snow drifted from a flannel-gray sky, as it had since morning.

Nicholas could still recall the way the nickel-sized flakes had looked from the barn where he watched through the crack at the doors—peaceful but significant, like messages quietly arriving. He studied their slow descent.

His father was drinking mulled wine from an iron pot full of it on the barn woodstove, and he had urged Nicholas to scoop himself a small mug to keep warm as the two of them examined the steamer trunk Aunt Louise had brought that afternoon as a Christmas present for Frank.

"This may be it, Nick! This may be the day!"

But after half an hour, Frank's search for document pockets, panels, or obviously loosened or reglued seams in the trunk became wearisome to ten-year-old Nicholas, who had begun to shiver in the drafty barn. His attention was revived by his father's occasional demands that he pay attention, but he longed to return to the festivities in the warm house.

Suddenly, Frank let out a cry of surprise. Nicholas's gaze flew from the gold house windows full of happy figures to his father's hopeful face as his hands urged a slip of onionskin from a thin panel of heavy cardboard covering the inside floor of the trunk.

"Ah!" Frank narrowed his eyes, then pulled off his glasses, wiped them impatiently, and shoved them back on. "Someone's... name. I see a capital...*S*, maybe *F*." He shifted so close to the floor lamp that his hair touched the shade and the onionskin paper glowed hot with light.

Instincts already attuned to the subtlest changes in his father's expressions and voice, Nicholas averted his eyes quickly to the floor, even before Frank knew for sure that what he studied was worthless. It was a familiar, faint slackening in the muscles around his eyes, perhaps, or a shift in the angle of his head as his urgency peaked, just before it began to disintegrate. Something pulled Nicholas's heart down even before his father's voice went flat and he tossed the paper into the trunk, shoved the thing away with his foot, and told Nicholas to go back to the party; they'd examine the trunk further later.

For years, Nicholas's mind had followed up the disappointing nondiscoveries with detailed imaginings of the moment when, at last, his father's stubborn dedication would be rewarded with an exquisite, perfect document undeniably written by the beautiful poet *after* the date of her disappearance. All of these hours, these disappointments and tensions, would be worth it. A person can struggle with a dream for years, even a dream that others don't understand, while missing out on other life opportunities along the way, because it's the outcome that matters.

For instance, Mary Walker's work was less valuable without a life conclusion, or so Nicholas had come to believe based on his father's long narratives about the young woman. And each of the poems already collected would possess more meaning once everything she had created was finally found and the collection was larger. Nicholas had spent years believing in his father and coming to understand the notion that the value of a life was determined by the opinions of those left behind.

Now, however, tension between his mother and father held them in a vice grip of frequent, ugly arguments, threatening— Nicholas feared—the family's ability to survive together. His mother was obviously fed up with his father's fruitless pursuit and the expense of it, and Nicholas realized that his father had propped just about his whole career on the hope of finding Walker writings and, with outrageous luck, the poet herself. At this point, his father's activities were looking foolish from the outside. Jack Kenilworth was only the most recent of many to hedge around the subject as if he were discussing a madman's humiliations.

Nicholas was just a page or two away from seeing it that way, too.

Thin rays of sunlight found Lydia asleep on the couch in her study the next morning. She opened her eyes to the sound of knocking on her door, and her consciousness flew instantly back to thoughts of Frank's cruel turn against her in their bedroom just a few hours before.

"Yes?" She spoke the word without invitation, her heart racing. The doorknob rattled a little.

"Door's locked." It was Nicholas.

Lydia closed her eyes and exhaled with relief. She unlocked it, then flopped back onto her couch. Nicholas slid into view, and she smiled at him. He nudged the door open farther.

"I'm going to school. Is everything okay?"

"Oh yeah," she said, wondering how much he had heard the night before from his end of the second-story hallway. "Dad and I were up late discussing business stuff. You know how I am once my mind gets going."

"Yeah. Okay. I hope your day is good, Mom." He looked at her closely for a moment, then pulled the knob and turned it silently to latch the door closed.

She stared at the light and shadows on the wall as her son's footsteps tapped down the stairs. The painful scene that had driven her to the privacy of her study filled her mind, and she lay back down and rolled to her side, watching that scene replay in sharp fragments. It had happened before. The fog of alcohol had allowed her to fall for the trick that worked so well on her. Frank would fabricate some sin on her part—she'd had an affair, she'd violated their literary or family values, she did not love him anymore—attacking with such violent drama that she reflexively replaced her own authentic emotions and perceptions with simplistic self-defense.

Minutes later, other heavier footsteps ascended the stairs. Alarm seized her, and she looked at the clock. Frank was almost never up this early when he didn't have to teach. But again there was a knock on her door. It opened, and there he stood. In his hand he held two mugs of coffee.

"Good morning," he said pleasantly. Lydia said nothing and didn't smile. He stepped in and offered her a mug.

"You can set it there." She nodded toward her desk. "What do you want?"

"Just—good morning!" His smile was unguarded. It was possible that he did not even remember the horrible last moments of the night before.

"You must have slept well," Lydia said, sitting up and pulling her knees to her chest and her blanket up around her collarbone. "You never get up early, and you never make coffee for me. So…what is it?"

He seemed to weigh his options and then spoke. "I said things last night that I should have probably framed more carefully."

Frank paused, watching her, but she simply waited. He tilted his head slightly and seemed to be searching for the precise phrasing of delicate truths.

"I confess, I can't really see how your new plan for our lives would work right now. I know that's disappointing for you. I admire you for searching for ways to keep your career alive, and yes, I do remember the dreams we shared when we were younger, Lydia. Of course I do. I, too, would like to feel so free and inspired again. Maybe I will. Maybe you can help me get there. Someday."

Ordinarily such a comment would have encouraged Lydia, but she eyed him skeptically.

"There are a lot of things I have appreciated about you for many years, Lydia, and your resourcefulness is certainly high on the list. You will make this happen if it's meant to be. When the time is right. Whether or not I see the vision."

It was a qualified endorsement, but more support than he'd offered in quite some time. She wondered if she had touched a nerve in his conscience. Or if he was just that masterful at manipulating her.

"There's something I want you to see," he said, moving his

gaze to the window. "And it looks like a really lovely day, so I think we should take a drive to see it."

"Oh?" Lydia could not think of anything outside that Frank might want to share with it her.

"I heard what you said about needing to move on, from romance writing to something new, and I think in one way that makes sense for you at this point. I also know that long ago Mary Stone Walker and the era she lived in inspired you."

"*Long ago?* They still do." Lydia had the sense that her husband had one static idea about who she was and could no longer perceive her in the moment.

"Well, today, there is a furniture auction in Portman, and… Hold on, hold on"—he held up his hand as Lydia shook her head—"there is a whole container load of items, from bookcases to linens to rocking horses, that were gathered from up and down Michigan's west coast. I thought it would be fun for you to do what I do…walk among the items and think about the lives those objects were part of. You're a master storyteller, Lydia— well, you are!—so I know it would amuse you. You've never been to one of these things, and I think it's time. Undoubtedly there will be some interesting items from the early nineteen hundreds. We'll make a day of it: go to the auction, get lunch, and walk downtown along the river."

"Come on. Do you really think you can attend that auction and not buy something, Frank? I don't want to be part of that." She stood up and stepped over to her desk where she began straightening the piles of paper. "I just don't think it's right anymore."

Lydia felt him looking at her as she sorted research notes from the impossibly flawed pages of her current romance manuscript, placing her notes on top of Ethel Van Zant's scrapbook and tossing her manuscript to the center of her desk to read as soon as she could stomach it. She ran her fingers slowly along the edges of the scrapbook, wondering if she should force Frank to look at it right now. Here was an antique that had relevance, right there in the room with them. A minute passed before she raised her gaze to meet his. His jaw was set, his expression cold.

"What is it?" she demanded. "You want me to forget your cruelty last night, your dismissal of my hopes and even my love, and we'll just go buy a few more antiques? What kind of an idiot puppet do you think I am, Frank?"

"*My* cruelty to *you*?" He looked off to the side and gave a huff of disbelief. "You want me to give up my own career plans and capitulate to yours, adopting your tired views on my life's work, but when I protest, *that's* cruel?" Lydia watched his eyes grow hard with anger quickly. She watched for a hint of uncertainty, of guilt, but there was none, and she groped through what had been said in the foggy hours after midnight to see if there was something she might have forgotten or misinterpreted. "Now, I came in here with coffee because I wanted to suggest a nice outing that would be a change of pace, some time together doing something fun, and again you've made it about you, your unhappiness, my failings. Is there a way out of this, Lydia?"

He would go to the auction whether she went or not, and if she let him leave with this chip on his shoulder, there was no telling what he might think he had a right to do or buy. She gave a short laugh, her heart pounding harder, her thoughts dissolving into familiar disorientation. If she did not choose a diplomatic response, there would be another nasty battle; in fact, the situation might already have slipped out of control.

"A way out... Hmm, a way out. Good question," she said, looking into his face and trying to lighten her tone. "Okay. How about if we *both* try to let go of hard feelings for the rest of the day? We'll go to the auction—as casual observers—and just have a good time. Have lunch, take a walk."

"Okay then, sure. You'll enjoy it," he said coolly. "I'll meet you in the truck in fifteen minutes."

Inside the Portman field house, Lydia pointed to a locked glass case containing vases, inkwells, silverware, and a set of coins.

"Special items?"

"Yes, those are more valuable," Frank said.

"That vase—the carved one with the little figurine standing on the base—how fanciful."

"Nineteenth century, art nouveau." Frank peered into the case. "Bidding will probably start around $3,000. Not a bad idea for your birthday."

"At that price, it goes from fanciful to silly."

Frank chuckled. "Lydia, where is the aristocrat in you? With higher standards, you would likely achieve greater wealth. That's how it works, you know. Oh, there he is. See the guy with the funky hat? That's our auctioneer. Grab a couple of seats. I'll meet you there. It's almost time."

Frank had been right. It was stimulating to wander through the place, browsing the unusual items in all states of renovation and disrepair, and contemplating the lives they might have been part of. For the last three hours or so, their conversation had gradually grown more lighthearted, and the change was encouraging. It had been... Well, Lydia couldn't remember the last time she and Frank had gone somewhere just to spend time together, with no agenda.

When Frank met her at the folding chairs near the back of the fifteenth row, he was holding a card with the number 610 on it. Lydia's stomach lurched.

"Your bidding number," she said, turning her face quickly to the front of the room where the auctioneer stood at a podium.

"*Our* bidding number," Frank corrected her. "Just in case you get a notion to bid on some special little thing. A footstool or a kitchen chair or something. It's a fun experience. If slightly addictive."

She nodded, staring ahead of her, and wondered how soon she could get him to leave. The bidding began, and Lydia watched as the auctioneer and patrons interacted so rapidly it was both impressive and comical. After half an hour or so of this entertaining exchange, she began to relax.

"That was pretty cheap for a bed like that, wasn't it?" she asked Frank.

"Yes and no. It needs a lot of restoration. Hours and hours and hours."

"Still, something like that would be fabulous even in a rough state."

He smiled and nudged her in the ribs. "That's why we have the number!"

When the auctioneer moved from the podium to a large oak dining room set, Frank sat up straighter.

"Huh. That's quite a specimen," he said, running his hand through his hair.

"Yeah, didn't you notice it when we were walking around? Little griffins carved on each of the chairs. But something like that—"

Frank held his hand out to silence her, listening to the auctioneer's details.

"R. J. Horner, circa 1880, solid quarter-sawn oak..." the auctioneer recited.

"I think I've read about this," Frank whispered, his eyes fixed ahead.

Lydia stared at his profile. "Where? What do you mean?"

"Wait—"

"Four fully skirted leaves, racetrack edging..."

"Jesus, I think..." Frank pulled at his mouth, thinking, listening, his eyes ablaze.

The auctioneer said something about the dining set's provenance, about western Michigan, the Huntington family.

"My God!" Frank grabbed Lydia's hand. "I thought I recognized that woman." He pointed across the room. "The woman in the white coat. Fox fur. See..."

"Yes. What about her?"

"Shirley Huntington. Her grandmother was a great patron of the arts in western Michigan. I bet the family lost the table, and she's trying to buy it back. Yes, I think I heard about that situation a while ago. Lydia, Mary stayed with the owner of that dining room table…that woman's grandmother!"

"You're kidding. Are you sure?"

"My memory usually serves me pretty well on these points." He squeezed Lydia's fingers so tightly the bones crunched together.

"Well, it will be fun to see this play out then, won't it?" Lydia said cautiously, watching his face. He nodded absently.

The bidding started at $9,000. A cluster of interested buyers was seated in the same far quadrant of the room, and they quickly drove the price up over $20,000. Just as the bidding slowed, and the auctioneer held a hand pointed toward the Huntington woman as he scanned the room, Frank raised his card high in the air.

"Frank! What are you doing? Jesus Christ!" Lydia said, pulling at his arm. He swatted her hand away.

"Hush! Don't act that way!" he hissed under his breath. "Come on, I'm just going to give her a run for her money. Anything that was part of Mary's life deserves a higher price tag."

Up the price soared. Frank and the stranger in the white fur volleyed the numbers back and forth, and at $26,990, the auctioneer pointed at Frank with his gavel, then banged it on the podium with approving finality. The Huntington woman stood up, shoved past the row of knees between her and the aisle, and walked rapidly out of the building. The auctioneer called for a break, and people stretched, walked around, and drifted toward the food counter.

Frank turned toward Lydia, smacked his forehead, and cried out with a laugh, "My God, what have I done?"

She stared at him, sick with anger and shock.

"You just spent over half of our savings." Lydia's voice was unsteady. "You tell me what the hell you are doing."

He put his hand gently on her arm. "Oh, Lydia, but look at that set! The Huntingtons owned it, and Mary stayed with them. I've seen photographs of the main-floor rooms of that house, and I'm sure now that I heard about Shirley Huntington's effort to reclaim all the heirlooms. Mary must have sat in those chairs, eaten off that table! She must have!"

"Frank Carroll…you cannot do this. I don't care who sat or ate there; we can't afford such a thing. And you know that." She glanced around them at a handful of people who were clearly aware of the topic of their discussion, and she whispered, digging her fingers into his arm, "Can you hear me? You've lost your mind."

"I know, I know, I know," he said quickly, shaking his head. "I went overboard, didn't mean to." He wiped at his mouth as if to remove the smile. "I'll take care of it. Wait here, and just calm down."

She watched him hurry toward the booth where people with numbers in their hands and checkbooks ready were lined up to pay for their purchases. When it was his turn, he spoke with animation for a few seconds, nodding, shaking his head, giving a laugh, and then pulling out their checkbook. Lydia rushed down the row of chairs, tried unsuccessfully to push quickly through the crowd, and got there just as he was turning from the transaction.

"What did you do, Frank? You wrote a check?"

"I told the guy that it was only as the Huntington woman was leaving that I recognized she was a family member, and I wanted no part in depriving her of her family's heirloom. The check was just a dummy check. Don't worry."

"Dummy check… What are you talking about?"

Frank was guiding her toward the coatracks near the front doors. "You know. Until the woman replaces it."

"Does this woman know she's going to replace it?" Lydia fought to keep hysteria out of her voice.

He gave an impatient little shake of his head as if she should know what he was talking about. "It's all arranged."

She grabbed his wrists and stopped him. "Look at me, Frank. Explain what you are talking about."

"The Huntington woman will be contacted today because she arranged to be the default buyer."

"That's an auction thing? That's how it works?"

"Yes, an auction thing." He smiled, handing Lydia her coat.

"So what did the guy say when you told him you won't be buying it?"

"He looked relieved, actually," Frank said.

"Ohhh. Okay. Phew! Do you want to go back in and look the table and chairs over while you can?" Lydia asked generously, her heart still beating too hard. They could go home now; they'd made it through without irreversible trouble. "Seems like it would be interesting."

But Frank was walking toward the door.

"Nah, that's okay. Enough antiques for today." His tone was crisp, as if his mind were elsewhere, and as they drove home, he responded to Lydia's comments distractedly.

"Shall we stop in one of these parks and walk around a bit? To fill out this pleasant date?" Lydia said, as they passed another lakefront town.

"If you don't mind, I'm feeling like I ought to get some things done at home," Frank said. "I forgot about a project that's overdue for some attention."

"Sure." She watched the fields, trees, and fences flow past with the sense of a disturbance that she could not quite bring into focus.

He glanced at her, then stared back at the road. "You know, you don't have to be a millionaire to acquire something like that dining room set, Lydia. You just have to have certain priorities."

She watched his face, waiting for him to qualify his statement, to smile, to thank her for going, to continue the connection with her somehow. But he said nothing more.

13

WHITE HILL, MICHIGAN—JUNE 1936

He had given her walls
She wished to burn, his body she wished to tear...
He was the dark, he was the house and sound.

~ Louise Bogan (1897–1970), "The Flume"

The blue pitcher on the table held milk purchased at the dairy that morning, and there was enough for Bernard to have a hearty glass. Mary didn't care for it herself, so it seemed even more of a gift that she'd gone across town into the outskirts of White Hill to get it for him. She eyed him as he handled the pitcher because it was one of the only things she still possessed from her childhood, and Bernard always seemed to be rough with it. He spotted her watching him and gave a curious smile.

"Well?" he said. "Ain't you hungry, Mary?"

She picked up her fork and looked down at the whitefish, given to her that morning by a friend of Bernard's, which she had fried for supper in corn meal and lard. She cut off a piece, stabbed it with the fork, then set it down. She was so rarely hungry anymore. Bernard returned to his fish and potatoes without waiting for an answer. As he lifted his gaze back to her, she averted her eyes and reached for her glass of water.

"What is it, Mary? What's wrong with you?"

"Bernard, nothing's wrong," she said. He asked this question often, sometimes with a daring tone, as if she should certainly have nothing to complain about, but more often lately with hope that she was sick with a pregnancy. "The heat puts me off eating."

"It's not something else?" He kept his eyes on her as he drank the glass of milk.

"No, Bernard, I'm sorry. It's just the way I am in summer." She stood up and took her plate to the sink, wondering how long it would be until he left the house for the tavern. Tonight she might walk until the moon set.

He scraped back his chair and stepped up behind her and put his arms around her arms, his hands on her belly where he wanted a child to grow. His mouth was on her neck, then slid to her ear, and Mary closed her eyes, flushed with a warring surge of emotional revulsion and physical desire.

"Let's try again," he whispered, the skin of his lips on her ear. "Right now." He slid his hands up her ribs to her breasts. "Right. Now."

Mary squeezed her eyes shut, then opened her gaze to the kitchen boards and shelves he had painted dark pink for her before she moved in. He pinched her nipples, his breath warm and wet on her collarbone. Rage flashed through her body and into her brain. She whipped around, grabbed his face and thrust her mouth onto his, kissing and biting, hands locked around his neck as he tried to back away. He finally caught her wrists and stood up straight.

"Goddamn it!" His eyes seemed even bluer when he was angry, and he was as handsome when he scowled as when he smiled. "What gets into you?"

She pretended innocence, lowered her eyes, and ran her finger along the top of his jeans.

"I thought men liked to play rough, Bernard. I only want to please you. You know that."

He drew the back of his hand away from his mouth, checked the skin for blood, and flashed his eyes toward her, nodding.

"Uh-huh, yeah. Everyone in town knows that. Ethel Van Zant, for instance."

Mary swallowed with difficulty. The old woman was an herbalist, and Mary had gone to her for help with her mental states. But the woman was discreet; surely she wouldn't have told anyone. Perhaps someone had spotted her coming or going.

"Ethel Van Zant knows I want to please my husband?"

"I mean the opposite. Why would you go see a witch except to do something you shouldn't?"

"A witch?" Mary gave a sharp laugh.

"Does she cure you of children? Is that what you go to her for?"

Mary's eyes roved his face for some sign that he was making a cruel joke, but his eyes were genuinely asking. Her heart shrank against him in these moments when he seemed so hopelessly stupid.

"She isn't a witch, for God's sake, Bernard. And furthermore, why do you assume I would do something like that?"

"You don't want children! You want to read and write and follow your thoughts around, like…like a child chasing butterflies! You *don't want children*, Mary! And *that* is one of the things you lied to me about."

It stung worse for the shards of truth in it. "Like a child chasing butterflies? That's how you're describing my work?"

"Yes! Wandering aimlessly, hoping for words to float by that strike your fancy and fit together just so. You told me in the beginning that you wanted to *really* work. Teach. Raise a family." Bernard glared at her.

"What would I have to teach if I don't learn? Do you want your children to have an educated, accomplished mother or not? And how can I mother them if I am not my true self, writing the poetry God intended me to write? *That* is my work!"

He gave a laugh and shook his head. "I know better than to believe that's what's going on here."

"You don't know that at all."

"Well, look what's happened so far in almost three years of sharing this house. I'd say you've spent a lot of time with your books and paper. But"—he feigned a searching look around the room—"you've kept my children away pretty good."

"So what are you saying?" The shaking began in her knees. It climbed into her chest and face, and she instantly felt that Bernard was growing farther away, the pink walls even darker.

He crossed his arms. "It's obvious."

"No, it isn't! What exactly are you saying? *What*, Bernard?" When he only stood silently, glaring, she lunged at him, flung her fists onto his chest, then stood back and stared into his eyes. "What do you mean? Do you imagine I can conjure up a child like I write a poem, just think it up and hand it to you? Maybe *you* are the problem, Bernard. Maybe *your* bag of tricks won't make children."

He raised his eyebrows and balled his right fist as if to strike her, but she didn't flinch. He sneered. "Such a common girl you are, really. College couldn't learn that out of you."

Mary reached up to slap him, and he grabbed one of her wrists, then the other, and held them both in one hand, while he twisted her around and bent her over before him. She kicked a leg back into his shin, and he winced as he shoved her skirt up and jerked her underwear down until the coarse denim covering his pelvis pressed against her bare skin.

"Now just give me a minute." His voice was husky, angry, lusty, as he bound her arms and torso with his right arm and ran his left hand up between her thighs before unzipping his pants. "Mmm. Yeah. Got to keep trying…" Mary stopped struggling and stared down between her legs at Bernard's boots. Her hair hung toward the ground. "Keep…trying."

She waited, and as soon as pleasure began to seize his body and he shifted his right hand, she twisted loose at the waist and bit his wrist. He yelled and grabbed her by the hair as she sent out fierce laughter. He dragged her over a few feet, then shoved her, chest down, on the table beside his dinner plate. Her body rocked with his thrusts, and when he groaned with climactic release, she cut her fingernails into her palms, angry tears wetting the wood beneath her cheek.

14

Egos crying out of unkempt deeps
And waving their dreams like flags—
Multi-colored dreams,
Winged and glorious...

~ Lola Ridge (1873–1941), "The Ghetto"

I'm going to Portman," Frank said the next morning, pushing open the door to Lydia's study.

She spun around toward him.

"To get the check back."

She glanced at the clock. "What about your class?"

"I called in, said I seem to have a recurrence of that flu."

"Why not just wait until after you teach?" Frank's inconsistent dedication to his teaching was a perennial source of concern to her. His expression began to sour. "I mean, I'm glad you're getting right on it. But—"

"I'll manage my own life, Lydia. See you later."

She listened to him quickly descend the stairs, his step light. She heard the back door close and considered how her mistrust of Frank had come to affect all of their interactions in recent months. She reminded herself that she'd gone with him to an auction and had some fun, and they seemed to be on the same page about not spending. She should just take things one day at a time.

Turning back to her computer, she composed a note she would send with Nicholas to Jack Kenilworth. Something about the idea of corresponding with him seemed risky to her, but she chalked it up to the clumsiness of their drugstore conversation. The fact that Frank's account of his interactions with Jack differed from Jack's did not necessarily mean anyone was being dishonest or that some problem existed. She would find out what she could about it if she could do so without alienating Jack. Right now, he was the best thing in Nicholas's life, and she would not risk jeopardizing that relationship.

Dear Jack,

When we ran into each other at the drugstore, I wasn't quite myself and I'm afraid I neglected to thank you for your mentorship of my son. Could you spare a few minutes sometime to speak with me briefly one-on-one about his work with you? I also have another question I'd like your opinion about, so if you're willing to chat a bit, I'll stop by your business whenever it is convenient.

~ Lydia Milliken Carroll

"Oh, I don't know about this," Lydia murmured.

If Jack Kenilworth was as reserved and self-protective as Lydia had always gotten the impression he was, a request for his opinion about anything might ensure that he never spoke to her again. She leaned back and tried to imagine him openly talking to her about Nicholas, or about the best people to interview regarding White Hill history who might either shed light on Mary Walker's fate or be useful for a new fiction project. These weren't difficult subjects, Lydia reasoned, not provocative. It should be fine. He didn't have to say much if he didn't want to. And if he seemed open and talkative, she could bring up the question of what he had tried to share with Frank.

She pushed the subject off to the side of her mind and turned to the printed pages of her romance manuscript. Her heroine, Jodi, had reenlisted in the marines but now found herself in love with a war protestor and reluctant to fulfill her military duty. Both Lydia's agent and her editor thought the premise gave her all kinds of room for meaningful drama and interesting dialogue, and they both found the war protestor hero appealing. But to Lydia, it was the same thing she had written twenty-five times already, and she was particularly sick of the hero, a self-centered, charismatic do-nothing with all the right words who, Lydia had realized recently, was modeled closely after her own husband.

She had been horrified. How could she have missed this likeness between Frank and her romance heroes over the course of fifteen years, twenty-five romance novels, and at least fourteen male love interests that acted just like him? It was suddenly a relief that Frank had never deigned to read one of her books, where he might have discovered Lydia's subconsciously generated parody of his strengths and weaknesses. But then again, the man was unlikely to recognize an honest portrait of himself in any form.

Focus, focus. There was work to be done. With a combination of dread and hope, Lydia took a deep breath and started at page one, reading, with fresh eyes, *The Few, the Proud, and the Hungry*. Her eyes roved the lines fast, then faster, impatient for something to believe in, and the modest stack of eighty-eight double-spaced pages was quickly over. Slowly, she set them down on her desk and stared blankly ahead. The writing was awful.

She turned her gaze toward the window at the faint sound of Canada geese passing overhead, their timeless voices calling. And suddenly, like a full moon, a new idea rose so clearly and completely in her mind that it felt like a vision. Here she was, living daily with questions about Mary Walker and now gathering information from the world beyond the poet's written words. *This* subject was alive for her. Why not develop it into her next novel? It was just what Lincoln Babcock had been afraid she might do, and he'd virtually warned her not to, but that seemed another persuasive reason to take it on. There was vitality in it.

Yes, it would be as alive as anything Lydia could imagine and would come together easily, because the words and ideas about Mary Walker had been with her since childhood. This was brilliant.

And there was an added attraction: by using her own imagination, she could end this endless story that threatened her marriage. Frank might object to her fictionalizing Mary Walker's life at first—yes, of course he would. But Mary Stone Walker was not *his poet*, his sacred property; he'd just convinced himself that she was.

Yes, Lydia's spirits rose. She could drop *The Few, the Proud, and the Hungry* and dig right into this story. There certainly was a rich novel here, and she had a right to it. And how hard could it be to bend a story about a beautiful, vanished poet toward the interest of her romance audience?

She would do as much research as possible into the real people and places that were part of the poet's life and then draw the girl, the woman, without romanticizing her life. And in her novel, Lydia would give the poet's life a conclusive ending. Within the raw texture of an actual, troubled existence in the nineteen thirties, Lydia could illustrate how the woman might have been driven by horrible circumstances to leave her home and maybe even her life, only to have that decision twisted into a pleasing myth decades later by the likes of Frank. Lydia took a spiral notebook from a stack of them on her shelf and eagerly began a list of details and questions about Mary that intrigued her as potential elements of a novel.

When Nicholas arrived home at three fifteen, he tiptoed up the stairs and knocked lightly at her door.

"Where's Dad?" were his first words when he entered.

Lydia set down her pen and looked at the clock. Frank had been gone for over four hours. He must have gone from Portman straight to campus.

"Running an errand," she said. "Why?"

"You guys were gone all day yesterday, so I didn't know if something was—you know—going on." She felt his eyes trying to read her thoughts.

"No, everything's okay as far as I know. Are you working at Jack's today?"

"Yeah, I told him I would," Nicholas said. "But I can stay home if you need me. If we need to look for Dad or something…"

She focused closely on him. "No, Nicholas. Honestly, it's okay. He really is just running an errand, and probably went from there to his office. But it's nice of you to offer." She went back to the file with the letter she'd written to Jack and printed it out, folded it into an envelope, and sealed it. "Give this to Jack, would you? I'm going out, so I can drive you over there."

"Sure, if you don't mind," Nicholas said. "What's the note about?"

"Ah, I want his opinion about something," she said. "Just some facts I might use in my next novel."

"You mean about building boats?"

"Not exactly." Lydia gazed uneasily at her son. "More general. I'm thinking about setting a novel in White Hill, and his family has been here a long time. He might be able to point me toward good people to interview about what life was like here in the past."

"Hmm. Maybe," Nicholas said. "But it doesn't seem like he ever leaves the woods and the lake."

Lydia chuckled. "Well, then it might be a very short conversation."

It was a quiet ten minutes as they drove to Jack's place. Lydia found her mind toying with the ideas she had been working on in her study, while Nicholas gazed out the window with something that seemed like sadness. But Lydia wasn't sure how to ask him about his mood without making him feel scrutinized.

"Do you want me to pick you up later?" she asked as he got out of the Jeep. "It's pretty chilly out."

"Yeah, if you can." He looked at his watch. "Three hours from now?"

"I'll be here. I'll come in for you so that you don't have to watch the clock. Okay?"

"Right."

"Hey, be sure to give Jack that note, Nick."

"Yep. See ya, Mom."

Lydia watched him disappear around the barn, then drove slowly away. She couldn't have him getting into worried states like this all the time. These were not his issues he was suffering over. The Jeep bumped down the narrow, rutted dirt drive as she thought about the pervasive tension in their home. Nicholas had been aware enough for quite some time to see the mechanics of it—even when they were subtle, without loud drama.

Where Jack's drive met the road, Lydia stopped and opened the window a crack. She could hear the surf faintly from far below. It was impossible to imagine that Frank had ever driven out here to speak with Jack Kenilworth. As avid as Frank's interest in Mary Stone Walker was, Lydia had never known him to investigate the woman's life beyond reading, conversations with other academics and librarians, and of course the damned antique searches. He claimed that he didn't trust "the locals," but Lydia had grown increasingly suspicious of this excuse.

On the road toward home, she felt reluctant to return to her house full of conflict. Instead, she shopped for a frame for the photograph of Mary's attic that she imagined as the cover for Frank's book, she walked the town with thoughts of how she might incorporate the details of downtown White Hill into a new plot, and she browsed local history documents at the library.

After two and a half hours, she headed back out toward the lake. At Jack's place, she parked the Jeep and walked around the barn as she had seen Nicholas do, then headed cautiously toward a closed door. As she stared at it, planning her words of greeting, she heard the storm door on the house behind her slam and she turned. She and Jack exchanged startled looks.

"Hi!" Lydia chirped. The sun cut into long clouds at the horizon, and the light over the lake behind Jack was lavender. "I'm taking you up on the offer to see what Nick's doing."

"Great! Come on in," Jack said, opening the door.

The barn was well lit and smelled faintly of a kerosene heater she could hear hissing somewhere at the edge of the vast room. Nicholas didn't notice her as she stood several steps inside the entrance and watched him. He was sprawled on the floor with his right arm extended, a thick pencil gripped in his hand. Jack walked over to Nicholas and leaned above the drawing, gazing back and forth across the lines the boy was drawing on the floor, then turned his face to Lydia and gestured for her to come closer.

"Got a visitor," he said to Nicholas, and the boy turned toward him. Jack nodded in Lydia's direction, and Nicholas sat up.

"Hey, Mom," he said with an embarrassed glance at Jack.

"Say, Nick, that's magnificent, what you're doing there." Lydia peered around at the lines that resembled those she'd seen tacked to Nicholas's bedroom wall. "Wow."

"This is a twenty-two-foot sloop Jack's going to start on soon."

"Made out of what?" Lydia asked.

"Mahogany," Jack said. "It's a replica of an early-twentieth-century boat for a client in Chicago. Don't forget that color code we talked about, Nicholas." Jack bent down briefly to tap a chart at Nicholas's side.

"Oh, right." Nicholas held a flat orange pencil, but checked the chart and exchanged it for a blue one.

After a few minutes watching Nicholas, Lydia mustered a cheerful voice to ask, "Did Nicholas give you my note?"

Jack stared at her blankly, opened his mouth, then looked confused. "I'm sorry?"

Lydia lightly kicked Nicholas's foot. "Did you give Jack the note, Nick?"

Nicholas also stared uncomprehendingly at her.

"The note I printed out at home and handed to you? In the envelope?" Lydia felt herself flush. "Nicholas!"

"Oh yeah. Sorry, I forgot, Mom. When I got here, Jack need help carrying stuff. I forgot."

As he stood up to go for his backpack, a woman entered the barn with a thermos and two mugs. She gave Lydia a friendly nod and set the things down on Jack's worktable, unscrewing the thermos as Nicholas produced the bent envelope.

"Never mind now, Nicholas," Lydia muttered, embarrassed. Was this Jack's wife or girlfriend? She had assumed that he had neither, but what had given her that idea? Jack took a steaming cup from the woman, and the two of them gazed idly at Nicholas, who was striding toward Jack with the note.

"Nick, never mind now," Lydia said again as Jack took the envelope and held it up, eyebrows raised to ask what she wanted him to do with it. "It doesn't matter," she said, pretending that it really didn't matter. But the fact was, Jack was almost a total stranger in many ways, and she suddenly felt as though she was assuming more familiarity than she should. "Is this your wife, Jack?"

The small, thirtysomething woman laughed. "Nooo. I like to say I'm the wind manager."

Jack glanced at Lydia, then held his coffee cup in a gesture toward the woman. "This is Dolly Atkins. She sews the sails. Among other things."

"Yes, I can work miracles with a needle and thread."

"Sails?" Lydia said. "How...vast! Isn't that difficult?"

Dolly lifted one shoulder in a shrug. "Stitch by stitch. That's how you do it."

The woman was so completely at ease, and her role there was so obviously essential, that Lydia felt reluctant to discuss anything personal with Jack. But he opened the envelope, apparently taking Lydia's lack of retraction as a go-ahead.

Lydia beamed her gaze fiercely down at busy Nicholas, but when she glanced at Jack, she saw that his expression had shifted, and she thought he looked uncomfortable. She averted her gaze to Dolly, who was searching for something in a set of drawers under the worktable. When Lydia looked back at Jack, he had folded the note closed, then in half, and again into a small square that he was sliding into his shirt pocket.

"Well, Lydia," he said, turning his side to her as he poured more coffee for himself. "Um...let's..." He glanced around the loft. "Come on back to Dolly's room for a minute. My office is covered with financial records. Taxes."

"Ooh, that's just a couple of days away."

"Wednesday. We won't be long, Dolly."

"I'm headed out. After I find that sharpener," she replied, her voice punctuated by clinks and shuffling as she ran her hands around in the drawers.

"Right. Take it easy." Jack led the way after briefly meeting Lydia's eyes. They entered a separate, simply finished room full of canvas in various stages of transformation. An industrial sewing machine hunched in the middle of a long table in front of two chairs on casters. Jack sat down in one of them, lifted his ankle onto his knee, and leaned back, hands linked together behind his head. He gestured for Lydia to sit in the other.

"Thanks for taking time out, Jack." She pressed her palms on her thighs.

"Don't worry about it," he said, straightening the stapler, tape dispenser, and other items on his desk, as he waited for her to begin the conversation.

"Mostly I am wondering how Nick's doing." As soon as the words were out, Lydia felt exposed. It was happening all the time now—any subject connected to her family felt dangerous and upsetting. It suddenly seemed out of the question to ask Jack about his interactions with Frank.

Jack looked surprised. "I'd say he seems just fine, but I'm just starting to get to know him."

"No, I mean how he is doing at the job. Here."

"Oh!" Jack was visibly relieved and shook his head. "Of course, yes. He's exceptionally good at this. And he learns very quickly."

"That's wonderful news. I'm so glad," Lydia said. "Nicholas hasn't had a lot of wins in the last year or so, I guess you could say." She paused, considering all she unexpectedly wanted to share with Jack. With someone anyway. He watched her face, raising an eyebrow.

"You look like there's more," he said.

Lydia allowed her gaze to remain hooked to his a couple of seconds too long and felt embarrassed. "He's…sensitive" was all she managed to say. "But so many of us are, or were, at that age. You might have been, I think. You were quiet."

"Maybe around you," Jack said with a small smile. "No, you're right. I was always quiet in public. But I found my out-lets. Nick will, too. Maybe he will even come to love boats. Like I did. Or something else fun that expands his horizons."

Lydia took the opportunity to put aside the intimate subject of her son.

"So how did it begin, your love affair with boats?" she asked. There was so much more personality and emotion visible in Jack Kenilworth's face than there had been when he was seventeen. But then again, she'd never studied him the way she was now.

"Let's see." He ran his hand on his jaw, tiny reflections of the track lights shining in his eyes as he aimed his vision above her face. "It seems like it had to happen, no way around it. We all loved the lake, but Dad was nuts for wooden boats. You run a fiberglass boat aground and it's garbage, he said, but you can drag a half-sunk wooden boat up from the lake and salvage it. Takes some doing. And a hell of a lot of cash. And time. But it's worth it. Granddad always said they have souls."

Jack nodded, his expression lifted by the boats—or perhaps the people—in his mind. "I guess it's that simple. My granddad had a great fishing sloop, and my dad and I worked on it a lot. I built my first boat, just a kayak, when I was fourteen, in my granddad's shop. Which was right where my house is now. Part of the shed where Granddad worked on his fishing nets and kept his tools is my kitchen. One wall and a window."

"Oh really? He lived and worked right here?"

"Yes indeed," Jack said. "With my grandmother. And they had one child."

"Your father."

"Naturally." Jack smiled.

"Your granddad was the one who taught you how to build boats?"

"Yeah, he was a pro. And quite a character." He laughed a little. "I got as much bullshit as boat talk from him."

"So he had a fishing sloop? What did he use that for?"

Jack gave her quizzical look. "He…fished. Mostly. You know…what fishermen do."

"Yes, of course. But did he use it for other things as well?" She realized it was incredible that with all the research she and Frank had done, she didn't know a thing about the fishing industry in White Hill during Mary's era. Did fishermen take people out on summer days to catch their own trophy fish like they did these days?

"Seems like with a boat he could give tours or travel…" She let her voice trail off.

"Usually not. That's a different sort of life you're thinking of. Not a working man's life." Jack gazed at her. "Why?"

Lydia shrugged. "I just…don't know much, I guess. And, um, that leads me to the other reason I wanted to talk to you today. I've gotten a start on researching Mary Stone Walker through interviews of people still alive who might have known her or known something about her. You know, firsthand, not merely through her writing."

Jack listened but said nothing when she paused, so she fumbled for more words.

"In all these years, Frank and I have never done that. Sought out real people. And it's kind of stupid." She watched his face for signs that he might want to share what he had tried to share with Frank, but Jack's expression was closed.

"Mmm-hmm."

"So I am wondering if you might have some tips for me. Ideas about people who might have known her, or known people who knew her. That sort of thing. People I could talk to."

"I'll give that some thought." Jack sat up straight and swung around to look at the clock over the sewing machine. "Tell you what, Lydia." He inhaled slowly and thrummed his fingers on the table. "Nicholas has probably run out of stuff to do out there. Let's…let's, uh, take this subject up another time. Okay?"

"Sure. Of course. Maybe sometime you could elaborate on what you told me today about your grandfather. His fishing business. Boats. If you don't mind." She lifted her purse. "I'd like to really understand that aspect of White Hill life."

"Well, the past is dead, as they say, but I suppose for novelists it really isn't, is it? Anyway, you're always welcome here." He stood up, and Lydia followed him out the door.

"Hey, Nicholas. Knock off for the day," Jack said, and he went to his worktable where a stack of papers seemed to capture his attention completely.

"Okay. I don't have much left to do on this," Nicholas said. When Jack didn't answer, he shrugged and put his supplies away, picking up his backpack. "See ya," he said as he opened the door.

"Good night, kid," Jack said over his shoulder. "You all be careful on the drive and don't get stuck. Mud's getting soft."

"Thanks for your time, Jack," Lydia said, confused by his abrupt dismissal. It was well after five o'clock. But maybe he worked crazy hours.

"Hey, good to see you." He gave her a half smile, then continued to sort through the papers.

When they reached the Jeep, Nicholas smiled at Lydia. "What'd you think? It's neat in there, isn't it?"

"Yes, it really is." Lydia started the ignition, turned around, and drove down the drive.

"Pretty cool guy, don't you think?" he asked.

Lydia was surprised to notice that Jack's presence in her mind was no longer threatening in the way that it had been since she'd begun to wonder if Frank was hiding the truth about meetings with him. In fact, it felt now as if Jack Kenilworth might possess—and share—something that would be extremely helpful to her.

"Yes," she said, smiling toward her son. "How great to feel that way about your boss. Is he...kind of moody?"

"Well, I don't know. He thinks about boats all the time, I guess," Nicholas said, watching her. "Nothing wrong with that, though. Right?"

Lydia nodded, trying to remember exactly what she had said right before Jack cut the conversation short, but her thoughts grew more scattered the closer they got to their house.

"Whoa, what's that?" Nicholas asked as Lydia pulled into their driveway.

She turned her attention toward the barn where Nicholas was pointing. The doors were open, and inside Frank was running his hand along the top of the oak dining room table from 1880, next to which ten chairs were clustered awaiting his inspection.

15

White Hill, Michigan—April 1999

I would give, to recall the sweetness and the frost of the lost blue
   plums,
Anything, anything.
               ~ Edna St. Vincent Millay (1892–1950), "The Plum Gatherer"

Barely able to breathe, Lydia rushed to the house without speaking to Frank, while Nicholas went to the barn. She was too angry and shocked to do anything but pace back and forth with a disbelieving glance out the kitchen window every time she passed it. He couldn't do this. He could not do this to her. Her heart whapped against her ribs. What would she do? How could she endure this? If she went out there now, her fury would be an incoherent spectacle, and she would not subject Nicholas to that. She had to preserve something of the peace that her son needed. She had to hang on to her self-control.

She took the stairs two at a time and rushed into her office. Fumbling wildly through a desk drawer, she pulled out the most recent statement for their savings account, which their checking account would draw from when presented with the $26,990 check to the Portman Auction House. The pages shook in her hands.

"How could he do this?" she whispered, her face rigid with anger. She sat down, grabbed a pen and a sheet of blank paper, and began to write in fierce, dark figures.

FRank—$52,098. That is the balance in our savings account as of yesterday. As of tomorrow, it will be $26,990 less. These are funds we have been saving for fourteen years. These are mostly funds I earned. You will not take this amount from me, from your son, from our future for your fucking dining room set.

"*God!*" she screamed, and she hammered her desk with her fist again and again, finally laying her forehead on her arms to weep. He had bought these antiques knowingly, with no intention of retrieving the check he'd used to pay for them. What else might he do?

Lydia sat up, wiping her eyes on her sleeve. She had to pull herself together. Her husband was acting irrationally, and she had to protect the family resources, her child, and herself, even if she could not protect Frank. She stared out the window at a distant streetlight, considering how to shame Frank into acting responsibly to correct this situation somehow.

After half an hour of trying to breathe calmly in spite of her explosive thoughts, Lydia went downstairs, pushed the kitchen door open, and was alarmed to find Drew Johnson arranging cheese, cold cuts, and crackers on a plate.

"Hi, Lydia!" Drew said with a half-embarrassed smile. "I hope you don't mind. Frank asked me to find something to eat in here. 'Anything,' he said." She laughed, still looking at Lydia, a package of ham in her hands.

Lydia wrapped her sweater closed tightly as a shaky feeling started in her core. "Order a pizza or something."

"Oh, no, that's too much trouble. This will do." She went about filling the plate. "Do you have any apples? I love apples with cheese, and we both know Frank does."

Against the darkness of Lydia's thoughts, the sight of Drew with her hair curled and pinned back, eyes and cheeks painted with bright makeup, was jarring. She opened the refrigerator, found two apples, and set them on the counter.

"Okay, now, where are your knives? And a cutting board?"

Lydia stiffened as she pulled out a knife and groped in a low cupboard for the cutting board.

"So Frank has you fetching his snacks now?" she said, staring at Drew, but the younger woman didn't look up.

"I don't mind. He's all absorbed. You know. Besides, he said you're mad at him and he didn't want to risk the distraction of an argument." She threw an unseeing glance sideways toward Lydia, along with a short laugh. "I know how that goes, I told him. No offense to you, of course."

Lydia considered an honest response to this comment but instead said, "Really? Mad at him? Why would I be mad at him?"

Drew seemed satisfied with the platter of food and lifted it, shaking her head. "Something about the furniture. You don't approve, he said. But really, Lydia, I think this is a significant find. It's so easy to imagine Mary Walker sitting with colleagues in literary discussions at this table, because it really was in the town where she was staying at the house of one of her benefactors that first summer after college! In fact, it's impossible to think she wouldn't have been getting attention from the arts crowd when she had published quite a bit already, and it's around this table that conversations with patrons and fans were most likely to happen! Frank thinks it's obvious, and so do I."

"Oh, so do I," Lydia lied. "Why else would I have gone with him to Portman to bid on it? Honestly. What a silly he is."

"You were with him? That must have been exciting." Drew stood ready and waiting to return to the barn with her feast. "We hardly know where to begin. Well, I better get back to it. 'Night, Lydia."

"'Night, Drew," Lydia said, but her grimace was wasted on Drew's back as the young woman passed through the door and into the yard, the storm door rattling as it slammed. The meat and cheese wrappers were scattered around on the counter. "I'll get these for you!"

Lydia watched Drew hurry toward the barn, disgusted with the young woman's adoration of Frank and cheered slightly by her own charade. Yes, maybe this should be her tactic. Devoted, unrelenting joy at Frank's acquisition. She would stay by his side and pretend to be sad when it ended as all the other searches had. Then she could be ready with contact information for the Huntington woman, who should have had the damn furniture to begin with, and they could retrieve their savings.

Retrieving the man she'd fallen in love with so many years ago was another matter entirely.

Lydia stared out the window at the barn where the light occasionally flickered as someone crossed in front of the lamp. Not so long ago, she would have been at Frank's side in that barn, searching relics that might have had some possible connection to Mary Walker. In her journals, the poet mentioned hiding things time and time again, so together Lydia and Frank had traced connections between the dates and locations, and then they'd done their best to reconstruct the settings so that they could make educated guesses about which items might have been in those settings.

But these days Frank bought items based on nothing more than rumors and whims, and Lydia wasn't sure what sort of checking he actually did. The last really strong clue they followed had been at least four years ago. For all she knew, the Huntington story could be Frank's fabrication based on some half-lost tale, albeit one he may have come to believe.

Lydia sighed. She remembered the first time that Drew had supplanted her as Frank's partner in this exploration. Drew was a new English instructor at the college, and Frank was obviously intoxicated by her fascination with him and his quest. One night, Lydia and Frank were listing the places Mary Walker had hidden the nine documents others had found over the decades, describing the objects and methods she had used, and trying to develop a theory of her psychological changes. Over the weeks, Frank had mentioned Drew a handful of times—his new colleague at Carson—and suddenly she was standing there in the dining room, young, cute, and full of a kind of energetic captivation that made Lydia feel completely outdated.

Now, however, it was perfectly, painfully clear that Lydia's true rival was not a living woman, but the imagined goddess of an unfinished life. Frank had idealized this martyr, as he saw her, a poet driven from White Hill by an insensitive husband who not only did not want her poetry, but who also, Frank was certain, mocked her tender desires to have children. The fact that she had never given birth was actually an asset in Frank's calculations, Lydia knew, but he would never admit that. As an unloved, unappreciated, but beautiful and tragically childless artist, Mary Walker was Frank's perfect damsel in distress.

In recent years, Lydia had attempted, with no success, to compete with Mary Stone Walker. She had even humiliated herself one night by bringing out the manuscript of her own poetry to share with Frank, who had always described that early work of hers as promising. To reminisce, she'd said aloud to him, but also, she had to admit to herself, to reassert herself as a poet before her husband. He had seemed distracted, then a phone call from a student ended the one-sided conversation entirely. It was not the first time, or the last, that he'd made it clear that as a writer and a poet, Lydia Milliken no longer interested him.

Recently, Nicholas had asked to see her poetry. It was typed up and bound with a cover, which seemed naive and pathetic to her now. He had been full of flattery, dear Nicholas, asking to borrow it to read the entire thing. She assumed it was still in his bedroom. When he had finished, he asked if she had any others, any at all that he could read, and he had averted his eyes when she said she didn't. As if perhaps he was disappointed. So she had thought and thought…but no, she'd been through this before when she assembled the manuscript. It contained everything she could find, even the lesser creations. And sadly, nothing more recent than 1990.

Just a few days ago, Nicholas had sent her an email from the downstairs computer in the middle of the night, declaring how much he loved all of her poems. "Why didn't you ever sell them?" he wrote. "They're the best!" This was one more reason to begin the process of self-publishing. The world of self-expression and art was difficult, lonely, and competitive, and she had often told her son not to wait for external approval before embarking on his dreams. She should set that example.

Suddenly, it occurred to her that there might be an unexpected benefit to the disappointment Frank would feel when this dining room set offered no Walker documents: it might open his mind about creating a publishing company. After all, the insanity of this purchase indicated that he was desperate for some way to move forward, but had ceased to be able to think in terms of anything but finding documents in antiques. It was possible that with the powerful disappointment that this furniture was sure to disintegrate into, the timing of an independent press would be perfect for him after all. The set could be resold for close to what they had paid, and the savings account would be nearly intact. She inhaled deeply and slowly exhaled. Perhaps the outcome would not be disastrous after all.

This new perspective lightened her heart, and hope wormed like a drug through her veins. She went to the window and gazed at the barn, her breathing beginning to feel normal. Maybe their family life could be calmed and even improve over time.

Lydia made a cup of tea and turned off the kitchen light. She'd heard Nicholas go to bed an hour before. Frank had a morning class to teach and had just skipped his class today, and yet he was still out there playing around. Could he be finding encouragement, having some success? That would be…so different that she didn't know how to think about it. She shook her head.

Lingering over his obsession was not unusual for him at all, and if he had an early class, that was his problem, not hers.

It was *her* lingering over his obsessions that was no longer acceptable. She would confront Frank in the morning and give him an ultimatum about reselling the furniture. And she would concentrate on gathering material for the novel focused on Mary Walker, beginning with whatever information she could gather from Jack about his grandfather's life during Mary's era.

She felt a quiet rise in gratitude as she thought about her personal good fortune, which had nothing to do with her home, her marriage, or even her son: there was always so much to hope for in the creative process. Once a project came alive for her, every day was filled with possibility, inspiration, and the work of trying to meet her ideas with language. For this novel based on Mary Walker, even seemingly unimportant firsthand accounts could add texture to her understanding of the poet's character and fate, details of all types that Lydia could use to build fiction.

And the process would serve another purpose: she would get closer to the truth that had eluded them for so long.

She sat back, thinking, trying to calculate. Like Lydia, Jack was born in 1962, or thereabouts. In the 1930s, when Mary Stone Walker was in her twenties, Jack's grandfather would most likely have been a few years older than that... Well, possibly ten years or more. He would have been a mature adult, with a house just a few miles from Mary's marital home. Could he have known her? It was possible, Lydia supposed, but how would they have crossed paths? Lydia was fairly certain from her own reading that Mary had never written about the Kenilworth family. Which made sense because she had been something of a snob, if comments in her letters and journals were taken at face value, spending most of her social time connecting with people who might assist her career.

Lydia pictured the dining room table that was out in her barn, imagined Mary Walker sitting at it with fellow academics or patrons of poetry, and the old heat of fascination flashed. If only they could discover that the poet had survived! But Lydia was too weary of the vision to give any more of her life to it. What they needed to conclude this tale were real-life clues and witnesses—not more antiques and imaginings. And as it happened, that was also what she needed to create a novel that was alive.

When she was in bed, under the covers, a memory flashed of an early night with Frank in his Ann Arbor apartment seventeen years before. Shirtless, he was leaning out the street-side window on a clear, cold night, and even from the bed, she could see stars in the black sky around his head. He had turned and said, "My sweet young poet, I have never loved like this before. Together, you and I will make poems of our days."

It was dramatic, and overly romantic, but that was how their little private world had been back then. Daily life was transformed by the energy between them, and every moment was made extraordinary. He had seemed to understand her mind better than she'd imagined someone could. But today... Well, now her goal was nothing more than a return to the simple tolerance they had managed over the last few years.

Knees close to her chest, Lydia gradually fell into sleep, where she was besieged by a chaos of dream fragments and only awakened near dawn by the sound of her husband pushing heavily through their bedroom door.

16

The heart's laughter will be to her
The crying of the crows,

Who slide in the air with the same voice
Over what yields not, and what yields...

~ Louise Bogan (1897–1970), "The Crows"

Bernard said it brought good luck to watch the sun set, especially if you stared at the sun until there was no more of its dark red left on the horizon. His mother had told him this, and the proof was that she had seen it sink into Lake Michigan hundreds of times and given birth to seven fine sons who had all survived to become adults.

Mary walked with him to the White Hill lighthouse on the last night of September to watch the sunset from the end of the pier where the lake water broke against the rocks, and he carried a bottle of corn whiskey that his brother had brewed. They planned to sit with their backs against the lighthouse wall and drink until their bodies warmed despite the cool night air.

But shortly after dark, Mary grew restless and stood up to walk slowly toward the edge of the pier. After several minutes, she gasped, pointing across the lake.

"Bernard!"

He was looking over the fish caught by a couple of men a few feet away, and he ignored her.

"Bernard, look!" She glanced around, then pointed emphatically again. "City lights! I can see lights right out there in the lake!"

Bernard stood and directed his eyes where she pointed, then turned away and laughed at something one of the other men said. A distant line of phantom streetlights, along with the floating headlights of cars, was dim but undeniably visible to Mary.

"We're seeing a city beyond the horizon!" Her voice trilled like a child's. "The Fata Morgana! Master of illusions! I've heard of this sort of mirage, but I never dreamed I would see it!"

"No, she ain't drunk," Bernard said in answer to one of the men, but intending for Mary to hear. "She imagines things all the time. I might have to trade her in."

Mary turned away from the lights, stepped toward him, and flung a fist at his chest. "Look for yourself, you bullheaded—"

"Don't you be telling me what to do, woman!" Bernard gave a laugh as he easily caught her wrist and jerked her toward himself, his other hand open to slap her buttocks, but at the moment he was loosening his grip to turn her around, Mary pulled back as hard as she could to break free. He lost his grip entirely, and she lurched away from him and teetered precariously before stumbling backward over the edge of the pier, her body bouncing along the rocks of the jetty like a doll. Her scream was enveloped by the lake.

"Holy Jesus!" Bernard was shocked out of his mischievous whiskey fog, and the two fishermen dropped their poles and rushed to his side. Mary's body bobbed against the rocks, her left arm caught in the piling boulders at water level. Her long hair and heavy coat billowed in the dark waves. Bernard scrambled down the boulders and sank into the water beside her.

"*Mary!*" He lifted her head from the water, and she twitched with pain, spluttering, gasping for air. One of the fishermen lay on his stomach on the pier and lowered a rope to Bernard.

When he looped it around her chest, Mary emitted a watery scream and tried to speak, but her words were unintelligible. All light had left the sky, and the lake's temperature was barely fifty degrees.

"Mary! Can you hear me? Answer me!" Bernard's voice was desperate, but her eyes stayed closed, her body limp, and her groans sounded more like an animal's than a woman's.

Twenty-four hours later in Mercy Hospital, Mary's body temperature had stabilized, but she lay listless, recovering from a powerful anesthesia that had been administered for an operation on her arm. Breaks through the wrist and hand were so numerous and complex that the doctor predicted he would have to operate at least two more times to return the bones, muscles, and tendons to even a moderate level of functionality. Bernard gazed at the guileless face of his wife and her mangled arm wrapped in gauze, his thoughts black with the prospect of her being even less able than she already was to accomplish anything beyond minimal cooking and cleaning.

He watched the surgeon raise a hypodermic needle from a tray and touch Mary's skin with its fine point, and although she was barely conscious, she twitched at the pain. The doctor emptied a barrel of morphine into her blood, and it wasn't long before peace came over Mary's whole body, lending a slackness to her facial features that months later gave the appearance of boredom. And one year into her dependence on the powerful drug, that look of boredom took turns with a frenzied wildness that few ever saw.

17

WHITE HILL, MICHIGAN—APRIL 1999

The rain has taught us nothing.

~ Edna St. Vincent Millay (1892–1950), "The Bobolink"

Lydia!" Frank's voice was urgent and rough.

Lydia woke, confused. "What? What is it, Frank?" She glanced at the clock. It was 6:39. Her alarm clock would sound in six minutes.

"Lydia," he said again, collapsing onto the bed. "You've got to call the college for me. Tell Janet in administration that I won't be there this morning." He lay still, fully clothed, breathing hard.

Her eyes scanned the ceiling. It wasn't like him to cancel a class simply because of a hangover, but it had happened before. "You're just coming to bed now?"

"You don't need to monitor my activities, Lydia. Just make the call. I can't go in. That's all anyone needs to know."

Lydia considered telling him to go to hell, but she heard Nicholas moving around in the bathroom. She left the room, closing the door behind her, and hurried down the stairs to avoid her son. Had Frank found something in the furniture that kept him up celebrating?

In the kitchen, she flipped through the address book for the college's administrative office numbers, found Janet's, and stared at it. Was she really going to do this for him at this point? Was she going to play along forever with his games?

But if she did not call, Frank would receive some comment from the college, and there would be even more tension in the house. She dialed the phone number, and it rang and rang. The answering machine with instructions for reporting information came on just as Nicholas entered the kitchen. She hung up.

"Hey, Mom," he said.

"Good morning, Nicholas," she answered, and busied herself cleaning the wineglasses and platter that Drew, no doubt, had brought in from the barn.

"How did Dad's furniture thing go?" Nicholas pulled a box of frozen waffles from the freezer. "He was pretty excited about it."

"I'm not sure." She would call the college after Nicholas left for the bus.

"I thought I heard him talking just now."

"Yes, he's sick. Can't teach today."

"Oh. Bummer." Nicholas ate a banana while he waited for his waffles and spoke with his mouth full. "Hope I don't catch it." He downed a glass of milk and pulled the waffles from the toaster to eat them as he walked to the bus stop.

"Yes. So do I," Lydia said, watching him put on his coat and backpack. "See you this afternoon, Nicky."

"Yeah. I think I'll go straight to Jack's from school."

"Okay. Thanks for letting me know." She opened her arms to hug him good-bye.

"Have a good day, Mom," he said, glancing into her face before he headed out the back door.

"You, too, Nick."

The door shut, and Lydia turned to look at the barn. Should she just go out and see if there were any clues as to what had gone on during the night? Why not? She went to the back door, put on her boots, and walked out into the chilly morning. In the trees she heard the whistling of robins as dawn light seeped into the yard. At the barn door she hesitated. It was closed and was always difficult to open. It would make noise, and Frank might hear it. She looked back at the house, dark but for the kitchen light. Nah, Frank wouldn't hear anything.

As she pulled the door open, shadows bloomed from the dark, full interior, and she waited for her eyes to adjust. Her ghostly imaginings of the beautiful furniture with yellowing Walker pages spread carefully out on the mahogany were smudged out slowly by the reality that the thin light revealed. She gasped.

There, scattered around on the floor, were the seats of the chairs, all removed from their frames, fabric and stuffing torn haphazardly. The table was on its side, the legs removed. Lydia felt light-headed. She drew her hand up to her mouth and bit down hard on the knuckle of her forefinger. Every piece of the valuable set was damaged. As if…as if attacked by a lunatic.

A wave of nausea gripped her. Slowly, she stepped to Frank's favorite chair and sat down, gazing around for only a moment longer before she lowered her face to her hands. Her fingernails dug into her scalp. Something like a sob seized her throat but went no further. Her husband had lost his mind. She pressed the heels of her hands into her eyes, thoughts racing. What would she do? What was she to do? He'd never done anything like this before. He'd never *destroyed* any of his treasures.

For several long minutes, Lydia could not stop the spinning of her thoughts. Then it came to her: that sailmaker. Dolly, wasn't it? Maybe she could sew the seats back together. She glanced around. Maybe Dolly could do it without letting on to Frank or telling anyone in town about the mess. Lydia stood, her muscles jellylike, and picked up one shredded seat. She'd take this to Dolly and ask. She'd do it right now. The thing shook in her hands as she examined it. Most of the fabric was still in one piece. They had to get it back together before they could think about selling it.

But maybe Frank had found something…maybe. She set the seat down and walked from piece to piece, from surface to surface, searching for any encouraging clue. If he had finally found something in this dining set, then it could be okay. It *would* be okay. It would be okay, and Frank would earn back what he'd spent from their savings. He *would*—

But what was she thinking? A sharp, unrecognizable sound shot from her mouth, something between a laugh and a cry. How could she still believe in this preposterous fantasy? She was as crazy as he was. A creature of denial. The chaos before her eyes was a horrible representation of the madness of the entire long search. Tears tightened her throat, and she held her abdomen where she felt shots of pain.

"My God!" She kicked the nearest piece of mahogany. "The bastard!" she cried, picking up a chair seat and screaming into its torn, ancient-smelling fabric. She slammed it down, marched back into the house, and went to the basement, where a basket of clean laundry waited to be carried upstairs to her closet. Jeans. T-shirt. Sweatshirt. Socks. She dressed with angry jerks that made the task take twice as long as it should have.

Back up in the kitchen, she listened for sounds from upstairs. Nothing. Frank was unconscious. Of course he was. She grabbed her purse and car keys and went to the barn for a chair seat, threw it into the Jeep, got in and backed down the driveway in a crazy zigzag that missed the birdbath and the blueberry bushes by sheer luck. She'd get help with the seats before Frank even woke up.

There must be someone who could assist Frank in reassembling the wood to a state near its original condition, which was the only way they could recoup even a portion of their investment. Maybe the damage was not as bad as it appeared. And Frank would be contrite when he came to his senses, surely, eager for her help and grateful—if it worked—for this idea of having Dolly the sailmaker fix the upholstery without anyone else having to know.

Lydia approached a yellow traffic light and sped up to get through it, glancing around for police cars as the light went red. House lights dimmed as the sun rose. Passing Lottie's Bar and

Grill, she noticed two or three men ambling toward the front door for breakfast. Lucky bastards. Lucky, sane, hardworking bastards and their lucky wives.

Her thoughts darted from images of Frank's drunken body on the bed to the shards of his latest hope in the barn. She trembled as if she'd chugged a whole pot of coffee, and she wanted to ram the Jeep into a building. On the country roads that ran toward Jack's house, her thoughts spiraled to visions of parking the Jeep and abandoning it while she ran off into the woods. To be gone and finished with all of this. Through with Frank and all of his messes.

Because the truth was that he would not be grateful to her for thinking about restoring the furniture. He would be angry. He would probably accuse her of having an affair with Jack, or God only knows what. Her heart rate felt dangerously fast. How could Frank do this to her? He was the deluded one, and she was just trying to keep things together, so what was she afraid of?

She was afraid because he had convinced her, deeply convinced her, that she was constantly violating something rare and important as she failed him in ways she wasn't even aware of until he accused her. She lived in fear of his mind and the rules that it imposed on her and her son.

When she reached Jack's private road, Lydia considered turning back home, but the thought was fleeting. She had no other plan, and she couldn't think clearly enough to conjure up any other idea than to fix the furniture, starting with the simplest thing, the cloth. Surely Dolly did this sort of thing from time to time. It wouldn't seem that strange. Lydia rolled slowly down the dirt drive and glanced at the Jeep clock—eight fifteen. A light switched on, and yellow rays cut through the shadows near the house. She rolled the window down a couple of inches, and the wind in the pine tops shushed like lake waves. There was the slam of a door, footsteps. Moments later, a light went on in the barn beside her, just fifteen feet away.

She slid down and watched what she assumed was Jack's

silhouette moving against the pale window shade. But the thought of actually walking in there… How could she approach him with this…this pile of seat bits?

And why was she running away? This morning, right now, she should be sitting in her own kitchen, calmly waiting for Frank to explain everything. Let him carry the weight of the disaster, not her. What was she running from, and what made her think she could or even should try to fix things?

Frank would fix nothing. That was the fact she was running from. Again and again. That was what she couldn't bear and what she fled: the fact that he would speak the same words he always did, brush off her confusion and fear as if she were the one who was unreasonable, and then she would join him to live in that lie, with the vague hope that the lie would eventually fade away. But life would get worse in the meantime. She rested her forehead on the steering wheel, aware of the thud of her heart in her throat as it punctuated loud, shallow breaths. When she lifted her eyes to the barn moments later, the shade in the barn window was up and no one was visible within.

There was a tap at her partially open window, and Lydia gasped and jumped. Jack stood a couple of feet away, gazing in at her. She lowered the window with the same embarrassment she had felt doing so for police officers.

"Hi, Jack," she said apologetically, glancing at his concerned expression, then turning her face down. What excuse could she make?

"Hey," he said querulously, apparently not willing to pretend that her presence here was normal. "Is anything wrong?"

Lydia knew she looked as if something was indeed wrong. She could feel the gummy thickness of disturbance in her features. At least she was not in her pajamas. There was nothing to do but follow through with her plan.

"In a way," she said, trying to meet his eyes, but only briefly glancing as high as his collarbone. "It's been…a difficult morning."

Jack stood back from the door as she opened it and stepped out. "I have a problem. I was hoping your seamstress assistant might be able to help me."

"Oh...Dolly?"

"Yes." Lydia opened the back door and pulled out the chair seat. "Can Dolly sew upholstery? Things like...this?"

Jack eyed the thing in her hand. "What is it?"

"It's the seat of a dining room chair." Together they stared at it. "It's gotten rather torn up." Lydia attempted a smile, but Jack's face was still troubled, and she felt her explanation die in her throat. She turned her face toward the barn.

"I don't know, um... Dolly's here. She stayed the night. Yeah, she's probably up by now. Let me check." He started to turn toward the house. "Come on in. You want coffee?"

"Oh, no, that's okay. But, yes, I'll come in. If you don't mind."

"Sure, come on," he said. She followed a couple of steps behind him as he crossed the yard and opened his back door. Inside, Lydia smelled coffee and other things she couldn't identify...the odd mix of scents in another person's house. So Dolly was there with Jack overnight, and Lydia had shown up at the crack of dawn like a crazy person, intruding on their privacy. Jack walked lightly down a hall, and Lydia stood in the kitchen, hands clenched around the chair seat, her body calmed somewhat by the distraction of other lives.

He knocked on a door, and Lydia heard a woman's voice. He opened the door a few inches and spoke too quietly for Lydia to hear his words. Minutes later, Dolly emerged, dressed in jeans and a sweatshirt, her curly, shoulder-length brown hair pinned back behind her ears.

"Good morning," the woman said brightly, going to the cupboard for two mugs and pouring coffee. She handed one to Lydia. "Cream and sugar?"

"Black is fine. Thanks," Lydia said, accepting a yellow mug

with a red trucking company logo on it. A semi with a smiling face on its metal grill winked a large, blue eye at her.

"Well, you're up with the birds, honey. What's goin' on?" Dolly sat down at one of the kitchen chairs and pushed another out with her foot for Lydia.

"I have a problem," Lydia began, but she felt as if she might cry at the understated claim. "I have…" She faltered. "Here." She lifted the seat she'd set down beside her chair. "This is, as you can see…" She stared at the stupid thing, silenced again by her tight throat. "Do you ever sew—in this case, repair—upholstery?"

Jack and Dolly both gazed at her and then at the object in her hand. After a weighty silence, Dolly turned her eyes to Jack, who looked down into his coffee, then moved to the refrigerator. Lydia could hear him fishing for things and setting them on the counter as she turned the seat over for Dolly to look at it.

"It needs to be fixed, and I know that might be difficult, but I'm just hoping…" Lydia hadn't really examined the fabric until this point as she felt Dolly doing so. It was maroon velvet with a paisley jacquard design, its threads loosening at the edges where Frank had sliced it, and the yellowed, lumpy stuffing falling out. Dolly took the seat from Lydia, running her fingers over the fabric to do what Lydia had not dared to—to attempt to fit it back together to see if it would even cover the stuffing and meet the wood.

"Well," Dolly said thoughtfully. Lydia could smell bacon cooking and glanced up to see Jack breaking eggs into a bowl. Dolly continued to finger the fabric. "Hmm."

The friendly clink of a fork on glass as Jack beat the eggs gave Lydia a spark of strength. "My husband bought the set and hopes to fix it up to sell to the family who originally owned it." She lifted her mug, glanced at Jack's profile as he poured the eggs into a hot pan on the stove, and went on. "This is a kind of side business he's gotten into. He's a professor. But if we can fix this up, we stand to bring in a profit on it."

Dolly nodded as Jack lifted three plates from a shelf and lined them up on the counter. He moved quickly, opening cupboards, the refrigerator, pouring things, scooping, buttering. Lydia felt relieved and suddenly hungry. That was a good line she'd come up with about a side business. Who needed to know Frank had torn up the seats? Dolly pulled the fabric toward the edges, flipped the seat over, flipped it back, rearranged stuffing, pulled again and pursed her lips.

"Tell you what," Dolly said, still absorbed in her hands' efforts. "After I grab a bite here, I'll take this out to the workshop and see what I can do, okay?"

"Great! That would be really great." Lydia smiled, beginning to feel almost normal as Jack set a plate before her. "Honestly, I can't believe I've interrupted you all so early. You're nice to accommodate me."

Dolly's smile was oddly intense and sympathetic when she reached over to squeeze Lydia's fingers. Jack, too, turned his gaze onto Lydia as he lowered himself to his chair, and something in the look—was it pity?—unnerved her. She forced her eyes down to the yellow eggs, brown toast, and bacon, her appetite gone in one self-conscious instant. Woodenly, she picked up her fork and speared a piece of egg, raised it to her mouth, and chewed slowly, passing another bite onto her tongue before she'd swallowed the first. Three, four bites, and she lifted her coffee to her lips, feeling as if every move she made was testimony to the transparent lie she'd just told and the thoughts she couldn't bear to even acknowledge.

Lydia focused studiously on the food and gradually relaxed as Dolly and Jack discussed an article in the newspaper about lakeshore erosion. She forced herself to ask with detached composure if either of them had been to the park written about in the article. Jack said that he'd seen most of Michigan's shoreline from the water, as well as Illinois's and Wisconsin's, and that there was plenty of erosion everywhere. But the conversation didn't last, and after a minute or two of silence, Jack shoved his chair back, cleared his place, and said he had to get to work.

"Thanks for the breakfast, Jack," Lydia said with as much cheer as she could muster.

"Anytime." He threw a half smile to the general area of the kitchen table and left the house.

"Well!" Dolly said. "Shall we see what we can do with your chair?"

"Yes." Lydia's plate was half full, but she had stopped eating. "Jack was so nice. To cook breakfast."

"He's a good one." Dolly stood up and ran her hands through coats and sweatshirts hanging by the door, apparently looking for something of her own among them.

"You're lucky! I can't remember the last time a man cooked breakfast for me." Lydia rose also.

"I am lucky," Dolly said, pulling an orange sweatshirt over her head, then tossing her hair free of the hood. "Most employers don't keep a spare room for you and make meals for you when you're a wreck. But he knows I don't cook worth a damn and probably wouldn't eat if I stayed home every night. My husband did all that. The household stuff. Craig. He was another good one."

Dolly moved to the kitchen counter and refilled her coffee mug. "More?" She held the hot carafe up toward Lydia, whose eyes grew teary. She shook her head lightly, and Dolly set the pot back, then put her hands on her hips.

"You're sad for *me* now? Hey, he's been gone a while, my husband. Two years and four months. Colon cancer. I'm finally starting to find some peace."

Lydia turned her gaze toward the small window that faced a patch of lightening grass and fiercely bit the inside of her cheek to keep from crying. This irrepressible, bold thing, love… Considering the fullness of her heart, how could she have woken up this morning to a marriage that love seemed to have no part in?

Dolly put her hands on Lydia's shoulders as Lydia looked down at their feet on the wide pine boards of Jack's kitchen. Dolly's, in blue-and-white-striped canvas tennis shoes, were even smaller than Lydia's.

"Lydia," Dolly said. "I don't know what's in your head, but I do know this. There's only one person you can save in this world...one person you're left with when all is said and done. And there are people who want to make you completely forget that."

"I'm okay," Lydia said with rapid shakes of her head and a small wave of dismissal. She started to glance up but stared instead at what suddenly seemed to be childishly small hands as she opened them, then partly clenched them shut.

"Of course you are. Strong as ever, right? Well, maybe I'm out of line. But the thing that made you rush over here this morning... It gives me a bad feeling. Like you did it because somebody's got a fix on your mind. I've seen that kind of pain before. Grew up around it. Now, my marriage was different. Craig spoiled the hell out of me. But I think I did to him what my father did to my mother—tried to control him. And now look... I'm alone. Maybe I'm even part of the reason he got sick. I'll never know."

Lydia met Dolly's eyes. They were green, and Lydia noticed strength in them that she hadn't before.

"Come on." Dolly opened the door and picked the seat up from the floor. "Marriage is crazy and really shouldn't be discussed before noon. For now, we'll see if we can at least do something about this little problem."

"But..." Lydia began. The words clawed at the walls of her mind: *There's no way out.*

She cleared her throat and heard a strange version of her own voice ask, "Would you ask Jack if I could store a few things here? Just for a little while. I would ask him myself, but I don't want to put him on the spot. He might... Well, my husband... I probably won't actually need to do it—"

"Don't worry. Jack's barn has a huge storage area for special items," Dolly said, gazing at Lydia while her fingers fiddled with the ragged edge of the seat's fabric. "So does his heart, for that matter."

18

A bright spark
where black ashes are;
in the smothering dark
one white star.

~ *Elinor Wylie (1885–1928), "Incantation"*

In the barn, Jack pulled out his list of tasks for the day, but his mind hadn't left the kitchen. So the crazy professor had been tearing furniture apart again. And now Lydia was here before sunrise trying to put things back together? What went on between those two? Angrily, he sharpened a pencil and sat down on a stool to make notes.

Nothing Jack had ever seen in Frank inspired his respect, and he did have respect for other professors, so it wasn't the academia that pissed him off. No, it was the arrogance he'd picked up on immediately and which had been confirmed by the man's refusal a few years before to hear the information that Jack had finally convinced himself he should share. He'd deliberated about it for years, finally choosing to attend one of Frank's readings, where he'd waited around afterward while Frank played up to a covey of college girls for what seemed like hours.

At last, the group dispersed, and Jack was alone with Frank in the room. He'd approached the professor, introduced himself, and gotten straight to the point, but the experience had been humiliating. Jack told Frank his grandfather had known Mary Stone Walker.

"Did he now?" Frank said, gathering his papers.

"Yes," Jack answered. He had expected more initial interest, but maybe the man had heard this sort of thing a lot. "He was fond of her."

"Ah yes, so many were." Frank stood up, and he was a tall man. He'd peered over his glasses at Jack with an attitude Jack could only call condescending. "One of those who claimed to be a lover of hers, perhaps?"

"No. Not at all." Jack recalled that Frank's expression had seemed more tolerant than curious. "He was a fisherman. Happily married, by all accounts."

"Isn't that what men say when they're married? They're all happily married." Frank had chuckled. "Especially when they're talking to their grandsons, I'd imagine."

The comment had angered Jack. It was just the sort of asinine remark he'd expect from someone like Frank Carroll, who spoke about the romantic love of poets as if it were sacred, but couldn't imagine love between a fisherman and his wife. Jack had almost left right then, especially because his grandfather would have predicted just such a sentiment from a professional dreamer. *Keep what you know to yourself*, Jack heard in his head.

But his grandfather was dead, long gone, and so was the woman in question, and Jack had come to the conclusion that he himself, being alive and part of this community, might owe the truth. He mustered up the patience to try once more.

"No, I don't think that was the case, Mr. Carroll."

Frank gave a plastic smile. "I've been investigating Mary Stone Walker's life for years now, Mr. Kenilworth."

"Well, then you may have heard some of this already. My grandfather, Robert Kenilworth, knew Mary Stone Walker as a troubled young woman. He assisted her at a difficult time."

"I see. So that was his tale. I'm sorry, Mr. Kenilworth. I

guess I've just heard too many false claims." Unbelievably to Jack, Frank walked toward the door, essentially dismissing him. *Could this really be the man Lydia Milliken married?* he remembered thinking. *Poor kid.*

"Mr. Carroll, speaking honestly, that's disrespectful." Jack didn't follow Frank, who stood by the door with his hand on the light switch. "I'm a serious man. If you decide you'd like to hear more of what I know, I'd be willing to talk to you. Here's my number."

He handed his business card to Frank and nodded as he passed him to leave the room.

"It probably won't be necessary, Mr. Kenilworth," Frank said to his back. "I've researched her life exhaustively through her own words. There's no mention of your grandfather or any meaningful problem she might have received a stranger's assistance for in any of her writings. And the woman was, as you may have gathered, a prolific journal writer."

Jack considered suggesting that Frank do some interviewing around town, that no investigative reporter would do any less. But instead, Jack walked away, down the hall and out the front door without further words. That was four years ago, and Frank had never contacted him. In his disgust, Jack had worked up a good, solid determination that he would never again attempt to speak about the past as he knew it from his grandfather—those things Robert Kenilworth had seen with his own eyes and felt with his own hands and heart. After all, promises had been made, and in order for Jack to be a proper caretaker of those intimacies, they should not be released to the public.

As fate would have it, however, Jack and Frank were reintroduced a couple of years later by a mutual acquaintance at an Elks fund-raiser. The lummox was more congenial and feigned a jolly uncertainty about whether or not they had met. Since the Elks event was being hosted to raise funds to buy canoes for the city park, Jack had been asked ahead of time to speak briefly about the joy of being on the water, but after leaving half a dozen phone messages at his house that he chose not to answer, the organizers had apparently asked Frank Carroll to speak instead.

He spoke eloquently, of course, integrating a handful of verses by various poets into his text, as was his specialty. The last was a mysterious phrase about the mingling of light and water, by Mary Stone Walker. Stuck in Frank's vicinity again after the speeches were all made and the fried-chicken dinner consumed, Jack could not resist prodding him.

"Don't you wonder about that last day?" Jack asked Frank in a conspiratorial tone.

"Beg your pardon?" Frank asked him, his gaze hardening as he focused on Jack's face.

"Mary Walker. She stood at the edge of that very lake she wrote about—you know, in the verse you read up there—and then she just"—Jack sent his hand out flat into the air—"disappeared. Ended her life as a writer, for all intents and purposes. Right? No more Lake Michigan verses."

Frank looked to the plate he held in his hand and pushed a strawberry and a square of cake around with his forefinger. "I think we may have a difference of opinion on that, Mr. Kenilworth." His eyes were cold when he aimed them at Jack. "I do recall our other meeting now. You wanted to share some information with me. Is that right?"

Jack nodded. "I'd still be willing to talk to you."

"That's kind." Frank placed the berry in his mouth and chewed thoughtfully as he let his eyes rove over the crowd in the Elks' fluorescent-lit meeting hall. "But unless you've found her body, or—it was your grandfather, if I'm not mistaken?— unless he was her doctor and saw her die or something, there isn't anything new to say about her fate." A smile played around Frank's mouth, and then he shrugged. "It's all speculation."

Jack had gazed at the floor, considering the best response to this comment. When he raised his head to reply, Frank had turned his back and moved away to speak with someone else.

Subsequent encounters in public had been comprised of terse acknowledgment and avoidance, but Jack's conscience was clear. He'd made two overtures, direct invitations to speak with the man, and those offers had been rejected. Because Frank Carroll was the individual most passionate about the girl—as far as Jack knew, he was the only scholar still hoping to find documents written after 1939—Jack felt the unspoken could be left that way. Perhaps in time Frank would ask for Jack's thoughts, and if he did, well, Jack could consider it if that happened. Any reasonable person would have let that unsupported theory fade away by now, and Jack assumed all men eventually conceded to reasonableness when enough reality was heaped before them.

But now, in 1999, the fool was still ripping up furniture in his futile—and no doubt expensive—little hobby. Jack was fuming at his worktable when Dolly and Lydia entered the barn.

"I'm going to see what I can do with this," Dolly said to Jack with a significant look as she passed him. Dolly was a good soul who was probably going to try to help Lydia out of this crisis. Fine, but the destructive effects of Frank Carroll's fantasy couldn't be shoved under the rug forever. Jack turned around to look at Lydia and smiled at her.

The poor girl looked like someone had killed Santa Claus. He'd seen that same look on Nicholas's face. They were clearly regular victims of Frank's misguided energies. The son of a bitch didn't deserve either one of them.

"So, Lydia," Jack said impulsively, deciding to attempt to cheer her up in the only way he knew how: through work. "You're curious about boats. Maybe you'd like to see one of my works in progress."

"Why, sure." She nodded.

"Right this way."

The construction room, which was how he referred to the

portion of the barn full of sawhorses, uncut lumber, tools, and working plans, had grown full over the last fifteen years as his reputation had become secured.

"Now this," Jack described as they approached a nearly completed kayak, "is eighteen feet of light, sturdy mahogany that will give a hell of a ride."

He pulled two sheets of sandpaper from a nearby shelf and offered one to Lydia. "Why don't you help me out for a few minutes? You'll get an idea of what the wood feels like. At this stage, you have to get every imperfection out, or it will be magnified by the varnish."

"How do I do it without screwing up your boat?"

"You just...do it." Jack smiled and started sanding. "Work with me on this side, and just do what I do for a few minutes."

After a minute or two, Lydia seemed to be genuinely concentrating on the sanding. Sawdust misted the barn with a pungent scent that was the only thing Jack liked about sanding. The work grew tedious quickly, and even a kayak grew enormous if he didn't focus on each inch without thought to the whole.

They worked silently for fifteen or twenty minutes, then Lydia stood up and said, "Boy, it's harder than it looks."

Jack smiled. "Unfortunately, it's also more important than it looks. People get their boats new, and let me tell you, they notice things like scratches, even when they have no idea if the thing will keep them safe in the water. Then when they're out in the water, they forget all about the surface and knock into every damn thing."

"That must be sort of sad for you."

"No, not at all. That's the life of boats." He kept sanding. "It's the same with people, isn't it? They come out all new, and you're examining every detail. By the time they're eighteen, you just hope they survive."

Lydia laughed.

Jack set down his sandpaper and turned to flip on the radio.

"You've got yourself a new dining room set, I gather?" he said, immediately regretting the words.

Lydia frowned but kept sanding. "It's a boondoggle, if you want to know the truth. I feel bad that I said it's an investment. It's just another fucking mess."

Jack started to laugh but took one look at her face and stepped back to gaze at the area she was sanding instead.

"My husband was searching through the seats for hidden documents, and…well, the whole set looks like that seat."

"I see." Jack decided to feign ignorance. "Hidden documents. An academic quest?"

"That's certainly what he would say."

"Not what you would say?" It wasn't like him to quiz someone like this, and he caught himself. "None of my business. I apologize."

"Doesn't everyone know about Frank's endless treasure hunt?" Lydia's tone was bitter.

Jack felt her looking at him, so he met her gaze and shrugged. "I guess. I mean, I don't know much, just that he's a very determined scholar who believes in…" But words failed him.

"Believes in…?" Lydia watched him, and he shrugged again.

"Well, to be honest, I don't know. You tell me."

"He would say he is trying to right a wrong. To elevate Mary Stone Walker's place in history from that of a semi-memorable regional female poet to one of the great, immortal American poets. By finding more of her work and getting it out there for people to read. But it isn't just that; his own ego is tangled up in it. He's gambled many years of his life's work on her literary value and the prospect of increasing it. So I guess that's how he keeps believing. He just…has to."

Jack smiled at her candor, and Lydia went on.

"He expects to find significant literature that he is theorizing she wrote while hiding somewhere for years, work of higher quality than anything she ever published. But do you think that's possible at this point? Quite a few pieces were found decades ago, but it's been so long now."

Jack had not expected to be questioned in return, and he wasn't about to be so open in a discussion of someone else's spouse. "You mean, would I keep trying to do something that had never panned out?" She gave a sort of nod, and he said, "Maybe."

"But it isn't just that it hasn't panned out. From the start, it was a long shot requiring a great deal of luck. I was once a huge fan of the idea myself, and plenty of other people have been, too, but Frank has based his whole career on it." She gave a shake of her head and clammed up then, as if maybe she was afraid of betraying her husband.

"What would he do if he weren't doing that?"

Lydia's gazed wandered. "That's almost impossible for me to imagine. He has literally been on this quest for as long as we've been married, sadly enough."

"Why is that sad? It could have worked out. Maybe it will yet."

"I don't think I've said this out loud, but...I'm pretty sure he loves his idea of Mary Stone Walker more than he loves anything in his actual life. Including Nicholas. And me."

"Now *that* is sad. If it's true, it's not just sad. It's a crime."

Lydia's mouth turned down in a small, shaky frown. He was doing a marvelous job of distracting her and lightening her heart, he observed. Apparently, that was not what he'd wanted from this encounter.

"Well, you might be able to guess what my prescription is for anyone who wants to brighten up their life."

"A boat."

"You *are* as smart as I remember! And I have the perfect one for you. A Swedish folkboat I've been given because she's so far gone someone's going to have to put hundreds of hours into her repair before she's seaworthy."

"Hmm...sounds like an adventure for sure. But look who you're talking to, Jack."

"I am looking. Anyone's life can be improved by a boat, and anyone can not only learn to sail, paddle, and navigate, but also learn to do the repairs."

"You really think so?"

Jack thought he saw interest in her face.

"I do. Furthermore, I would help you every step of the way." He paused, picturing it. "The trickiest part might be learning to *want it* in the first place."

Lydia's gaze shot to Jack's, and for a moment their eyes locked. He lifted one shoulder in a shrug, looked back at the boat's hull, and told himself to cut the talk and stop imagining that she could be part of his life. The fact was that while a boat might or might not change the life of a beautiful writer, there was no doubt whatsoever that a beautiful writer could change the life of a boatman.

19

I have wandered over the fruitful earth,
But I never came here before.
Oh, lift me over the threshold, and let me in at the door!
~ Mary Elizabeth Coleridge (1861–1907), "The Witch"

Light snow began to fall in the dunes when Mary was halfway to the fisherman's land. Against her chest, she braced the jar of maple syrup for him in her damaged left hand, while her right hand held the flashlight. The sweet-smelling pines were dense and the path narrow, but she had visited him three times before, so she was sure now of the way. All that mattered was that she get there. She would feel peaceful then. He would speak of the lake, whitefish and sturgeon, the lingering winter ice, and he would listen to whatever she wanted to say of simple things. He would look at her with that amused, gentle focus and laugh. Robert always laughed as if he understood the mercurial nature of life, and every tragic or absurd thing that he heard only confirmed it.

She couldn't analyze what she felt for him—it was unlike any other sentiment she had ever experienced. The first moment she saw him still lived in her heart as a turning point. Standing in the cemetery for the funeral of young Hattie Barber a couple of years before, she had suddenly spotted a handsome man across the grave. He was several years older than she was, someone she had never seen before, and he was looking directly at her. Their eyes met, and warmth shot through her entire body. But it didn't feel like sexual desire or the sort of common thrill she got when she knew she was stirring a man's interest. No, it was strange; it felt more like…recognition.

She tried several times to catch his eye again, but he was focused on the prayer book, the hymnal, the older woman on one side of him who was perhaps his mother, or the pregnant woman on the other side who was clearly his wife. Yearning lit in Mary's heart and stayed there. He seemed as dignified and intelligent as Bernard was reckless and rude. "To have someone like that," she had murmured out loud under her breath. *To have someone like that.* It was a wish, a prayer, and it became something that never completely left her mind. Her life would be safer if she had someone like that. To have someone like that in her life would mean this world, and even her marriage, would feel less bleak.

The day after the funeral she had visited the herbalist, Ethel Van Zant, specifically to ask if she had seen the pregnant woman with the blue cape at the funeral, and did she know who she was? Ethel had looked at her in that way she had that made Mary feel understood beyond her words and accepted nevertheless.

"Yes," she'd said, settling into her rocking chair to watch Mary's face. "That's Robert Kenilworth's wife. He's a fisherman. Good man."

Mary had nodded, asking nothing more, and Ethel had chuckled. "Don't you want to know her name? The *woman* you asked about?"

Mary had given her a half smile, slowly closed her eyes, and said nothing.

No, she didn't want to know the name of the woman. She didn't know what she wanted. But Robert Kenilworth had something to do with it.

Now as she approached the top of the hill, Mary could see

light from Robert's lantern falling from the fishing shanty into the gray afternoon woods. Snowflakes drifted like tiny moths through the lantern's glow at the window. She saw his hands at work on a net, and she was suddenly embarrassed to be interrupting him again with another trivial gift. Uncertain, she stood outside the shanty waiting for her courage to return, but he must have sensed her presence or heard her steps, because he stopped what he was doing, looked up, and then opened the door.

"Mary Walker," he said, gazing at her, and he said no more.

Hand gripping the door, he waited, not inviting her in, but not stepping out into the cold spring air. Mary saw a woodstove burning inside and longed to be part of the warmth of his space, but his stillness froze her thoughts, and she stared at him, mouth open to speak but speechless. He looked to the jar in her hands. She held it toward him.

"For you. Hello, Robert."

"For me?" He stepped forward, removing the jar from her hands carefully, as if to avoid touching her. His expression was studious. "I can't imagine why I deserve another gift from your kitchen."

Her face reddened, and she could not lift her eyes from the jar.

"But, ah… This is maple syrup, isn't it?" he said kindly.

"Yes," she replied. "I tapped three trees this year. I just…" Her eyes sought his and found them resting on her without judgment. "I just wanted you to have some. I imagined you enjoying it."

Again there was silence, and as Mary allowed herself to return Robert's gaze, she realized that it was ridiculous to try to pretend this was an ordinary, neighborly gesture. What she had vaguely considered might be inappropriate behavior was, in fact, just that. And Robert Kenilworth was not only completely aware of that but unwilling to pretend not to be.

"Mr. Kenilworth, I know that it seems odd. Well, that it *is* odd. For me to visit you alone. Again." The only reason Mary could think to offer was the truth, but to be so honest was risky. "I'm sorry for any discomfort I'm causing you."

Although it was April, the ground was cold enough that snowflakes didn't melt, and they began to collect around the soles of her boots where her gaze was fixed. She knew she should not stay; he had almost said as much. She heard a shuffle, then the thump of the jar being set down on a table in the shanty, and she raised her eyes. The fisherman stooped in front of the woodstove to add another log to the fire. Then he walked back to the threshold and leaned against the doorframe.

"Mrs. Evans."

"My name is Walker. Not Evans."

"Miss Walker."

"Yes."

"First of all…I think it would be simpler"—he paused, appearing to assess something he saw in her—"if you call me Robert. And I call you Mary."

She smiled and felt her muscles begin to relax. "I agree, yes."

"I must tell you that my wife, Elizabeth, and I have enjoyed your gifts very much. But I think you should explain why you are bringing them to me."

She turned her face toward the icy lake and after several seconds of silence felt a shiver begin at her core.

"Forgive me," Robert said. "It was rude of me not to suggest you come inside where it's warmer. Please come in, Mary. Just for a few minutes."

She hesitated but, with a flash of resolution, stood where she was and looked straight into his eyes.

"I am bringing you gifts, Robert, because…" Her heart pounded so heavily it felt it would interrupt her speech. "I am bringing you gifts because there are…things that make me feel lost. In my own life. To be frank, I believe that you have a character that opposes those things. I have found it to be unwise to act on inclinations born of fear, but this is just the opposite. You make me feel a kind of hope, so I have sought a reason…to be around you. To be welcomed by you. Just…that."

Robert Kenilworth's eyes widened slightly. "I see. Just that."

He gave a small laugh and walked to the stove, using a stick to push around several palm-sized stones that lay on top of it. "Please…come in for a moment. You have a cold walk back, I think. Please don't start it off with a chill."

"No. Thank you." She eyed the gold flames with longing. "I have interrupted you longer than I intended to. I hope you will enjoy the maple syrup."

"Mary." Robert absentmindedly brushed splinters of wood and threads of netting from his denim pants. "I think you shouldn't bring gifts like this anymore. I think…this is wonderful"—he gestured toward the syrup—"but more than enough."

"I understand." She took a step backward, tightening her scarf.

"Please…wait."

She wanted to disappear.

"You have a serious injury there." He nodded toward her hand. "And a long walk from your home to this place. Wouldn't it be more appropriate for you to bring something easier to carry?"

She looked up.

"You've told me you are a poet."

"I am."

"It seems to me a poem weighs almost nothing."

They looked steadily into each other's eyes for several seconds, constructing an agreement that neither one of them consciously understood.

"You could even read a gift like that to me while I work on these." He nudged a fishing net with his foot.

"Yes, I could do that," she said quietly, joy flickering in her heart. "Thank you."

Robert picked up a rag, wrapped it around one of the hot

stones from the stovetop, and crossed the rough shanty floor-boards to Mary.

"Where's your pocket?" he asked in a low voice that she could feel in her spine, and when she pulled the black wool coat pocket up to his hand, he bent near her and dropped the stone in. One side of his mouth lifted in a smile. "Safe passage, Mary Walker. Hurry home."

20

White Hill, Michigan—April 1999

The anguish of the world is on my tongue.
My bowl is filled to the brim with it; there is more than I can eat.
Happy are the toothless old and toothless young,
That cannot rend this meat.

~ Edna St. Vincent Millay (1892–1950), "The Anguish"

As she left Jack's workshop, Lydia's mind clung to imaginings of an escape on Lake Michigan in a sailboat, and she felt a swell of wistfulness followed by guilt. Her life was a good life that she had built over many years. It just needed some adjustments—and the courage to enact them.

It wasn't yet noon when she rolled up the driveway, where there were no signs that Frank was up. His truck was parked as it had been, the barn door was open as she'd left it, and she didn't see any lights on in the house. She got out of the Jeep and headed into the dark barn to gather the torn seats into a pile. As she searched around for them, she wondered what Dolly would charge her. If she could fix them at all, the work was likely to be extensive and tedious.

Lydia tried not to let her eyes rest too long on the pieces of wood from the furniture, tried not to determine just now if they were un-repairable. She could do that later tonight. She had just spotted another seat leaning against the new armoire when she felt the air in the barn change. She saw the sunlight dimmed by his body before she heard Frank speak.

"What are you doing?" His voice was flat.

Lydia whipped around to see him silhouetted in the doorway, his arms crossed.

"You lied to me, Frank," she said, matching his emotionless tone.

"You aren't someone I can be honest with anymore, Lydia."

"Oh. Oh, I see." She emitted a hard laugh. "By what code of behavior would it be okay for *anyone* to spend half of their family's savings on a dining room set so they could tear it apart looking for scraps of paper?"

"It's obvious we don't share the same values anymore," he said heavily.

"You've got that right, Frank. Marriage and common decency require that such choices are discussed beforehand."

She turned back to the furniture, heart pounding, and picked up the seat, willing herself to be calm. Holding it in her hands, she walked toward him, intending to pass to her Jeep. He blocked the opening and didn't move.

"Excuse me," she said.

"What are you doing?" he asked, and when she stood without speaking, he said, "I asked a simple question, Lydia. *What* are you doing?"

"What do you think I'm doing, Frank? I'm taking these seats to be repaired. Let me by."

Still he remained where he was, so she forced herself to look into his face. It was not angry, as she'd expected, but held an expression of poisonous, patronizing amusement.

"Oh, I see," he said, nodding, smiling. "You're doing the right thing. Getting everything back to normal. Nobody around to interfere with the task. You *thought*."

His words so closely echoed her actual thoughts that she searched his eyes for a shard of genuine understanding.

"We can't leave things like this." She waved her free hand back toward the dining set parts behind her.

"No, I guess *we* can't," he said. "*We* have an investment to take care of, don't we? Can't sell it back to the old biddy like this."

"Right," Lydia said. The caustic note in his voice and the loose attempt to mimic her attitude were the same tactics he had used in countless such exchanges of the past, and they rattled her as they always did. Just like that. "Well, Frank, are you going to tell me you don't agree? That you have some better plan?"

"You know...I don't recall that you were really part of this project, Lydia," he said, reaching down to take the seat from her, but she held on tightly. "You going to wrestle me for it?"

"Frank." Lydia stepped back from him, holding the seat with both hands. "This has gone far enough. You lied, you spent half of our savings, then you tore up the furniture. You don't see what's wrong in all of that?" She stared at him. "It's *insane.*"

"I don't know, Lydia. You're leaving out so many of the facts." Frank's voice was light and chiding as he pasted contrived concern on his face and shook his head. "Where should I begin to discuss all you've violated...in just this one morning?" He followed this with a loud exhale of disappointed astonishment and the slap of his left hand to the door's frame.

His face appeared hideous to Lydia in that moment, not the face of the man she knew in real life, but a mask molded by a long, artificial drama. She gave a brief laugh of horror.

"Do you seriously believe that this was a rational thing to do? Buying this on a whim and tearing it all up like this? Look at it, Frank!"

"I looked at it all night, my dear. I'm through looking at it. Let's look at you for a minute. You're half-crazed with your money lust."

"*I'm* half-crazed? *Money lust?* If I look half-crazed, it's because I don't know what to think anymore: about you, about our marriage, about our lives."

Feeling as if the ground were shifting, Lydia fleetingly wished she could grab Frank for stability, and that his intelligence would force him to admit to the obvious. But staring at his body set to block her from leaving the barn, she knew without a doubt that such support from him was not an option anymore. Maybe it never had been.

"I stayed up all night trying to find what I believed, for good reason, I would find," Frank said in a measured tone, his hands linked before him as if he were lecturing a class. "Once again, I was endeavoring to uncover a document that would change our lives. And here you are, the morning after, running around like a scavenger, snatching, peering, picking"—his features contorted in disgust as he hunched forward, matching his words with rapacious gestures—"trying to put together pieces you can sell. Did you even give me enough respect to ask about the search before you proceeded here? Of course you didn't."

"Should I? Look at the rest of this shit just sitting around abandoned while you slept off your hangover."

"Then I woke up," he went on, ignoring her, "to a phone call from Cal Stringman at the college. He was wondering why I wasn't there this morning and didn't call. 'Not acceptable, Frank,' he said."

Lydia's stomach clenched. After calling the college that morning and getting the administration answering machine, she'd completely forgotten to call again. Frank's head tilted to the side, his gaze directed at the ceiling, as if he were remembering. He removed his glasses to wipe the lenses.

"I told him that you called, but he said no. No one had called."

"I tried—"

"And now here you are, the person who said she would call to protect my reputation—"

"Oh, do you really think a call would manage that at this point?"

"—fishing around in this most important work of mine without knowing a goddamn thing about it. So I want to know,

Lydia Milliken…" He paused, put on his glasses, and took a few steps toward her. "What else are you doing to my life? Huh? Where are you taking these seats? Are you telling everyone in town that you have to clean up after your crazy old man? Are you fucking around with our money now, too, trying to make sure you can enforce spending rules? Huh? What else is going on behind my back?"

His voice was harsh and edging out of control. He jabbed several fingers against Lydia's breastbone so hard she was thrust back half a foot. She scrambled sideways, and he continued to step toward her.

"Nothing is going on!" Her voice rose with alarm. "Nothing except my efforts to try to recoup some of the funds you threw away. Can't you see that I am trying to make things right? Pick up after your destruction? You ought to be grateful." Her heart beat so hard she could feel it in her throat.

"So tell me just what you've been doing this morning in your determination to *make things right*. Where were you off to with the chair seats, for instance?"

"I was taking them to an upholsterer," she cried. "What do you think? What the hell else could I do?"

"What else?" He laughed, then quickly scowled. "You could leave me and everything in my private life alone!" He bit his lower lip and nodded. "That is an excellent plan, and right this minute would be an excellent time to start."

"*Your life*. What about Nicholas? Me?" she asked, anger rising. "You think this is just your life you're affecting? Does it help you to pretend we don't matter? Do you erase us from your thoughts because you can't handle the mess you've made"—she slid to a chair frame and kicked it—"of your life"—she kicked it again—"and all this garbage?"

She swung around, breathing hard, to find him smirking at her.

"Go ahead, Lydia, Throw your little temper tantrum. Always

got you what you wanted with Daddy, didn't it? And next come the tears."

"*Who are you?*" she screamed at his face, tears pressing out.

"Who am I? Oh! How thoughtful of you to ask. I'm the man you married because we both believed in something. We believed in the transcendence of art, its power—not, as you have apparently interpreted it, as a source of tainted income. I don't know what you believe in anymore. But I don't tell foolish lies for cash. No, I have continued along the path we chose in the beginning."

"I see, I see. Your pursuits aren't a lie, huh? This elaborate daydream you tell yourself about a dead woman, a minor poet you want to save from obscurity so you can be the hero. Can't do anything original, nothing on your own, can't even support yourself, much less a family, so you feed off this dream that Mary Stone Walker was the saint of poetry and womanhood. She's the unacknowledged goddess of the written word, and you're going to raise her from the dead. Do you even realize that's what's going on? You're sacrificing real life for *a daydream*, Frank. I would not have imagined you had that in you, and I certainly never signed on for it."

Frank raised his hands as if to crush her, then froze. They glared at each other.

"So. That's how you feel about it all," Frank said with venomous control, eyes glittering with fury.

"No, that's not how I feel about *it all*. It's how I feel about *your choice* to allow this search you've been on for almost twenty years to interfere with every other aspect of your life. A search funded almost entirely by my 'foolish lies,' as you describe my career." Lydia's tears were gone, and she stared into his face with the closest feeling to hatred that she'd ever felt for anyone. "Do you know how your son watches you, watches us, and suffers?"

"That's right, play the Nicholas card."

"It's not a fucking card, Frank, and he's not just a prop on your stage. He's a real, live boy. Part of *a living reality* far bigger than you are. Wake up."

The hardness in Frank's face fractured momentarily. He took a few steps away from her, deeper into the barn, shoved his hands into the pockets of his pants, his head bent toward the floor.

"But we are not powerless," Lydia said passionately, hoping to reach him through what she perceived to be a crack in his rage. "We can *choose* to build our lives back. It's gotten crazy, but it doesn't have to stay that way."

He stood motionless, and in the silence and stillness that went on for minutes, Lydia believed that Frank was considering what she'd said.

"I'll help you with this. I will." She walked toward him, her hands extended. "We can move on, get back to the way things once were…if we try."

She was about to touch his arms when he leaned down, picked up a chair, and turned his face toward her.

"Do you think so?" he said quietly.

"Yes."

Frank gave her a smile that made her lower her hands in fear.

"And you're in charge," he said. "You know how to fix everything."

"No. But I know… I think I know where to begin."

"Well, how…" He hurled the chair ferociously against the fallen table, and two of its legs shattered off. "How do we fix that?" He took long steps to another chair, jerked it up as if it were made of balsa wood, and hurled it the same way. It hit and shattered with explosive finality. "And that?"

"*Frank.*" She rushed to him, grabbed his arms, and tried to get him to look at her. "Stop! You're making everything worse!"

He threw her off and pushed her in the direction of the door. "Get out!" he cried, stepping around broken chair parts toward his old armchair. "Get out, I'm warning you, Lydia!" He pressed his face into his hands.

Lydia gripped his shirtsleeve. "Listen to me."

He knocked her hand away.

"My God, what has happened to you?" she cried.

He tilted his face down toward hers. "You don't get it, do you, Lydia? Don't get it at all."

She took a few steps away from him, shaking.

"I'm alone," he said, shaking his head as his eyes roved the barn. "I am alone in all I care about. You can't even see it." He laughed softly, disbelievingly. "Even as I try to hold on to your better self for your own sake. I'm alone in my beliefs." He sat in his chair, removed his glasses, and pinched the bridge of his nose with his fingers. "Maybe you'll come to see your mistakes, maybe you won't. My dream is not a dream… It's a reality not yet uncovered. You just gave up on such things, Lydia. You gave up on the elusive. *Genuine* romance. Poetic thought. Fine art."

He nodded, eyes roving blankly toward her. It felt to her at that moment as if she could have been anyone to him. "I can't give up, though. And you… Well, you'll learn in time. Or not."

"What nerve you have—"

"Go, Lydia. Don't try to respond. Get out of here. Your childish words, the sight of you… They bring me nothing but disgust. You sicken me." He lowered his forehead onto the heel of one hand as if his head hurt and, with the other hand, waved her away. "Go."

Too furious to speak, Lydia stalked off, picking up two more seats on her way out of the barn. She hurled them into the back of the Jeep with the others, locked the doors, and went in the house, where she paced in the kitchen, slamming the counter with her fist and kicking the floorboard. She ran the water, filled a plastic cup, and bit the rim as she tried to swallow. Water ran around the edges and down her chin. Frank did not emerge from the barn.

If sitting in there with the debris around him did not eventually awaken some of the same horror she had had at the sight of it all, then there was nothing she could do. There was no way to resolve anything between them. Not yet…not in the state they were both in.

But it came to her that this was not merely another argument, not just a horrible fight. No. Something fundamental had slipped. Frank was sick. He was mentally ill. Fear shot through Lydia's body.

Okay. She paced. *Okay, get a grip*. She pulled out a cookbook and flipped to a familiar bread recipe. She had to do something simple that was good. She had to keep things normal somehow. Nicholas would be home before long. Yeast. Molasses. Corn meal. Flour. She slammed them all onto the counter and pulled out her measuring spoons and cups. Impatiently, with trembling hands, she ripped open the yeast packages and measured warm water. It would smell good in here. It would smell healthy and happy in the kitchen when Nicholas entered.

After sprinkling the yeast on the warm water to let it begin growing, Lydia went to the closet and pulled out a paper grocery bag, placing one after another of her most essential cooking tools into it. Then another bag—she flapped it open and wrapped several coffee mugs and plates in newspaper pages, filling it. She took the two bags to the back of her Jeep and came back for a pot, a frying pan, and a hot plate from twenty years before when she had sometimes lived in places without an adequate kitchen. She would take these things to Jack's and store them in case she and Nicholas had to flee soon to a hotel. The part of her that was an animal, that had instincts, knew the danger and moved without consideration of her emotions. She would pack more essentials tomorrow, just in case.

In case what? In case she had to rent an apartment or a house for a while. *That is unthinkable*, a voice in her said as the animal part tossed the things into the Jeep and closed the door. With a glance at the barn, she simply locked the Jeep and returned to the kitchen, composing a mental list of what she would pack next.

Then Lydia mixed the bread ingredients and kneaded them. Frank stayed in the barn. Her hands worked automatically, her mind circling precautionary measures that she should take. Nicholas would be home in a few hours. Perhaps she could keep thoughts of the ravaged furniture out of her mind, and Frank would calm down long enough for them to get through this night. She put the dough in the oven to rise. Perhaps they would eat this bread together this evening, the three of them, and by morning be able to speak like reasonable people. It was not that much to ask, she thought with a deliberateness that felt something like prayer. It could happen.

21

Do you ask for a scroll,
parchment, oracle, prophecy, precedent;
do you ask for tablets marked with thought
or words cut deep on the marble surface,
do you seek measured utterance or the mystic trance?

~ H. D. (1886–1961), "Demeter"

When Nicholas arrived home, he found his mother cooking. She turned and gave a cheerful hello.

"What are you making?" he asked, throwing his backpack into the corner.

"Beef stew. And there's bread dough rising in the oven. Weren't you going to Jack's today?"

"Oh. Yeah. I was on my way there and remembered that it's tomorrow I'm supposed to go," he answered, watching her. "Kind of wasted my time."

"Have much homework?"

"Some. Where's Dad?"

"In the barn."

"What's he doing?"

"I have no idea." She didn't meet his eyes. "He's been out there for quite a while."

Nicholas felt a flurry of worry. "Did he find anything in the furniture?"

"I believe he did not." She opened the oven, leaned down, and took out the two loaves of puffy, uncooked dough and set them on the counter.

"Yum. You haven't made bread in a while."

"Seems like a good day for a hearty meal."

"Think I'll say hi to Dad."

"He might not be very friendly. He's feeling…disappointed."

"So what's new," Nicholas murmured as he left the house. He trotted across the grass to the barn and peered in at the door. "Dad?"

There was no answer. "Dad?" he said again, stepping inside. He heard a shuffling from the back of the barn. "You here, Dad?"

"What is it, Nicholas?" Frank's voice was gravelly.

"What are you doing?" Nicholas's eyes adjusted to the darkness, and he saw his father sitting on a folding chair among his antiques.

"What do you need?"

Nicholas didn't notice the scattering of broken furniture parts until he tried to walk closer to his father. When he realized that something had been more or less attacked, he froze. What had happened? There was no way he was going to ask.

"I wanted to tell you… Um… Brad Kramer called. He left a message yesterday saying he's got some books he wants you to price. Two boxes."

"Okay, Nick. I'll take care of it."

"Are you going to, you know, go look through them?"

"I'll get to it. I have a lot on my mind today."

"But he sounded kind of urgent. Said they looked pretty good and he needed your advice as soon as possible."

"Okay. I said I'll take care of it. Don't worry about Kramer. He's full of himself."

"I thought you liked him."

"I like him fine. I have other priorities."

Nicholas noticed that his father had a pad of paper and a pen in his hands, and his curiosity increased. What was going on?

"What are you doing?" he asked again.

"I'm cataloging everything I have here. All the antiques." After a moment, when Nicholas still stood waiting, Frank looked up at him. "You want to help?"

"Sure." It was the last thing Nicholas wanted to do but pretty obviously the only choice.

"Okay. Come on back here."

Nicholas picked a path through the old shapes, some of them familiar, many too dusty or ordinary to clearly recall, until he stood next to his father.

"I'll tell you what to write." He handed the paper and pen to Nicholas. "Okay. Silver candelabra. Circa 1930. Two hundred fifty."

"Two hundred fifty what?"

"Dollars. Just write it down."

"Is that what you paid for it?"

"It's what I'm estimating it's worth, Nick. Write down the details I just told you."

"Alright." He continued his father's itemized list of antiques.

"Dressing table. Oak. Circa 1900. Four hundred eighty."

"How do you know the values?" Nicholas asked, writing.

"I get around. Auctions, catalogs. You got it?"

"Yeah."

This process continued for half an hour, slowing down as Frank slid things around to examine them.

"What's this list for?" Nicholas asked, wondering if his father really planned to include every item in the barn, as Nicholas was starting to fear he might.

"Whatever I might need it for," Frank said, then exhaled heavily and sat down on a rocking chair. "I should have done it before. Retrieve some of the funds locked up in these antiques."

"Oh. Well, I do have some homework—"

"Go then. Go on. I'll finish."

"But…maybe you should take a break. Mom said you've been

out here a long time." Nicholas watched his father's weary-looking face stare vacantly, and it unnerved him a little. "Why don't you go to the tavern? Look at the books? I'll go with you if you want."

"I thought you had homework. So you can take time to go look at books, but not to help me out here?" Frank propped his head on one hand and gazed at Nicholas.

"It's just that…I've been thinking maybe I should try to get a job at Jacob's. I thought I'd apply. That is, if you'll be there. You know, to bring it up with Mr. Kramer."

"You don't need me to bring it up with him." Frank eyed him, and Nicholas felt his cheeks begin to flush. "Besides, I thought you had a job. Things not working out with Kayak Jack?" A smirk brought a shade of cheer to Frank's face.

"It isn't that. Summer's coming and…sometimes Jack has work, sometimes he doesn't."

Frank said nothing for a moment or two. "Okay. Yeah, okay. I could use a drink. Go tell your mother where you're going. And get my keys."

Nicholas ran to the house.

"We're going to Jacob's Tavern, Mom!" Nicholas called out when he didn't find her in the kitchen. "Mom!" She answered from upstairs somewhere. "Dad and I are going to Jacob's!"

He heard rapid steps on the stairs, then Lydia appeared in the downstairs hallway. "Why?" she asked.

"Brad Kramer got some books in, and Dad promised him he'd take a look at them."

She looked skeptical. "Okay. Be back for dinner, though. Please."

"Sure thing!" Nicholas ran back to the truck where Frank was brushing dirt and dust off his clothes. They opened the creaky doors and climbed in.

When they reached the bookshop and tavern room, Brad himself was removing liquor bottles from the shelf behind the bar and replacing them with new ones. He turned around.

"Hey, old man, what can I get you?" he asked Frank.

"Ah…" Frank began. "It's been a long day. What the hell, I'll have a double scotch on the rocks."

"You want something, kid?"

"A Coke," Nicholas said. "On the rocks."

The two men chuckled.

"I hear you got some books in," Frank said a few minutes later, taking a sip of his drink. Already he seemed younger and happier than he had been in the barn.

"Yeah, I set them out there for you." Brad pointed across the room with the sink's spray nozzle. "No rush, though. Drink your scotch."

"But it's urgent, you said?" Frank asked.

Nicholas stared into his Coke, calves tightening around the barstool.

"As always," Brad laughed.

Brad's ruddy, watchful face was always friendly when he talked to Nicholas's dad, and he laughed a lot at Frank's candid, often cynical remarks about people in town and at the college. They also shared similar tastes in wine, beer, and scotch, a subject that generated an unbelievable amount of conversation, in Nicholas's opinion. He looked at the clock as he swung off his barstool to meander toward the shelves full of books. Half an hour had passed already.

"Nick!" Frank said over his shoulder after a few more minutes. "Didn't you want to talk to Brad? The man's gotta leave here soon."

Nicholas walked heavily back to the bar.

"Yeah, I was wondering what jobs you might need people for this summer." He scratched his head self-consciously, avoiding Brad's eyes.

Brad's gaze flicked back and forth between Nicholas and Frank. "Truth is, while I do get lots of tourists in the summer, I also have students who are out of school lined up for those jobs. September comes, more work hours usually open up."

Frank cleared his throat. "I'll have a stout, Brad." Frank gave a rueful expression. "It seems that for Nicholas here... Well, the boatbuilder's job isn't panning out quite like he'd hoped."

Brad nodded as he slid a glass of black beer toward Frank's hands. "Could be we'll be shorthanded at some point. Tell you what, buddy... Come see me on your own sometime after school gets out in June. Toward dinnertime I'm usually here. There might be a position open. You never know, and we can talk about how things work here. Okay?"

Nicholas nodded, smiled, and let his eyes rove toward the boxes of books while Brad was still watching his face. As if, in fact, Nicholas's expression reminded him, Brad wiped his hands and told Frank again to take his time with the books.

"Let's see what you've got," Frank said, slowly rising to walk to the couch near the boxes.

He sat down and set his beer on the coffee table, then leaned back, and his thoughts seemed to float off to some distant point. Nicholas rapped his fingers on his knees, but his father stared at nothing, oblivious.

In his mind, Nicholas counted the drinks his father had consumed. Two double scotches and this beer. Thinking of past experiences with him, Nicholas calculated that he should still be able to concentrate. In fact, if only he'd get captivated by the books before he had any more drinks, his dad might become really lively. Nicholas had seen it happen plenty of times.

"We better get going on these boxes, Dad."

His father shifted, sipped his beer, and sighed. "You know, Nick, I'm awfully tired. Of everything." He tapped one box with his shoe.

"So, what... You're going to just forget about them? How can you do that?" Nicholas leaned over to pull a book from the box closest to them. "Rudyard Kipling. *Gunga Din and Other Favorite Poems*. Gold-leafed pages. Looks pretty nice."

Frank closed his eyes and leaned his head back against the couch. "What's the copyright date? The most recent one."

"Let's see…1966."

"Worthless."

"How do you know? Your eyes are shut."

Frank opened his eyes, sat up, and pulled the volume from Nicholas's hands, flipping through the pages. "It's okay for Brad, and it might look nice on somebody's bookshelf. But a collector won't want it. Write four dollars inside there. On the very first page. Here." Frank fished around in his shirt pockets until he came up with a stubby pencil.

"So what about this one?" Nicholas pulled a fat book from the box. "Never mind." He thumped James Michener's *Texas* onto the floor. His father owned thousands of books and had assisted in numerous estate appraisals over the years, another subject he loved to go on about, so Nicholas's mind possessed bits of knowledge about what his father did and did not value. He searched the titles.

"I haven't heard of her," Nicholas mused as he pulled up another book.

"Who?"

"Elinor Wylie."

"Really?" Frank's attention increased.

Nicholas handed his father a slim book, and he examined it.

"Hmm. Interesting book collection. Both Michener and Wylie. Still, worthless for any collector. Five dollars."

"You men want dinner?" Brad asked.

"Mom's cooking," Nicholas said softly to his father.

Frank turned toward Brad and said, "No thanks. To tell you the truth, Brad, I just don't have the brain for this tonight. Maybe later in the week?"

"Sure, Frank," Brad said, slipping coasters onto the bar for another couple as they sat down.

"But, Dad—"

"Nick, I'm just damned tired." Frank removed his glasses and rubbed his eyes.

"Maybe we could do this at home," Nicholas suggested.

"That's fine, if you want to take them home," Brad said. "I'll accept your help any way I can get it."

"Good lord, Nicholas, I have papers to grade," Frank growled softly at him. "Okay, you're so keen on this, you can carry it. Just one of them. Come on, let's get out of here. I've got to get to bed before dawn."

"It's just that books always cheer you up, Dad," Nicholas whispered nervously. His father gazed at him for a moment, then patted his back.

Nicholas lifted one box to the coffee table to take home and carried the other one back behind the bar.

"This is *not* getting you out of doing your homework tonight. Come on."

When they reached the house, Frank told Nicholas to put the box in the barn next to his chair.

"But—"

"Just do it, Nick. I don't want your mother thinking I'm spending more of her precious money."

His father went into the house ahead of him. After he'd put the box in the barn, Nicholas wrestled the door shut and went inside to find his mother ladling stew into three bowls. He sat down, and she brought the bread, butter, raspberry preserves, and bowls of stew to the table.

"I thought Dad came inside."

"He did. I heard him go upstairs," Lydia said. "I assume he'll join us in a minute."

They waited a while for Frank to join them at the table, one or the other occasionally saying something trivial that didn't grow into a conversation. When ten minutes had passed and he hadn't shown up, Lydia sliced off a few pieces of bread, handing one to Nicholas and placing one on her own plate. They buttered the warm slices in silence and began to take small bites of their stew.

"How was your outing?" Lydia asked.

"Okay."

"Any interesting books?"

"Not really. But there are a lot left to look through."

"Has Dad cleaned up in the barn?"

"What do you mean?"

"The torn-up furniture. You must have noticed, unless he's already cleaned it up."

Nicholas recalled the pieces he had stepped on and processed for the first time just what they were. "Oh. Yeah. What's all that about?"

"The usual thing; he was looking for poems. I guess he got impatient."

Nicholas almost laughed at the understatement, but looked up to find his mother distressed. She stood and walked to the sink where she rinsed her dish.

"So I guess he didn't clean it up yet," she said over her shoulder.

"No. He was doing something else. With the other stuff." Nicholas's mind groped for words that might cheer or console his mother. He wanted to tell her that things would get better soon. They *had* to get better because it was impossible that they would stay this way. He wanted her to know that she wasn't alone, that she had him, but the words that came to his mind were more like questions than reassurance.

"Well, I'm going to do something else, too," she said, drying off her hands, her voice strident. "I'm going to look harder for the answer to this Mary Stone Walker question in the real world. I'm going to put an end to his searching, his tearing up antiques and throwing away our money. I'll keep talking to people until I find someone who knows something helpful, and I'll track that woman down.

"She was a person with a life and a place in the world and

a body…and her body didn't just evaporate. She went somewhere, she did something, and chances are she died somewhere along the way. If we look for information in other places than inside furniture, maybe we can put an end to this endless quest, this"—she pulled the towel in her hands from both ends—"this madness. Before it ruins our lives completely."

She held her fingers to her brow to cover her eyes, and Nicholas could see her upper body quake slightly. He walked to her quickly and put his arms around her narrow shoulders in a hug.

"Something good will happen, Mom." She felt so small and fragile. His heart turned with sadness. "I promise it will."

Nicholas was old enough to know that promises should not be made only to comfort someone in pain. But he also knew that his mother was losing hope and that he had to try to help her get it back.

22

White Hill, Michigan—August 1937

Strong flux of life,
Like a bitter wine
Out of the bloody stills of the world.

~ Lola Ridge (1873–1941), "The Ghetto"

The creature crawled in through the window. It was the size of her palm, shaped like a star and pulsating like a heart. A long thread unwound from it into the thick night beyond the windowsill, and Mary could make out its glowing trail all the way back into the trees and then across the black lake. She took the sharp point of her fruit knife and hesitantly reached for the thread. It looped around the tip, and she felt her heart speed up with hope. But then the thread sagged and clung with an infant's weakness. Mary's throat tightened with grief.

Before the creature came in the window, she had been writing. The words flowed easily, even though the subject was difficult: the death of her mother in a Detroit hospital. Mary had been only three, but she felt she could almost remember the details since she had begun using the medicine. The doctor said morphine could cause hallucinations, but it seemed to Mary that her visions were real memories unfolding from kernels of buried experiences. They enriched her understanding of her life, and she was grateful.

The star creature throbbed like the chest of a frog as it floated off to hang in the night. And then it seemed to speak. Mary's eyelids felt heavy. She looked down at the page.

Nothing there but yearning, where a mother once
   had gently
held her—hands forever useless now, and cold…

The star spoke. It spoke in a threatening tone, cursing as it bent around the branch of a tree. It growled.

No. Oh no. It was not the star speaking—the sound was from someone on the stairs. It was that intruder again in the hall. Mary took the sheet of paper she'd been writing on and quickly rolled it, then pressed it flat. Her breathing was fast; her heart was afraid. She heard herself whimpering slightly and listened with pity, as if the sound came from someone else. The rolled poem fit into that hole at the window frame. She had used the spot before to hide dangerous poems with dangerous thoughts that she could not recall now. She lifted the curtain, although it tried to pull away from her, and crammed the rolled poem inside the gap between the window's frame and the wall.

The intruder knocked. Then after a few seconds he banged on the door. She didn't answer. The star creature was nowhere to be seen, and Mary felt bereft. She coughed out a sad cry and put her head down on her arms on the desk. The banging continued, louder and more violent, then came the screeching grind of the chair she'd used to bar the door as he shoved through.

"What the hell is going on in here? You're barricading a door against me in my own house? Against your own husband? You're out of your soft little mind!"

The intruder stood at the violated threshold, then charged across the room and shoved her aside to grab at the paper on her desk. She stood up to protect herself from him.

"Just what sort of trash are you writing, anyway?" He flipped the sheets around, saw they were empty, and wadded them up to hurl them to the floor. He grabbed her by the jaw to turn her face toward his, wrenching her neck.

"Stop it!" Her voice was garbled and pinched. His fingers pressed into her cheeks, then the nails dug in.

She began to lose her balance and reached back to the desk, palm landing on the paring knife she'd been using to play with the star. The intruder's expression was contorted with cruelty and disgust until her hand snatched up the knife and sliced his face into tender ridges of skin that moved delicately like a mouth, letting out a long tongue of blood that spread thick and wide. The intruder screamed.

It was confusing how quickly and easily it happened, and before she knew it, the intruder had knocked her down to the ground, his voice wild, his eyes glaring above her. But then, in one shocking instant, he was just Bernard.

Bernard's left cheek was cut in a jagged six-inch diagonal, and he was reaching for the shawl draped on the back of her chair to press against the blood. She screamed, stood up, and backed slowly into a wall, unable to pull her eyes away from her husband's torn face as he drifted toward her, then staggered slightly and sat down in the chair.

"Oh God! Bernard! What happened?" Weeping seized her, and she knelt on the floor, crying as she inched forward with pleading eyes until her head was near his knees. He knocked her away with the back of his hand, but she went toward him again and lay her head on his lap, choking on sobs and clinging to his legs as he tried to kick her off once, twice, three times, until she could feel that the bruises on her thighs would be deep, but still she clung. He let loose a single, strangled cry of pain and hit her back with both fists. She lost her breath.

"*Why*, Mary?"

His voice was so weak that she could barely understand it.

"What secrets are you trying to hide from me?"

Aware that his rage had been defused by pain, Mary released her grip on him and stood up. Her legs and back throbbed from his blows. When she looked down at his face, it was so bloody that she gasped. She stifled a perverse urge to laugh and pulled gently at the shawl he held against it to view the tear.

"I'll get another cloth for you, Bernard," she said quietly. "Don't move."

But downstairs as she soaked a clean strip of cheesecloth with water in the kitchen, she heard his steps on the floorboards above her head and knew that he was coming after her with renewed anger. Dropping the cloth to the floor, she yanked the back door open and ran into the cold night. So hard to move fast enough, to breathe deeply enough. *Oh God. Help me, God.* There was only one place she could go, and she ran for that shed to curl among Robert's fishing nets with the hope that when the fisherman found her there before the sun rose, he might touch her kindly as he had before, because her fear was so enormous she felt it could completely swallow her mind.

23

WHITE HILL, MICHIGAN—APRIL 1999

And she will slip
Down silently and leave our hill alone,
And hide where dark leaves drip…
We caught the sun forever there—the shadows are our own.

~ Elizabeth Bishop (1911–1979), "Imber Nocturnus"

After refusing to disclose further information about Mary Walker or the Evans family, Lincoln Babcock told Lydia on the phone that there were more records on microfiche than there had been when she and Frank were doing research a dozen years before, and he was right. While Lydia had not even been aware that the weekly paper had existed, the *Carson County Gazette* had been in print for eleven years between 1931 and 1942 and was now available on microfiche.

"I remember these names," she murmured as she sat in a tiny back room of the White Hill Library with the microfiche machine, taking notes. "Helen Hall. Josephine Baxter. Ruth Donovan."

In September 1936, someone had written a short announcement about Bernard and Mary's wedding, listing the groomsmen and bridesmaids beneath a photograph of the Evans-Walker wedding party. Lydia peered into the fuzzy photographic images. The overpowering observation was that both Bernard and Mary were strikingly handsome and confident-looking individuals who appeared to be full of joy on their wedding day.

The other articles she found offered limited, familiar information about Mary's era, so she focused on a search through Michigan telephone books for Halls, Baxters, and Donovans, knowing how unlikely it was that she might stumble upon one of the ancient women or a family member. But just as she was about to put the task aside, she found R. E. Donovan-Lee on Eighth Street in Holland, Michigan. That looked promising. Lydia added the name and number to her list, and when she returned home, she dialed it first. An airy, thin female voice answered the phone. Lydia introduced herself as a writer and researcher, and the woman said her full name was Ruth Ellen Donovan-Lee.

"Are you the Ruth Donovan who was a friend of Mary Stone Walker's?"

There was a long pause on the Holland end of the phone line.

"What a strange coincidence that you're asking me that on this particular day," she answered. "I had not thought about Mary Walker for years, but last night she came to me in a dream. Decades ago, I grew weary of thinking about her, always wondering." Lydia heard sounds that might have been sighing or tears. "Goodness...Lydia? This is astonishing. I think you must come visit as soon as you can. We were meant to talk."

Lydia arrived in Holland in time to share a late lunch with Ruth Donovan in her apartment. She was a tall, elegant woman in her eighties whose white hair was pulled back into a bun held fast by a jeweled hairpin. At a round maple table for two, she had set lace place mats, cloth napkins, and a small vase of artificial rosebuds. They shared a chicken casserole as they talked. Ruth's blue eyes were sharp with intelligence and curiosity.

"So..." she said, gazing at Lydia for several seconds as she unfolded her napkin. "What brought you to the study of Mary Walker? We always thought she was a genius, but I have to admit, I never imagined she had created a large enough body of work to be remembered." Her head shook slightly, and she paused often in her speech. "What are you hoping for from me?"

Lydia explained the theories that she and Frank had shared over the years and described the quest for documents hidden in antiques that they believed Mary had owned or had access to. Ruth looked thoughtful, then pursed her lips.

"I saw her do that once, and I wondered what was wrong with her. I saw her tack a poem with dots of sticky pine resin between the lid of a trunk and the lining, you know. I'll never forget it. I have no idea what she thought she was doing, but she was quite startled by my interruption. I remember that look she gave me…fearful, then angry." Ruth gazed out the window. "She was difficult at times. A bit mad, I used to think."

"Do you think she could have made the choice to leave White Hill when she was in a state of…madness, as you say?" Lydia's gaze took in the lines of Ruth Donovan's face and tried to envision what Ruth might have looked like at twenty-five.

"Well, I did wonder about that," Ruth said. She lifted a bite of casserole onto her fork and held it above her plate for a moment as she talked. "Back when I heard that she had disappeared, it did cross my mind. Bernard contacted me, you know, and asked if I knew anything. His desperation was sad…but scary at the same time. They must have had some terrible rows. In her letters, she never said much about their life together. She was one for long walks when she was troubled, though, and she spoke of many walks."

"Was she in love with him in the beginning?" Lydia was enthralled. To be talking to Mary's close friend—able to ask direct questions about the poet who had become almost like myth to Lydia over the course of her life—was not something Lydia had ever thought possible. And Mary would look this way if she were alive. She would be an intelligent, beautiful woman of more than eight decades.

"Oh yes, she was wildly in love. If you can call it that. Powerful attraction. He was so physically handsome and so strong." Ruth clenched her fist and held it up to represent Bernard's persona, and then her smile seemed to focus inward. The memories she sought seemed extremely far away. "But I don't really know how long it lasted. She did write to me at least once about hoping for another sort of life somewhere else. But that longing might have emerged no matter whom she married. She was a restless sort. It was early on, as I recall, that she began to dream of running away from everything she knew in White Hill to become that great poet who had no other concerns but writing."

To hear testimony to Mary's dream of leaving White Hill to build a life of letters somewhere else sent a current of excitement through Lydia's body. What she and Frank had long imagined had been something Mary had actually discussed with her close friend.

"Then it's possible that's just what she did, isn't it?"

"I don't know. There were practical problems I am not sure she would have been able—or even willing—to figure out. She had no money of her own, for instance. She didn't have relatives with any means. I know that I myself was still living on a shoestring, rooming with three other girls in Detroit, until I got married. Conditions were hard back then. And Mary and her father seemed very much alone in the world. He died just a year or two after she married Bernard Evans."

Lydia watched Ruth Donovan's face with the sensation that she could almost see the past scenes playing behind her eyes.

"Poor girl. She had some bad luck. Some sad luck. Mary's gifts—her poetic gifts, I mean, and her beauty—never seemed worth those burdens. And she was strong, but not consistently. Did she make a go of it somewhere else? Well, I suppose she might have. More likely to happen in the company of a man, though, and it's true that she was never without admirers. Bernard knew that, and from the very start, anyone could see how it drove him crazy. My first thought when I heard she'd vanished was that he'd locked her away or killed her himself. Lord have mercy. That family had loads of money. I suppose he could have done whatever he needed to do to pull it off."

Her eyes were lit by this question that she had wondered about for sixty years, the thin fingers of her right hand spread along her jaw.

"Did something change your mind about that?" Lydia asked. It had never made sense to her that Bernard was not considered a more serious suspect.

"Actually, I don't think the man was capable of lying. Everything he thought and felt was obvious all the time." She tilted her head with a little shrug. "A good quality in some ways. Or in some people. In Bernard, it often came off as bullying. He just knew everything because it was all so obvious to him in his black-and-white world. But at any rate, his distress about Mary—his rage that she had run away from him, with or without another man—was brutally sincere. He hid it from no one."

"You say *rage*." Lydia's mind filled with questions. "What about fear or sadness? He never thought she might have drowned? That was the leading theory by the time I heard about her life."

"Well, at first, no one knew what to think. Because just two people had seen her out in the night, and only one had seen a woman actually standing on the pier. The man who saw her could not possibly have been *sure* it was Mary from the distance. So there were all kinds of speculations. My dear, would you like something else to drink? Maybe some tea?"

Two people saw Mary on the pier?

Ruth pushed her chair back and began to stand before Lydia could answer. She walked toward the kitchen, and Lydia followed her.

"We had a tea for Mary," Ruth reminisced as she filled a silver kettle with water and dangled two tea bags into a ceramic teapot. Silently, she turned on the flame and watched the kettle. "Yes, we had an afternoon tea for her before she got married. Goodness, it's strange to think about these things...such old memories that they seem like imaginings. Like children's stories!

Many beautiful, very young girls who brought sweet gifts. Small gifts. I think her favorite was a scarf Helen knit for her."

When steam began to rise from the kettle, Ruth poured water into the teapot and pulled two cups from the cupboard. They carried the tea and cups to the table and sat down.

"Back to that night in White Hill. When Mary was seen on the pier," Lydia said, watching Ruth's face for recognition of the subject. "You said *two* people saw her? I thought there was only one witness."

"There was the man," Ruth said. "That older man with the house on the hill in view of the pier. He saw a woman pass his house, carrying something, he claimed. Then ten minutes later, he saw a figure walking along the pier, and he assumed it was the same person. A day or two later an open, empty suitcase was found rolling around in the water, which made people sure she had been murdered, robbed, and her body disposed of. Bernard said the suitcase wasn't hers, and I hoped he was right."

"I remember reading those details. But I don't recall anything about another witness. Who was it? Do you know?"

Ruth poured tea into their cups.

"I think that man was the only one who would actually testify."

"But who was that other person?" Lydia felt the woman's concentration begin to fade.

"Yes, there was another, but it didn't amount to anything. It was just the talk around town. A fisherman's wife said she saw Mary walking that night. Toward the pier, she said. But then she retracted her statement. She said she just couldn't be sure."

"A fisherman's wife? Do you remember her name?"

"Heavens no. Her name. Hmm." Ruth put her finger to her lips and gazed out the window a long time and then sat up straighter. "Oh, yes. That's why I got this shoe box out." She leaned toward a box on the floor near her chair and opened it, drawing out a stack of old composition books.

"My journals," she said with a smile toward the books. She

looked at the dates on the front covers, found the one she wanted, then leafed through it. "Well, silly fool, all I wrote was 'E. K. said she saw Mary rushing across the sand and toward the pier. A fisherman's wife. But she has retracted her statement because it was "too dark a night to be sure of anything," she said. I ask you, when is the night not dark?'" Ruth lay the book down on the table. "Such an astute character I was, wasn't I? I'm sorry, I don't know her name. I wasn't much of a journalist. But as I recall, she was several years older than me, so she has likely passed away."

Lydia's mind spun quickly and hooked onto a coincidence that seemed impossible. She knew of only one fisherman from that era in White Hill, and his last name began with a *K*—Kenilworth. Was it possible?

"Do you think her last name might have been Kenilworth?" Lydia asked.

"I just can't say. I never knew the woman. And I didn't know any fishermen at all. We just heard stories and names thrown about for a few weeks. Bernard, his family, everyone who had a thought—they were putting their two cents in all over town, and that's what the newspapers printed. Just gossip that didn't lead anywhere. Even a couple of years later when I returned to White Hill for a college event, Bernard's brothers were still making up dramatic explanations, for one thing claiming that Mary had run away to Detroit to be a prostitute. Wicked men! And all the rest of us old college friends with our sorrow. They were too hateful."

"I don't understand why they didn't fear for her life, Ruth. I have never been able to get over that. It seems unnatural." Lydia sipped her tea, a familiar frustration rising. Had no one in White Hill loved Mary Walker?

"It was because of specific Evans family belongings that were missing, I think," Ruth said. "Valuable things like jewelry that had belonged to Bernard's mother. Things that Bernard said proved to him that she planned on making a new life with someone else. Though I never thought of Mary as a thief. She was too impractical!"

Together they laughed.

"But even if there were things missing, she could have been kidnapped, murdered, drowned," Lydia said. "She could have intended to leave but met with some disaster before she could. She never contacted anyone, did she? Ever in all of these decades?"

Again Ruth gazed at her, and Lydia felt a shot of wild hope that the woman was about to reveal the secret that she and Frank had believed in—that Mary had made contact after that October night. Ruth lowered her eyes to her lap.

"I have forgotten many things," she said. "Eighty-six years is... It's such a long time to live. But I will never forget the shock and intoxication I felt one day when a telegram arrived a few months after my friend Mary disappeared. It said simply, 'Spring will swoop in and bathe our hearts in light, dear Ruth! Prepare your best dress, love, and we will go dance in the green.'" She gave a little laugh.

"You see? I still remember those beautiful words. It was something Mary said many times during every one of those long, draining winters that we shared. And we actually did prepare our dresses. Meticulously!" She chuckled brightly and shook her head. "So, as one naturally might, I passionately wanted that telegram to be from her! No one else admitted to sending it! Not until a full year had passed and the Mary we were praying for still had not made her existence known.

"But it was one of us. It was Josephine Baxter. As far as I could tell, she imagined she was keeping Mary alive with that little trick of the telegram, as if pretending could conjure her up. For some reason, the loss, Mary's absence, and the not knowing had troubled Josephine more deeply than anyone else I know. I didn't dare tell her how upsetting her telegram hoax had been for me...how much it hurt my heart, and then when I saw through the trick, how it angered me. Poor Josephine. I think some people are too sensitive for this world, don't you? She didn't live long either."

Lydia believed that most human beings are too sensitive to bear the weight of human existence, and so they build their private shelters of delusions, addictions, and dreams. She watched Ruth Donovan's brow grow troubled and her composed expression shift to confusion that seemed to flow in from the past.

"Oh, it was so awful," she said at last. "So awful. So many times when Mary first disappeared, I saw her dead body floating in the water. In nightmares. In those dreams, it was obvious that she was dead, on the lake right there near the college. Her dress was purple with cold water, her face barely recognizable and bloated. Oh, so awful. I would wake sweating. Weeping.

"But in the dream I had last night, Mary was floating along in the water as if on her way somewhere. So strange! And she was not in White Hill; no, it was someplace else. I could see trade docks and ships." Her hands gestured the imagined shapes, then she directed the question in her eyes toward Lydia. "And this time her eyes were open. In the old dreams, she was clearly deceased, her eyes closed, her limbs lifeless. So maybe this one…maybe you could interpret that as a sign she lived on past her disappearance."

After a few moments, Ruth Donovan gave a long sigh and leaned her fragile body back in her chair. "But I don't believe that's what happened." Her mind seemed perfectly, painfully clear as her eyes gazed out the window into the late-spring afternoon. "I have had a long career as a teacher. I have loved and buried two husbands, raised three children, and watch them bear children. I have traveled to many of the destinations that the very young Mary and I once dreamed about. San Francisco. Paris. The islands. And all that time, all those decades, she *could* have been living, too." Ruth Donovan looked directly into Lydia's eyes, as if this fact were so elusive that they needed to agree on it. Then she shook her head. "It boggles my mind. But you see, I don't think it happened, although I often tried to imagine it. And sometimes pretended it was so. No, I'm afraid she has been gone a long, long time."

Her voice began to shake a little. She sipped her tea, then stared into the cup. After a moment she took a long breath.

"So if you and your husband are trying to keep her poetry and her name alive, that's a nice thing. She would have been glad, that girl I knew sixty years ago. But I don't think there is ever going to be anything more to say. Her life was cut short, and that was a tragic turn. Ours go on. I have had to accept that I will never know what happened to my friend. It is just another shadow in this world, which, while beautiful, has often made me violently sad."

24

It was as though I curved my hand
And dipped sea-water eagerly,
Only to find it lost the blue
Dark splendor of the sea.

~ Sara Teasdale (1884–1933), "The Net"

T his one's not so bad," Dolly said as she and Lydia started examining the chair seats the next afternoon. She lifted another. "This one's cut near the center."

Lydia eyed the torn fabric and padding with continued disbelief.

"Do you really think any of these are salvageable, Dolly?" She stared at the debris into which half of her marital savings, and a good portion of her hope for the future, had vanished. "The woman who wanted to buy this set would be horrified. I'll be lucky if I can sell four of them with the table for a hundred bucks. What a mess."

"Well, maybe we'll have some luck," Dolly said. "Don't give up yet. I'll shoot for Friday and give it my all."

Moments later, Lydia heard Jack and Nicholas enter the main room of the barn, and when she left Dolly's sewing room, she pretended not to notice Nicholas's surprise at the sight of her. She picked up the briefcase she had brought.

"Hey there," she said. "I don't want to interrupt whatever

you guys are doing. But I wonder, Jack, if you might have a few minutes to speak with me?"

"Sure, we can talk in my office."

In the tiny room, he settled into his desk chair and gestured to a folding chair across from it, looking at her with curiosity. "What can I help you with?"

She cleared her throat and lifted the briefcase onto her lap. "I have been thinking about the fact that you tried to speak with Frank about Mary Stone Walker," she began, her hands growing moist on the leather as she directly broached the subject she'd hoped he might bring up on his own. "I know that we need to be gathering information from living people. This is a conviction, for me. I've been trying to persuade Frank to join me in it, but until he does, I am taking it on myself. Not long ago, I drove to Misquers to meet Ethel Van Zant's granddaughter."

"Who is Ethel Van Zant?" Jack asked.

"She lived here in White Hill and worked as an herbalist, almost a doctor to some, it sounds like," Lydia said, opening her briefcase and passing the scrapbook to Jack. "This was hers. Her granddaughter wasn't willing to talk to me about it. Just wanted to get rid of it."

Jack spent a few seconds looking at the first page, then the second and third. "Oh wow," he murmured. "Nice. Stuff right out of the twenties, thirties, forties. Huh. Some from the fifties." He flipped back toward the beginning of the book and paused at a photograph of the Evans Mill.

Lydia had spent a long time examining that simple photograph of the warehouse with a large sign over the entrance and two open-bed trucks out front, and she'd tried to read between the lines of the short paragraph, but there just wasn't much information there. Three pages later, Jack paused again, peered closely into the page for a good minute, and then closed the scrapbook.

"Sorry, got distracted," he said. "Mind if I hang on to this for a couple of days?"

"Of course not. I'm not sure what to do with the information at this point. I've looked through it, taken some notes. It's good background information, but I can't glean any clues specific to Mary Walker's life. You'll notice the articles are all just loose, so be careful. Frank took the scrapbook out of my study the other day and went through it looking for hidden documents." She gave a small shrug. "As he does."

"The glue is old, yeah," Jack fingered an article, looking at the back of it. "Won't hold up to much."

"So you'll let me know if you find something I might have missed that sheds light on Mary?"

He gave her a nod. "I will do that."

It was clear that he was waiting to hear if the scrapbook was the reason she had asked to speak with him, or if there were more questions.

"Well, I also visited with one of Mary's friends, Ruth Donovan."

He raised his eyebrows. "Interesting."

"Do you know the name?"

"No, I can't say I do. I don't know much about the people of that generation, except my grandparents. Good conversation?"

"Oh yes. But I guess I was hoping for more. Something to go on. You know, to convince Frank that there are valuable facts to be had out there. Beyond antiques." She tried to read Jack's face as he nodded. "She did mention something curious that I wondered if you might know about."

He shrugged. "Try me."

"She said that when Mary Walker went missing, there were two witnesses—at first—who saw a woman walking toward the pier that night. Over the years I've only heard of one. Ruth said the other retracted her statement because she just couldn't be sure."

"Okay." He gazed at her steadily, and she found an apology rising into her mind. She felt like a suspicious cop trying to corner him.

"Ruth Donovan's journal mentioned that the other witness was a fisherman's wife. She couldn't remember the woman's name, or the fisherman's, but she'd written down the initials E. K."

Jack's gaze shifted away from her to the wall behind her, and his mind seemed to be working.

"You're wondering if I know anything about what the fisherman's wife saw, and who she was," he said at last, focusing his eyes back onto hers. "I really don't. But I applaud your effort to find real people's stories about Walker. I mean the woman is *still* causing trouble, so I sometimes wonder if her memory should just be dropped. You being one of the major victims of all this…obsession."

"I see what you mean. But for me at this point, finding out facts could potentially *free* me from the obsession, as you call it. Jack, I don't mean to put you on the spot—"

"It's okay," he said, leaning forward. "It's fine. E. K. My grandmother was Elizabeth Kenilworth. So I guess it could have been her. Although there were many, many fishermen in this area. But I was never privy to anything she did or thought about that night, so this only sets up a question in my mind that I will never be able to answer. You see? What good does that do? For me or you?"

"I do see." She looked down at her hands.

"Don't get me wrong, Lydia. I see the bind you're in. But as far as a story like this goes, I don't really want to know if my grandmother was involved," he said. "Their lives were their lives, and these events were over and done with so long ago, with so little left behind in the way of words or letters or anything, that I'm hopeless to understand stuff like this that comes up. To me, it is not a fascinating mystery or trivia for a doctoral thesis. It's just unsettling questions about people I loved and won't ever be able to speak to directly about anything I'm left wondering about."

"I'm sorry, Jack." Lydia tried to gauge how much damage she had done. He seemed to grow angry as he spoke. "I shouldn't have bothered you with it. I'm just looking for a way to close this chapter of our lives."

"I know. And I think that's a good thing. But realistically… for you and Frank, what would that look like?" He laughed briefly. "I don't think your husband is going to stop doing what he does until he constructs some sort of ending that fits the story he likes. That's a strong impression I got every time I encountered him. And you're very kindly assisting him by perpetuating the interest. Believing it still matters." Jack's expression softened. "You're in a tough spot, kiddo," he said. "And undoubtedly Mary Walker's true reality is not nearly as much fun as these stories of her surviving and writing in secret, so I'm guessing he's not going to want anything you might dig up."

She straightened. "Frank may be interested in a romantic story about Mary Walker, Jack, but *I* want out of this game of antiques and fantasies. It's expensive, and it's robbing me of the things I care about, like my husband, and a peaceful home. I want the truth."

"That's good," he said quietly, reaching for a pencil that was on his desk and turning it end over end on his thigh. "Because the truth usually comes out in the end."

There was no invitation in his voice, no hint of facts he would like to disclose, and Lydia was wary of jeopardizing a friendship based thinly on shared school days and his special relationship with her son.

"I have not been clear on where you stand on issues of your family history, Jack. I truly don't mean to pry. But some time ago you wanted to tell Frank something about Mary Walker," she said cautiously.

"Yes, that's true, I did offer some information to Frank. I heard he'd been looking for unpublished works by Walker for many years and was also interested in her life story. But a man can't hear what he doesn't want to hear. Your husband isn't the only one who has taught me that."

"But you can help me now if you would be willing to tell me

whatever you would have told him. If I can find out something that will lead Frank away from his fantasy, I could get free. We all could… That's what I am going to try to do." She was holding her hands out beseechingly and noticed that they shook slightly.

"I would bet my workshop that nothing will lead your husband away from his grand quest, Lydia. I'm sorry, but that's how I see it. I'm just a naysayer to him, and anything I told you would only put you in the middle. Between him and his dream."

She considered this as she fought back tears of tension and fatigue. After a minute, when Jack shifted to lean back in his chair, she returned her gaze to his face. He looked as if he was trying to guess her thoughts.

"I wish you would move on. With or without Mary Stone Walker. Nothing is worth all of this fuss. And you… Well, I personally feel that you deserve more." He looked over his shoulder toward the hall. "Somebody there?"

Nicholas pushed the door open.

"I just wanted to tell you," he said, smiling at Jack. "I figured it out."

"Great, Nick! Okay." Jack smiled, then aimed a friendly pointing gesture toward Lydia. "Back to work. Next time we talk boats?"

"Sure." Then she was alone and spoke quietly to his empty chair. "Or whatever comes up."

After leaving the barn with Nicholas ten minutes later, Lydia could see Jack's silhouette in the doorway as he watched them get into the Jeep. She fumbled with her keys.

"Jack's an interesting guy," she said, trying to draw a veil over her mood. "He was telling me the other day that we should fix up a boat and learn to sail. Seems like a fun idea, doesn't it?"

"Yeah, but do you think Dad would agree to it? I can't picture him on any kind of boat."

Lydia stared at him for a moment without answering, and he looked back at her uncomprehendingly. They were halfway home before she spoke.

"Nicholas," she said, as they passed the Phillips 66 gas station at the edge of town. "It's important that we stop thinking first about what Dad wants or is going to feel every time you or I want to do anything." She glanced at him. "It's an old habit that we have fallen into because we're nice people who want everyone to be happy. But it's not right to do that anymore. Not for me. Not for you."

"What do you mean?"

"If we imagine that Dad is the only person in the family whose opinion matters, then we devalue our own lives. You see? And that's not right."

"I know that."

"Do you? Think about it. All the little parts of your life. The little parts of mine. They matter *just as much* as his do. Not *almost* as much. Each piece of your life matters *every single bit* as much as Dad's."

Nicholas stared out the side window into the passing darkness. She could feel his relaxed mood turn to tension, and she regretted saying anything. They rode in silence the rest of the way home, and when they pulled slowly into the driveway, the first things Lydia's headlights lit up were the rear bumpers of four visiting cars.

"Jeez, what's the deal?" Nicholas said, his eyes wide.

"I don't know." Lydia barely spoke the words. They pulled up onto the grass beside the driveway, got out, and walked rapidly toward the barn. Lydia placed both of her hands on the barn door and shoved, while Nicholas reached above her hands and pushed, too. Inside, Frank sat like a king in his chair with six other people gathered around him. All faces turned toward Nicholas and Lydia.

"Hello, Nicholas," Frank said jovially. "Hello, dear wife." He raised a glass of wine in their direction. "I have found something utterly wonderful."

25

One morning she saw how the first autumn had changed
The splayed repeated figures on the ground
Making them leaves, and not the shadow of leaves.

~ Louise Bogan (1897–1970), "The Flume"

From the window of the Stevens Hotel dining room, Edith Evans watched her son part ways with his wife and head toward the hotel. Bernard and Mary didn't touch or seem to speak good-byes, but this didn't surprise her. What *had* surprised her was the animated way the two had talked and laughed during the first few months of their marriage.

Mary. A small sadness crossed Edith's mind as she recalled the way Bernard had said Mary's name when he first spoke of her. He had possessed an interest in girls for years but had never been smitten like this. Taking care of her and the children they would have together, that had been what mattered to him—and look how things had turned out.

The girl had been breathtakingly beautiful at the wedding. It wasn't the first time Edith had met her, but it was the first time she'd had such an extended opportunity to assess her. Bernard had married her so quickly after their meeting that Edith had had to pay extra money for the hastened completion of a proper wedding gown. The girl had nothing, no skill to sell, no mother, and a father who lived hand-to-mouth. The pitiful man was fading from life even at the wedding, in Edith's opinion—barely forty years old but unable to sustain himself, let alone his daughter.

And the apple didn't fall far from the tree. Whatever constitutional weakness had pervaded Leonard Walker's being and compromised his health, it was there in his daughter, too. In her case, manifesting as a weak mind. The knife incident proved it. Slashing your husband's face with a knife because you're out of your mind on morphine. God help us.

"Hello, Bernard," Edith said as Bernard approached her table from the front door.

"Mother." He nodded and met her eyes briefly, huffed an exhale, and sat down. He flagged the bartender and ordered a beer. "Damn hot summer."

"Start your workday earlier."

"I start early enough."

"Is the sun any different this year?"

Bernard ignored his mother's question and remained silent until the bartender came around with his beer. He raised it to his lips and drank a third of it down.

"Well, let's discuss the important matters right away," she said.

"I don't know if getting rid of Mary is gonna be the right thing for me, Mother."

"I understand, Bernard. But it's important to have a plan in place. It's hard to say how bad things could get." Edith leaned across the table and spoke in a fierce whisper. "After all, you never could have predicted she would go at you with a knife. And she could have blinded you. Killed you!"

"I know." His voice was taut with irritation.

"It's for her sake as well as yours."

"I know, I know. You've said these things already, twenty, thirty times."

"And she just doesn't matter. You'll find another woman to take care of your needs at home."

"There are plenty of women, maybe. But Mary…" After a moment he shrugged.

"We need to get to the point and be brief. Your father expects me. Is she coming back here to walk home with you?"

Bernard looked out the window and down Water Street, shaking his head no.

"Let me see that injury." Edith raised her hand toward his face, and Bernard turned his left cheek toward her for a moment, then brushed her arm away.

"It'll heal."

Edith swallowed hard and raised her chin. "The scar will be a ragged, terrible one, Son."

He let his hand fall with a slap to the table. "Okay, so what do you want me to do about it?"

"I am only saying that you should prepare your mind for that. And place the blame squarely where it belongs."

"It's the habit. The morphine."

"She is responsible for her own actions, regardless."

"I try to keep the stuff from her. I don't know how she gets hold of more." Bernard gazed around the room, anywhere but at his mother.

"The Devil always has ways. She can blame it on the injury, but that was over a year ago. It's nothing but an excuse. She is simply weak. Like her father."

"I should hit her. Teach her what she doesn't seem to know."

"And start a cycle that ends up in more trouble for you?"

"A man shouldn't put up with the kind of things I put up with." Bernard finished his beer. He ground his teeth together and shook his head slowly.

"She's a sick woman." Edith watched the rise of a temper she was intimately familiar with in her men, and she wanted to protect him from it. "Put her in an institution with others of her kind. Safely far away from your life and our business."

"Maybe I should just turn her out on the street." Now Bernard looked directly into his mother's face. "Let her figure out how good she's got it. But I can't stand the thought of another man having her. No, I cannot stand it. I'd rather see her dead."

"*Bernard.*" Edith's voice rose in warning as she glanced around the room.

"It's true."

"I understand. But you must be careful with your words around other people. And certainly with your actions. In public, *you keep quiet.* She isn't worthy of such powerful attachment. She could ruin your life."

For more than a minute, Edith watched her son's mind follow sordid thoughts and his face twitch with angry jealousy. When at last he spoke, his voice was vengeful against an imagined rival. "All right. What do I have to do?"

Edith inhaled deeply. "Protocol at the State Hospital for the Insane requires that she be examined by two psychiatrists. Your story about her behavior the night of the stabbing, as well as this addiction, will be enough to have her committed. I have connections, and we can get it done quickly."

"What do you mean, connections?"

"In college I knew a young man who is one of the doctors there now." Edith was proud of her year of college at Michigan State University and of the friendships she had managed to retain, but she instantly regretted explaining the acquaintance that way. She always paid a price for the details she revealed about her feelings or her past to her sons and husband. "You don't need to mention that doctor to your father. You know how he is."

Bernard gave something like a laugh as the bartender came to the table with a pitcher of beer and refilled Bernard's glass. "Father and I don't talk about you, Mother."

Edith's neck grew hot, and her sympathy for her son thinned somewhat, as it did eventually whenever she spent enough time with him. "That's just as well. I will tell Dr. Davison that you will be bringing Mary in soon, and things will go quickly from there. You will have your life and freedom back, and you can move on."

"How am I supposed to even get her into the car?"

"Watch for another time when she's just as affected as she was when she stabbed you. By your accounts, it shouldn't take long."

Bernard drank a few sips of beer and leaned back, more relaxed, with a slightly amused expression. "And while she's gone, maybe I'll look around, find some incriminating things she's written down. Put her in her place for good; make it clear who's boss."

Edith studied her son's expression and saw that he had not thought things through completely yet. In a firm tone she hoped would not revive his anger, she said, "Make no mistake, Bernard. She may never come back. The point is for you to move on. *Without her.*"

He gazed at his mother for a few seconds, then shrugged and looked out the window, as if seeking Mary's form on Water Street. "Fine. As long as I don't have to wonder where she is. Or who the hell she's with."

26

White Hill, Michigan—April 1999

I have forgotten which of us it was
That hurt his wing.
I only know his limping flight above us in the blue air
Toward the sunset cloud
Is more than I can bear.

~ Edna St. Vincent Millay (1892–1950), "There at Dusk I Found You"

Lydia was speechless. The clutter still lying around in the barn looked like remnants of a nightmare, and the staring faces of Frank and his visitors all seemed to taunt her with secretive smiles.

"Don't you want to know what I have here?" Frank held up an old volume of Sara Teasdale's poetry collection *Strange Victory*, his face smug. A few seconds of silence followed.

"Well, of course," she said, pushing her hair back around her ears. "Good evening, everyone."

"This is Dr. Richard Albert from the English Department. I don't believe you've officially met," Frank said, gesturing to a stout, fortysomething man to his left with wire-rimmed glasses and piercing eyes. He nodded to Lydia. "You know George Vanderkley, of course, and Drew. This is Shane Harding, one of Drew's graduate students, Lilly Schmidt from the Carson library. And Sylvia Gilmore."

Lydia nodded to each one, unable to smile. "So what have you found, Frank?"

"I don't think you'd believe me if I told you." Frank chuckled. "It's really something, though." He perused the end pages of the book. "Nicholas, you're going to be pleased. After all these years of searching, it's here at last."

Lydia looked over her shoulder at Nicholas, whose eyes seemed especially round and bright.

"Well? Just tell us!" she said, her passion for Mary Walker's work overshadowing her discomfort.

"This modest volume, *Strange Victory*, Sara Teasdale's posthumous collection, contains a fascinating addition to it. Lilly here, and Dr. Albert, feel optimistic that these handwritten, original lines of poetry scribed in the back are authentic." Frank nodded his head, smiling.

"Well, not by Teasdale, obviously," Lydia joked, and she heard a murmur of chuckles.

"No, not Teasdale. Who do you think they might be written by?" Frank's happy face contained a vindictive shadow especially for her.

"Why don't you just tell me?" Lydia said, finding it difficult to suppress her rising anger.

"Why don't you guess? It's fun!" Frank set the book on his lap and locked his hands together as he gazed at her.

"I don't want to bore your guests, Frank."

"Come on, Dad," Nicholas said quietly.

"Nicholas, aren't you pleased? Brad Kramer's boxes of musty old books from the Tavern shop have always been disappointingly dull, but not this one!"

Drew, sitting to Frank's right, put her hand on his arm, looking sympathetically at Lydia. "He did the same thing to us, Lydia." She gave a burst of laughter. "Although it's pretty obvious where his literary love lies! Who else would he be this excited about?"

"Now, Drew," Frank said, feigning displeasure. "Say nothing more. You're giving it away."

Lydia took a couple of steps forward into the circle, accidentally bumping the graduate student's arm so that wine slopped onto his pants.

"Just let me take a look," she said, extending her arm.

"Oh, no, no. Can't risk it. Got to hang on to this item," he said, lifting a bottle of wine to fill his glass. "We were just discussing how to handle it. Such a small, precious treasure. Wouldn't want it to be carried off by a doubting Thomas."

"He's very possessive about his poet," the graduate student, Shane, said sardonically, pressing a paper napkin to the wine stain on his leg.

Frank's eyes gleamed. "Shane, hush now!"

"Frank, pass the wine, would you?" Drew said, and he handed her the bottle. She filled her glass and held the bottle across toward Dr. Albert, who declined.

Lydia stepped back and put her hands in her jacket pockets.

"Nicholas, I bet you can guess. You've always believed it would happen, haven't you?" Frank said, giving his son a wide smile. "Come on."

Nicholas crossed his arms over his chest. "So…Mary Stone Walker?"

"Excellent! Cheers! You've been listening all these years!" He grabbed the bottle of wine from Drew, pulled another glass up from the floor, and said, "Give the young man a drink."

"Frank," Lydia protested.

"It's time to celebrate, dear wife. No harm in some enlivening spirits." He filled the glass half full and passed it around to Nicholas.

"I don't like wine, Dad," Nicholas said.

"I'll handle it." Shane, who had offered the glass up to Nicholas, poured its contents into his own.

Lydia's thoughts spun. Could it be? Unknown lines inscribed into a book? It could be authentic if Lilly Schmidt thought that it was real. She'd heard of this quiet, prematurely gray young woman who was often called upon throughout Michigan to examine documents, although as far as Lydia knew, Lilly's professional training didn't extend beyond library science.

"Lydia, you've had so much to say about this issue recently," Frank chided. "And here you are without words! I'm surprised."

She hoped he would read the lines out loud, but his attitude was so antagonistic toward her that she didn't want to risk further embarrassment by asking. Surely this caustic mood would pass if she left him alone with his cronies. She imagined him bringing the volume into the house later, after the guests were gone, brimming with excitement to share it with her. She would give him a piece of her mind about his rudeness after that.

"I suppose I won't be able to persuade you to guess what year this was written, since you're being such a spoilsport. But that might be the most exciting thing of all."

Lilly Schmidt and George Vanderkley nodded.

"Thrilling," Lilly murmured, smiling. "You and Frank seem to have been on the right trail all these years!"

"Yes, I was in it for the long haul." Frank chuckled.

Lydia watched him, awaiting a look of acknowledgment, a word about her own efforts.

"The mystery goes on," Shane said. "And on and on."

Drew leaned in toward the center of the circle, her hands tense and excited. "If she wrote this in 1940, if it's authentic, and it was found in Michigan, then perhaps she sailed up the Michigan coast from the pier that night."

"If it was even her that old Ambrose Smith saw on the pier," Frank said with one eyebrow cocked, lifting his wineglass. "This opens up all kinds of possibilities. Because I think you're right. She must have stayed in the state. At least for a while. Obviously she didn't drown. What do we really know from Smith's account? Almost nothing."

Lydia watched as the conversation knitted back into a tight circle of speculation that she could see Frank did not want her to join. Without another word, she rushed out of the barn. Nicholas followed a few steps behind her.

"Mom!" he called softly. She ignored him, pulled open the back door of the house, hurried inside, and threw off her coat as if it were some nasty, clinging creature. Nicholas opened the door as she leaned against the kitchen counter, her face burning.

"Mom!" he said again. "What's wrong?"

"That was humiliating." She fought back a wave of angry tears.

"Dad's just being Dad," he said with a note of pleading. "He'll come around."

"Won't even *pretend* to act civil to his own wife in front of his colleagues. Asinine." She almost felt faint with rage and with fear that she did not fully understand. Would he push her away completely? Now that Frank had finally gotten what he wanted, would he forget their bond through all of the years when she had patiently attended his outlandish excuse for a career?

"He was just showing off."

The back door opened again, and Nicholas and Lydia both whipped their heads toward the sound. Shane stepped inside, wiped his feet lazily on the mat, and looked from one to the other of them.

"Got chips or something?" he asked. "Frank sent me to ask."

Lydia wanted to refuse, but her manners were too automatic. "Nicholas," she said, "would you see what we have and help this young man, please?"

Shane whistled a breathy melody, letting the notes trail off as Nicholas opened and shut cupboard doors, and said, "I'm sorry to say it, Mrs. Carroll, but your husband's an ass sometimes." Shane's expression was rueful. "Well, actually, most of the time, if you ask me."

She stared at him, unsmiling, and he stared back. Not a single retort came to her mind. She heard chips jingling into a bowl, then Nicholas set it, along with a jar of salsa, on the counter in front of Shane.

"He's bonkers about this poet. She's not great enough to spend your whole life on, as you probably know. And hey, let's face it…" He pulled his head back, held out his hands, and lightened his expression flirtatiously. "There's no way she was as pretty as you are."

Lydia rolled her eyes. Even this kid who barely knew her or Frank had picked up on the fact that Walker was Lydia's competition.

"Wait till you're an old fart like he is, Shane. You might prefer phantoms to real women yourself."

Shane gave a hoot of laughter and waited, hands on the bowl of chips, for her to meet his eyes. "Thanks," he said, smiling. He backed up to the door and left.

"Jeez, what a jerk," Nicholas muttered.

Lydia shook her head. She watched the young man cross the dark grass and reenter the barn, as someone's hands came up to close the door behind him. For minutes she stared at the crack of light there. How long she had hoped for this day, and look what it was actually composed of: rejection and meanness, in equal parts to an excitement that she was excluded from. The mystery of Mary Stone Walker had corroded her husband's mind and their marriage, and Lydia knew suddenly that although these newly discovered words had always been the point of the struggle, they would not heal either one.

As she started to turn away from the window to retreat to her bedroom, a sharp, bright star over the barn roof caught her eye, and a vivid image of her father filled her mind. He had always thought Frank was a myopic dreamer who "does not give a damn about reality" and had even said once shortly before he died that she should always follow her own intelligence, because it was deeper and steadier than her husband's. The star visibly flickered, and she yearned for her father's expansive heart and the kind of generous love that was no longer part of her world.

Frank framed his life inside little inked lines and fantasies, but her life was not so much differently framed. She had certainly had her victories, and now he seemed to be having his own. Now perhaps he had found what he'd been looking for so long. If so, she would be sincerely glad for him. But the situation that she needed to accept here and now was that they no longer shared the same values. In fact, her belief that they did was a fantasy that for years had been as seductive for her as Frank's dreams of Mary Walker had been for him.

When she turned from the window, she was startled to find Nicholas sitting patiently at the table.

"Nicholas…I thought you'd gone to bed."

"How can I go to bed, Mom? This seems like such an important night. Doesn't it?"

"Yes, it does." She gazed into his large, blue eyes.

"Are you glad about it?" he asked.

"Well, sure. Cautiously glad." She sat down at the table with him and picked up a box of matches and shook it. It sounded full, and out of a habit that extended back into the early years of unforgettable marital poverty, she felt faintly gladdened by the thought that there were at least plenty of matches in the house.

"What do you mean, 'cautiously'?"

"Lilly Schmidt out there may think it's real. People respect her. But if Carson Community College or some other institution is going to purchase the document, they'll have to have it more thoroughly checked out."

"Oh," Nicholas said as he nodded. "I was expecting Dad to just keep it. I mean, that was the point, wasn't it? That he wanted something of hers? Something she wrote?"

"Sure, but it wouldn't make sense for it to sit here in his library. And if he wants to write about this new poem as part of Mary Stone Walker's work and life, its authenticity will have to be confirmed, whether or not he sells it." She studied Nicholas's unsettled expression. "I could be wrong; he surprises me sometimes. I hope the library will buy it if it's real. They have a Mary Stone Walker collection."

"I know." Nicholas bit his lip, looking away from her.

"But we shouldn't jump the gun here and get too excited yet. Not until we know for sure. What are you worried about, Nicky?"

"Nothing."

They were silent for a few moments.

"We've been waiting for something like this for a long time, haven't we?" she said, placing her hand on top of his.

Nicholas looked up at her and found her smiling, and he returned an unconvincing smile.

"I just hope you're glad, too," he said sadly.

"Well, sure. Of course I'm glad. You're right. Dad will come around, and he'll bring that book in here and share it with us. Then…" She gazed blindly toward the kitchen ceiling, considering such scenes, trying to imagine how everything would unfold. Jack had asked her what Frank would do if he weren't searching for hidden poetry. Now he would just keep searching forever—this guaranteed it. If there was one complete poem written into a book in 1940 and Frank had managed to get his hands on it, then there were bound to be more. Somewhere. And maybe a poet, too.

"Do you think this will make him famous?" Nicholas's face appeared oddly young, as earnest as the small, serious boy he had been at nine or ten.

"In a certain circle." Lydia nodded. "It will be exciting to the literary world at large. Yes, it will definitely bring him… prestige. And inspiration, which is even more important. There's probably every reason to believe this is a significant find, but let's not conjure up too many specific ideas about it just yet, okay?" Wearily, she stood up. "I'm going to go upstairs to check my email and then get to bed."

She turned at the door to look at Nicholas's back as he stared out the window toward the barn. His uncombed hair and tense, bony shoulders wrenched her heart. Poor kid. Trying to be a strong man, and left so often lately to figure out unpleasant things on his own with a mind that was still so childlike at times that it startled her. If she and Frank could continue to live with each other—if they could make peace in the wake of his theft of their savings, and if they could get past all of the disrespect of recent days—then life in this house had to change. With or without Frank, she would construct a safe world where she and Nicholas could be happy, and where as a family, they could all accept each other without meanness. If the result was a respectful, joyless coexistence, that would be an improvement.

In her study, Lydia struck a match, lit a candle, and set it on the windowsill. A chill ran through her body. When had Frank gotten so mean to her? How long had it been like this? If she didn't take action, Frank's self-absorption and obsession would become an even larger feature of their family life. For there in the barn he held evidence that every step of his expensive, absurd preoccupation had been valid. Mary Stone Walker had written more than anyone knew and survived past October 1939.

She wanted to believe that the discovery might motivate Frank to work hard and finally complete his book, but it seemed unlikely. Instead, Lydia suspected he would keep searching for hidden documents and never again so much as tolerate her warnings about the waste of time, money, and life. The search was where he lived now…where he had been living for years. Twenty years for one poem. On this timeline and with these methods and no standards whatsoever to meet, there would never be a conclusion to his "work."

Staring out the window at darkness pinned by a single streetlight, Lydia tried to order her thoughts. She would have to focus on her own writing, her own income—her own life. She would make this immersion in Mary Stone Walker *benefit* her instead of being merely a source of worry. She would write a novel based on all she knew about the poet, and even though using this material for fiction might be a difficult thing to get used to after so many years of framing the woman's life and work exclusively as academic research material for Frank, that was another issue that she needed to take a hard look at.

Because after all, the woman was *not* purely academic for Frank. No, she was a romantic escape no less than any other mistress would be, and Frank had chosen that preoccupation again and again over the years, without concern for any damage it was causing to his marriage, family, or career. He deserved to be described in a novel for what he was: a man using a dead woman's life and work to give his own life meaning and make himself a hero. At this point, Frank's dedication had come to look like nothing more than a weird and lazy sort of lust. It sickened her.

Turning from the window, Lydia sat down at her desk with determination and turned on her computer. She would write that book. The process would be invigorating, and at least for her, it would offer a path to closure around the issue of Mary Stone Walker. The first thing on that screen that her eyes lit upon was an email from her agent.

Lydia, you're worrying me, my dear. If you're going to drop *The Few and the Proud*, you must get me a proposal for your new idea. Call me immediately. Barbara

It was going to be difficult to break away from the novels people expected of her, to create literature with an uncertain audience and possibly face criticism and even failure. But all of the skills she had honed should easily carry her through any story, and a novel about a poet inspired by Mary Walker would practically write itself, driven by so many elements Lydia found fascinating that she would hardly know where to begin.

After a while, she slid from her chair to the recliner in her study, pulling a blanket up over herself and falling at last into sleep. But sometime in the deep stillness of the middle of the night, she startled awake. She threw back the blanket, stood up, and opened her study door. Silence. Darkness. She went into the bathroom, leaving the light off, and gazed into the backyard. The glow at the door of the barn was gone, as were the cars. Her heart began to pound. She turned and tiptoed down the stairs, listening. Nothing. She walked through the hall, and her gaze was caught by light beaming under the closed door of Frank's study. She thought of knocking on it, but felt frozen where she was.

"Lydia?" Frank's voice came muffled from behind the door, then she heard him step across the floor and open it. "What are you doing up?"

"Something woke me."

"Can you believe it?" he said, his voice warmed by happiness and wine. "Can you believe this is finally happening?"

She exhaled, waiting for the right words to come to her mind, but they didn't. "No," she said.

"But indeed it is happening! As I knew it would!" He raised his arms as if inviting an embrace. "Goddamn it, I was right all along!"

"Maybe so."

"Oh, come on, Lydia, it's real. Schmidt and Albert were both electrified by what they saw." He laughed. "And the poem, Lydia… It's indescribably exciting. Innovative. Profound and strange. Among the most provocative she's written. So far."

"So far."

"Well, there is no earthly reason not to believe there are more out there. I'm telling you, the woman lived on after White Hill. We have proof now."

"Is it dated in the same hand?"

"Thank God, yes, it is…1940."

She gazed off to the side, her eyes meeting an eerie, incomplete reflection of herself in a wall mirror. She turned away from it.

Frank walked over to her and raised his hands, saying, "I've done it. You can be proud, Lydia." He gave her a small smile and pulled her to his chest, and she could hear his heart pounding heavily. She pushed away.

"I'd like to read it," she said, one hand on his shirt.

"In time. Lilly Schmidt has the book tonight. She'll do what she can to analyze it for authenticity. You wouldn't steal the book away, now, would you? When you finally see it?"

"Why would you say that?" Lydia stared at him in shock. "I'm just as excited as anyone else. In fact, more excited than everyone else who was here tonight! Seriously, Frank…what are you thinking?"

He laughed as if this were a question they both knew the answer to and pulled her toward his body again. "Come on, let's go to bed. I could hug you all night."

His affection was oddly impersonal, Lydia observed, and she felt a simmering revulsion, even as she tried to crush it by focusing on Frank's happiness. This might, after all, be the first step back through the wreckage to the familial peace that she had just been daydreaming about.

27

Why is grief.
Grief is strange black.

~ Gertrude Stein (1874–1946), "Preciosilla"

G uess what? The woman from the Library of Congress
called," Lydia told Frank as he entered the house near dinnertime the next day. "A couple of hours ago. Nicholas and I
looked all over for you before we realized your truck was gone."

"No kidding? Already? What'd she say?" Frank tossed his hat
onto the coatrack.

"Nick wrote out a message before he left."

"I hope he got the facts straight. Where is it?" As Frank
passed, Lydia caught the smell of alcohol.

"I didn't even know you'd left," Lydia said, pointing toward
the refrigerator. "Partying somewhere?"

"I put in an appearance at Richard Albert's house, if it's all
right with you. He had people there from the college. They're
all excited about the poem."

He stopped at the large yellow sheet of paper stuck to the
refrigerator. Excited, jagged lines encircled the words in royal-
blue marker from Nicholas.

DAD! Judith Tomlinson from the Library of Congress
called to say CONGRATULATIONS!!! Lilly Schmidt sent her

a fax of the poem. Hopes you might visit with the original ASAP. She is a special fan of Mary. Please call as soon as possible. 202-555-0125.

Lydia leaned on the doorframe, arms crossed over her chest.

"Better detail than usual," she said. "He's so excited, Frank. I hope you'll include him—"

"He's been there through the whole search," Frank said absently, pushing in the phone number.

"I haven't seen him like this since—"

"Shhh!" Frank held up the yellow note, then said quietly, "Damn. It's just an answering machine. Yes, Ms. Tomlinson, this is Frank Carroll from Carson Community College in White Hill, Michigan, returning your call. I'm available at this number any time, and I will wait for your call. Until then, I do want to say that we're impressed by the authentic nature of the document and the provocative character of the poem. I'll do whatever I can to meet with you personally if that would be helpful. Thank you."

He hung up, drummed his fingers on the counter, then grabbed the phone book. "You know, Lydia…"

After a moment she said, "Yes?"

"We might as well have a few key supporters over. Tonight, in fact. I think we should. Lilly Schmidt, Sylvia Gilmore, Drew. Maybe a couple of Drew's students."

"What for?"

"For a little party." He stepped close to her and smiled as he ran the tips of his fingers along her temples and gently pushed her hair back. He held her head in his hands and leaned down to kiss her forehead. She closed her eyes. He said gruffly, "You remember back when this all started, sweetheart?"

Lydia turned her head away, but Frank nudged her cheek with a knuckle to urge her to look into his eyes. "Yes. Of course."

"Do you? Do you remember the two of us, before you

were even publishing, before Nicholas came bounding into the world... We'd stay up all night talking. About poetry. About love."

Lydia shifted her weight from one foot to the other, tilting her head out of Frank's grip. "Mmm-hmm."

"We heard about that candelabra, that first candelabra, the one thing left that was available from Mary's home right here in town—"

"I remember. That forty bucks we spent on it felt like a thousand would now."

"We just kept on," Frank said, running one finger lightly over her mouth. "Determined. Nicholas isn't here, you say?"

"He's at Jack Kenilworth's," she said. "Working late and staying overnight."

"Aha," he said. "Let's go upstairs for a minute, Lydia baby."

"Frank. Where is this coming from?"

"What are you talking about?" He put his hand on her breast and gave her an expression of complete confusion.

"One second you're wild to make phone calls, and now you've got to have sex." She stared at him. "Right? We're talking three minutes, tops. And"—she pointed at the wall clock— "if you want guests, you've got to arrange it now. It's after six. It's really too late."

He leaned forward and pressed his mouth onto hers, sliding his hand down the back of her pants. Before she could either relent or protest, he withdrew his hand and his mouth, giving her breast a pinch as he headed for his study with the phone book. She watched him walk away and marveled at his bright mood. She had forgotten how unhappy he'd become. She really hoped she would be able to help him enjoy this hour, in spite of her hard feelings.

After a few calls, Frank leaned into the hall and shouted Lydia's name. "I told everyone eight o'clock!"

An hour later, Lydia turned the chandelier light low over

the dining room table. Violets in small vases surrounded by pussy willow sprigs were clustered around three tall, white candles in pewter candlesticks. She had set half a dozen different swatches of lace at angles across the table, and the wedding china dessert plates were stacked beside silver forks and a fanned stack of pink cotton napkins. In the kitchen, a pound cake sat cooling on a rack, beside a white bowl filled with chopped strawberries and a mixing bowl full of whipped cream.

The doorbell rang, and of course it was Drew, who was consistently fifteen minutes early for everything. She helped Lydia open three bottles of wine and set wineglasses on the table as Frank searched around in the stacks of CDs.

"Ah, one of Mary's favorites," he said, removing a CD from its case, and as the Chopin nocturnes played, the other guests arrived.

Lydia watched Frank's face as he focused on the music, his expression dreamy and joyful. Cleared of tension, his features had become more youthful looking literally overnight. Memories unfolded one after another in her mind, poignant and distant recollections of the man she'd fallen in love with and the conspiratorial alliance of passion and work they had shared. As they sat down with their champagne, cake, and all of their guests at the table, Lydia felt a warm longing for such convivial days—a longing that was part remembrance and part hope for the future.

"I wish Nicholas could be here," she said with quiet excitement.

Frank waved his fork full of cake dismissively. "He'd be bored."

"I don't think so." She smiled, glancing at him. "I can't even believe how keyed up he's been. Wait'll you hear him talk about it. He thinks of himself as your right-hand man in all this, you know."

"In some ways he was." Frank nodded. He held his finger up,

his ear toward the stereo. "Listen. This nocturne always conjured thoughts of loss for Mary, remember? Particularly losses at sea."

He turned his gaze to Lilly Schmidt, and when she smiled back at him, he tapped his wineglass with his fork, standing up as the guests grew silent. He held his hand open toward Lilly, and she set *Strange Victory* carefully on his palm.

"Most of you," he said with what Lydia knew he intended to be reverent gravity, "have heard what I am about to read. Some of you have not, and you're in for a treat. Just a couple of days ago, we sat around in the old barn, wondering if we'd stumbled onto a remarkable literary find." He paused, letting his gaze glide from face to face. "And now we have been confirmed. By the Library of Congress. Tentatively," he added, raising one forefinger, "but we are confident."

There was applause, along with some whooping from Drew.

"We knew, some of us, that this day was likely," he went on. "Mary Stone Walker left behind nine other hidden documents that we know of and, significantly, when she disappeared did *not* leave her body." There was laughter, then Frank grew solemn, his voice bending in a familiar, bittersweet tone as he went on. "She lived. Mary lived past that October of 1939."

He inhaled and pulled his glasses off for a moment to look around at everyone after he wiped his eyes. "In some ways, the poem is shocking for its time. Shockingly revealing, too, about the deep connection Mary felt to the mother she never really knew, which was a subject she had not approached often—a subject that perhaps we'll find becomes more common in her mature years, as we continue to discover her legacy. I suspect that you will see what I mean and be impressed, as I am, by her courage and her honesty.

"So…" he said, replacing his glasses after an adequately contemplative, grateful pause, "I will read the evidence. It is signed *Mary S. Walker*, with the date of 1940."

He cleared his throat. The air wavered. He began.

The Study of Lakes

They found a calcified infant
curled like an ear
in the womb of an eighty-five
year old woman.
How many years was it frozen,
motionless—
drowned.

I spend my days in motion
listening to the trains' deep
chromatic call and answer—
like a conch shell and foghorn.
At 5:30 every morning,
their echoes reach my house.

Have you ever walked out
to the middle of the lake
in winter?
Some spots the ice is clear,
and I try to see underneath.
You can write letters there
and leave them. Yes,
I have.

Once, I imagined my mother.

During the day, I walk
and walk so that I am lost.
It's a game I play to find her.
Houses I've never seen
with their trees and walkways

and wooden gates'
unkindly promise.

I think the old woman
must have known
the entire time—
this is how some of us
hold
on.

~ Mary S. Walker, 1940

Frank drifted slowly through the last lines and closed the book silently, to a ripple of whispered comments and sighs. He had lowered his eyes toward the table as if saying a prayer, and Lydia watched him in disbelief, waiting for his gaze to seek hers, waiting for some acknowledgment. When none came, she scraped her chair back from the table, nearly knocking it over backward. She rushed from the room, her hand pressing her pink cloth napkin to her mouth, and she heard the conversation behind her like a performance scripted to mock her.

"Well, Cap'n," Shane Harding said. "Congratulations again. It's damn cool."

"Every time I hear it, it gives me chills," Drew said. "Every single time."

"When I told Judith Tomlinson at the Library of Congress about Frank's find," Lilly Schmidt said in her soft voice, "she said she always thought Mary might have lived past 1939. This is a gift directly from her, and her audience will be overjoyed."

Trying to be discreet, Lydia slid barely into Frank's view, gesturing for him to come to her. At first, he was so caught up in the excited talk that he didn't seem to notice that she'd left the table, but then he spotted her and responded with a stony glare. Could he really be doing this? She felt dizzy, disoriented. If he didn't come quickly, she didn't know what she would do, so she said his name once, loudly. He gave her a fierce look and nodded once in angry acquiescence, but it was more than ten minutes before he finally came to the kitchen. She stood, hands flat on the counter, the fine curls against her neck and shoulders trembling.

"*What is it?*" he demanded.

"Frank," she said evenly, staring at him. "That poem."

He waited. She said nothing more.

"What?" he demanded.

Still she only stared. *What?* Did he think the theft didn't matter?

"*What?* Do you disapprove? Can I not just enjoy this hour, for Christ's sake?"

Her eyes were wide and shocked. "No, I don't think you can. I don't think that's appropriate. *That poem? I* wrote it."

"What?" He gave a howl of laughter. "That's a good one, Lydia. A new twist." Her eyes bored into him. "Christ, what is this? You're being ridiculous, Lydia. You look positively insane."

He tossed the napkin he'd been carrying onto the counter and spun around to leave.

"Frank!" Inside her head, her voice sounded gravelly and strange. "I wrote that poem. Mary Stone Walker did not write that poem."

He narrowed his eyes at her. "Lydia. You did *not* write that poem. Did you see the book?" He pointed behind him toward the dining room, lowering his voice. "Is that your handwriting that Lilly Schmidt recognizes as Mary's?"

"You are not going to stand there," Lydia said with difficulty, breathing hard, "and honestly tell me that you don't remember it?"

"It's kind of an unusual subject, Lydia. I think it would ring a bell."

"Exactly."

"But…it does not." He enunciated sharply, holding his finger up as if he were scolding a child, and gave her a stern, warning stare. "You hear me, Lydia? Nothing in that poem ever entered my eyes or my ears…until I found *Mary's* book. Okay? You got it? Mary Stone Walker's book. Mary's poem. Now pull yourself together."

The kitchen floor creaked, and both Frank and Lydia turned to see Shane standing there—for how long, it was impossible to say. Frank let out an irritated sigh. The kid wore an inquisitive expression.

"Honestly," Frank said, his voice artificially heavy. "Listen." He stared pointedly into Lydia's eyes, demanding her cooperation. "Sweetheart, you've got to take it easy. Get some rest now." He took her arm in his hand and didn't let her pull away. "You have gotten overexcited. What do you need, Shane?"

"Looking for water, actually," he said, ambling to the sink, opening a cupboard, then another, pulling out a glass and whistling casually as if he lived there.

Lydia glared at Frank, and he glared back at her.

"I want you to lie down. Please, sweetheart. You've done so much for me tonight, and you're tired. I'll be up shortly with some aspirin. Okay?"

Lydia's mouth twitched with rage, but as long as Shane stood at the sink sipping his water and gazing out the window toward the dark backyard, Frank knew she would say nothing more.

"All set?" Frank said to Shane, clapping him on the back.

"Sure. Your wife sick?" Shane asked without looking at Frank as Lydia lightly took the stairs.

"She has"—Frank used a low tone that Lydia could still hear from the upstairs hall—"some nerve issues. Please don't mention it. And don't worry about it. She's fine with medication."

"Aspirin?" Shane said.

"Of course not." Frank scowled. "That's what I say to avoid embarrassing her. Her prescription ran out. I'll…have to run to the pharmacy for her later." There was the jingling of car keys being removed from the hook on the wall. "When we finish up here. Don't want her driving, not feeling like she does. But if she'll just stretch out upstairs…in the dark, the quiet…she'll fall asleep almost instantly, no doubt. That's the way it goes with her."

They left the kitchen, and from her bedroom, Lydia heard a burst of laughter and a toast to Frank Carroll and Mary Walker from the small group gathered around her dining room table.

28

CARSON COLLEGE, MICHIGAN—JULY 1938

The heart of a woman falls back with the night,
And enters some alien cage in its plight,
And tries to forget it has dreamed of the stars,
While it breaks, breaks, breaks on the sheltering bars.

~ *Georgia Douglas Johnson (1877–1966), "The Heart of a Woman"*

It would be unusual for Carson College to hire a twenty-four-year-old woman to teach literature, the dean of the college had warned her the week before as he scratched her name into the schedule of upcoming interviews. However, in the course of her days as a student, three of Mary's professors at Carson had explicitly suggested that she pursue a collegiate teaching career to support herself while she wrote poetry. She was told she was brilliant, charismatic, and a precociously serious scholar. Before she was twenty, Mary Stone Walker—author of a collection of original verse that had won two regional awards—believed that a place in American letters and a future as a college literature professor were certainties for her, and all she really wanted.

She had not been able to sleep the night before the interview, and seated now in the wooden chair across from the dean's desk, nerves fired throughout her body, making her knees shake and upsetting her stomach. In her lap she held the expensive leather satchel Bernard had purchased for her twenty-first birthday, in the first year of their marriage when he had still liked the idea of his wife being a writer. She had brought a copy of her published volume, *Sea Shadows*, an additional eighty-three typed sheets of new poetry, and approximately two hundred pages of essays, mostly literary criticism. The satchel was slightly damp where her hands clutched it.

Dean Wilson Hart entered his office, shut the door softly, and sat down before her in his generous leather chair, locking his hands together on his desktop. The smile he gave, tipping his head forward to look at her over his reading glasses, was formal and brief, although he'd known Mary Walker since she'd entered Carson College at seventeen.

"First of all, Mrs. Evans, let me say how proud we all are of your dedication to the art of poetry," Dean Hart said. "As I hope I have expressed before, the publication of your book adds to the prestige of our Humanities Department. And I understand you have continued a rather prolific production of verse?"

Heart knocking in her throat, Mary adopted the dean's serious attitude as she said, "It's just Walker. Mary Stone Walker. I did not take my husband's name because I have a career to think of. And yes, sir, I have the manuscript here, along with—"

Dean Hart shook his head. "I won't need to see that today, Mary."

"Perhaps I can leave it with you, and you can read it at your leisure?" she offered. "I have brought my literary essays as well. Three have been published, and I have copies of the journals in which they appeared."

The man shifted to lean back in his chair, removing his glasses.

"Your achievements are impressive. But let's make sure we are both clear on this teaching job and our mutual values before we go any further."

She furrowed her brow. "Isn't it true that the open position is for a professor of English, to begin this fall?"

"Yes, but I'm thinking more fundamentally than that, dear."

"I'm sorry, sir. I don't know what you're getting at." She

bounced her knee, keenly aware of the slight rustle of cloth that the action created in the quiet room, but unable to stop.

"We are seeking a professor of English literature—all genres, not just poetry."

Mary exhaled with relief and her voice lifted. "I am well versed in those works most commonly understood to be the pillars of English literature, Dr. Hart. This is why—" She reached to unbuckle her satchel.

Again Dean Hart held up his hand. "Please. This is not a position that will necessarily allow the chosen candidate to teach the writing of poetry, which would be your strongest asset and might at some point offset weaknesses."

"Of course I understand. If you are asking about my long-term career aspirations, I don't feel I need to teach the craft of poetry writing, per se. I am deeply passionate about the value of all kinds of literature as an enrichment to every individual's life, and that will be clear when you read—"

"Miss Walker." His voice was stern.

Mary looked up in confusion. The man's face was set.

"No one would question that your young efforts have displayed talent. Your ability to hold the interest of a group of people during readings is also inarguable and exhibits a valuable teaching quality. However, for someone in my position, there are other concerns that must be taken seriously."

Mary's jaw clenched.

"Artists have, throughout history, famously destroyed their lives one way or another through vice. But this is not acceptable for a professor at Carson College, someone who will be a leader of young people. Wouldn't you agree?"

Mary said nothing but looked directly into the dean's mud-colored eyes as he gazed back at hers.

"Close to a year ago, I saw your husband on Water Street, leaving Dr. DeBoer's office, the left side of his face covered in bandages. Bernard Evans's mother, Edith, has been a generous donor to Carson College, and we do not forget our patrons or their family members. Concerned, I asked Bernard what had happened."

Dr. Hart stared accusingly, said no more, and appeared to be waiting for a response from Mary, who froze in mortified disbelief that Bernard had disclosed personal problems to the dean of her alma mater. Her mouth grew instantly dry, and she could think of absolutely nothing to say.

"You see what I'm getting at now. Violence. Inappropriate drug use. Addiction. Your talents mean little in the balance, frankly."

Suddenly the flat leather case in her hands felt like the last board of a wrecked ship she was clinging to, foolish and unprepared, in a poisonous sea. She couldn't bring herself to look at Dr. Hart's face again, more from anger than shame. Such men, such men.

"Miss Walker." The dean's voice had softened slightly. "Do be careful. There is no reason a man like Bernard Evans would feel the need to take care of a childless woman with such problems. He does not strike me as a highly sensitive or intellectual individual. But he can provide for you. Marriage does require sacrifices."

Mary gave a short laugh toward the leather satchel in her lap. After a moment, she stood up and locked her gaze on Dr. Hart's empty desktop.

"We were always told, by professors here at Carson College, to investigate the truth for ourselves and not rely on hearsay," she said. "With all due respect, Dr. Hart, I think it would have been more appropriate for you to ask me about my life than to lecture me about some version of it that is based on the words of others. I withdraw my application. Good day."

Rigidly, Mary Stone Walker left Dean Hart's office, closing the door firmly behind her. As she crossed the campus green, it was blurred by unwanted tears and a million drifting cottonwood seeds.

29

What do I care, in the dreams and the languor of spring,
that my songs do not show me at all?
For they are a fragrance, and I am a flint and a fire.

~ Sara Teasdale (1884–1933), "What Do I Care"

Lydia locked herself in her study, breathing heavily. She stood before the mirror on the door and stared at her reflection.

"I wrote that poem," she said to her own image, her voice shaking with indignation. "I wrote that poem. Lydia Carroll. Lydia Milliken. I wrote that poem."

She stared at her face, which was chalk white, mottled by angry red splotches, and her eyes looked wild even to her. Water filled the rims of them. She felt pity and dislike for the pathetic creature in her mirror.

"The Study of Lakes" she had titled that poem so long ago. She'd forgotten about it, left the original in a college notebook somewhere. But now a flood of detail returned to her from those weeks when she was studying poetry writing at Boston University's Master of Fine Arts program. She'd written the poem to send to Frank who was in Ann Arbor working on his PhD. One of their romantic nights together during a return visit to Michigan had led to pregnancy, and all of the people closest to her were upset—her father; her sister, Louise; and most depressingly, Frank. As if it had been some reckless plot of self-sabotage, in the view of her father and Louise, and as if it were cruel and intentional imprisonment of him, in the case of Frank.

Oh yes, she remembered the pain she'd felt at their unsupportive alarm and the frustration of wondering why the event of pregnancy was somewhat universally assumed to forecast failure of the mother's personal endeavors. This turbulence had hurled her into renewed anguish over why her mother had borne Louise and then Lydia, only to leave them forever when they were young children. Altogether, it seemed to her that the act of bearing a child was often perceived as both a punishment and a crime.

In the echo of her poem being read as if it were Mary Stone Walker's creation, Lydia's mind struggled with the disorienting sense that truth was malleable. She sought grounding in the image of herself in the mirror, but as reality shape-shifted, even that face looked like an illusion. Was she somehow misremembering some part of this piece of history? She paced. Her brow was damp. No, there was no imagining such a poem, one's *own* creation. But why had she never run across it in all these years? Where had Frank kept it? She had forgotten about it, although it was one of the most difficult things she had ever written. She smacked the wall with her fists. How could he stand there and claim he'd never read it before?

She could remember the night she'd asked him to respond to those lines, when they spoke on the phone a few days after he received the poem in the mail, and he had been tense. She had asked him if he understood the emotions she was explaining, and how important the issue of bringing the child to term and giving birth was to her, especially in light of her mother's psychotic abandonment. She needed his support, she'd said, to do right by this unborn human being and herself throughout the child's life.

"Do you understand that?" she had pleaded from a thousand miles away, staring onto the light-speckled darkness of Boston Common from her apartment window. The phone receiver had grown slippery in her hand from nervous perspiration, she suddenly remembered as memories unwound in her White Hill bedroom. And to all of her questions but one, Frank had said they should not try to talk about the issues on the phone. And that one: was he at least moved by the poem enough to hear its plea? To which he'd responded, simply, that it was not among her best.

It was a horrible memory, and no wonder that she'd shoved it deeply out of view for all of these years. That night, she had cried until she fell asleep, certain that she'd alienated Frank even further with her well-intended lines of poetry and afraid that he was not the man she'd believed him to be. At last, he'd said that he felt it would be best if they left the subject of her pregnancy alone for a while to give them both a chance to come to terms with it on their own. He'd never mentioned the poem again.

So, did Frank think that because nearly sixteen years had passed, she would not remember her own thoughts? Had he so diminished her value as a human being and an artist over the years that he believed she did not even own her own experiences? Her own words?

She rushed to her desk, jerked open the top drawer, and collected everything she could find related to their bank accounts. At some point, enough was simply enough. She needed to be ready to separate from him. She left her study and went to her bedroom with the feeling that she was being watched, that someone stood staring from the shadows. She locked the door.

Opening the closet, she reached inside to wrestle a gym bag from the back corner and rifled through her bureau drawers, pulling out socks, underwear, and T-shirts, enough for several days, to stuff into the bag. She tucked the bank statements and checkbooks securely under the clothes, then went to the closet for two pairs of clean pants, pushed them on top of the other things, and zipped the bag closed.

After changing from the dress she'd worn to the dessert party into a pair of jeans, a T-shirt, her warmest sweatshirt, and her hiking boots, she groped around beneath her side of the bed for the flashlight she kept there. She snapped it on. The beam was bright. She stood at the edge of the king-size bed she'd shared with Frank until he had begun sleeping most nights in the guest room a few months ago. On his bedside table a half-empty glass of amber liquid stood next to a magazine, some papers, and a book set open, facedown. Tennyson's *In Memoriam*. On her bedside table there were an alarm clock her father had owned and a water glass. Everything else was intentionally out of view, a habit she had developed when Frank had begun making comments about many of the things that she bought or read.

Through every degrading fight, every fresh indignity and insult, she had always looked for reasons to believe that the situation would improve. This was her habit of mind. But it was time to face the fact that her life with Frank was a lie that she had been telling herself for a long time, and leave. She didn't know where she was going right now, but the sense that this was the prelude to a permanent departure flickered ominously in her mind. She hoisted her purse onto her shoulder, then the gym bag.

She was downstairs at the back door, unnoticed, when she remembered that Frank had her Jeep keys in his pocket. God! Had he intended to submerge her in this humiliation, unable to escape? She began to feel nauseated from the racing questions about her husband.

He couldn't have forged that poem. He just couldn't have willfully pulled off the details of a trick like that. He would have needed to be able to pretend he wasn't involved. Her thoughts turned frantically to other possible candidates. Drew? She seemed incapable of such deception or such artistry. No, she seemed too genuinely thrilled by the "discovery." Who else was close enough? Nicholas? He was capable with a pen; that was certain. It occurred to Lydia that he had even had access to her poetry—but not that poem. No one knew about that poem but Frank. And how could young Nicholas have even conceived of such a scheme, especially knowing how much it would hurt her? Impossible. Perhaps it was someone else connected to the university—a student or someone else? Someone who would show up later wanting credit or money to remain silent.

Her heart beat wildly with a dozen emotions. Frank had filled the house with people toasting his victorious discovery, while she was forced to slink away like an unwanted pest. How much farther down was she going to let herself sink?

She twisted the door handle carefully and pulled it shut silently behind her. She would walk to Kathy's in town, or Veronica's, and one of them would drive her to a hotel. Or something. Although to let either of them and their husbands and children see her like this was unthinkable. Within a day, the whole town would know that something had happened.

Lydia walked blindly down her driveway and onto the street, quickly crossing to a narrow dirt road where she imagined she could think clearly. Nicholas. Of course she couldn't leave Nicholas to simply wander back unknowingly tomorrow to the emotional swamp of their home. And Nicholas, she could protect. So that's where she went—to Jack Kenilworth's home.

Through the darkness, she walked so rapidly that the over-stuffed bag and her purse banged painfully against her hip, but she was too removed from her body to care. She followed the lakeshore. When at last she neared the parkland that adjoined Jack's property, she climbed up through saplings, wild grass, shrubs, and sand, tossing both the gym bag and her purse up the hill ahead of her a few feet where the hill was steepest, then picking them up to toss them ahead again. On the top of the hill, she stood at a weary angle and stared at the lake, which was visible only as streaks of moonlit ink through the pines and oaks. She could barely catch her breath.

Had it been this way for her, for Mary Walker? Had she, too, been scrambling away from some man, only to end up separated forever from life itself?

A few hours earlier, in Jack's workshop, Nicholas and Jack had laughed over a series of mistakes Nicholas had made in calculations for a new set of boat lines. Mistakes so problematic that they would have led to the construction of a massive ship with ridiculous features, but Nicholas had caught them himself, just before Jack did. He told Jack that he was distracted, and Jack had said that was obvious, but that his distraction seemed to be one avenue to creativity. About then, Jack decided it was time for a break and made ham sandwiches that they ate as they sat at his kitchen table. When he opened two beers, Nicholas glanced up at him, flattered.

"Well, you aren't going home tonight, I figure," Jack said. "It'll help you sleep on that foldout bed."

"I've never had a beer before. It'll probably be easier to sleep here no matter what I'm sleeping on," Nicholas said, then bit into his sandwich.

Jack gave him time to say more if he wanted to, then asked, "Your mom doing okay?"

"I think she's happy. Yeah."

"Oh?" Jack studied the teen's face, but Nicholas didn't raise his eyes. "Well. That's good."

"Yeah."

"And your dad?"

"He's happy, too."

"Hmm." Jack felt his heart speed up. His curiosity was insistent; he felt an unpleasant flash of jealousy and found himself reluctant to let the subject drop. Had they already made up over the pulverized antiques? "What're they up to these days?"

Nicholas shrugged, taking a careful sip of his beer. "Well, right now, probably celebrating."

"Oh?"

"Dad found a poem written by Mary Walker. Finally." Nicholas flashed a smile at Jack.

"You're kidding. Where?"

"I guess she wrote it into some old book she owned. On the last page."

Jack sat back and took a long breath to collect himself. "Well, that beats all. And it's signed by Mary Walker? It's authentic?"

"Signed by Mary Walker. Yep."

"What exactly does the inscription say?"

"Umm. Mary S. Walker. 1940."

"Nineteen forty?"

"Yeah." Nicholas nodded. "That's what Dad said."

Jack dropped the front legs of his chair to the floor. "Nicholas, Mary Walker left Michigan in October of 1939. She was never seen again. She didn't write anything in 1940."

"That's what people thought. But apparently that's not the case." Nicholas took another bite of his sandwich.

"Has your mother or anyone else seen it? Is this a big deal at home?"

"Heck, yeah. Huge deal. Lots of people have seen it," he said, taking his glasses off to rub his eyes. "They think it's really hers. So."

"What does your mom say?" Jack asked.

"She's really happy," Nicholas said. "She hasn't seen it yet, though. I don't think. I haven't either, actually."

"Listen, Nick, I hate to be the voice of gloom, but...it *cannot* be true," Jack said, trying to remain calm.

"Why not?"

Jack shifted and looked at his watch, wondering if he could give Lydia a call. It would be strange, and it would be unwelcome, but this whole thing was going too far.

"Because Mary Walker wasn't alive in 1940," Jack said sternly. "I know this."

Nicholas's eyes met his. "*How* do you know?"

Jack gazed at him. He felt furious at Frank Carroll for persuading his own kid that his self-serving charade was so vitally important. Jack didn't want to be the one to burst everyone's bubble. But Christ almighty. A silly theory was one thing, but forgery and outright lies were quite another. "Are your parents at home tonight, Nick?"

He shrugged. "I don't know. Probably not. Like I said, I think they were going out someplace special."

"I think I should call your mother. I need to talk to her."

"Why?" Nicholas asked, emptying his hands and brushing off crumbs.

"Because there is information she should know. I tried to talk to your father a long time ago about these things. More than once. He wasn't interested because he's very specific about the kind of story he wants to find for Mary Stone Walker. It didn't matter then. But now it's gone too far."

"You mean because now my dad found what he wanted?" Nicholas's voice had an edge to it.

"No, of course not. *Because it isn't reality.* It isn't... I could explain the whole thing, but..."

Jack shook his head, sorry for Nicholas. He weighed the bulk of what he knew about the woman in question with what he ought to say to this boy who, in his opinion, should not even be involved in this drama.

"Well, how do you know anything?"

Jack locked his fingers together on the table and sorted his thoughts. He needed to be careful.

"It's very simple," Jack said. "I know she died. In 1939. I... know someone who knew her."

"That still doesn't mean anything," Nicholas said quickly. "It's all just speculation if you haven't seen her dead body."

Jack nodded. That was Frank's line. "I'll just talk to your mother. It's not too late."

"I don't think she'll be there," Nicholas insisted.

"Then I'll leave a message." Jack stood up, tossed his napkin onto his plate, and carried it to the sink.

"But..." Nicholas said, eyes wide.

"What?" Jack asked.

"I don't think Dad would like it if you were calling Mom," Nicholas said.

"I don't care if he likes it," Jack said with an irritated smile. "He doesn't get to write the whole story of everything that happens in your house. Does he?"

"But...he just hates you," Nicholas said, then looked alarmed at his own words.

"I don't actually care if he hates me, Nicholas," Jack said firmly but, he hoped, kindly enough to make Nicholas understand that nothing he said was going to make Jack flip out. "There are more important issues here. It really doesn't matter what he thinks or doesn't think about me or about Mary Stone Walker. There's a reality that is independent of his stories—or anyone else's, for that matter. Do you know what I'm saying?"

"Yes, I know what you're saying," Nicholas said rapidly. "But you don't know how he is. He'll be mean to Mom."

"Okay. You call her then, Nicholas," Jack said quietly. "Ask her to call you here. Then I'll talk to her. Is that fair?"

"In the morning," Nicholas countered.

Jack spread his arms, shaking his head. "All right. First thing tomorrow, you call your mother. You leave a message if no one answers. Because, Nicholas..."

"What?"

Jack waited for the boy to look up at him. When Nicholas lifted his eyes to Jack's, they were distinctly frightened.

"Being honest about all of this is going to make things better," Jack said sincerely. "I promise. Maybe not in the first five minutes. But it will. In the end, it will."

30

Sweet Burning gave the red side, and the white
Is Meadow Milk.
Eat it, and you will taste more than the fruit:
The blossom, too,
The sun, the air, the darkness at the root,
The rain, the dew,

The earth we came to, and the time we flee
                    ~ Louise Bogan (1897–1970), "The Crossed Apple"

A thread line of bloody red rode the western horizon, and Jack stared into it as intensely as if he expected that lingering seam of water and sky to give birth to something he needed. From a certain perspective, it could be said that this whole dilemma was his fault. He thought of how much he despised Frank Carroll for his marathon of foolishness. No, this wasn't Jack's fault, but he might have stopped it. His thumb flicked at the matchbook in his right hand. He shook his head, eyes narrowed toward the swelling darkness.

"Fuck." He kicked one foot against the blanket of pine needles underfoot and pulled a pack of cigarettes from his shirt pocket. He'd been relieved to find the stupid things in his coat closet. He'd thought there were some there, but then he'd tried to forget. It was always crazy people that drove him back to smoking.

The night was clear. It was cold. He lit a cigarette and paced very slowly. After ten minutes or so, he heard a shuffling, thumping sound. He jerked his gaze up toward the dune ridge trail and saw nothing. He glanced back at his house where the kitchen light was still the only one glowing. It didn't look like Nicholas was up.

The question now was exactly what to say to Lydia, who was already pressing him for what he knew about the past. There was no need to dump all the gory details out, no need for him to harm the memory of anyone. But he'd never been skilled at carving half-truths from his knowledge. Silence he could handle, and that was usually his choice.

Thumping and shuffling again countered the rhythmical shush of water below, this time accompanied by the faint note of a voice. He heard his name, and then from behind a line of trees and moon shadows, Lydia appeared.

"Jack?" she said again, sounding uncertain. What was she carrying?

"Lydia?" He walked toward her, his arm out for the bag that seemed to be pulling her over. He lifted it from her, tossed his cigarette down, and tried to see her face. "What are you doing here? Did you walk?"

She coughed as she nodded.

"I had to. Frank has my car keys. But I couldn't stay there with him another minute. He's…" She was panting for breath. "He's gone too far this time. He's lost his mind."

He let her walk in silence, leading her toward the barn, and when they reached the open room, he strode to his worktable and set down her bag. He was about to turn on the overhead shop lights but thought the better of it and felt around the shelf beneath the worktable for his kerosene lantern. He lit the wick and looked at Lydia, whose features were distorted by something he didn't have time to interpret before she covered her face with her hands and shook with weeping.

Instinctively, he reached his arms around her body to hold her. In the presence of her pain, his mind groped the darkness for what to say, what to do. He couldn't have said how much time passed in this way or when she finally began to slump away from her brittle tension and let her hands fall from her face. When at last she exhaled with a shudder of distress, he pulled back from her.

"Come on, sit down," he said, and they walked to a couch, where she sank into the green tweed cushions.

"I'm sorry to come here, Jack. I didn't know what else to do. I wanted to be near Nicholas. And also you, I admit."

"I'm glad," he said quietly. After a couple of minutes, he stood up. "I'll be right back."

In his office, he dug out a quart of whiskey, set the bottle on the desk, and waited for his storm of thoughts to ease up. With deliberate slowness, he selected two glasses and walked back to the couch, stooping down in front of Lydia, whose hands were loosely locked between her knees. She raised her eyes to his.

"I'm going to pour you a drink," he said, setting the glasses down, unscrewing the bottle, and pouring. "Not because I want you to spill your guts and tell me everything on your mind." He gave her a small smile. "It's just to calm your nerves. Think of it as medicine."

He held the glass to her and she took it.

"Thanks, Doc."

She tried to smile but looked beat up. When Dolly had been a mess so many times after Craig died, she had leaned against Jack on the couch in the house, watching movies, basketball games, anything. He'd talked easily about nothing, feeling that every word, every laugh from Dolly was a victory, a step of healing. But Dolly had always been like a sister. Jack's feelings for Lydia were more complicated.

Lydia took a sip of whiskey and slumped down farther. Jack poured himself a drink and sat next to her, careful to leave space between them.

"My life's a farce, Jack," she said at last. "That sounds dramatic. But in the truest sense, my life is a farce. I am a woman pretending she has a loving husband that she's helping in his work. But really I'm just aiding his lustful delusions about an imaginary lover and telling myself lies about it."

Jack could think of nothing to say. She looked at him, then away, taking another small sip of whiskey.

"Now he claims that he's discovered a poem by Mary Stone Walker," she said. "Not in the furniture. Not in any one of the hundreds of items crammed into our chaotic barn or in the junk he's been insanely scrutinizing for almost two decades. He found this poem in a used book. Just *happened* to find it in a box of junk books from Brad Kramer. The guy who owns Jacob's Tavern and Books."

Jack stared into his glass. Frank didn't strike him as the sort of guy with any artistic skill. He couldn't imagine him pulling off a forgery. Maybe he'd managed to persuade a talented student who was captivated by the tale. Jack had a flash of the adoring looks he had seen on some of the young female students' faces at Frank's readings. "You've seen the poem?"

"No. *I* still haven't seen it. But tonight we had guests over at the house. And he read it. Performed it, you could say. There at the dining room table we all sat, listening, eating the silly shortcake I baked for his special occasion." A brief cry broke into her speech. "I'm such a fool! He read it to us all, but he'd already shared it with just about everyone else there. Everyone but me. I could have stopped this disaster if I'd only seen it. But of course he didn't show me, because I would have ruined everything."

"Jesus," Jack murmured.

"I'm getting used to his…meanness. But the poem…" She took a gulp from her glass, giving little shakes of her head.

Jack waited for a moment, expecting her to mention the date and her own disbelief. He didn't know anyone except Frank Carroll who still truly believed Mary Stone Walker had gone on to live incognito as an active poet. It was an entertaining notion and a lingering question in White Hill, her hometown, but Walker was too minor a poet, too brief and unknown a life for the masses to still be wondering what happened to her.

Lydia turned her eyes toward him.

"Yes...the poem?" Jack prompted.

"The poem he read out loud... It was mine."

Jack didn't know what she meant. "You mean he was kidding around?"

"No!" she cried. "Not kidding around. He read a poem that I wrote—*to him* in 1983—and said it was written by Mary Stone Walker." She held up her hands. "My poem... He read it as if it were Mary Walker's."

Jack was still confused. "You mean he was passing it off as hers? He actually told them she wrote it?"

"Exactly. I confronted him in the kitchen, and he acted like I'm insane. Like I'm a liar. Like I was just trying to screw things up for him. He said he'd never seen it before it just appeared in this book, but I'm telling you, no one else even knew about it but him. And it was important."

Jack stared into the dim recesses of the barn. "Do they believe him? Do they think it's real, these other people?"

"Yes! Some local scholars have looked it over, and even some librarian at the Library of Congress saw a facsimile of the page where it's inscribed. They all think it's genuine. It's the talk of Carson Community College."

Jack considered this. "So we know it's not authentic."

She emitted a guffaw. "Of course. Obviously." She turned to him. "You don't think I'm making this up, do you?"

"No." He shook his head emphatically. "No, I know you aren't making it up. Lydia, listen. You've got to tell him that it can't be authentic."

"I did tell him!"

"But, I mean, the facts—"

"Oh, I've lost all my credibility. He has shut me out. I said…" She stared vacantly and seemed to lose her train of thought. "Do you know what it's like to have someone betray you like that, Jack?" Her voice wavered, and she shook her head. "It's like I don't even exist. It's like I have no personhood to him."

"Lydia." Jack drank his whiskey down. "There are things you can tell him that are inarguable."

"Like what? There's no official dead body, so every imaginable outcome is still a possibility, and that man is willing to believe any notion that crosses his mind—"

"I know. I know his position on the subject. I've heard it before."

"So you *have* talked with him about this?"

"I'll tell you," Jack said, trying to sound reassuring, but also wondering just how much he really needed to say if the forgery was so clearly a fraud. To the academics, and even to Nicholas, he would come off as a troublemaker at this point. "I approached him a few times, but he always cut me off immediately. If it would help, I'll tell you what I tried to tell him, but…just remember: I did offer, and he wasn't interested."

Lydia's expression did not change and he couldn't read it. "What do you know?"

"I told him that my grandfather knew Mary," Jack began, and his heart thumped harder. "What I didn't get a chance to tell Frank was what he really needed to hear. He just didn't want to."

"He refused to listen to you?"

"Well, yeah, I think it's fair to say that. I don't make a habit of speaking to the backs of men who've just dismissed me."

"So he was rude."

"That isn't the point." Jack felt irritated at the mere thought of Frank's condescending face. "There are things I would have shown him if he had cared to have a serious conversation."

"Like what?"

"I had not shown anyone anything to that point, or ever discussed any of this, because I promised I never would. A very serious promise, mind you, one of those deathbed commitments, Lydia. And it would have been bad for everyone involved if the story got out."

Jack had a sudden realization that had surfaced before, but he had shoved it away: this emotionally drained woman, who'd come to him more than once for help, could logically blame him for everything. Her husband's fantasy had torn up her life, and all along, through every passing year of Frank's obsession, Jack had known the truth. Of course Lydia would blame him. Why wouldn't she?

"I told my father I would respect my grandfather's vows. If I hadn't, and if my father before me hadn't, there might have been a lawsuit, or…I don't know, maybe even murder. The Evans family is a vindictive, violent bunch. That much of what Frank says is true."

"Murder?"

"The Evanses could be ruthless, my grandfather said. The grudge they held against Mary Walker for disappearing is legendary. I'm sure you've heard that. But the details of the story… They're ugly, and it won't help anyone to know about them at this point. Let's just discuss the bottom line."

He stood up and moved reluctantly toward the photo of his grandfather's fishing boat on the wall. On the floor beneath it, an eighty-year-old toolbox sat inside an even older crate stamped Stratton Bros., Greenfield, Mass. It was his grandfather's last box of prized possessions, a cherished few items that had survived the twenty years of sorting that took place after his wife's death and before his own.

Ordinarily, Jack kept the crate in his house, double-locked in a closet. People would steal anything, his dad always said, though Jack had never been robbed. But he'd brought the box up here a week ago, planning to show Nicholas the beautiful Negus pelorus, an instrument for taking relative bearings at sea, and the two nineteenth-century sextants in their cherrywood boxes. He had even hoped to teach both Lydia and Nicholas how to use the devices in those bright, future days he had foolishly allowed himself to imagine, when he would instruct them on everything they'd need to know to sail the Great Lakes.

He lifted the sextants out and set them on the floor. Who was he kidding? Nicholas and Lydia, both of them, would not only resent his secrecy, but also kick him out of their lives forever when they realized he'd been sitting on the facts that would have awakened the lummox to reality. There had to be some way out of this confession he'd set himself up for here. Lydia could never understand how he'd wrestled with the issue. For *years*. He'd never be able to make her see how his family and his principles mattered so much that to betray them would permanently damage some essential structure in him. People don't think that way anymore. No, they expect you to be what they want you to be. If you aren't, there's something wrong with you, and you become expendable.

The complicating element here in 1999 was that Jack had had no idea Frank Carroll was making such a fucking mess of his life over his Mary tale. And if that rainstorm hadn't driven Nicholas to his barn, Jack still wouldn't know. He wouldn't know that Frank Carroll had based his entire academic career on it *and* planted it at the center of his home life. How could Jack have conceived of such a phenomenon?

From the spattering of Frank Carroll lectures he'd attended or heard about over the years and the occasional blurb in the paper, Jack had thought it was a hobby for the guy, an entertainment. His own distaste for the bullshit of it was, he guessed, largely because he identified more with the pretty girl he grew up with than her arrogant husband. Not to mention a strong sense of Mary Walker being a real person who deserved an accurate, unromanticized biography or none at all. Jack had never wanted to submit himself or the memory of his grandfather to need-less town gossip, and he still thought it was wrong to do so. However, his silence would perpetuate the suffering of these two people he had stumbled into caring about.

From the crate Jack lifted the plastic bag thick with the letters, postcards, and other papers his grandfather had valued through the end of his life, and he carried it to the couch. Lydia had stretched out, one arm bent under her head, her knees pulled up toward her chest, her eyes closed. He sat down gently and, with a change of heart, tucked the bag out of view under the couch.

"You're back," she said lifelessly. "I think I drifted off for a second. Were you gone long?"

"A couple of minutes. I was looking for the papers I want to show you," he improvised.

"It doesn't make any difference," she said. "It's not fixable. You said it yourself. Frank doesn't want to hear anything that doesn't fit his story. And I can't accept him passing off one of my poems as hers. Our life together is over."

"Lydia," Jack said, guilt pricking his mind. "Listen. The one fact that matters most is that she did not live past 1939."

"Yes, that would discredit this document. Since my word means nothing. But…what makes you sure?"

Parsing up the past into what was harmful to discuss and what was not, he suddenly couldn't think at all. "It's a long story."

Lydia sighed heavily, wearily. "Jack. I have time. I have waited almost two decades for a genuine new fact to surface. Please tell me what you know."

She sat up, and his gaze caught in hers. He couldn't imagine that a man who'd fallen in love with those eyes would prefer the imagined eyes of a dead woman. "My grandfather knew that she died. It's a very unhappy story."

"I understand it's not happy. I'm not surprised." After a pause she added, "Don't you think you've borne the weight of your grandfather's knowledge alone long enough?"

Jack's gaze darted to her face, sure he heard judgment in her voice. "Don't forget, Lydia, it wasn't mine to share. My grandfather promised her that he would never, ever tell anyone what she'd done or where she went." He started to bend down to reach for the bag, then gripped his hands on his knees instead, feeling the burn of old anger. "I did not ask to be in this position. But I don't believe that just because someone publishes poetry, their life belongs to others. Even after they're dead."

"I agree. But…"

"But what? The only reason I even considered telling your husband anything was because…well, because he was your husband, frankly. And because of the little bit I knew of you from when we were kids, I didn't like to think of you being made a fool of." He looked at her straight on. "How could I know he was making such an enterprise out of the question? That he was tormenting you and Nicholas with his…his self-serving fantasy?"

"I don't think it was intended to be torment, Jack," she said evenly. "He's a scholar. It's one of the things scholars do. They become obsessive in their quests. He wanted to save Mary from obscurity—"

"Christ, Lydia! Why are you still defending him? He wanted to make a name for himself through a tale that he became married to. He wanted to live in a romantic story about a woman with a certain mystery and appeal around her, simply for what it would do *for him*. For his career! And if you don't see that, I don't know how to show you."

"Well." Her face tensed, and she tightened her body into a smaller form on the couch.

"He did not have the truth of Mary Stone Walker's life in mind, or he would have sought more information from people that knew her. Like me. Okay, he took a disliking to me for some reason. But there are numerous others. No, real life did not fit into Frank Carroll's mission. He wanted her life to turn out to be a thrilling page-turner with a nice stack of literature he could publish, right? Best way to ensure that was to stick to partial truths. But we don't get to design the story of other people's lives merely from plots we like…making devils and angels out of ordinary men and women, whatever suits us, to hell with the messiness of real human beings' lives."

He grew agitated as these thoughts that he'd repeated in his own head many times emerged as spoken words. "I think he should have at least *sensed* that maybe there was something dark and not at all that glorious about her…disappearance. But no, that wasn't in his viewfinder. He wouldn't peek past his own version of Mary Stone Walker, even when I offered him significant suggestions that I knew more. He didn't want it, and that should tell you a lot about the man. He didn't want *her*, not the real her. Just like he doesn't want the real you."

He was shocked to hear his own final words. "I'm sorry. That was out of line."

"Yes, it was. And how would you have any idea about that?" she asked shakily. "Marriage is a complicated thing."

"Oh, yes, so I see. Marriage is a complicated thing. Like Mary's, for instance." He pulled out a cigarette with a wry laugh. "Angel of White Hill now, but in her own time, and in her own *home*—" He couldn't go on. The self-censorship on this subject was too old. He lit his cigarette, inhaled, then blew the smoke away from Lydia. "There's no end to the complications of marriage, it seems to me."

He stared away from her, fully aware that she was probably also looking away from him.

"My grandfather talked about this stuff to my father because he was tormented by the fact that Mary had come to him in a time of crisis, and that because he cared, he ended up playing a part in her premature death. Eventually he couldn't keep it in. He completely blamed himself. Completely. Furthermore, Granddad knew firsthand how jealous Bernard Evans would be that he'd ever even spoken with Mary, and he knew how violent that man could be. Bernard Evans had put at least three other lumbermen in the hospital, can you imagine? His own employees. And then there was the whole clan of Evanses, and Granddad was sincerely afraid that one of them would take revenge on one of us." Jack looked at her without seeing her.

"Do you think I was anxious to let that demon loose? And how could it be right under any circumstance for my grandfather, Robert Kenilworth the fisherman, to go down in local history as the bad guy in a story about the beautiful poet Mary Stone Walker?" He grunted. "I know this town. That's exactly what would have happened. What *will* happen if I open my mouth. And then maybe I'll die at the hand of some pissed-off Evans prick. Who knows? People are insane."

He could hear his own heart pounding.

"Wow, Jack," Lydia said quietly after a few moments. "I see why you've wanted to keep this to yourself." For minutes neither of them spoke. The kerosene lamp hissed softly as both of them stared into the barn's shadows.

"Okay," Jack said. "I knew this stuff and wanted to protect Granddad. But still, Lydia, there were facts out there you all could have found. Even that scrapbook you brought to me had bits of information that relate to Walker. And that thing found you; you didn't even have to search! You might not have been able to tell what things meant without a whole lot of work or talking to someone like me, but her story is out there."

Jack walked to his worktable and pulled the scrapbook out from under a magazine, setting it on his knees, next to Lydia.

"Here's one example. Look." He opened it to the page with an article about Koslowski Boat Works. "This is from December 1939." He read: "'Damage during inhospitable October winds left this fishing boat in need of Peter Koslowski's expertise.' Well, 'this fishing boat' is the *Fata Morgana*." Jack nodded toward the photograph of his grandfather's boat. "You can see." He pointed at the old newspaper clipping. "I can tell. Look. You can see the word *Morgana*."

"What is the connection to Mary Walker?" Lydia had pushed herself up and leaned against Jack's arm to see what he was pointing to.

He shook his head. He'd stepped right into the story he didn't want to tell. "I don't know, Lydia."

"You brought it up! You said this photograph would have told me something. Well, what? Was your grandfather on Lake Michigan with Mary?"

He looked at her. "So you see my point. That question would be a good place to begin. Frank could have learned much, much more over the years by looking for things like this. By digging up and identifying the pieces of her life's history in this little world of White Hill."

"And now? Can't you share the true history now? *What happened to her?* Please, Jack, help me."

The lateness of the hour and the emotional pain of the night had drained Lydia's face of color, and her features seemed almost blurred.

"Frank won't want it," Jack said flatly. "He won't even be able to hear it. I'm sorry, but it's pretty obvious to me that that's the way it is. And I'd prefer to keep as much of my grandfather's information as I can to myself."

"You can't do this to me!" Lydia's voice bent with despair. "I should at least tell Frank that you know for certain she died in 1939. Don't you think so? There must be some kind of proof that you can share with us."

"Yes, I have her death certificate."

"Would you agree to show it to him? Maybe he'll understand that this will save him from humiliation later."

"Yes, I'll do that."

"Okay." She took a deep breath and pressed her palms on her thighs. "Thank you. I'll call him. He needs to see once and for all that the basic premise of his search is false. And that there may be more detailed information available through you." Jack thought he saw hope in her face.

"You do that. I'm tired of the whole thing, and I'm sad to see what it's done to you and your son."

He finished his whiskey but felt no relaxation from it.

"If anything can make him give up this charade, surely proof of her death will," Lydia murmured. "Surely it will."

Jack nodded, but the hope he had held for that outcome had dwindled as he'd spoken and thought about the hidden past. It was too ugly a tale. No one wanted any of it. Hell, even Nicholas would be disappointed. Jack ground his teeth and wished Frank Carroll would vanish, too.

"What time is it?" Lydia's voice wavered.

He looked at his watch. "Going on midnight."

"I'll call right now." She stood up slowly. "Will you talk to him? After I do?"

"Sure." He nodded, staring at the floor, and thought of all the things he'd like to say to the son of a bitch. But he would stick to the facts he had documentation for, no more, no less, and no commentary. Let the chips fall where they would. "The phone's on the wall by that worktable."

Lydia moved lightly across the room, and Jack watched her. He stood and walked to the door at the far end of the barn, pushed it open two feet, and stared through the still-bare tree boughs and pines at the darkly flickering lake.

31

We shall remember that a new moon sank
Into a quiet lake, or that a bough
Of leaves sighed over us; not lips that drank
For the last time, or eyes that slowly filled,
Or stricken voices muted on a word,
Laughter that groped and faltered and was stilled.

~ Mildred Amelia Barker, "Not Again"

Mary took the colored fishing floats out of a wooden crate and turned it upside down to sit on it, avoiding Robert's eyes as she spoke. At first he sharpened his knives as he listened, but then he stopped and leaned against the worktable, watching her profile.

"I'm ashamed to admit it, but I don't fully understand the science of my own body." She spoke furtively. "It's terrible commentary on my education and on our society, but I suppose it's also because I had no one. I didn't have women in my life when I was growing up. The point is, there is no way to explain all of these things I am experiencing except by admitting to myself that—" She broke off, and when she turned her eyes toward him, they were filled with tears. "Oh God, Robert, what am I going to do?"

He wanted to make sure he understood. His heart beat faster even as her words made it feel heavy.

"Please explain, Mary."

"Oh. *You know.*" Elbows propped on her knees and hands clasped together in front of her mouth, she tried to speak, then covered her face with her hands. "I'm pregnant. I'm just sure that I am."

Robert stood and looked out the window, peering through the woods toward his house, then stepped outside briefly and scanned the road and dunes. It seemed there was no danger of anyone interrupting them. He stooped beside her and put an arm around her shoulders. Instantly she gripped him as if for her life, fingers digging into his back. He felt her shake against him, felt the fabric of his shirt quickly dampen with her tears, and he closed his eyes. She smelled of cloth, soap, and pine.

"You know how I feel about my life!" she cried, pulling back to look at him. "I can't do it. Robert, *I just can't do it.*"

He watched and said nothing. A child inside her. A child of Mary's that would come into this world. Of course she was afraid. But his first thought was that he could help her. Perhaps he could even help her raise the child somehow. Yes. He would, he must. Mary's child... The thought of it suffering Bernard's cruelty the way that Mary did was dreadful, unthinkable. And he did not believe that a child would change the man unless he *wanted* to alter his behavior. Robert did not know any men of Bernard's violent temperament who had ever learned self-control. He took her shoulders and looked straight into her eyes.

"Mary, listen. You must try to think differently. I will help you do what you have to in order to take care of yourself and your child. I'll help you find a way."

"*What?* Help me how? You can't help me!"

Robert thought she almost laughed, and her expression was a stubborn mix of hopelessness and anger.

"That isn't true. Together we can figure something out." His hands tightened on her shoulders, and his voice toughened.

"You can't give up so easily. These are *lives* you're talking about. A child's. Your own."

"Give up? *Give up?*" She threw his hands off. "I have lived with this man for five years, and tried and tried to believe it would get better. He gives me just enough kindness that I, like a fool, keep hoping. But he's a brute, Robert, and he'll never think of me as anything more than his chattel! God, I would think you of all people would see that."

He stiffened. She was pushing him to step into the drama of her tragedy, but he would not be a pawn to her tears or her temper. He would only help in a way that might lead her to a saner life and better health. He stood up and held his hand down for her to take.

"What?" She looked up at him pitifully. "Do you want me to leave?"

"Yes." He tried to keep emotion out of his voice. "I will help you take care of a child, Mary. I swear to you I will. I'll find a way. I will help you get off the morphine and build the life you want, but I can't just watch you give in to fears and weakness. I won't abandon you, but I will not help you continue to run from your own responsibility."

"*My responsibility?* Fine, Robert!" She stood, falling into a storm of angry tears. "But I don't see how I—*or you*—can do any of those things. None of them. They are *impossible*. Your ideals can't change the way things really are in this world."

"Changing Bernard into a gentle man may be impossible. But the things I have just said I will do—the things you can do for yourself to make your life better—are not impossible. I don't believe that." He fought to maintain an even tone of voice.

"But how—" She lost her breath to sobs. "How can you stand there and say that? You can't help me raise *my child*. You have a wife and child of your own! You can't pay for doctors to help me with the morphine or anything else when you are barely eking out a living. It's true! I don't know what patriarchal desire to control my actions you are speaking from. But if I listen to you, I will spend my life in misery and never, ever will my unborn poetry see the light of day."

As she spoke, her attitude exploded from chagrin to indignation. She glared at Robert.

"I thought you understood," she whispered venomously and turned to leave.

Reflexively, Robert lunged after her, putting his hand on the door to keep it shut. He was not finished.

"Listen to me, Mary. There is nothing in me that wants to control you." He spoke in a low tone. "It is something else that moves me...something you don't seem to understand yet."

She crossed her arms and waited, but he straightened, continuing to stare at her, and said no more. Their eyes locked for seconds upon seconds, at last softening, and Robert put his hands on either side of her face and pressed his lips to her forehead where her hair clung in damp strands against feverish skin. Then he held her head to his chest and closed his eyes.

"For over two years now I have listened to you, watched you in your life, and tried to help you," he said. "I know your struggles, and our moments together have not occurred without effect. You know this. That's why you come here to me. We have this between us. We're no longer powerless."

Robert Kenilworth's mind rarely left the realm of reason, but in this moment it was deluged with passion and a kind of wishful thinking that he had never experienced before, and he followed its buoyant seduction.

Her blue eyes, when she pulled back and looked into his, were grateful but sad.

"Oh, Robert. You're forgetting...you are forgetting Bernard. He will kill me. Or you. Or he will have me locked up in a mental asylum. If I don't conform to what he wants, he will kill my soul somehow. You can't stop that. Not if he knows where I am."

The concept of Bernard Evans assuming the right to snuff out this woman, who was barely more than a girl and whose soul was not anyone else's to decide the fate of, jarred loose Robert's inner control, and he felt a seething hatred and rage that frightened him. He pulled her against his chest, his eyes searching the twilight for some consolation that wasn't there, his heart rocked by confusion.

"We will find a way to keep you safe, Mary, you and your child. We *will*...because we *must*. Go back to your house," he said. "And please think. As I will."

He dropped his hands and turned away. And just as Robert's wife, Elizabeth, entered the wooded path that led to her husband's workshop, Mary closed his door behind her and raced home against the red sun, through the trees.

32

WHITE HILL, MICHIGAN——APRIL 1999

Gather together, against the coming of night,
all that we played with here...

~ Sara Teasdale (1884–1933), "In a Darkening Garden"

Lydia dialed her home phone number from the phone in Jack's workshop, letting it ring seven times until the answering machine clicked on and she heard her own recorded voice. She hung up, stared at the wall, then picked up the receiver again and redialed. After six rings she heard Frank's muddy "Hello."

"Frank."

"Lydia?" His tone was confused. "Where are you?" She heard him shift around. "It's after midnight. I thought you were here. Where are you calling from?"

"Listen, Frank. There's something very important I need to tell you. Are you awake?"

"*Am I awake?* What's going on?"

"I have found a source of firsthand information about Mary Stone Walker. It's extremely significant."

"Lydia—"

"Listen."

"No, you listen. Where exactly are you?"

"It doesn't matter. Could you please just let me say what I have to say?"

He sighed heavily and said nothing.

"There is written evidence available right here in White Hill of what happened to Mary Stone Walker. Evidence that will prove she could not have composed a poem in 1940...since you aren't willing to believe me about the authorship of the one in your book."

"Oh my fucking God. You're just dead set on killing this document, aren't you? What... Are you calling from a pay phone at a bar or something? Hanging out with your friends and plotting against me?"

"Oh, yeah, that's my style, Frank." Lydia glanced over her shoulder. Jack was no longer sitting on the couch. She spoke quietly. "You've got to retract that poem. Somehow, we have to make everyone understand that it was a mistake." He was silent. "They'll understand. I'm sure we can make them understand. And you will have new information to offer. Brand-new information to offer to the academic world and to incorporate into your book."

She was thinking that Frank wouldn't even have to say who forged the poem since it could have been anyone really. The only thing necessary was to get the information Jack possessed in front of the right people, and surely Jack would agree to that. Only a few things needed to be said.

"Frank?"

"I don't know why you're doing this."

"I'll come home right now and bring you the evidence—"

"I don't want to see some stupid thing you've come up with out of the bowels of your imagination."

"I have not *made anything up*." She hesitated. She had to tell him where the information came from. "In fact, I am waiting to hear all of the details until I am with you. Jack Kenilworth has documents in a box of items his grandfather left behind, and he knows—"

"So that's where you are? You're at Kenilworth's?" He gave a harsh laugh. "That's priceless."

"Frank, he knows the truth. His grandfather was close to her—"

"*Lydia. Quit.* I've heard enough. First, you wanted to tell me you wrote the poem, and now you've run off to your con-man friend, and you're calling me to say that this White Hill nobody knows the whole story. His grandfather happened to have had a secret relationship with the beautiful Mary Stone Walker, Lydia? Come on! Oh, and by the way he has never discussed this with anyone before, but he wants to tell me right now, tonight. Just quit, would you? Give it up. I've made an important discovery that gives absolute credence to my theory, and apparently you can't handle it."

"You're completely wrong."

"Look. I don't know what your plans are, but I sincerely hope they don't include returning to this house tonight."

Lydia heard the clatter of his phone and stood motionless with the receiver at her ear for a long time in the thick silence of the dead line, because she couldn't bear to hang up and turn to Jack. Her skin crawled with humiliation. Silently, she replaced the receiver but leaned her head against the wall, eyes closed, and didn't turn around for several minutes.

"Jack?"

The voice came from darkness at the barn door. Lydia jumped and turned around.

It was Nicholas, who saw her at the same moment she saw him.

"Mom? What are you doing here?" He moved slowly toward her.

Lydia tried to compose her features as she heard Jack approaching.

"What are you doing up, Nicholas?" she asked as calmly as she could.

"I… Dad just called. To Jack's." He pointed toward the house, his face alarmed. "Why are you here? What's wrong?"

"What's up, Nicholas?" Jack asked, approaching them.

"My dad just called you." Nicholas's eyes flickered toward Lydia, then back to Jack.

Lydia tried to keep panic out of her voice. "What did he say?"

"I answered it because the phone was right by my head," Nicholas said.

"He wanted to talk to me?" Jack asked.

"I guess."

"Nicholas, what did he say?" For a moment, Lydia hoped that Frank might have asked to meet Jack.

"He said... He said for me to tell Jack to stay out of his business."

Lydia's hands fell to her sides. "Didn't he say anything else? Nicholas, didn't he say he wanted to talk to one of us?"

Jack put his hand on Nicholas's shoulder. "He's just upset. It isn't anything for you to worry about. Your mom was trying to talk to him about something that he feels strongly about."

"But why? I mean, what did he feel so strongly about?" Nicholas asked suspiciously as he stepped backward, away from Jack. "What did he mean about staying out of his business?"

"He's angry about things that have to do with the distant past and his own ideas about it," Lydia said recklessly. "He doesn't want to see evidence of the objective truth. He wants his fantasy just as he likes it."

Jack let his gaze rest on her, and the humiliation burned all over again. She wanted to hug Nicholas to her, even as her son looked at her with something she could not read—was it anger? In the last few hours, life had turned inside out for her, and the one thing she could believe in, that she must be able to believe in, was her son. Frank could steal her poem, deny her credibility, and tell her not to come home, but he couldn't take her son.

Could he? What if he started telling everyone she was crazy? What if he told Nicholas she was insane, and Nicholas believed him because for his entire life, he'd cherished the hope of finding Mary Stone Walker's work and now Lydia seemed to be trying to tear holes in this dream come true for no apparent reason but jealousy? Her mind sparked and spun until she had to press her hand to her forehead. She walked to the couch to sit down.

"Nicholas, come sit with me for a minute. Would you please?"

With obvious reluctance, he walked to the couch and sat next to Lydia, not meeting her eyes.

"You know the poem Dad found, Nicholas?"

He nodded, still avoiding her face.

"Well. The truth is…Mary Stone Walker didn't write it. Jack knows that she died in 1939. His grandfather knew her."

Nicholas clenched his hands, and his breathing grew audible.

"I know it's disappointing, Nicholas," she said anxiously, reaching for his hand, but Nicholas pulled away.

Nicholas's gaze turned up toward the ceiling of the loft. Lydia thought she saw tears in his eyes. His voice was small. "I don't understand how you can know that."

Jack spoke. "It's a long story, Nicholas, but Mary was a troubled person who needed help, and my grandfather was a friend to her. In White Hill, he was her closest friend, and he knew what happened to her at the end."

"But how could she die?" Nicholas said with frustration. "She was young."

"Sixty years ago, more people died young than they do today," Jack said quickly.

"But what difference does your grandfather's story make? It still doesn't mean anything," Nicholas said, his jaw set.

"Nicky, of course it means something," Lydia said with alarm. "Sometimes there are *facts*. Testimonies. Documents." She searched his eyes. "If she died in 1939, then the poem in Dad's book isn't really hers."

"How do you know for sure?" Nicholas's voice rose. "Jack's stuff might be fake. Or maybe the date on the poem is wrong. You know, if she was sick, maybe she didn't know what she was writing."

"That's not very likely," Lydia said firmly.

"But it's possible," Nicholas said stubbornly. She stared into the face that did not remind her of her husband, even though his denial did.

"No, it really isn't," Lydia said.

"In the end she wasn't well, Nicholas. She wasn't writing much of anything," Jack said.

"You don't know!" Nicholas said angrily. "How would you know? That was sixty years ago! You weren't even born."

"Nicholas, you're sounding as close-minded about this as your dad." Lydia tried not to sound bitter.

"*So what?* I am his son," Nicholas said. "I don't understand why you came here. I don't see why you had to find this out. *Why?*"

She gazed into his eyes, confused and riled by his anger. "*Why?* You mean you think we should just pretend that she didn't die, like we have been all along, even though we know differently now?"

"I don't see why this had to happen," Nicholas said desperately, his voice breaking at the end of his sentence.

Jack gazed at him.

"It's okay, you know, Nicholas," Jack said. "The truth is a good thing in the long run. Things will be all right. Even though it doesn't feel like they will be right now."

"No, they won't," Nicholas said certainly, shaking his head. He glared at Lydia. "You didn't want Dad to find a poem. I thought you did, but you didn't. Otherwise, you wouldn't have come here tonight. You would have just been happy with the way things were going."

"I came here tonight, Nicholas," Lydia said, "because the poem in that Sara Teasdale book is mine. I wrote it."

Nicholas shook his head.

"Do you hear me, Nick?" She pulled his arm.

He mumbled something.

"Nicholas, do you hear—"

"*Yes!* I hear you!" He whipped his face up toward her, his eyes bright with tears and something she didn't recognize.

"Do you know what this means?"

"What does it mean?" he said belligerently.

"Well! It means it… It's obvious. It means it couldn't be Mary Walker's poem, of course. It means it's a forgery."

Nicholas turned away.

"It means that we have to bring the truth out." Lydia felt flustered. "I told your dad—"

"You told him it's your poem?" Nicholas faced her. "What did he say?"

"Well, he wants to believe it's hers. He claims he has never read it before."

"Maybe he hasn't," Nicholas said, as if this proved something important.

"But that doesn't change the fact that it is mine and not hers." Lydia glanced at Jack, whose gaze remained fixed on Nicholas.

"Why don't you just let him have it?" Nicholas said flatly. He was rigid, his hands locked together between his knees. "It'll make things better."

Lydia stared at him. She felt as if he'd slapped her.

"What's the worst that could happen?" he asked, his voice strange.

"You must be kidding. It's a lie. The worst that could happen? If I just went along with his delusion? Nicholas, people can't live like that without suffering negative consequences. That's what's been eating at this family for years. Your father's delusion, his worship of a dead woman, a *story* that he cares about more than real life. A story that it turns out isn't even true!"

"But no one would know but us. Right?" Nicholas voice sounded cold, and his face, when he looked at her, seemed hard and unreasonably determined.

She stood up, the whiskey and emotion making her vision swim.

"Lydia," Jack said, walking toward them. "Let me talk to Nicholas for a minute. Okay?"

Shaking, she strode silently a few feet away and crossed her arms, staring blindly into the barn's old rafters. It wasn't possible. Nicholas could not have been so thoroughly brainwashed that he, too, cared more about the myth than reality. Had Frank made Mary's life so huge, so glamorous, and so critical to their lives that her own son was ready to believe that they should do whatever was necessary to keep that fabulous story alive?

Through search after search, Nicholas had been by his father's side, hoping, and the woman's poems had been read in the house like Bible verses. Frank had established Mary Stone Walker's ghost in their family with a vitality that the rest of them had never been allowed to attain. Lydia gouged her fingers into her arms. It was absurd, but it was true. She was the only one who could have stopped it, and she had let it happen.

"We have a tricky situation here, Nicholas," she heard Jack say. She glanced back at them. He was seated cross-legged on the floor in front of Nicholas, who was staring at his hands. "Forgery is a crime. So someone has committed a crime by copying that poem into the book and signing Mary Walker's name to it."

A silence followed.

"Now, lots of times the forger is never discovered, as you probably know." Jack cleared his throat. "But it's a crime for a good reason. Because pretending that a document is a real piece of the past is like…like claiming that something happened that never did. And if we treat history like fiction or a game where we can move around the pieces, then we have no genuine history at all. No real sense of who we have been. Who we are."

Lydia wondered why he didn't just tell Nicholas the details, make him understand that his grandfather was a witness to the woman's death in 1939. Was he worried about Nicholas's feelings for Frank?

"A forged document could also be a lie in another way. It

could suggest that something didn't happen when it really did. Think about it. In this case, your mother wrote a poem. Now that poem is being presented as someone else's. So for all time, that poem would have another woman's name on it, and your mother would never, ever get the credit. Like she didn't live the life and do all the work to create it. You're an artist. Imagine what that would be like. I know that if someone claimed a boat I built was their own, it would really hurt. Piss me off royally, as a matter of fact, no matter what their reason was. You know?"

Lydia heard nothing from Nicholas.

"So here's a poem your mother wrote when she was a young woman. And I guess you've gathered from your father that every poem—like every drawing or every boat—is a work that matters, whether the person who created it is alive or dead. Whether or not they are a professor, a poet, a novelist, a fisherman, or a child. See what I mean? It's a product of someone's life, their time on earth."

After a few moments, Nicholas said, "So what do they do about forgery?"

"You mean as a crime? What's the punishment?" Jack's voice was still mild.

Lydia turned around slowly. Nicholas shrugged at Jack, then gave a nod, his eyes still cast down.

"Well, nothing if it's never analyzed. Which, of course, it never would be if the document were destroyed. Otherwise, I don't know exactly. But even more important than any legal consequences would be…" He paused and looked off to the side as if he thinking. "Well, you know, the sadness of the whole thing. The lie. Hard to live with a lie like that. Over time. Especially if it hurts someone you love. Better to have it out."

Nicholas inhaled deeply and seemed to hold his breath, his face stiff. Lydia's heart began to race. For a long time no one spoke. Nicholas glanced up at Lydia, then lowered his face to his hands.

"But what will happen to us—to all of us—if Dad never finds what he's been looking for?" he said plaintively. "I mean… everyone's so…miserable." He lowered his face again and his shoulders shook.

Lydia felt frozen, but she heard herself speak. "Nicholas…"

He continued to weep; she could hear him struggling against it. She rushed over and stooped down beside him.

"How? You couldn't have!" But disparate pieces of reality locked quickly together into the logic of Nicholas's forgery.

"No one would ever know, Mom!" He lifted his red, tear-streaked face and wiped his sleeve across his nose. "I thought you'd be happy. Happy to fool Dad with your poem. It's as good as her stuff. I'm sorry. I'm sorry. But I really thought that after all this time, it just had to be done…"

"Oh, Nicholas!" Lydia cried without thinking. "My God! Where in the world did you even find that poem?"

He didn't answer. She stooped down and tugged his arm away from his face. His eyes met hers, and they looked utterly crushed. It was a sight that pulled her own heart lower, and she sat down to think, but saw nothing in her mind but fog.

"That was a poem I wrote for your father. Did he put you up to this?"

"No! No, I…" His voice faltered.

"You what? How did you get your hands on that poem, Nicholas? It was his. I sent it to him before you were born, and he must have—"

"I found it," Nicholas blurted out. "It was in the attic in a box of his stuff. It was in an envelope. From you. I could tell it was from you."

"That poem meant a great deal to me," Lydia said faintly. "I was pregnant with you when I wrote it. He knew it meant a lot to me."

"No."

"What do you mean, no?"

"He never opened it." His voice was barely more than a whisper. "It was sealed shut. With sealing wax."

"What do you mean, he never opened it? He must have! We talked about it. Back then. He said—"

"It was sealed shut with sealing wax. *I* opened it, Mom."

"But…are you *sure*?"

He nodded. She had almost forgotten Jack was there. She glanced at him, but his face was turned away.

"I don't know what to think. He just pretended? All this time?" She shook her head and gazed blankly around. "I don't know what to think about any of this."

Then it occurred to her that a major part of her horror at his disregard earlier in the evening was unwarranted: Frank had *not* known the poem was hers. Now he could be told that Nicholas had done this, and he would finally see, not only that the poem was just what she'd said it was, but also that their son had been so agitated by the state of their marriage and family life that he had come up with this elaborate solution. A weird sense of relief ran through her. Frank would see that what she'd said was true and that she had not just been trying to destroy his dream. Some order and connection to him might be restored after all.

"Nicholas," she said firmly. "We're going to go home and explain everything to Dad. It will make things better."

He looked up, his face full of despair.

"Come on, Nick," she said with energy, trying to take his hand. "We'll go there right now, and when he sees what you have tried to do—for him, for all of us—he'll start to understand. Understand everything you've been going through."

"No, Mom! He won't!" Nicholas looked afraid. "He'll kill me!"

"Of course he won't. You are his son. It's the right thing." She tried to fill her voice with encouragement. "He doesn't want to lie. He just thought the poem was real. Truly. Now come on. If he gets mad at anyone, it will be me. Try not to worry. I will help you explain."

She stood and found that Jack was staring at her. "Lydia, maybe it would be better to wait on this. Wait until morning."

But Lydia couldn't bear to wait; she had to straighten everything out immediately. No, she couldn't let Frank's anger build one minute longer than necessary. She knew how he was once he got started on an idea. By tomorrow he would be unreachable.

"I don't think so, Jack. This is one of those situations that has to be addressed immediately. Would you be able to drive us to the house?"

"Yeah. Of course, but..." He stood up slowly. "But I can't just drop you off, okay? I'll wait down the street."

"No, no, really—"

"No, I mean it. It's okay. If it all works out, fine. I'll drive on home." He sighed, lifting his coat from the back of a chair. "If not, you know I'll be there."

"But, Jack." She didn't want to admit that Frank would become even angrier if he detected Jack's presence. "I'll get my keys and I'll have my Jeep, remember. I can leave quickly if I have to. It isn't as if I've never dealt with his anger before."

Lydia glanced at Nicholas, who stood with his arms drawn in straight and tight against his body, hands in his pockets. He looked cold and nervous as he passed her and walked out of the barn.

"Just drop us off, if you don't mind," she said, hurrying to follow Nicholas to the pickup truck. "We'll be fine."

Jack pulled out his keys and gazed at her, unsmiling. He didn't agree, and she didn't wait for him to, hurrying through the damp night air with the urgency of prey seeking cover.

33

Time for the pretty clay,
Time for the straw, the wood.
The playthings of the young
Get broken in the play,
Get broken, as they should.

~ Louise Bogan (1897–1970), "Kept"

A heavy silence in the truck persisted until they reached a corner two blocks from the house where Jack had to make the last turn. He stopped at the intersection and stayed there.

"Lydia," Jack said at last.

"Yes."

"We could still turn around and come back after a few hours of sleep."

"Yes, Mom." Nicholas came to life. "I really don't know what I'm going to say."

"You're going to tell Dad the simple truth, Nicholas. It isn't complicated. Hard, yes. I know. But you can just stick to facts, and I will be there at your side. Okay? Honesty is the shortest route to understanding, even if it's uncomfortable."

"Mom, he won't understand at all, ever," Nicholas stated, his teeth chattering.

"But it won't be any better in the morning," she said. "He'll brood about things, get more stubborn... No, it won't be any better if we wait. And he *does* have to know."

Nicholas turned his face toward the window again. Jack pressed the accelerator, and they slowly rounded the corner, inching along until the house came into view. They rolled past it and out of sight of its windows. Jack turned the truck off, and they all sat there without speaking.

"Okay," Jack said. "I'm going to wait here for an hour or so. Just in case...I don't know. Just in case."

"Open the door, Nicholas." Lydia's voice was not as calm now. "Thanks, Jack. Thank you so much for everything. As soon as we can, we'll let you know how it goes. The door, Nicholas."

Nicholas moved haltingly, as if the seat were sticky. The two of them walked through the darkness of the road, then onto the front lawn where the grass was long and damp, its spring growth not mown yet. She reached for the front doorknob and turned it. It was locked.

"Damn it," she whispered. "Okay, wait a minute, there's a key under here." She stepped down to the garden and turned a turtle-shaped pot over, retrieving a key. Nicholas stood behind her, shivering. "You wait in the living room, and I'll get Dad."

They walked inside, where the familiar smells of the house's furniture, books, and food wrapped around them like old friends.

"Oh, Mom, this isn't going to work," Nicholas whispered.

"Be brave, Nick."

She stood at the bottom of the stairs, hand gripping the banister, and called Frank's name. When he didn't answer, she called again. After a minute or two, they heard his weight on the upstairs floor, then he appeared at the top of the stairs.

"Oh, for God's sake, Lydia, what now? I hope you're here to apologize."

"I'm sorry, Dad," Nicholas said.

Frank gave a short laugh and began down the stairs. "Okay. One down."

"Nicholas has something important to explain. This is hard for him, so please try to open your mind and just listen."

Nicholas's face was rigid with fear. Frank crossed his arms and waited. The hall clock ticked like a rat with a hammer.

"Out with it, please. I'm tired." He yawned, ran his hand over his face, which was puffy and red, and looked like he had consumed a few extra drinks after the guests went home.

"Dad," Nicholas said with difficulty. "The poem by Mary Walker. It's... When I..." His breath was shallow. Lydia wondered if he would be physically capable of finishing a sentence. "Dad, I found..."

Lydia's chest filled with anger. "You've made your own son terrified of talking to you. Are you proud?"

"Dad, I wrote that poem in the book," Nicholas blurted.

"So now *you* wrote it? Just what do you two hope to gain from all of this nonsense?"

"Frank, I told you I *composed* the poem. What your son is trying to get out is that he found my poem and copied it into an old book because he thought that would make you happy. And you know why he found it? You know why you've never seen it before? Because I sent it to you in 1983...in a letter you never even opened. You *said* you opened it—long, long ago when it mattered—but you didn't."

Frank's face edged from sarcasm to wariness.

"It was a poem that I wrote when I was pregnant with Nicholas," Lydia pressed on. "I sent it to you from Boston, and you told me you'd read it. You actually *pretended* to discuss the contents. Said you didn't think much of it."

"I don't remember what night, what envelope—" Frank began.

"You don't remember," Lydia went on, "because it didn't matter to you. Not like things should matter if you love someone. Nick found it in an envelope that was still sealed shut with my sealing wax, with my seal."

Frank shuffled to a chair and sat down.

"I loved you, you know?" Lydia's voice quavered. "But you—"

"Hold it. Stop." Frank held up his hand, avoiding their eyes.

"There is no way," he said firmly, "that this boy could have created a forgery like that. If he had, it would be obvious." He raised his shoulders. "No, there's no way. You're both lying. I cannot fathom why. But perhaps *that* is what you should be honest about."

"Nicholas," Lydia said urgently. "Get the envelope."

"But Mom…"

"Don't you have it?" she asked with alarm.

"Yes! Of course I have it, but—"

"Then please go get it this minute."

He stood up and hurried toward the stairs.

When he returned to the living room, Frank and Lydia were staring away from each other in silence. Frank took the envelope from Nicholas's hand, briefly examining the address and postmark. He pulled out the paper and read, holding the sheet for a long time without speaking.

Lydia watched as a familiar, dark disappointment entered his features.

"Pulled a fast one, didn't you, Nicholas Carroll?" Frank said after a long time. His voice was hoarse and low. "Quite a job you did, huh?" He lifted his eyes to Nicholas. "Fooled everyone. Such a talent. Who knew?" Frank's mouth formed a crooked, irritable smile. "And you." Frank tilted his brow toward Lydia, glaring at her over his glasses. "Was this your idea, or did our boy genius think of it all on his own?"

Nicholas sat back down on the couch and opened his hands, which trembled. "I did it secretly, Dad. I wanted you to have a Mary Stone Walker poem. I thought it would make you happy. That's all. I didn't mean to fool anyone."

Frank nodded. "Well, of course you meant to fool people, Nick. Why would you do it otherwise?" He emitted a sour chuckle. "Why else would you do it if you didn't want to fool me, fool everyone? Huh? With your mother's very own poem. Mmm-hmm."

No one spoke as Frank shook his head and stared at the pink paper. "Wow. And here I thought you were wasting all of your time on boat plans for the fool in the dunes, keeper of secrets."

"Nicholas wanted us to be happy, Frank," Lydia said. "Surely you can see—"

"Lydia, don't talk. Okay? You don't really have any part in this, according to our son, so…just keep out of it. You wrote this poem. I see that. You, a romance novelist, wrote a poem that was passed off as the work of a fine poet. Must give you a kick. Must have really tickled you." He mimicked a false gesture of delight.

"You know it doesn't tickle me, Frank," she said, hardly able to process all of her husband's insults. "You heard me in the kitchen earlier tonight. I was horrified."

Frank nodded and pursed his lips.

"Listen." She reached her hand out on the coffee table with nervous urgency. "If you deal with it correctly, this doesn't have to be a big deal. It doesn't have to be an embarrassment, Frank. Because we now have definite evidence of what really happened to Mary Stone Walker. Jack Kenilworth is willing to tell you what he knows. If we share all of that with your colleagues, then they'll know the poem is a forgery. But they never have to know who did it. This sort of thing happens all the time."

"Kenilworth again. Mmm-hmm." Nodding absently, Frank folded the sheet of pink paper and slid it back into its envelope. With difficulty, he scooted his heavy armchair up to the coffee table.

"Yes," he said mildly. "You told me that earlier on the phone." He nodded for several seconds. "Jack Kenilworth has the real story about Mary. Huh. However…" He reached across the coffee table for the ashtray and a box of matches beside it, sliding the wide art-deco glass piece toward himself. It rattled on the wood. He set the envelope on the glass and snapped a match to life. "This copy of the *new* Walker poem"—the pink paper flared in flame and Lydia jerked forward, but he knocked her hand away—"will no longer exist."

"Dad!"

The paper bent and curled, alive with flame, one edge left unburned in the ashtray as another triangle fell to the coffee table and turned to ash.

"That isn't fair, Dad!" Nicholas cried. "That was Mom's poem!"

"You didn't seem to care about that before, Son."

"I thought it would make her happy, too. I thought when she saw how much you liked it…just as much as Mary Stone Walker's other poems…that she would be happy. And I thought that you…"

Nicholas's voice trailed off. He stood, fists clenched, staring at his father. Then he snatched up the unburned fragment and unfolded it, but there were no words on the pink scrap.

"You'll be sorry, you know," Nicholas said angrily.

"Now, now, Nick," Frank said venomously. "This can all remain between us. No one needs to say a word. Your mother is not a poet; she's a romance writer. She should be glad to have one of her poems immortalized as a Walker poem. You were right about that." He leaned back, staring at no one and nothing. "It's done. It's over. This confession. Your secret is safely buried."

Lydia stared in disbelief at her husband. "You can't actually mean you want to keep up this pretense."

"Well, at this point, of course I do," he said, blinking at her with a false smile, straightening the front of his robe and retying it. "There's no choice. The word is out. It's well spread, as a matter of fact. The Library of Congress even has a copy of the poem, as you know. There's no turning back. Not when Nicholas here is our forger and he wants it that way. We can all live with that. The alternative would be far too humiliating. For everyone. No, it's not an option."

"No, Frank, *the lie* is not an option." Lydia faltered. "It would be poisonous for Nicholas. It would be poisonous for all of us,

Frank. Do you hear what you're saying? You aren't thinking about this clearly at all."

"Oh yes." He laughed coldly. "I'm thinking quite clearly."

"I won't allow it." She stood up.

"On the contrary." He turned his face toward her, and it was full of contempt. "You will not stop it."

"I won't allow my son to be forced to live with this!"

"You have no choice, my dear. I've made my decision."

"Frank." Lydia stood up and stepped slowly toward him. "A lie like this will kill something in all of us."

"You come one step closer," he hissed, "and I will knock your fucking head off."

She drew back. "*You're crazy*. You'd prefer your charade to your family? I can't believe this." Her hands rose to the sides of her head and pressed as if she were trying to hold it together. "I'll go to Lilly Schmidt. I'll make them understand. I will. I'll—"

Frank stood and surged with the force of a bull to thrust his hand at Lydia's throat, and he shoved her hard against the fireplace mantel.

"Dad!" Nicholas cried, pulling at his father as Lydia kicked at his legs.

"You"—Frank was pressing close to Lydia's face—"keep your shitty little stories to yourself, or I swear I'll kill you. I'm sick to death of your sabotage." He tossed her away, glaring and pointing at her. "I mean it. I'll find you, and I'll fucking silence you, you hear me? You've stood in my way long enough, you silly little whore."

Lydia pulled at Nicholas, who stood frozen, and dragged him toward the front door.

"I know every hole you can possibly hide in, and I'll follow you if you make one single gesture to betray me. I will find you and smash your life like you've tried and tried to smash mine."

Lydia pushed Nicholas out in front of her and slammed the door shut behind them. Frank's voice was reduced to garbled threats as he continued to rage. The sleeve of her coat caught on the storm door handle, and she tried to jerk away from it again and again, but it didn't come loose until she stopped, violently shaking, and deliberately unhooked it. When she turned around, Nicholas was nowhere to be seen. Her eyes groped the darkness in every direction as she began to run, but there was not a trace of him. The moonlit road gleamed eerily.

"Nicholas!" she shouted. "Nick!"

Silence swelled around her. Peepers sang in a nearby marsh. Darkness further dimmed her thinking, until the small beam of a flashlight swept the grass several yards away and Jack's whisper reached her from the shadows.

"Lydia!"

Lydia ran across the grass. "Is Nicholas with you?"

"Nicholas... No."

She turned toward the yard and scanned the entire scene, watching closely for any shift of light or form, but if her son was part of it, he was invisible.

34

Carson Woods, Michigan—September 1939

For frosty things and blazing things
and things that fly and hide
have crafty ways of visiting
a door that swings too wide.

~ Fannie Stearns Davis (1884–1966),
"Oh, Never Leave Your Door Unlatched"

Elizabeth Kenilworth tucked her child in his crib, added a second blanket, and stroked his back for several minutes until he was calm. Robert watched her from the front door of their small house. He knew she'd heard him enter, and he was aware that she did not want to greet him. Throughout the two weeks since Mary's visit to his workshop to confide in him about her pregnancy, this had been Elizabeth's pattern. Tonight he would speak with her about it directly. Her refusal to engage in any conversation with him was painful for both of them, and even the baby seemed to be crying more.

"Lizzy," he said quietly as she continued to linger over six-month-old Gregory.

She turned in the shadows and gestured for him to be silent. He sighed, walked to the kitchen, and studied the food she had prepared. Corn bread, fried onions with sausage, and applesauce. They were all still warm, and the table was set. He heard her exhale wearily behind him before he noticed her light footsteps as she approached the stove. He waited for her to speak or touch him, hoping for her eyes to meet his, but she merely picked up the corn bread and walked to the table. He followed her with the pan of onions and meat, and the bowl of applesauce, and sat down. The silence and warmth of the modest main room were soothing, as they always were after a day on the water.

"Elizabeth," he said, his heart speeding up with trepidation.

"Robert." She glanced at him, and her eyes were lit with something he didn't recognize.

"It's been quite a while since we had a conversation," he said. "And I feel like it's because you don't want to talk. To me."

"Mmm. I don't know what to say about that."

"That's what it seems like. Is that right?" He set his knife and fork on the plate with two clinks and waited. She continued to take small bites without answering. "Lizzy, this is ridiculous. It's beginning to feel unkind."

She set her own knife and fork down and folded her hands together with artificial patience. "Unkind? Wouldn't want that to be said of me. Talk. I'm listening."

Robert shook his head, chuckling.

"I want *you* to talk. To me. That is what I miss."

"I have nothing new to say. My life is the same every day, Robert." The words were clipped. "You are the one who goes out on the lake, into town, works on your boats, has drinks with friends. Receives visitors in your workshop. *You* talk."

His gaze probed her face, and she stared back at him. He reached for her hand and wrapped his fingers—still cold from the lake—around her fisted ones. She pulled away.

"I have had one visitor in recent weeks. Mary Walker came to see me. Nearly two weeks ago." He wanted to say more, but he was silenced by the frightening memory of kissing the poet's forehead.

"Why would Mary Walker visit you, Robert? That's odd. Or isn't it? Could it be that *she's* the lumberman's wife who has brought you gifts? The one whose name you always neglected to mention. The coffee? Candies? Maple syrup? Do we owe those treats to Mary Walker?"

What had seemed like an obvious, clear line of discussion in his mind suddenly looked like treacherous water. He eyed his wife's hard stare, the tension in her crossed arms, and remembered the warmth he had felt during Mary's confessional visit, and then all through that night and the following week as he'd recalled the closeness they had shared. Had it changed him? Had Elizabeth noticed?

Robert's eyes darted to the bedroom where Gregory slept, and his thoughts clouded even more. His face flushed hot, so he stood and walked to the front door and opened it a few inches. Elizabeth didn't move. He breathed deeply of the pine-scented air, calmed somewhat by the shush of wind in the high boughs.

Closing the door, he decided in a rush of sober conviction that he would not tell his wife about Mary's pregnancy, that he must no longer encourage Mary to believe that he was available to her for any level of intimacy, and that he would only help the woman in ways that he could tell Elizabeth about. He did not know what he'd been thinking. What kind of depravity would allow him to endanger his marriage, his child's future—his own life, when it came down to it? Had the devil possessed him? He would take a stand against his own weakness. For now and always. He would not be ruined by it.

He walked slowly to Elizabeth and stood behind her, gently placing his hands on her shoulders. Her dark hair was shiny, pulled back into a braid. It was true. Her life was the same every day. It was part of their arrangement; it was part of what she gave him so that he could do the work he knew how to do. She took care of their home, their child, his needs, and he tried to earn enough money for their food and shelter. His life had been happier, healthier, sweeter since they had married.

Mary was… What was she? Another man's wife. An addict

and a person without steady values that he could discern. She was trouble to both herself and others, no matter how much beauty or loving inclination she might possess.

"It is odd for Mary Walker to come to me, yes. But the reason, Lizzy, is that she has problems. And she has no one else to talk to." He heard how it sounded. What a fool his wife would think him, falling for a needy woman, thinking himself her savior. "But I'm not taking on the role of some cheap hero. They are her problems. She will take care of them. She only wanted my opinion. And for that help she did bring gifts occasionally. For both of us."

Still Elizabeth did not move. She didn't speak. After a minute Robert felt a tremor under his hands, and he stooped down next to her, turned her face toward his, and found her silently crying, her eyes squeezed shut.

"I can't compete with her, Robert," she whispered. "She will win. She will fool you. If you step any closer, you will fall for her beauty and even for her desperation. Don't you see? That's how some women are."

"No, Lizzy. This isn't like that." Robert held his wife's face in his hands, just as he had held Mary's, and he gritted his teeth against that memorized image. Even now, even in this awful moment of his wife's pain, he was thinking of a wayward, sensual encounter with another woman. He stood to lose everything he had built here, to lose the genuine love of a good woman and the respect of his own son as he grew. He could not let himself become that sort of man. What, *what* had he been thinking to ever let himself fall into boyish, romantic impulses and moments of friendship that were far too intimate to ever admit to Elizabeth?

"Maybe it isn't like that for you. But you don't know what it is for her." She untangled herself from Robert's hands, carried her plate to the kitchen, and turned toward her husband, eyes glittering. "Be careful. If you choose her—even if you don't act

301

on it every day, Robert—if you choose her in your heart, and she remains a part of your life, I will take your son and I will go back to my family in the Upper Peninsula. I will not endure watching you disintegrate into another woman's plaything."

Robert raised his chin and looked directly into the eyes of his wife, and from a murky well of regret, his eyes grew damp.

"I have not chosen her in my heart, Elizabeth. And I promise you, I never will."

35

White Hill, Michigan—April 1999

Having left the sea behind,
Having turned suddenly and left the shore
That I had loved beyond all words....
  ~ Edna St. Vincent Millay (1892–1950), "Mist in the Valley"

As Lydia stood with Jack in the shadows on the road watching for Nicholas, Frank's truck backed wildly down the driveway and lurched off in the direction of White Hill. She took off running toward the house, yanked the front door open, and went inside, calling her son's name. Then she was stopped in her tracks.

"Oh God, no!" Furniture was overturned and smashed, books strewn from their shelves, the large mirror over the fireplace mantel shattered.

She heard someone enter, and she turned toward the sound, hoping it was Nicholas, fearing it was Frank, and confused for a moment by the sight of Jack Kenilworth.

"What has he done? He's lost his mind!" Her knees and her jaw shook, but her body seemed far away. Jack stood in front of her with his fingers wrapped around her wrist. He caught her attention and held it.

"Lydia, these are just things. Replaceable *things*."

"Jack," she whispered intensely, staring into his eyes. "My husband has lost his mind. Something has snapped. *And where is my son?*"

She pressed her fist against her mouth. Part of her mind flew through imagined spaces in search of Nicholas, while the other was frozen, half believing that if she just sat back down on the couch and willed it, she could undo the events of the last twenty-four hours.

"Nicholas!" she shouted toward the back of the house. "Nick!"

"Yes, Mom. I'm here."

Lydia and Jack whipped toward the darkness beyond the living room where Nicholas's form took shape in the hall. He stopped before he entered the shattered room where the argument had taken place. Lydia rushed to him, but something in his demeanor prevented her from taking him in her arms.

"Nicholas...what are you doing?" She held her hands out toward him, but he said nothing and didn't move.

"What are we supposed to do now, Mom?" Tremulous as his voice was, the words were angry.

"I will figure that out, Nicholas. Don't worry."

"What if Dad comes back and smashes up the rest of the house?"

"I don't think that's going to happen."

"Why not? Why did he do this?" He struggled to maintain control of his voice. "All because of that poem?"

"No, certainly not." Lydia stepped up to him and gripped his hands in hers. "He's not well. You can see that! This is not a normal reaction under any circumstance. He needs..." She glanced at Jack, whose face discouraged any words of sympathy for Frank. "He needs to really take a good look at himself. Come on, let's go to the kitchen and sit down for a minute."

"No! I don't want to be here when he comes back!" Nicholas said with an edge of fury.

"It's okay, Nicholas," Lydia said, reaching her hand out toward him. "I just need some water. And I think I should call the police."

"The police? That will just make him madder! Please don't, Mom!"

"Okay, Nicholas, calm down. I'll think about how to handle this." She urged him toward the kitchen, where nothing seemed broken. Her car keys lay on the floor as if Frank had thrown them down, along with the coats and scarves from the wall hooks that must have been in the way of his own. Her hands shook as she ran the water, then passed a cup to Nicholas, who took it but did not drink. In the light of the kitchen, he looked excessively pale, the natural shadows around his eyes very dark.

"Nick, do you have any idea where your father went?" Jack asked.

Nicholas shook his head and pointed to the kitchen door. "I sneaked in this door and then hid in the bushes while he was leaving."

"You mean you came *in here* while he was destroying everything? Nicholas, what for?" Lydia cried.

"I had to…for just a minute. I heard him smashing things. I was trying to think how to stop him, but…it didn't seem possible."

"No, of course it wasn't possible! Oh, Nicholas!"

"Lydia, I think we should all get the hell out of here," Jack said.

"Yes, of course. I'll gather some things so we can stay away for a day or two. Could you take Nicholas to your house, and I will come as soon as I can?"

"What's wrong with right now?" he said.

They looked at each other. *How strange*, part of her mind mused, *that I am standing in the ruins of my marriage with this man I hardly know.*

"I will hurry," she said firmly. "Please go. I promise I will hurry."

"All right. Let's get you out of here," Jack said to Nicholas, and they started quickly for the front door.

"Wait." Nicholas started up the stairs. "My backpack."

Jack took a few steps back toward Lydia. "If you aren't at my house within an hour," he said in a low voice, "I'm coming back. You got that?"

After watching the taillights of Jack's truck glide down the road, Lydia faced the eerie silence of her house with the sensation that she was a ghost returning. She left lamps that were on still lit, and those that were off she did not touch. The pale-green lights of the stereo gleamed silently, and the furnace breathed on with a commonplace rattle and huff.

On the hall table, the violets and pussy willow sprigs she had clipped for Frank's gathering opened into emptiness. As if the house occupants had left because of an invasion or a house fire, abandoned wineglasses and coffee cups containing cold sips were clustered here and there on the white linen of the dining room table, and dessert plates held bits of shortcake, whipped cream, and strawberries, some stacked together, some remaining at their places with forks and knives resting on them like clock hands. Habit tempted Lydia to straighten up the messes everywhere, but it felt like any attempt at order would be unseemly. After all, there was a death underway: the family she'd been part of would never live here again.

But somewhere, she told herself with a stubbornness born of despair, home could be made right again for her and her son. Somewhere. This house was only a building, and the years lived here were irretrievable for repair. A longing to correct the past should not define the future.

Her gaze caught on the bough of a lilac tree bobbing in the wind outside the kitchen window. She moved to the sink and pressed her hands on its cold edge. The lilacs by the window would bloom pink in a few weeks; the ones by the barn would be dark purple. Their leaves were emerging already, and she might not be there to smell their blossoms. The truth of this twisted like a cruel hand in her chest. But there were lilacs in other soil. And there were millions of kitchen windows.

Then suddenly they were lit, the lilac leaves by the barn flashing white with the beams of headlights. Her heart raced, and she caught her breath. It was Frank. And then beside his lights on the barn, another set. Quickly she leaned forward to see—*a police car.* Lydia shrank back into the shadows, her hands instantly damp and cold, her eyes darting around the room. Why would he bring a policeman? Could Frank be searching for them? Maybe he was frightened at what he'd done; maybe he'd realized his own madness. Her heart thudded in her chest.

Should she face them right here, right now? No. She could not let them see her. She looked around with an adrenaline-cleared mind. Had she left anything out to betray that she was here? They would enter right at this door. She had to hide immediately.

Lydia heard their voices outside, approaching. Somewhere far behind them, a train whistle sounded. Again, she ran her gaze around the room and along the path to the staircase, finding no accidental clues of her presence. Silently, she flew up the steps to the dark second-story hallway. From that spot, she could hear. From that spot, she could also slip easily over to her study and lock herself in if she had to. But that was ridiculous. She had as much right to be in her home as Frank did.

The kitchen doorknob rattled, there was the nibbling sound of a key in the lock, and the door creaked open. Their voices floated inside, and then their footsteps.

"In here mostly." Frank led the policeman across the kitchen floor.

"It was this door that was left open?" The voice was that of Tom Epson, a White Hill police detective Frank had sometimes traded stories with over coffee. She wondered if he had told Epson about the argument and their disappearance afterward, or if Frank had spotted Nicholas and was now seeking to track him down.

"Yes, this one was wide open."

Lydia's mind clung to the idea that Tom was somehow being enlisted to help straighten things out because Frank had realized his mistake. But the dialogue began to suggest something else.

"Holy shit," Tom said, his voice slightly muffled to Lydia's ears.

The two men were standing in the living room Frank had torn to pieces. "Why would anyone do this?"

"I know. It's unbelievable." Frank's voice was strung tight, but he was trying to sound somber. "I can only speculate."

"It's doesn't... It's not quite the look of someone searching for something."

"Vandalism. Rage."

"Over the book?"

"Jealousy."

"Over a book."

"You gotta *imagine*, Tom. It's out of your usual realm. It's... it's not even academics. It's collectors; it's possessive townspeople; it's three generations of Evans kin. God only knows what it is. There is a whole history behind that woman and her writings and her unexplained disappearance. Sixty years now. I don't know who would do this, but I can give you a long list of people who might have. Here. Look." Lydia heard Frank walk a few steps away, then back.

"This is it?"

"Open it up. Last page. See? Torn out. Gone. The literary discovery of a lifetime. Scheduled to be sent to the Library of Congress. Ripped. Out."

Tom Epson was silent for several seconds. Lydia noticed that she was holding her breath and that her eyes stung from staring without blinking. The page with the poem on it was gone?

"Yeah, you told me about this... But who would know where to go, where to look...back there in your office?"

Frank guffawed. "Obviously they didn't."

"But they did. They came here to your house, and they did find it. It's not like there's been a newspaper article or anything. And Jesus, you have thousands of books. How would anyone pinpoint the one? It just doesn't seem—"

"Well, I see where you're coming from. I can't answer everything." Lydia could picture Frank's broad disarming shrug as he shook his head. Then he sighed heavily. "I hate to say this. I really do hate to say this. But in my heart, I haven't completely ruled out family."

"You mentioned that. The Evanses are all over the place now, though there may be a few remaining in Michigan."

"No, *my* family. My son. My wife. There are... There's something abnormal, even mentally unsound, about Lydia's reaction to this discovery."

"Huh...really? How so?"

"She seems to feel threatened by it. Almost like Mary's a rival. Taking her place in the form of this poem. Back from the dead." He pretended a laugh. "If you will."

"Mary?"

"Mary Stone Walker. The poet..."

"Oh, yes. Yes."

"Lydia's always wished she were a poet herself. When this poem was discovered, she even started to think it was her own. I don't know, don't understand it, and I don't think she did either. She has seemed worried about her own state of mind, actually. Maybe I never should have involved her or my son with this work. Never should have shared my passion for it. Some people need simpler lives."

"Hmm. Frank, uh...it sounds like I need to speak to Lydia. Seems from what you're saying that she might be the most likely suspect."

"Yes, it does seem so. I don't know. I mean, I say that, and I can't rule out the possibility, but at the same time it's hard to imagine."

"Well, I agree with you there. I can't picture it. I mean...is she even tall enough to get a good whack at that mirror? Somebody had to. It looks like the main hit was near the top there."

For two or three minutes, neither man spoke above a murmur. They seemed to be walking around the room assessing damage. So vivid was her recall of the wreckage that Lydia felt she was invisible and examining with them, every detail, every angle of each broken thing against the memory of the way it should have been. She was no longer poised to dart away with her back against the wall; she had sunk to the floor with her arms around her abdomen, her breath pinched and shallow, as she suppressed an urge to hysterically decry Frank's charade. If Tom Epson had climbed the stairs and found her there, he would have believed Frank's tale that she was insane.

"I tell you what, Frank. I'm going to go back to the station to get a camera. Should have brought one. Don't move anything. In fact, why don't you come with me and fill out the forms?"

"I'll do that. You go on ahead, though. I have a couple of calls to make."

"I don't know if you're aware, but it's well after midnight. After two, actually."

"Yes, but there are people, close colleagues, who will want to know. They might have ideas."

"All right, but if you could come promptly. And do not touch anything, much as you might be tempted."

"Sure, sure."

As Frank walked Tom to the kitchen door, Lydia slowly pulled herself up and edged down to the landing. Frank returned to the dining room where she heard him open a bottle of wine, then heard the bottle clink on the edge of a glass as the wine glugged into it. She craned her neck and could see in the fractured mirror a reflection of his hands holding the glass as he sat down on a dining room chair. He sighed, took a long drink, then set the glass on the table.

Elbows propped on his knees, he lowered his head to his hands. A sound like weeping accompanied the clenching of his hands fiercely together. Lydia's breath caught. She could almost see his whole form.

Frank picked the wineglass up again and turned it slowly. "My love." His voice was broken.

He raised the glass as if in toast, and Lydia wished for him to lean forward so she could clearly see his face. Would his features contain that expression of affection that she knew well once but had not seen directed at her for months, maybe years? His hand and the wine were both shaking slightly.

"You're the only one," he said mournfully. "The one woman capable of understanding the point...of all of this...of everything. And, my dear, I will remain devoted. Sweet Mary, nothing will stop me... I will resurrect you."

Lydia swallowed against a rise of bile.

Frank emptied his wineglass in one gulp and clumsily set it on the table.

Then he left. She heard him shuffle through the house, shut the door behind him, and start his truck.

She bolted to the bathroom and retched into the sink, heaving, crying without tears. No, it just couldn't be. His warped mind really had cast her aside for a dead woman.

This time, the old denial had no power against the voice inside that said, *So...that is that.* It was a cold, detached voice as she teetered on the edge of shock. At last—at long last—she saw things as they were.

> The stone bird called,
> and all that seemed living
> was dead.

They were Mary Stone Walker's lines from the hundreds of lines a younger Lydia once memorized. What a fool she had been. For so very long. Frank had been devoted to a fictional figment, nothing more. He adored the ink of Mary that he animated with a handful of photographic images. Together, those pieces formed the perfect skeleton to hang his heavy idealism on. He kept a dozen or so photos of Mary in her twenties by themselves in a box that he locked, but Lydia knew that he took them out regularly to study the lines of the dead woman's arms, brow, jawline, shoulders. It was from these reimagined details and the snatches of Mary's mind glinting in her poetry and journals that Frank had created a blueprint for the perfect woman, his imagination's lover. Ah, the seduction of a woman without skin or a beating heart. And every inch of the way in his descent from reality, she herself had supported him.

Lydia reeled from the bathroom to the hall and fumbled down the stairs, her eyes moving mechanically around the shadowy walls where scenes from the protracted drama of the night seemed to replay: Frank's hideous scolding of them all around the table as he burned her poem, Nicholas crying out to him that it wasn't fair, Frank's description of Lydia as an unstable woman who wished she were a poet, and his pathetic toast to the cherished woman he never knew, who today would be almost eighty-five. *That* man in those scenes—*that man* was her husband. What fantasies had *she* been surviving on all of these years?

She was not stupid, so how she had missed what was happening? And now…it was too late. It was far, far too late.

There was something else that Frank had said to Tom Epson—that the poem in the back of the book had been torn out. Had Frank done that himself to heighten excitement around the poem? Or to implicate her? Or maybe…was he considering ending the charade? If he didn't do it, had Nicholas come back into the house in the middle of his father's storm for *that*?

Her son had devised and executed a forgery. What else was he capable of? What else might he do? What had he been going through? Driven by a desire to solve family problems, he'd committed a crime. Through his entire life, Nicholas had shared the search for valuable hidden literature, believing that it mattered more than almost anything, and that they were all in it together. And now she saw the childlike view he held of his own potential for mending the situation, and how this mending would bring his family peace and keep them together. *All of us happy again*, he must have imagined as he scribed Lydia's poem in Mary's handwriting.

She would pack clothes. She must pack a lot of clothes for both of them and take her computer. She thought that she might have half an hour left before Frank returned from the police station. In her effort to prepare for a temporary escape to a hotel room, she had already carried a box of Nicholas's clothing to Jack's barn during the previous week, along with three other carloads of belongings. But there were some critical things left to gather.

Roused to this singular focus, Lydia felt like she was moving faster than she ever had before. Within thirty minutes, her Jeep was ready to go. For a few moments she stood beside it, regarding the quiet house. Her family's home. A crime scene now.

While another woman might have seen the truth of things earlier and grown outraged and protective of her child—and herself—long before such extreme events, Lydia had continued to believe in Frank's best self as she remembered or imagined it, and in the resilience of them all. Or maybe it was just denial that had dragged her forward, on and on. Belief. Denial. Where was the line between the two?

There was one more thing to do. As some habituated part of herself protested, she reentered the house and picked up the phone. The number for the White Hill Police was taped to the wall with other emergency numbers, and she dialed it.

"This is Lydia Carroll. I'm calling about my husband, Frank Carroll." Even now, it wasn't too late. She could corroborate Frank's tale, say she was worried about him because there had been an intruder at the house and he was nowhere to be found. But she heard herself say, "He has threatened my son and me and damaged our home. And now he's gone."

She looked at the hunching barn where more evidence of Frank's physical violence lay in pieces on the dirty, damp floor. "No, he isn't armed. We don't own a gun. No, my son and

I weren't physically harmed. The threats were… Well, I'm concerned because… How do I say this? He was not in his right mind. He was violent against the house.

"Yes," she responded. "A danger to himself and others; yes, both. Mostly us, not strangers. I just want someone to know. It's our house at 1322 Thirty-First Street. I appreciate that. I will. In a few hours. I have to take care of my son right now. Thank you."

She hung up and stared at the plastic phone in terror. The deed was done. It was irreversible. He would never forgive her, never. She had no idea what he would do.

What *he* would do? What *he* would forgive?

What would *she* be willing to forgive?

She hurried from the house and locked herself in her Jeep. And as she drove away from the house and left the paved roads to head toward Jack's home, a wind swept down from the sky, hurling a rain so heavy that her windshield wipers flapped feebly to no effect, and her headlights illuminated only water. She slowed down and kept her vision pinned to the blurred windshield where at last appeared the murky smear of a light shining from one of Jack's windows.

36

Imperfect dream
we pull the grass,
we slash the wind, before us
is the winter.

~ *Mary Stone Walker (born December 1913), "The Shore House"*

A violent wind slammed the front door of Jack's house behind Nicholas and Jack as they returned from the Carroll home.

"How about if I make something warm to drink?" Jack turned to Nicholas, who was standing just a few steps inside the front door, his hands shoved into the pockets of his jeans. Jack gestured toward the living room couch. "Go ahead and sit down. In fact, go ahead and lie down if you feel like it, Nick... Rest."

Still the boy didn't move from the foyer, but Jack went ahead to the kitchen, started water boiling, and pulled a rectangle of cheddar cheese, a knife, and a box of crackers out, setting them on the round oak table that had dwelled in his grandparents' home for decades. This whole mess was criminal, in his opinion: treating a son and a wife the way Frank Carroll had tonight. He himself wouldn't know where to begin to fix the situation, or what punishment for the man would possibly be adequate.

"What do you think will happen, Jack?"

Nicholas had slipped silently into the kitchen, and his voice startled Jack from his thoughts.

"Ah, well, I think you and your mother will stay here for a night or two. Or as long as you need to. Let everyone calm down."

"I mean, do you think we'll all still be able to live together in our house?"

Nicholas's expression was difficult for Jack to read, but he had crossed his arms stiffly over his ribs and seemed to still be shivering slightly.

"I don't know your parents well enough to guess how this will all play out. But worse things have happened in families and they've stayed together." He gave Nicholas a brief smile.

They sat down together at the table with cocoa too hot to drink, silently nibbling at crackers, while Jack sliced cheese that neither of them ate.

"Maybe you'd like to watch some television," Jack said after a while.

For a moment Nicholas was silent, and then he said, "There's something I don't get."

"And what's that?"

He hesitated. "Why you never told my father about Mary Stone Walker being dead. If you were so sure."

Jack eyed the boy whose face reminded him so much of his mother, a face that was that of a stranger just a few months ago, and one which was, at this moment, Jack thought, slightly hardened with blame. *He's just a kid*, Jack reminded himself. A scared kid so desperate about his father's and mother's unhappiness that he had created an extravagant, volatile lie.

"I tried to, Nicholas. Several times. Do you remember I mentioned to you that I'd met him a few times?"

Nicholas nodded, fingering a slice of cheese and folding it in half.

"Well, those times were when I tried. Years ago. He didn't want to hear anything at all from me."

"But...why didn't you just tell him anyway? I mean, what were you waiting for him to say?" Hints of anger roughened

Nicholas's voice in a way that Jack suspected he did not allow himself when he had similarly difficult questions for his father.

"I don't think there's anything right about sharing something with a man who treats you like dirt, Nicholas. That's advice you may want to remember as you go through life."

Jack stood up with some agitation and went to the window to check for Lydia. It had been nearly an hour since they'd left her behind at the Carrolls' house.

"I wasn't going to plead with your father to listen to me. And I had to be thoughtful with the information I had. There are times when you have to protect the dead from gossip in this world, because they surely can't protect themselves. And these were people whose reputations were left in my care."

As he stared into the black night and the threatening wind, Jack's chest filled suddenly with a familiar anger, amplified by the tension of the night's events. He didn't need this, any of it. He should forget about the Carrolls and their problems. Their fantasies, their troubled personalities, and their games. Their issues were not his. And really, at this point, neither were those of his grandfather or Mary Walker, left behind by them for him to keep safe. Protecting the dead... What the hell did that even mean? No one in the world was worth sacrificing his own peace for, nor ever had been. He could see it clearly now—in Lydia's life, in Nicholas's, and in his own: one person's lie becomes another innocent person's mean little hell to endure.

He could fix nothing for anyone involved. Yes, maybe at some point in the past if he had shared his information and documents with some other scholar after Frank refused them, something might be different now. And a part of him certainly wished that he'd done just that, and that Lydia and Nicholas had been set free long ago from the painful side effects of Frank's delusion.

"It seems to me, Nicholas, that you are a good person caught in a very difficult situation—and you believed that you could help your parents in their struggle to be happy."

Nicholas looked down at his hands and squeezed the cheese flat between two fingers.

"That's what a good-hearted person who loves someone else tries to do. Right?"

Nicholas shrugged. "It didn't work," he said after a few moments.

"It didn't work the way you *hoped* it would. That doesn't mean it won't shake things up and bring the best outcome in the long run."

"Bad things are bad things. Everything that happened tonight was bad," Nicholas said darkly. "Where are my mother and I supposed to even live now? Out in the barn with all the other junk Dad doesn't want anymore? He hates us."

"Of course he doesn't hate you." Jack tried for a dismissive chuckle, looking again at the clock. Now it had been well over an hour. Should he leave Nicholas here, locked safely in his house, and go out and find Lydia? Would she still attempt to reason with that lunatic if he showed up while she was at the house? Is that what was going on?

"No, he hates us." Nicholas's voice was certain, and he looked directly into Jack's eyes. "And I hate him."

"Nick, listen. It's been a very long, horrible night, and your father was at his worst. From here, the three of you will *have* to move forward, away from this stuff, because underneath those feelings of anger, you love each other. It might take time, but things will work out somehow. They won't just stay this way."

"You don't know that," Nicholas said quietly.

And it was true. Things certainly could continue to deteriorate. Look at Mary Walker. The reckless events of her life had led to misery and disasters, and then she died. In fact, the disastrous episodes of that young woman's life were still manifesting misery in White Hill this very night. Sixty years later. It was enough to make a man start to really wonder.

White light beamed suddenly from headlights on his driveway, reeling into the room, across the walls, and pulling Jack to the window. When he saw Lydia's figure rise from her Jeep into the rain, he closed his eyes and exhaled slowly. Then he opened them, alarmed. The unwanted thing had happened: the hope within him that he might know her well, without boundaries— this troubled, married woman—had intensified into an almost tangible animal, a force he had no other word for but *love*.

37

White Hill, Michigan—October 1939

Bethink thee of oaths that were lightly spoken,
Bethink thee of vows that were lightly broken,
Bethink thee of all that is dear to thee,
For thou art alone on the raging sea…
~ Elizabeth Oakes Smith (1806–1893), "The Drowned Mariner"

The fog was so thick as Mary ran through it that it weighted her clothing like ice. Winter was coming… It was closing in around her even now.

She knew where to find Robert. He would have gone out on the *Fata Morgana* before dawn to catch fish and would return early because of the fog rolling in, but he would not be at the docks for long. When she'd visited him last, he had spoken to her as if she were a child, telling her that she needed to take care of her problems without his interference, and that he, likewise, needed to tend to his own. He had stupidly suggested that Bernard might grow into a good father for this unwanted child if she could bring herself to help him try. Robert had withheld his touch, his warmth, and she had privately vowed never, ever to seek his company again, but then she had realized that his love for her was what had altered him. He was afraid.

And if he had such love for her that he was afraid of it, then she could persuade him of almost anything, she knew.

They were no longer two completely separate people; they had become intertwined.

The milky-gray air dissolved all light and form as she approached the fishing docks, but she could tell she was close because the Shuttle Point foghorn that sounded with forlorn regularity was louder, and she perceived the white pulse of light-house beams pressing into the fog. Beneath the rumble and hiss of the surf, she could hear the clank of invisible sailboat rigging and eerie snippets of male voices as she approached. She slowed down as the sand beneath her feet hardened to dock boards.

"Robert!" She tried her voice in the fog as panic flashed through her from sudden disorientation. She was not even sure where the dock stopped and the water began. It might be impossible to find the way back to land if one were to fall into the water in such weather. She shivered, and her hand tingled with physical memory of her disastrous plunge into this powerful lake years before.

"Kenilworth!" a strange male voice called. "Someone's looking for you."

How would he find her? This was ludicrous! He was probably no more than fifty feet away, but how would she find him?

"I hear," Robert answered. Then there was nothing more but the low slaps of boats on water, the foghorn, the short calls of a lone gull.

"Where are you?" his disembodied voice called, and Mary could picture his expression. "God help us, I can't see a thing!"

"I'm... I don't know!" She tried to return his greeting with a laugh. "At the edge of the sand."

"Oh! Mary?" His voice grew quieter. And then he was visible, just five feet away, his wool-clad form woven with the mist as if he were already a ghost.

She cringed at the chill in his tone. He didn't want her there. She took a long step toward him, hesitated, then wrapped her arms around his neck and clung to him. He smelled of fish blood, diesel fuel, and cigarette smoke. After a few seconds, she felt his arms come around her body, at first as lightly as a cloak, but then protectively. She exhaled heavily, smiled on his shoulder, and cried with relief. To anyone farther than five feet away, their images were completely erased.

"Oh, Robert," she whispered into his skin. "Without you I would have no hope at all."

"That isn't true, Mary," he whispered back. He pulled away from her. "Come with me, come here."

With care, he led her from the docks, his hand gripping hers, and they took slow, blind steps down the fogbound October beach. Occasionally a froth of the water's edge emerged from the milky nothingness, then a scattering of stones or a floating log. In the shelter of sand hillocks pinned with dune grass they sat down, bodies huddled together. Robert turned to face her, closing both of his hands around hers, and after a minute he spoke.

"Mary. I can't…" His voice was strong, but as he met her eyes, it faltered.

"Robert, please don't pretend." She watched his jaw set. "Don't lie to yourself."

"It isn't a matter of lying to anyone, Mary. I have my life—"

"And you have me. You have my heart. I have never felt as I do when I am near you, or even when I think of you. I feel hope—"

"*Stop.*" His voice was firm. "This is not a story, Mary. This isn't a fairy tale. I have a wife and child. You have a husband, and you will have a child."

"Oh, you're wrong. I will not have a husband and a child in this way. No, not in this life here. I will not, *I cannot*. You have to trust what I know of myself. Please… I am begging you now… Please take me to Chicago. Secretly. On your fishing boat. That's the only way I can get there without anyone knowing, and the only way I can think of that I can be allowed to have a life without Bernard. And if I don't escape…I just can't say what will happen." She watched his gaze sharpen and take on a certain shrewdness, and she grasped at what she thought he might be realizing—that his life would be simplified if she, and all the questions she brought to his life, were gone. "Then you will be free of me. Whatever exists between us can't harm you."

They stared at each other, emotions chaotic. Robert took his hands away and clasped them fiercely together. A cold wind pulled an opening in the fog over the lake as Mary studied the face of this man whom she had originally sought specifically as a lifeline. Green eyes capable of warm understanding and cold analysis within the same conversation. Angles in his face that suggested strength of character capable of guiding his heart. Yes. She would marry such a man, it occurred to her suddenly; she could believe in someone like Robert Kenilworth. She was a different woman than the girl who'd chosen Bernard Evans.

"You could join me there someday." The idea rose like a star in her mind, yet she was horrified to hear herself speak it out loud. She felt him stiffen. "Later, Robert. When Gregory is older. Sometime maybe, just if things change…for you. We could be together in the city. Share a different life entirely!" Her mind filled with bright, enticing visions that had never entered the realm of possibility for her before, and she spoke them out loud, relieved as she watched Robert listen and think, even though he did not take his eyes off the lake. "I will make my name as a poet. I'll teach. I will work so hard… You know that I will. And I can stay with my mother's relatives. They can help me raise the child. Robert, say you will take me away, please. I will be destroyed here!"

He turned toward her, eyes stormy with pain.

"You are the only one who can save me!" This, she knew as she spoke it, was almost true. This was her life. *She* was the only one who could save herself, but without him, she would have to do that right here in White Hill.

A long time passed, it seemed to Mary, before Robert spoke, and in those minutes, her imagination flew from vision to vision.

She was imprisoned beside the woodstove in Bernard's home, rocking a child under her husband's fierce domination. She was reading poetry to a large, appreciative audience in Chicago. She was reuniting with Robert Kenilworth at Union Station, and he was joyfully embracing her. In that hour of fear and hope in the October fog, she did not envision a single thing that would actually come to pass.

"All right then," Robert said without looking at her. "I will take you to Chicago. Tomorrow I will meet you again right here at sunrise to devise a plan. If we are crossing the lake, we must go as soon as possible, Mary. It will be November and the weather is turning. It's almost too late."

38

Love's the boy stood on the burning deck…
While the poor ship in flames went down.
…And love's the burning boy.

~ Elizabeth Bishop (1911–1979), "Casabianca"

Their eyes were like dark lamps, glimmering. Her son. This man who had become a friend. Together they represented safety, except from the fear of her husband's mind. No one could protect her from that. As she entered Jack's house, the two of them watched her, their spirits hovered close to her, and their hands were quick to assist her. Opening the door, taking her raincoat, handing her a towel, and leading her farther inside to offer her tea.

"I'm fine." Lydia found herself struggling a little bit for breath. "I was delayed. But Frank didn't see me."

"But *you* saw *him*," Jack said. It wasn't a question.

"It's okay." She tried to dismiss the subject. She didn't want to discuss in front of Nicholas the fact that his father had returned to the house with a policeman and another set of lies. "I'm so confused at this point that it would be best for me if we could talk about everything after some sleep." Her attempt at a reassuring smile felt like it might tear her dry lips. "I saw Frank in passing, but he did not see me. I managed to get the things Nicholas and I will need in order to stay here—for a few days."

"Good." Jack lifted his hand to touch her but lowered it to his pocket instead.

"Nicky, I want you to rest." Looking at him, Lydia felt her voice waver. "Let me give you a hug. Then let's find someplace for you to sleep."

She wrapped her arms around her tall son, and tears filled her eyes. She clutched him tightly and felt his arms tighten around her as one strangled sob rose from his chest.

"I'm so sorry," she whispered. "I'm so sorry for all of this, Nicholas."

"It's all my fault, Mom," he said miserably.

She pulled back to look at his flushed face.

"Listen," she said. "You are not responsible for your parents' choices and behavior over many years, and it is there that all this trouble began. Do you hear me? The poem you forged was just an attempt to stop the pain. A well-intended mistake."

Nicholas was silent before reaching into his back pocket. Hesitantly, he pulled out a small object. For a moment he just stared at it, then he held out his hand. Lydia opened her palm, and into it he placed a wad of aged paper, folded to a tight square and damp from the rain.

She looked at Nicholas, heart hammering, and then began to pull on one edge. Like the mouth of some strange creature, it opened slowly. And there before her lay her own words...in the likeness of Mary Stone Walker's script. Like a magic trick. Expertly forged lines with pauses and little scrolls of ink forming Lydia's own words gave rise both to memories of writing the poem in Boston and a flash of the first time she'd seen Mary Walker's handwriting in the Carson Community College library.

"Oh my goodness," she whispered. She folded the paper down and slid it into her back pocket. "You were very brave to go back in and get this, Nicholas," she said, awestruck.

"My feet just took me back in there. I didn't have a chance to decide."

"It was the right thing to do. For everyone." Lydia squeezed his hands and exhaled heavily. "Now. Let's try to rest. I hope you can sleep until dinnertime," she said, and after watching him walk away, she went to the kitchen and sat at the small table, staring through the window at the storm.

When Jack had made sure Nicholas was settled in the bed in his den, he returned to the kitchen, and Lydia waited for him to meet her eyes.

"Mr. Kenilworth, my friend. In all this madness, some interesting facts have arisen and been swept away."

"To the sawdust bin where they belong," Jack said, busying himself with dirty dishes in the sink.

Lydia almost stopped herself from continuing. Who was she to demand that he talk—about anything? "I don't know about that," she said, and then her voice sank to a whisper. "I could have used your help a long time ago."

"But I had no idea." Knowing immediately what she was referring to, he kept his voice low. "*No idea* of your problems or Frank's thing for Mary Stone Walker. Now, however, I want this all over with, and I want peace. I no longer care if my grandfather's friendship with Walker becomes common knowledge if it makes you happy somewhere along the line and gives Nicholas some room to live his life. That's how it is from where I sit."

"I can't imagine Frank listening to me at this point. I don't know what's going to make him see reality, but I don't think it will be me."

"Oh, Lydia. Listen," Jack said after a few moments of silence. "Let's cut to the chase. I'll help you any way I can. If you think it would help your family, please take the death certificate to Frank in a day or two. Or whenever. It has to have some impact. He can maybe save a little face and base his next phase of research on it."

"His next phase of research?"

"He can go to Chicago, which is where the document shows

that Mary was buried, and seek out evidence and maybe even witnesses there. Tell him you just want peace for your family. And maybe—with the patience and effort that you are obviously skilled at—maybe in time everything will work out for the three of you."

The concept of the official death certificate was still so fresh and strange that it was difficult for Lydia to fit it into her personal understanding of Mary Walker. She was dead. She had been for six decades, just as her old friend, Ruth Donovan, had feared, and it was suddenly clear to Lydia how deeply she had hoped that the woman had survived 1939. "What exactly does the certificate say?"

"I can show it to you."

They left the house together, locking the front door behind them and dashing through the rain-filled wind into the barn where they sat side by side on the couch. Jack pulled the bag full of his grandfather's papers from the floor.

"You keep it in a plastic bag on the floor?" Lydia asked, alarmed.

"I got this out earlier tonight. When you first arrived." He fished through the papers. "My intention was to show you everything."

He found a yellowed envelope, opened it, and showed her the simple document inside from the Cook County coroner. She held it. This paper created by someone who'd seen and testified to the poet's dead body was the closest she had ever come to the flesh-and-blood Mary Stone Walker.

"But it says 'Mary Williams'!" Lydia's gaze shot to Jack's face.

"She used her mother's maiden name. As I said, she did not want anyone to find her or to ever know what she'd done."

"How can you be sure it's the same woman, Jack?" She regarded his face anew. Did he look like someone who could be stuck in a fanciful old family tale, as Frank had assumed? Jack's expression was weary and not entirely patient as he closed his eyes briefly.

"She wrote to my grandfather with her new name and address,

explaining why she was using that name, why she wasn't staying with her Williams relatives in Chicago as she had supposedly planned to, and...some other things."

"Do you have that letter?"

"I do." His jaw shifted.

It seemed to Lydia that he might be growing angry.

They looked at each other, then he held his hand out for the death certificate. "Would you like a copy?" he asked.

"Yes, please. I have my own reasons for wanting to understand all of this. But I'm not sure I'll ever be able to talk to Frank about this subject again."

Jack walked to his copy machine, turning back to look at her as he set the death certificate on the machine's glass.

"Is that so?" he said doubtfully. "After you've worked on this so long together, that's hard to imagine."

As he passed her the page, his eyes seemed to be trying to read her face. She picked up the plastic bag.

"What about the letter, Jack?"

He took the bag from her hands and replaced the original death certificate inside it.

"Why don't I read parts of it to you. So that I can explain it. Then I'll make you a copy."

The sound of the wind grabbing with fierce gusts at tree limbs and the eaves and corners of the barn was suddenly accompanied by the low grind of a car engine, and a flash of headlights hit the house. Then another set of lights followed the first. Lydia and Jack hurried to the window where she recognized Frank's pickup truck. She raced to the barn door and unlocked it to leave.

"Lydia, no, stay in here!"

"We can't let him go in the house!"

"I locked it, remember?" Jack came up behind her and put his hands on her shoulders to pull her back from the door just as Frank and two other people burst in.

"Ah, there they are," Frank said. "The thief and her accomplice. Embracing?"

Beneath a hood trimmed with white fur, Drew Johnson's mouth formed a grim frown. Slightly behind and between Drew and Frank, Shane's face had a similarly angry cast.

"How dare you come out here after all you've said and done," Lydia said. The barn seemed suddenly isolated and vulnerable.

Frank pointed a finger at her while glaring at Jack.

"This is my wife, Kenilworth. I don't know what you've been trying to pull with her, with Nicholas, but I'm warning you right now that you're looking like a home wrecker. And a con man."

Trembling, Lydia gave a short laugh. "Give it a rest, Frank. Your games are completely transparent."

"Were you the one who told her to call the police to claim I'd trashed our house?" Frank went on. "I didn't know who destroyed everything, but her phone call certainly put an end to that question."

Lydia could feel Jack's eyes on her.

"I didn't smash those things," she growled, "and you know perfectly well who did."

"Did Nicholas help you?" Frank furrowed his brow. "You can't be left with your son, dear, if you're going to engage him in destructive, illegal activities. You know, I was at the police station when you called. About me." He gave her a critical frown. "And they told me that. Even though he's fifteen, your care can be put off-limits if you're criminally inclined."

"Don't even listen, Lydia. It's nonsense," Jack said.

"Is it? You know her so very well, do you?" Frank tilted his head. "Better than I do?"

"I know what I see. Your son's a basket case, but it isn't because of his mother."

"Watch it, Kenilworth. You're getting a little close to accusations you *will* regret."

"Please, Lydia," Drew said, her voice shaking with a mixture of nervousness and anger. "That poem is so special. And it was all we have left of her. Please give it back."

Lydia stopped the words of outrage that she wanted to spew and shook her head. "Drew, you don't know what you're talking about."

"Let me set all of you straight. And then you can get off my property. Lydia is here because she wanted me to tell you, Professor, what I know about Mary Stone Walker. There are inarguable facts that I tried to pass along to you years ago, but since you never wanted to hear them, I'll assume your interest is limited, and I'll be brief now. The woman left White Hill on October 29, the night she disappeared in 1939, to go to Chicago for medical attention. She died there about four weeks later, and I have a copy of her death certificate and a letter she wrote from Chicago. To my grandfather. There were no poems written in 1940 because she was no longer in this world. The page you are speaking of, miss, is a forgery."

The roaring of wind and crash of the surf on the shore far below accentuated the silence in the barn.

"Give me the poem, Lydia." Frank's voice was low and threatening.

"*My* poem?"

"Mary's poem. Give it to me. Now."

"You can't hear me, Professor?" Jack said evenly. "Mary Walker has been dead for sixty years. She died alone in a tenement in Chicago in November 1939 when she was twenty-five years old. Dead. Forever silent. She wrote no more poetry. Get it through your head, man."

"How do you know all this?" Shane spoke up.

"That's too horrible," Drew said softly, eyeing Jack. "It can't be true. How could she die?"

"I know that it's true because my grandfather befriended Mary and helped her get to Chicago where she sought medical help. She was a morphine addict."

"Ah," Shane said, nodding. "I always wondered."

"That's hogwash," Frank said with an unfriendly glance at Shane. "No evidence for it."

"And she had other problems that drove her to leave. My grandfather was a kind man, and he pitied her."

"Oh, *he* pitied *her*, did he?" Frank chuckled. "If she knew him at all, it was undoubtedly the other way around. You see, Lydia, how it is? Even your pal here wants to make Mary Walker into a pathetic little female who could only survive with the help of a man. Doesn't that rile you?"

"Here, Frank." Hands shaking, Lydia held her copy of the death certificate toward him and he took it. "The certificate of her death in Chicago. She was using her mother's maiden name, Williams, in order to hide."

He scanned the page and laughed. "*Williams?* Mary *Williams?*" He let the paper drop to the floor. "What kind of fool do you think I am, Lydia? What kind of fool are *you?*"

"Well, I guess *I* am the kind of fool who married someone who wants to pass my writing off as someone else's."

"Get the poem, Lydia," Frank said, his tone suddenly light, as if he'd just thought of the idea. "If it isn't part of Mary Stone Walker's body of work, you know it won't ever be read at all. You know that." He straightened the collar of his coat, shook his hair back, and stared with intention at her. "We talked about that."

"Hmm. I think you have a problem here, Cap'n," Shane said after a few seconds, staring at Frank with doubt. "This does not sound good."

"You could have avoided this whole situation, Frank," Lydia said. "Long ago, you could have talked to people who knew her. You could have found out more than your imagination can whip up from gazing at her pictures and poems and fantasizing about her life. You could have written an honest account of her life, her struggles, her work. That would have been a genuine scholarly effort and meant more than all of this—"

"Stop! I was pursuing the truth through the only thing that matters—the written legacy of a genius. You would have had me speaking to people like your friend here?"

"Or maybe Bernard Evans himself," Jack said.

"He hasn't a whit of sense left, Kenilworth. You must know that."

"What do you mean?" Lydia asked, her eyes darting from Frank to Jack, who glared at each other. A fractured image from a recent experience crossed her memory as she asked again, "What are you talking about?" The image involved Lincoln Babcock and Mary's old house. "Bernard Evans is dead."

"Bernard Evans is in the state hospital. The asylum," Jack said, his eyes on Frank. "He has been there for years. Decades."

"But…" Her mind filled with the image of the old man pointing up to Mary's attic window and screaming at her as if he knew her, and as if…as if whoever he thought she was, was part of his madness. "I saw his obituary ages ago. It must have been over fifteen years ago."

"It was fake. He had a twisted plan, you see. He thought if she believed he had died that Mary would return," Jack said. His gaze was sympathetic as he took in Lydia's alarm. "He's crazy."

"That was a futile hoax that proved his stupidity." Frank laughed. "He was an idiot, and there was no point in trying to talk to him."

"You knew he was still alive, Frank?" Lydia's voice sounded slightly unhinged.

"Why would a woman who was constantly degraded by such a lout ever return to the place where she met with such treatment? Such constant abuse? Demeaned daily in her own home. It seems pretty obvious that she was too good for that."

"And I'm not," Lydia stated as Frank's description of Bernard's treatment of Mary sounded viscerally familiar.

"*None* of this is about *you,* Lydia!" Frank cried. He rammed a

fist down hard on Jack's worktable. "Do you hear me? None…
of this…is about…*you!*"

"Except for certain key points," she said, putting her hands
on her hips as Frank moved toward her, her fingers digging into
her own bones.

"No, woman, none of it is. You gave up literature. You
gave up on Mary. And you gave up on me," he said. "You're a
romance writer, not a poet, and what's done is done."

"What's done is done."

"Yes."

From her back pocket she pulled the piece of paper Nicholas
had torn from Teasdale's book and held it in both hands. Just as
Frank was recognizing it, she tore it in half. He cried out and
took hold of her wrists, trying to immobilize her hands.

"Goddamn you, Lydia. Stop right now! I swear if you don't
let me have this victory, you will not live to remember this."

She began to tear at the two sides, wildly, haphazardly, again
and again, as Frank shoved her to the wall and tried to grab the
remaining pieces from her hands. Jack pulled at his body from
behind, and Frank rammed his elbow back at him but only
grazed his head.

"You've come to the end of this road, Professor," Jack said as
he and Shane wrestled Frank's bulk off Lydia.

Breathing hard, Frank looked around at the faces all directed
toward his own.

"All of you are out of your minds," he said, breathing hard.
"We had this chance, this one chance, at last. To resurrect her."

"Okay. I'm outta here, Professor." Shane pulled his keys from
his pocket and headed toward the door.

"I'll ride with you, Shane." Drew clutched his jacket sleeve.

"Oh, no, no, no," Frank said, leaning back against the door,
effectively trapping them all inside the barn. "We can't have
everyone leaving with different stories. Let's make sure we all
understand the way things are, okay?"

It was then that Lydia noticed, like an image dreamed and stored in dark amber, her son's face watching from a dimly lit window of Jack's house. And moments later, the sound of police sirens erupted a mile or so away and quickly grew louder. The five people in the barn froze, helpless against their meaning: Nicholas had called the police.

"To hell with you all." Frank pretended indifference, but his body and face were suddenly alert to the reality of what was going on around him, and he moved with the agility of a thief, opening the door and slipping out, taking off at a trot over the same sandy earth that Mary Walker had eagerly crossed sixty years before to reach Robert Kenilworth.

Shane and Drew hurried out to Shane's car as four policemen emerged from two squad cars. Shane pointed toward Frank, and the men followed his dark form into the woods.

Besieged by shock and a weeping too deep for tears, Lydia backed away stiffly and sat down on a wooden chair at the table, while Jack continued to stand at the door and watch, awaiting the officers' return. The wind howled, the rain splattered in bursts, and Lydia's eyes roved the room in a daze. Everything looked strange. The intricate, varied tools hanging from hooks, the drawings pinned to the wall that fluttered now and then in the wind from the open door. The random objects of ordinary life—an ashtray, a broom, a phone book. Durable, fragile ordinary life.

Strangest of all was the photograph of the *Fata Morgana* that seemed to stutter and shake in the storm. Robert Kenilworth's boat. Lydia had noticed it before, yellowed and so faded that it appeared it would one day vanish altogether off the paper. Could Robert Kenilworth's boat have been damaged on Lake Michigan because he had carried a desperate Mary Walker away from White Hill when he never should have been on the water at all? Lydia stood and slowly walked to the photo, her gaze catching flashes of the ghosts there.

Of course he had. And he'd regretted it.

She could not have said how long she stood in the trance of Mary Walker, Robert Kenilworth, and the *Fata Morgana*. As if the sudden rift in her own life had opened her to these other energies, she felt an intimate connection to their spent lives.

"Frank is gone," Jack said after a while, just behind her. "Nicholas seems okay, but I told him we'd be with him in a minute."

Nodding, Lydia turned around. Jack stood right there, his face so serious, so sad. She wanted to scream and cry; she wanted to fall against him; she wanted to run away.

"I loved Frank, Jack." Her thoughts were splintered, and her voice sounded like a stranger's. "Doesn't that seem mad? I loved him so much. The crazy man who just ran into the woods to flee policemen…that man who threatened to kill me tonight. I loved him so much."

"Of course it isn't mad," Jack said quietly. "It's what we do." He took hold of her hands gently. "Listen. They found him, took him for some questioning. One of the officers told me that Frank will be kept overnight and most likely taken to Grand Rapids for a psychiatric evaluation. You can go by the police station tomorrow. Everyone has left now."

She returned her gaze to the *Fata Morgana*, but the photograph was completely blurred by tears. Jack's hand touched her right shoulder. "I'm so sorry, Lydia," he whispered. After a long silence, he said, "And I want to say… I do see what you mean."

"About what?"

"About marriage being complicated."

She gave a broken laugh, but as she turned around toward him, she collapsed into tears, and for a moment, she clung to him. For a moment, she allowed herself to close her eyes and simply feel the warmth and safety of the boatbuilder—a man who had unexpectedly been willing to help her cross dangerous water.

"I have a proposal for you, Ms. Milliken."

She stood back and tried to look into his eyes but felt awkward and confused.

"This boat you've been staring at here." He stepped over and pulled the *Fata Morgana* from the wall, then walked to the couch and sat with the photograph in his lap. She eased down next to him. "She needs a biographer. A good one. She has…a *lot* of stories to tell."

"Does she." Lydia pulled a tissue from her pocket and wiped her eyes.

"So many. Some happier than others. But we can get into that later." He turned the photograph over and began to pry back the metal stays that held the cardboard backing. "What do you think?"

"Oh, you know I am interested." She tried a smile but was unable to maintain it. "It's time for me to retire from writing romances. I have become unsuited for the subject matter."

Jack nodded slowly.

"The *Fata Morgana* had two owners before my grandfather. She lived in two other lakes before this one, believe it or not. Huron and Superior. A well-traveled lady. Hardworking." Sighing, he pulled the cardboard away—and between it and the photograph lay a sheet of paper. "She even provided sanctuary and a writing table one autumn for a poet in search of… something. Running from something. A very lost poet, you might say. Who was then chased through history by people who wanted her to be something she just wasn't."

His hands rested on the paper, and he looked up at Lydia. She grew alert, her breathing shallow. One corner of his mouth rose.

"It was the last poem the woman ever wrote. Sadly." He held up his hand as if to stop any objections. "But *definitely*. The last." With his thumb and forefinger, he gently turned over the aged and fragile leaf that weighed barely more than a breath, and it quivered in the light and air. "Do you recognize the handwriting?"

Epilogue

CHICAGO, ILLINOIS—NOVEMBER 1939

...I have been sad;
I have been in cities where the song was all I had—
A treasure never to be bartered by the hungry days.

~ Edna St. Vincent Millay (1892–1950),
"For Pao-Chin, a Boatman on the Yellow Sea"

In the chill of late autumn, the city felt cruel. Robert Kenilworth had been to Chicago but rarely beyond the harbor, and the streets lined with shops and apartments writhed with people rushing against an icy wind. The map he held was flawed, but Robert was not a man who was easily deterred or confused. When at last he found the building that matched the address Mary had sent him, his knock was answered by a middle-aged woman whose appearance was as battered as the tenement's front stoop.

"At last," she said curtly in response to his introduction, then led him upstairs. One flight, two, three—narrow, creaky, and unlit. She pushed open a stained pine door with a crack down the center and no lock. "Here."

The small room contained a narrow bed, two shelves, a crude counter, and three lines of string strung from nails on the rafters for drying clothes. One sock remained pinned there. He turned toward the other side of the room. A single window with yellowed curtains faced the back side of an identical building, a wooden frame chair set before it.

"No toilet or sink," he stated.

"She knew that when she signed. Water's down the hall. Running water is a lot to ask for nothing, mister. And I provided a bucket and a pitcher. That's more than most do."

"Okay," he said, firmly enough to stop the rant that he suspected would flow as long as he let it. "What did she owe you?"

"Well, it was eighteen dollars for what she didn't pay me, and it was forty-one dollars that she still owed the doctor. I don't know who paid for the burial."

"You paid the doctor the balance she owed?"

"I plan to with what you give me," she said, raising her chin. "I've worked with him before."

"Fine work he does, too." Robert scowled, pulling his wallet from his coat pocket. "I'll give him twenty dollars. And that's too much. See that he gets it, and make sure he knows that she didn't live long after."

She tucked the money into her waistband.

"He knows already," she said. "Says it was her own fault, you know."

Wickedness. Robert stepped to the window and tried to open it, but it was sealed shut. *Ignorance.*

"Where are her belongings?" he asked.

The woman pointed, and Robert's gaze followed the direction of her finger to the hanging sock. He gave an empty laugh and glared at her.

"Where are the *rest* of her belongings, ma'am?"

The woman shrugged, eyes wide, lower lip stuck out.

"Came with nothin'."

"I know what she came with," he said. "I brought her here."

But that wasn't entirely true. He had dropped her off at Hull-House, a way station from which she had said her relatives would pick her up. At that time, she had had two modest bags and the sewing box, and he knew from the one letter she'd sent him that she'd carried all of those things with her to her "new place." He'd expected her to stay with relatives. That is what she had claimed she would do when she'd recited her plan back in White Hill.

"So you were the cause of her having to have that operation? That was *your* child?"

Robert Kenilworth glared down at the floor, the dirty, splintery floor where untold numbers of strangers had pissed and cried and toiled their way through the days. *No, no, no.* No, if it had been *his* child… He shook his head, and a wave of desperate grief passed through his body like nausea. There was no reason to talk with this woman any more than necessary.

"If you can find the remaining items that belonged to Mary Williams, I will make sure you're compensated. She had a sewing box that meant a lot to her. You haven't seen that?"

The woman shrugged. "Like I said, she didn't have nothin'."

"Well. If it turns up," he said, writing his name and address down on an envelope that he handed her, "this is the same address you sent the telegram to. I will pay for your efforts. Likewise, if you will give me the names of her visitors. I need to inform her Chicago kin, if you have not."

"No visitors. No kin that I ever saw. She never left the room those last two weeks, and no one called for her. I don't know what she ate or how she lived…as long as she did, that is."

"She had nothing to eat? For heaven's sake, you didn't help her?"

"Mister, she didn't want help. She said that right to my face. She was too good to accept anything from me, you know."

Robert tried to control his voice as he said, "So you left her alone. Informed no one of her ill health. She died. Then you had her buried. Do I have it right?"

"I didn't have her buried. She was nothing to me. It's required by law, and the police took care of it."

"Tell me where."

"You will have to ask them. She died right there on that bed. They came and got her. Now I will have to replace it."

Robert glanced at the horrible little bed, observing the deep depression in the middle where Mary had undoubtedly settled for her last breaths. He gave a small nod and stepped toward the woman.

"I'd like to be here alone for a few moments, please."

"I can't allow—"

"Mary was a relation of mine. I'd like some time to honor her passing."

When she refused to move, Robert handed her a dollar and the woman turned to stand in the hall. Without apology, he closed the door between them, leaned back on it, and looked slowly around the room. *Holy Mother of God.* He could never have imagined this nightmare. Her letter after she arrived here had said nothing of the squalor. In fact, it had sounded almost…optimistic.

She had lied to him. She knew that he would not have let her come here alone if he suspected she could end up in a situation like this. She'd claimed that her mother's people, the Williams family, had generously invited her for a lengthy visit. They would help her with the child, she'd explained, and furthermore, they were going to help her secure a teaching position. They were fascinated with her poetry and had university and library friends who might be able to arrange readings. Had she believed these things, or were they fantasies? Or worse, were they just lies designed to disarm his concern? Why in the name of God had he fallen for them?

Oh Lord. It hurt him that she'd had such pride, even with him. How many times had he told her that he would not let her suffer if there was any way he could stop it? That was why he had brought her here, the only reason he had taken the risk of setting her out into this strange, enormous city. To free her from the abuse by her husband that had gone on for years with nightmarish episodes, and then the passionate, ridiculous reunions between the two of them. How many times had he listened to all of that, helpless to change anything or to protect her from harm?

Then there was the morphine, which had aggravated every problem. He had also begun to worry that the drug itself was going to kill her, so she'd sworn that she would seek a doctor's help in Chicago, another thing she felt she could not do in White Hill. When he had left her at Hull-House, she had promised to get help with the drug immediately to protect the child in her womb.

The child in her womb. When she had begged him to carry her secretly to this city on his boat, it had seemed to him one wish he could fulfill that might improve the quality of her life, as well as that child's.

But this—his eyes scanned the dark, dangerous, smelly room—this is what it had all come to. For a moment, Robert Kenilworth felt he could not bear it. He had not known enough of the truth to prevent this. She hadn't given him that opportunity. And now, just like that, she was gone.

His gaze groped for something, some scrap of her that must have been left behind. But there were no drawers where something could be stashed, no corners or shelves except for those nakedly facing him now. He stepped to the sock on the line and pulled it down, examining the coarse wool. Only this. His heart turned—he remembered seeing it with its mate, wet on the beach. He lifted it to his face.

The door opened.

"There is just this," the landlady said, and held out a full-length, black wool coat. "I'd forgotten."

Mary's coat. Robert stared, his mind tricked for a moment by the form so familiar and yet so utterly empty. He fumbled again for his wallet and pulled out two more dollar bills. When he passed them to the woman, she kept her hand extended until he gave her another. Then she folded the bills into her waistband, shoved the coat at his chest, and stood waiting.

"Thank you," he said, gripping it, and he started to close the door again.

"She cried a lot, you know, those last weeks," the woman said. "So I brought her tea sometimes. But she wasn't friendly. She wasn't grateful. I'm not surprised—"

"That's enough," Robert said, as he tried to block the visions her words gave rise to. "Have some pity. She was far from home. She was…" So many things occurred to him to say about Mary, but there would never be anyone to whom he could speak of her. "She was far from home."

Before the landlady could say more, Robert closed the door, held his hand against it, and listened for her to walk away. He waited three, four minutes, until at last her steps descended the stairs. He gazed down at the coat, took a deep breath in spite of the foulness of the air, and moved to the bed to sit down.

A different man might have wept, might have raged against the tiny prisonlike room that had played a part in the death of someone he loved. But for Robert Kenilworth, those moments would hit unexpectedly over the years to come. In a sort of stupor of grief that had begun when he received the telegram about Mary's death from the landlady, he continued to force himself to focus on doing what he could for Mary, on finding some way to bring resolution to the ill-fated journey out of White Hill. He thought there must be an appropriate ritual of some sort, a prayer—some formal acknowledgment of her life's passing that would have meaning. As he had traveled to Chicago on the train, he'd imagined that there would be a way to achieve a sense of peace once he arrived, though he'd had no idea how.

Here, now, there seemed to be nothing. She was dead. Her body was buried. He would consult with the police; he would find her grave and bid her farewell. Then he would take her coat back to White Hill and bury it deep in the sand near his workshop in the dunes where they had spent so much time together. But as far as his conscience was concerned, he was responsible for the tragedy set in motion when he agreed to her plan. *He* should have known better. He couldn't fathom what might ameliorate this wretched sorrow and guilt, but he had possessed some hope that visiting the place of her death would help.

From beyond the window, Robert could hear the thin cries of children playing. The sun was already falling low, and the November chill that penetrated the room had crept into his bones. He gazed down at the coat, squeezing the cloth to feel the weight and texture of it, picturing her lifting its hem as she'd handed him her bags and climbed onto the *Fata Morgana* with the sewing box.

"I will need this, Robert," she had declared of the box, using an attitude he recognized as the artificial cheer she mustered when she was afraid. "I will be so glad you helped me carry it to my new home. You might even be glad yourself, for I may sew something for you."

But when Mary sewed, it was embroidery, nothing more. Or mending. Or…with a little rush of hope, Robert lifted the hem of the coat to his lap and opened it to run his hands along the lining, and there at the center, back seam, near the hem, was a hiding spot like others she had told him about or shown him. How she loved to hide things, binding her words secretly into the things around her, as she said. She had made loose stitches with white thread, and those had already been mostly ripped out. His pulse quickened, and pulling back the fabric, he found an envelope inscribed with his name and address.

His heart raced. He was trying to decide whether to open it right then or wait until he was safely alone on the train when he turned it over to find that someone, undoubtedly the landlady in search of money, had already torn it open. He pulled out several sheets of hotel stationery, unfolded them carefully, ran his eyes along the first lines, then rapidly shuffled through more of the pages. It was almost entirely nonsense. Long lines of writing that contained no recognizable words.

His heart fell. Page after page, front and back filled with gib-berish, with random slashes of ink. What had she thought she was telling him?

But there was one sheet containing a poem that was written in her true, sober script, and another page with a letter that appeared to make sense, dated just eighteen days before. Before she was delirious with pain. Eighteen days. Eighteen days ago, she could still feel; she could write. Oh God help him, just eighteen days ago she could still think. It was too much…that she should be nothing now, her body like a fish on the beach. Nothing more than the dead gull they had noticed together once as it floated in to the shore, head twisted and wings splayed on the autumn waves. The two of them had watched, nearly indifferent—because they were among the living.

In the dim light, he struggled to focus on Mary's ink.

November 12, 1939

Dear Robert,

The saving grace of my new apartment is the patch of sky I can see from my window. It is sometimes the same color as it was at home over Lake Michigan. I receive my entertainment from the streets full of strangers whose faces and voices are from European countries, the Orient, Africa… From the front stoop the other day, I watched them pass for hours.

Robert, I have something to tell you that I'm afraid will make you unhappy. Four days ago I had an operation. It was the operation that I most needed, for I am not fit to have a child. I have known this for years, and I told you. I cannot give what is needed, especially not with the calling I have to do other work entirely. Thoughts of mothering terrified me.

Soon I will begin publishing and teaching. I just need to rest a bit more. The poem I have enclosed was composed on your boat — as you carried me into the unknown, my mind flew free. You see, even in the earliest hours of my departure from White Hill, I felt the thrill of my soul coming out of hiding. So already, it has been worth the cost of losing my home.

I can only be what I am,
Mary

P.S. Later this winter, please deliver this poem to Bernard. Perhaps he will suppose that it is about my love for him and how sorry I was to leave. Maybe then he will remember me kindly. Let him imagine I'm dead.

Robert's heart hammered furiously, and his thoughts raged. She had deceived him about everything. And he'd fallen for all of it, like a fool. She'd lured him into taking her to a strange city where she had no means of survival and no intention of keeping her child or quitting her addiction, leaving him to suffer guilt for her fate, and now he was to give this poem to her husband so that the brute she fled might love her? It was intolerable, all of it—the lies, the recklessness, the needless loss.

He stood abruptly, folded the papers together inside the envelope, and slid them into an interior jacket pocket. His unseeing gaze swept around the room once more as he tightly rolled up Mary's coat and tucked it under his arm. The poem would have to wait until he was on the train. He should have waited to look at any of it.

As fast as he could, Robert Kenilworth descended the three flights of stairs, pushed through the front door, and entered the twilit city street. He would take the coat and the papers home and get back to his work and the care of his family. His wife. His son. His livelihood and his soul. He would hide these remnants of Mary, bury them, hide all of the traces from himself. He must concentrate on his responsibilities and never be misled again.

There was nothing else to be done. For the cold fact was that the living needed him—and the dead did not.

That was all there was to it, and he would have to find a way to live fully within that reality. In spite of loss. And not crippled by dreams.

For my dearest,
In remembrance of our time together...

Unopened dream,
the tide comes in
and we so near the shore house
want for nothing.

(the burden of the boat
depressed the hull against the sea—
three outward-bound redemptionists
hunched low into the spray)

Imperfect dream,
we pull the grass,
we slash the wind; before us
is the winter.

(the burden of the boat
depressed the hull against the sea—
with nothing left before it
but the purple heel of day)

Enshadowed dream,
we've locked the door,

we've torn the bread and poured
the coastal wine.

(the burden of the boat
depressed the hull against the sea—
their hats were low, their coats were tight—
Fall shriveled on the quay)

Uncensored dream,
what voice is yours,
behold our anxious faces
around the table.

(the burden of the boat
depressed the hull into the sea—
three strangers rising into night
would not return this way)

Unopened dream,
the tide comes in
and we inside the shore house
want for nothing.

M. S. Walker
November '39

Reading Group Guide

1. *The Lake and the Lost Girl* focuses on Mary Stone Walker and Lydia Carroll, two female protagonists living at different times in the same small town. What are the similarities and differences between the two women, and how do their stories mirror each other? Which elements seem to be different because of the different time periods in which they live?

2. Mary Stone Walker finds meaning in life through her poetry. Do you have a passion or hobby that drives you forward in the same way, and if so, where does it live in your mind, and what emotions does it inspire?

3. Describe the Carroll family dynamic in the beginning of the novel. How does Nicholas relate differently to his mother than he does to his father? What family elements are having the most impact on him, and did you experience any similar pressures growing up?

4. Both Lydia and Mary are writers, albeit in two very different fields; however, would you agree they had parallel visions for their lives? How are their views of motherhood different, especially in relation to their careers?

5. Frank's hobby costs the family thousands of dollars in antiques. In one scene, he spends over half of the family's savings on a single piece of furniture. If you were Lydia, how would you have reacted in that situation? How far should a partner or family member go to be supportive of another's hopes and dreams (however ambitious or impractical)?

6. Nicholas said that he forged the poem in order to help his parents be happy. Frank was understandably disappointed, and Lydia was at first hurt and confused. If you were his parent, how would you handle this situation?

7. Jack Kenilworth claims he never shared the information he had about Mary Stone Walker because of a promise to his grandfather to protect her secrets (as well as his own). Do you think his secrecy was justified?

8. *The Lake and the Lost Girl* addresses at least two different addictions: Mary's addiction to morphine, and Frank's addiction to solving the mystery of Mary. Do you see any similarities between their downfalls?

9. How are addictions and delusions about reality connected in this story?

10. Lincoln Babcock says "a stack of poems, no matter how exquisite, does not make up for an immoral life." Do you agree with this statement? Do you agree that Mary Stone Walker's life was defined by immoral behavior?

11. If you found out your favorite author wrote his/her best works under the influence of a heavy drug addiction, would that change the way you felt about them?

12. How do you feel about the final chapters of *The Lake and the Lost Girl* and how you left the characters you met? Do you think Frank and Mary "deserved" their respective endings, and could they have avoided them?

A Conversation with the Author

What was your inspiration for _The Lake and the Lost Girl_?

We all see slightly different worlds through the filters of our limited minds. But sometimes this tendency seems to grow extreme. People turn away from living beings and issues, seduced by some story that they've made up or adopted from a group. Or they give over to an addiction, and that destroys their moral compass. I've seen so much damage caused by this preference for fantasies over reality, and I wanted to create a novel that showed this conflict play out. Frank is doing this in the most obvious way, but Lydia is also ignoring key elements of reality for the sake of her personal story line. Mary Walker is also hopelessly caught up in addiction, self-delusion, and an unhealthy marriage—she becomes a lightning rod for wishful thinking.

The theme of interpreting fragments of writing or the past just as we wish to is related to seeing the present through blinding filters, and this was also an inspiration behind this story. Reading a stack of texts left behind by a person and imagining we can really understand them or the past is similarly self-centered activity prone to delusion. I hope that juxtaposing scenes of Mary Stone Walker's life against the people of 1999 who are speculating about her illustrates that the past had as much vitality and complexity as our present and is not actually accessible through the handful of "clues" that have survived the destruction of Time.

***The Lake and the Lost Girl* is set along the beautiful, and often mysterious, Michigan lakeshore. Why did you choose this place for your story to unfold?**

The setting of a book is basically where your mind lives during the hours you are writing it, and I deeply love Lake Michigan and its coast—it's a place I always want to "be." I also know it and feel it in my heart, so to me it was as alive as any of the human characters and, in fact, could have had a much larger presence, had the plot allowed! As for it being mysterious, it certainly is at times; that liminal realm of the shoreline, where liquid meets land, the known merges into the unknown… This is where lighthouses are built, and the edge from which people and ships depart, sometimes forever… That is endlessly captivating to me, and a presence that intensifies the themes of so many tales.

Both Mary and Lydia are writers like you. Which character did you feel more closely connected to, and why? Do you see any qualities of yourself in either of them?

I felt more connected to Lydia, primarily because of the main condition of her life: balancing the emotional demands of relationships, day-to-day life, and creative work. We say that kind of thing all the time—"balancing career and family"—but what do we mean? In *The Lake and the Lost Girl*, Lydia needs to write genre fiction to support her family, so she has not been able to dedicate her time, her energy, her focus, or even her belief in herself to the task of writing something that might not provide income. Additionally, her husband's lifestyle takes from her financial resources and her mental health, and her son also clearly deserves her thought and time. So the question becomes not so much where to find the "hours" to do all of the things we care about, but how to *grow the self that can see* what matters most and what needs to be done, which might include important changes, sometimes extremely difficult ones.

Neither of these characters reminds me much of myself, although I tried to draw each one with that essential passion for language that brings life alive in the specific way that wanting to create with words does. Relating to those things I witness through language has been a defining feature of my personality for as long as I can remember, and I feel so grateful. For me, it is a quality that adds intrigue and possibility to life.

Do you have a favorite poem, and if so, why does it continue to resonate with you? We can easily conclude from the story that Frank's favorite author is Mary Stone Walker. Who are your favorite authors, and can you say their work shaped how or what you write?

These questions are worthy of long, long answers that would bore everyone except me. Favorite poem? So many of them, depending on the emotion and experience I want to immerse myself in. Favorite authors? The same.

But as a very general statement, the most affecting writers and poems for me have been those that capture something elusive, something that reflects qualities of life you rarely see captured in human expression except in dreams and other subconscious flickers. Then again, those same transcendent pieces of literature have a powerful and accurate grounding in the earthly detail from which the sublime arises. I try to learn from this—how to look, what to care about, what language, stories, characters, details might capture some slight filament of what I see and love.

Of the poets I used quotes from at the beginnings of this novel's chapters, I most adore Edna St. Vincent Millay and Louise Bogan. I am so proud to have a handful of their words on the pages of a book with my name on it.

***The Lake and the Lost Girl* has a wonderful past-present dual narrative. What research did you do to bring the late**

1930s Michigan to life, and what advice do you have for aspiring writers who wish to visit a period era?

I read a lot of books and online pieces about specific issues, including morphine addiction; abortion techniques and laws; the fishing and lumber industries in 1930s Michigan; clothing and other daily use objects; food and alcohol; the music, drama, and literary scenes of the time; furniture (future antiques) and furniture companies; Chicago tenements; medicine and herbal remedies; and every other related thing that arose in my imagination. I also read a lot of poetry by female American poets of the late 1800s and early 1900s, as well as critiques and biographies in some cases.

Not all of the information I read and jotted down was used, of course, but together, the details helped me have a sense of the era, as did reading some other nonfiction and fiction books set in that general time. I would advise that this process is the way to go: immersion in detail, creating a milieu in which your imagination can play with your story elements and characters until they come alive. A friend of mine who has written numerous history books about Michigan said that he could research endlessly and forgo the writing part. I can see why—it's fascinating to discover facts about the past that simultaneously reveal rich variations on the human experience and yet so many continuing themes. Fortunately for me, I find both the research and the writing completely engaging.

Frank has the strange, almost romantic hobby of "treasure hunting" for Mary Walker poems. What are your hobbies (and do you share a similar obsession with them)?

Frank's treasure hunts for Mary Walker poems *is* a romantic hobby, for he is driven merely by notions that delight him, almost nothing more. Except for writing, my own hobbies are less mysterious and not obsessive: reading, watercolor painting, gardening, kayaking, cycling, the study of Lithuania, volunteering at lighthouses, and other nonprofit work. I wouldn't fit well as a character in this novel, except perhaps as a random figure walking in the distance on a pier…or something.

If you could study one author and their works for the rest of your career, what author would that be?

Only one? That would have to be Shakespeare! I can't imagine another writer I would learn more from or whose works would keep me better company through all of life's turns. During college, and later in other periods when I've read a great deal of his work at once, I felt almost as if my mind began to vibrate at a different (more enlightened) frequency.

The fact is, I would like to study a number of authors more closely. And I am really grateful that it does not have to be just one.

Near the beginning of the book, Lydia stands in the attic where Mary crafted many of her poems. Do you have a special sanctuary where you do your writing?

I do. I have had more than one profoundly special sanctuary where I have written over the last twenty-five years. All of them had a door that shut, many books within reach, and at least one window revealing trees and a patch of sky and through which I was visited by breezes and birds' voices. I am incredibly lucky.

What would you like readers to take away from your novel?

That there is a high price to pay for ignoring reality.

Acknowledgments

To Elaine Fox and Beth Harbison, my marvelous sisters: thank you for being soul friends to me through every life journey, even the creative process. Elaine, this novel in particular owes you special debts. Deepest appreciation to my cherished friend Mark Nepo, spiritual mentor, nurturer of creativity, and helping hand into the publishing world. To Scott: for the gift of our shared writing journey, I possess love and an ongoing gratitude as it continues to unfold. Thanks to the inimitable Becky Cooper, inspiration in every area of life and brilliant poet who wrote "Lydia's" poem "The Study of Lakes." Marsha Nuccio offered just the right prompt, at just the right time and has always offered brilliant insight. Profound gratitude to Kevan Lyon, my agent, and Patricia Nelson, her assistant, for their transformative ideas and exceptional professionalism. My editor, Anna Michels, has also been a class-act partner in the understanding and fine-tuning of this work. Love and thanks to my "kids"—Chapel, Warren, Alexander, Jason, Ashleigh, Megan, Michael, Paige, and Karli—extraordinary souls who always provide light on the darkest parts of my path. Chris Smith, you hold the Truth near enough to believe in, and there are not words enough to express my gratitude. To Liga and Dawn, my incomparable friends with seemingly boundless hearts, I sing your praises in my heart daily. Paula and Melissa, you have been heroes in my life, through all things, and to Ballakeyll, I owe my prologue. Cheers and kisses to my amazing mother, who always believes in all of us...somehow. And to Bob, my beautiful man: thank you. Thanks for reading every version of this book, and for enjoying the process with me and caring so passionately about this part of my life. To say I miss you doesn't touch the feeling your absence has brought.

About the Author

Photo credit: Amanda Lemke

Jacquelyn Vincenta began her writing career as a police beat reporter for a daily Louisiana newspaper. She established a publishing company specializing in international trade issues and acted for many years as managing editor. She lives in Kalamazoo, Michigan, where she focuses on writing, environmental projects, family, friends, and nature.